The Girl Who Used To Be Me

Lynn Forth

First Crooked Love Cats Edition, Crooked Cat, 2019

To the wonderful memory of my bold Mum and Dad and their time in Spain.

And
To David, Stephen and Andrew,
Rosie and Fiona,
Ben and Barney, Molly and George
I love you all.

Acknowledgements

As a writer, you live in your head a lot of the time, having amazing conversations with imaginary people.

But it's the amazing and very real people who actually help to get these characters out there to readers.

My journey to publication started with a small group of local writers who guided and advised me on my first steps into the publication world and they continue to do so to this day. Thank you Morton S Gray, Janice Preston, Alison May, Georgia Hill, Nell Dixon and Liz Hanbury for your endless support and words of wisdom. I owe you all many cups of coffee and many hugs.

Their advice led me to join the remarkable RNA (Romantic Novelists' Association) who believe that what we do is important, as well as fun. Without the robust critique offered by its New Writers' Scheme, my first book would never have been accepted by my publisher Crooked Cat. I am forever indebted to my marvellous mentor and plot guru, Jules Wake, who continues to inspire me to further endeavours.

Hats off also to the vibrant and enthusiastic members of the Birmingham Chapter of the RNA who are always there with fun, friendship and fan-wafting at the annual Conference.

As ever, my gratitude also to my editor Maureen Vincent-Northam and to June Davis for giving her time and expertise so generously.

I will be forever grateful to my publishers, Laurence and Stephanie Patterson at Crooked Cat Books. It is thanks to them and their positive support that there is such wonderful pro-active collaboration in their community of writers. Thank you for your belief in me.

Thank you to all those friends who have read my books and continue to cheer me on to write more.

My heart-felt love to my warm and wonderful family for their unstinting approval and forbearance.

I would never have been able to write this book without my long-suffering husband, David, who has indulged me in this wonderful flight of fancy of being a published author. He is always willing to read through my work, offer help with the placement of a disputed comma and pop downstairs to make a reviving cup of tea.

But, in the end, it all goes back to my childhood where my parents encouraged my imagination and let me be their dilly daydream daughter. Boldly, in later life, they began their own writing endeavours as they documented their adventures after selling up everything, including their house, and setting off to travel the world with just two small suitcases. They often wintered on the Costa del Sol while they were planning their next big trip, be it driving across Canada, or Australia, or South Africa or the length of New Zealand. Their biggest venture was a year of journeying round the world, spending months in any location that took their fancy on the way.

That's why I'm so fond of the Costa del Sol as we spent over a dozen Christmases with them there in a house they rented. The memories are especially poignant as they both died there, just ten years apart, in that very same house on Calahonda overlooking the sea.

While writing this book, I have had my inspirational Mum and Dad constantly in mind as I retrace some of the places we used to visit. I have been thinking of them and how much I owe them, so this book is in loving memory of them and their very special attitude to life.

About the Author

Lynn went to live in Accrington when she was 11 and still has the accent to prove it. She now lives in Worcestershire where it doesn't rain as much.

Like most authors, she wrote stories from an early age and continued this fascination with words and people, by studying English and Psychology at University. Later, as a lecturer at the local College, she enjoyed teaching and transmitting this love of words to students of all ages. A very proud moment was when, in 2007, she was presented with a national award as an Outstanding Teaching and Learning Practitioner at a glittering Star Awards ceremony in London.

However, this demanding career, together with bringing up two sons, left little time for her to write down all the ideas whirling in her head.

Eventually she escaped the day job and, since joining the wonderful RNA in 2015, she has written and published three books in her room with a view.

To Tammy

The Girl Who Used To Be Me

with thanks and

fun and flamingos

x x x

Lynn.

PART ONE

Chapter One

June 1995
Birmingham

'Bloody bags!

Bloody heat!

Bloody Birmingham!' Kate was muttering mutinously to herself as she plodded homeward, heavily laden with shopping. The summer sun, reflecting off the nearby shop windows, was baking the pavement beneath her sandals. She squinted in the glittering glare and could feel a thin sheen of sweat covering her face and bare arms. The bulging plastic shopping bags were cutting into her hands. Already she was losing the circulation in her fingers and she knew she had a long, hot trudge back to her university flat.

Her first-year exams had just finished and somehow, once again, she had been lumbered with replenishing food supplies for her three flatmates.

Berating herself, she slogged on. *Why didn't I just go to the campus shop, even though it costs more? No, stupid me goes traipsing off miles just to save a bit of money.* She positively seethed with resentment. *I should be out celebrating the end of exams, just like them. Did they care that they'd eaten the kitchen bare? No. Did they once think about me when they finished all the cereal? No. Did they even leave enough milk for one measly cuppa tea? No.* Her inward fulminations continued with each plodding step back to the campus.

Glaring at the continuous stream of cars as they thundered past, she choked in the humid, fume-filled air. Clammy in the heat, she knew her thin summer T-shirt was sticking to her bosom, attracting leering looks from passing lorry drivers.

Her exasperation increased as she became aware of a car drawing up and slowing down beside her. Some perv hoping to pick her up, no doubt. She turned away in angry annoyance.

'Can I give you a lift?'

A furious 'Shove off' was just leaving her lips when she saw who it was.

Rob. Rugged Rob, looking cool and hunky in a dark blue T-shirt and an open-topped red sports car. Her heart missed a beat and her legs wobbled uncertainly. Why on earth was he stopping for her? And just as she was hot and flushed and hung over?

Dumbfounded, she just stared at the bloke she had been secretly fancying for so long now. The one she thought had smiled at her the other night before she realised she was sitting next to Selina. Slinky, sexy Selina, her flatmate, who had seductively lowered her almond-shaped eyes and whispered: 'That's Rob Frazier. What a hunk. I think he's after me.' Then Kate had watched in envy as Selina had artfully flicked her long, blonde hair over her shoulder before turning on the full wattage of her smile and beaming back at him.

But now, here he was, stopping and asking *her* if she wanted a lift. Why?

For a moment she was stumped. Then it hit her. Of course, he *does* fancy sodding Selina and he wants an intro into meeting her through me. Her shoulders slumped. This wasn't the first time hopeful blokes had used her to get close to her sexy flatmate. Well not again. Especially not Rob.

He can bloody well sod off. If he fancies her, I'm not helping them get together. She turned and glared at him.

A lorry roared behind the stationary car and gave an impatient hoot on its horn.

Hassled by the lorry, Rob reached across to open the passenger door. Seemingly surprised at her hesitation, he sought to reassure her about accepting a lift from him. 'Hurry up. The traffic won't wait. Don't worry; I'm after your shopping not your body.'

In spite of herself, Kate laughed and thought, *Oh what the hell, I may as well have a lift.* Thankfully she dumped her heavy bags into the tiny back seat of the snazzy low-slung sports car before clambering hastily into the snug bucket seat beside him.

The lorry behind them was edging closer and closer, so she had barely clipped on her seat belt before Rob pulled off into the stream of cars, giving an apologetic wave to the gesticulating driver.

He smiled at her and she was hotly aware of the close proximity of his bare tanned forearms and tight blue jeans. Grateful that the roar of the engine disguised the tremor in her voice, she shouted, 'Thanks, I was not looking forward to the rest of the walk in this heat.'

'No problem. You seem to have a lot of stuff.'

Above the car's throaty growl, Kate explained the post-exam non-sustenance situation and how she had been forced out to buy milk for her cuppa and somehow ended up getting more than she intended.

'Know the empty cupboard situation well. Luckily, Megan has kept us provisioned during our final exams.'

'Megan? You mean *my* flatmate Megan? Megan Price?'

'Yes, of course, *your* Megan. Didn't you know she's been living with us? Well, actually with Josh but she has been sorting out the rest of us as well.'

'So you're one of Josh's flatmates are you?'

'Yes. Oh, sorry. I thought you knew who I was. I'm Rob Frazier. And I believe you are Kate Caswell.'

'Yes. How do you do.' Kate suddenly blushed at the formality of her reply. Hastily she rushed on, 'I didn't realise that Megan had mentioned me.'

He nodded. 'Yes. I smiled at you the other night in the bar and you smiled back, so I thought you knew who I was.'

'Oh yes, I remember.' She blushed, remembering the thrill that had coursed through her body as she had returned the smile. Then the embarrassment of thinking it was clearly meant for Selina, not her.

She revelled in the knowledge that she had been right. *Up yours, bloody Selina. It was me after all.* Gloating, she sat back in the snugly padded seat and delighted in the sensation of being in such a swish open-topped sports car. It looked a bit old-fashioned with its gleaming wood-panelled dashboard, its simple round dials and its narrow wooden steering wheel. If only they were motoring along an open road, how dashing would that be? Pity the traffic hardly allowed them to do much more than crawl. But she could still feel the exciting throb of the engine as it pulsated through her body and the gusty warm wind lifting her hair away from her hot face and neck.

He grinned. 'You looked really fed up back there.'

'I was. I was enjoying a good old wallow in self-pity.'

'Post-exam anti-climax,' he pronounced authoritatively as he swerved through the arched stone entrance into the university campus. 'Feeling the same myself.'

Deftly he threaded the car through all the halls of residence till they stopped in front of her student building. Kate wondered how he knew the whereabouts of her flat without being told. Then her heart hit her boots as fresh doubts assailed her. Perhaps he had staked it out for Selina. He really was too gorgeous. OK he had smiled at her but was all this niceness just a pretence to get to know Selina? For a moment there in the car, she had been beguiled into believing he really was interested in her. With a sigh, she faced reality.

'That was great. Thank you so much,' she said, pretending nonchalance, as she clambered inelegantly out of the low-slung car.

But Rob had already leapt out, grabbed her shopping and was striding towards the flats.

Feeling a bit guilty, she trotted after him. What would he say when he discovered Selina wasn't there? But she wasn't going to tell him yet. Those bags were bloody heavy. Which Rob confirmed as he carried them upstairs.

'Phew, these bags weigh a ton. You must be as strong as an ox to have carried them as far as you did.'

‘Well, I don’t know about an ox, but they don’t breed wimps where I come from.’

‘Ah, sorry. Perhaps an ox wasn’t a very elegant analogy,’ he laughed. ’So where do you come from?’

‘A village no one has ever heard of near Keswick.’

‘Lake District?’

‘Yup.’

‘All mountains, Wordsworth, fluffy rabbits and Beatrix Potter?’

‘And rain and narrow roads and more sheep than people.’

‘Wow, I take it you’re not a fan of the place then?’

‘It’s OK to visit…just not to live there.’

She hadn’t intended for the bitterness to come through quite as strongly as it did and noted his look of surprise.

Opening the door to her hot, stifling flat, she teased, ‘From the way you are hefting those bags, I guess you must be vaguely northern. Are you?’

‘Vaguely? I’ll give you vaguely. I come from oooper north than thee, lass. I’m from Aberdeen.’ He puffed out his chest as he hoisted the bulging bags onto the cluttered kitchen table.

‘Oh wow. I bow to your superior claims of northernness.’

‘As so you should.’

‘But…well, you haven’t got a very strong accent.’

‘Curses, Moriarty, you have seen through my disguise.’

‘What?’

‘Although I was born up there in Aberdeen, my Sassenach mother got fed up with the dark Scottish winters and persuaded my dad to come back down south. So me and my family moved down to Worcester when I was nobbut a lad.’

‘Aha. So you’re a southern softie then.’

‘Nope, I object. I’m a macho man of the Midlands.’ He beat his chest with his fists like Tarzan. Then he gave a comic cough as if this display of machismo was all a bit too much for him.

His infectious grin lit up his warm brown eyes and she found herself laughing. For a moment they were both transfixed, just smiling at each other. Her heart gave an unexpected jolt as his eyes locked on hers. Then one of the shopping bags began to topple over. As one, they both rushed to grapple with the tumbling food.

'Can I help you put this lot away?'

'Ta,' said Kate, grabbing the large packet of cereal that had just fallen onto the floor. Was that really a flare of attraction between them just then?

But she had to make certain she wasn't being used, so she stood facing him, hands on hips.

'Look, Selina's not here. I don't expect she will be back for ages.'

Without pausing as he reached up to put stuff away, he said, 'Oh, you mean the tall, dramatic blonde one.'

'Um…yes. The one I was sitting next to the other night.'

'Oh yes, all hair flicks and preening. Megan's told me all about her.'

She blinked in surprise at the obvious disapproval in his voice. She knew there was no love lost between Megan and Selina. Selina's histrionics over the tense exam period and her snappy arguments with their other flatmate, Dee, had been one of the reasons Megan had moved out to stay with her boyfriend, Josh. And from his tone, it seemed Rob shared Megan's low opinion of Selina.

Thrilled, she tingled with sudden hope. Perhaps, after all, he was there because he really was interested in *her*.

Suddenly, she felt giddy in the airless heat of the flat. Tendrils of hair were sticking to her forehead and she was aware that beads of sweat were seeping around her neck and running in rivulets towards her bosom.

She was wearing her favourite turquoise V neck T-shirt that had become baggy with wear and now gaped invitingly as she bent to open the fridge. Glancing up she saw him noticing the trickles of moisture sliding slowly over her breasts towards her cleavage. The atmosphere was suddenly electric. His brown eyes flared, clearly mesmerised as his gaze followed the gliding droplets.

'Cold drink?' she asked, flushing as she peered into the fridge's cool interior.

'Love one,' he answered, hurriedly turning back to the shopping bags.

They both busied themselves round the kitchen, glad to be doing something to dispel the suddenly steamy atmosphere. Rob opened a window and, as she made him a drink, she spotted an angry bee that had flown in and got stuck buzzing at a closed pane.

She wafted it with a tea towel till it escaped through the opening.

'Poor thing. It shouldn't be trapped in a city.'

'I agree. Neither should we. Do you fancy coming out for a drive in the country?'

Kate turned in astonishment.

'Me?'

'Yes, you. Of course you.' He laughed at her surprise. 'Where do you fancy going?'

Sod her flatmates. She had done the shopping. They could sort the mess in the kitchen themselves. Looking at Rob's tall beaming figure, a reckless desire just to be with him swept over her.

Raising a quizzical eyebrow, he waited for her reply.

'My Cumbrian soul yearns for height and views and breezes,' she said. 'I don't suppose there are any hills around here?'

'Around Birmingham? There's loads.'

'Really?'

'Yes. Wonderful idea. A girl after my own heart. I'll take you up the Clents.'

'Sounds painful.'

He grinned. 'It won't be. It will be fun.'

Chapter Two

The drive out of the city cooled her down and gave her time to think. It was too much to hope he really fancied her. He had obviously taken pity on her with her heavy shopping bags and just wanted a companion to go on a sunny outing in his snazzy little car. It was no more than a friendly invitation.

Well, she could do just friends. Friendship with boys came easy to her. She loved the teasing, bantering exchanges with her fellow students and could give as good as she got. But nobody had grabbed her fancy for ages until the night she had spotted Rob across the crowded student bar. Standing there, laughing a full-throated laugh with Megan's boyfriend, Josh, he looked so at ease with himself and so much fun, he had definitely stirred her blood.

She had glimpsed him often after that but he was always heavy into studying for his exams, head down in the library. He had looked in her direction a few times and she had the distinct feeling that she had somehow caught his eye, until she was roundly disabused by Selina saying he was far too hunky to be interested in somebody like her.

Perhaps Selina was wrong. For once.

But she daren't hope and tried to dispel the image of that sudden steamy moment in the kitchen. This was just a fun trip out, which suited her fine. She had been going stir-crazy with all the swotting and exams lately and the heat hadn't helped. It seemed Rob felt the same and wanted to escape as much as she did.

The engine noise made talking difficult so she simply gazed around enjoying the drive out of the suffocating city and into the countryside. She noticed the car drew admiring glances from pedestrians and fellow motorists. Something about it dragged at her memory. Certainly it was a million miles away from Ma's ancient, bashed-up runabout, the one she had learned to drive last summer. This one seemed to need a lot of gear changing and the small windscreen in front of them made gusts of wind eddy about them, blowing her hair across her face at frequent intervals. It was very, very, noisy when at full throttle and so much fun. She could see Rob was enjoying it as much as she was. His brown eyes glinted with joy whenever there was a particularly deep throaty roar.

As they reached an open stretch of dual carriageway, Rob put his foot down and the car surged ahead with a mighty growl. Simultaneously they both threw their heads back and laughed in sheer exhilaration.

'Wonderful, isn't it?' he yelled.

She nodded, too elated to speak.

He pointed ahead at a long, low, tufted range of hills. The craggy peaks of the Lake District it wasn't, but they looked sunny and inviting. She grinned her approval.

'Picnic?' he suddenly bellowed above the noise of the rushing wind. 'Do you fancy getting some sandwiches and stuff. Not exactly haute cuisine I know, but we could stop at this garage and take provisions on board.'

'Sounds great to me.'

Rob drove into a large petrol station. He leapt out and swiftly returned with a bag full of sandwiches, crisps, fruit and drinks.

As she reached for her purse, he waved it away.

'My treat.'

'No really. I must give you something towards it. Especially as the prospect of being taken up the Clents is already a big treat for a hill-starved girl.'

How did she stop herself from saying 'sex-starved'?

'You could be disappointed. As you can see, these are Midland hills, just a small range of mounds about ten miles out of Brum. Not the mighty Pennine Chain or Lake District mountains or…'

'That's OK. Just some undulations will do me. Anything

green and hillocky without stair-rodding rain is just fine.'

Grinning, he put the car into gear and roared off. The sexiness of the throaty engine growl caused her to emit an involuntary whimper of desire, which she hid with a cough. She was acutely aware of Rob's long lean shape filling the seat beside her. His blue T-shirt was stretched taut across his strong rugby-playing shoulders. As he raced through the gears his firm jean-clad thighs flexed and tightened while his capable brown hands deftly manipulated the gear stick back and forth, stroking it neatly into place. A sudden flush of heat flooded her limbs. It was no good fighting it. Yes, everything about him excited her.

But how foolish to expect him to fancy her. As far as she could tell, Rob was just being friendly so she must get herself and her raging libido under control. Anything else would embarrass her, and him. And it was too nice a day to be spoilt by unrequited lustful longings.

The road wound up a hill leading to a busy pub car park.

'Here we are,' he said. 'The Clents.' He gesticulated at quite a steep path and a sizeable hill looming before them.

'Not bad, not bad.' She pretended a cool appraisal.

'And you should see the view once we get up there.' Looking keenly around he carefully parked his car next to a high hedge which would shield one side of it.

'Right come on, let's go.' Grabbing the bag of food from behind his seat, he leapt out and ran round the car. With a ceremonious bow, he bent down to open her low car door.

'Allow me, my lady.'

'Very well, my good man,' she said, trying to scramble out of the snug bucket seat with some degree of dignity.

Oops. Did she flash a bit of knicker there? Why hadn't she thought to change into jeans? Although her short denim skirt was much cooler, it was hardly appropriate for climbing hills. Tugging it down, she noticed Rob had kindly averted his eyes from her ungainly exit, but she still felt flustered as they walked towards the ascending path.

'Here we are,' he said, indicating a rough track. 'It's quite steep in places but should be fine for anyone like you, used to climbing your Lake District mountains.'

'Hmmn, we'll see about that. Personally I was a greater fan of all the valleys in between the high bits.'

Very aware of her short skirt, she indicated he should go first with a wave.

'*Lead on, MacDuff* as they say. Although strictly speaking it should be *Lay on, Macduff* which means something totally different but…' She stopped. What was she wittering about? Suddenly nervous in the presence of such a ruggedly handsome bloke, she knew she was burbling. She must stop right there or else he would think she was a gibbering idiot. 'Oh, anyway, you go first, seeing as you know the way.'

He laughed, 'OK, but it's not as if we could get lost. It's just straight up.' And he strode off swinging the carrier bag containing their picnic.

Following him, Kate watched his long loping strides, his broad, confident shoulders and his neat bum. It did nothing to cool her down.

The first part of the climb was fine but then it got steeper and she was mortified to find she was soon panting in the heat. Hearing her, Rob glanced over his shoulder and slowed down.

'Come on, Katie lass. It's a Midland mound, it's hardly Helvellyn.'

'Thank God. The hell that is Helvellyn. I said I lived there, I didn't say I liked actually climbing up any of them.'

Astonished, he asked. 'What? You mean you don't enjoy a good climb?'

'Do I look like a goat? I've told you, I'm strictly a valley girl. I don't mind *looking* at them but after a hundred feet I get vertigo.'

'Seriously?'

'No, you daft thing. As all my friends will tell you, I'm prone to exaggerated exaggerations. But after nearly a year down here on the flat, I think I'm definitely out of condition.'

'OK. Come on, valley girl, grab hold.' Laughing, he held out his hand. She took it gratefully and felt goose pimples erupt over her body as they touched. What a wonderful strong grip! Feeling a definite wobble in her legs, she hung on tightly.

Steady girl, steady, she told herself. *He's still out of your league remember. Keep it fun, keep it friendly.*

Half way up she gasped, 'It's no good. I'm going to have to stop and admire the view. All right, you've guessed, that's a euphemism for I'm totally puffed out. I'm really not used to climbing in this heat.'

Grinning, he stopped. Embarrassed by her flushed face and heaving bosom, she pointed at a nearby bench.

'Oh, quick, there's an empty bench. We could actually sit and stare at the view. It might take a while for me to recover my composure.'

Laughing, he started to pull her gently towards the indicated spot. Then they stopped short as they were overtaken by a sprightly middle-aged couple who obviously had designs on this self-same seat.

'*Too late. Too late. The maiden cried,*' Kate declaimed theatrically, flinging her hand to her brow in mock despair. Seeing his bewilderment, she explained, 'Oh, sorry. I also have a terrible tendency to quote stuff as well. It's one of my Ma's favourite sayings.'

'Oh, I should have guessed as much. My mother's always doing that.'

'What?'

'Quoting from books, poems, anything.' He looked around. 'Anyway, benches are for oldies. Let's find somewhere nicer. And I don't know about you, but I'm starving. What do think? Here?' He guided her towards a quiet, secluded area of grass enclosed by bushes. 'Let's sit on this bank.'

'I know a bank whereon the wild thyme blows,' quoted Kate as she flopped gratefully down.

'Oh God, she's off again,' he grumbled good-naturedly, plonking himself next to her and dropping the carrier bag of make-shift picnic within her reach. 'Do you know a poem about everything?'

'You'd better believe it, brother. And a song too. Test me.

Go on, test me.'

'OK, OK. But not right now, I'm too hungry and I'm sure there's a poem that says don't get between a hungry man and his butties.'

'There must be. Let me think…'

'Nope. Now do you want the ham and pickle or the cheese and pickle? That's all they'd got, so if you don't like pickle, we're stuffed.'

'Like 'em both. Shall we split the packets and have one of each…um...each?'

He carefully prised the packets apart and allocated a triangular sandwich each.

Kate was surprised to find she was hungry as well. Then remembered, of course, she'd had no breakfast which is what had sent her out shopping in the first place. The pickle was tangy on her tongue and the cheese had a welcome sharpness.

As she munched, Kate looked in surprise at the vista before her.

'Actually, this view is stupendous. You can see for miles. Although I do confess to a tendency to disdain hills and stuff, I hadn't realised how much I missed being up high. And the fresh air.' Taking in great lung-fulls of air, she felt quite dizzy with joy at her surroundings...and the hot closeness of Rob's body as he lay sprawled beside her.

He nodded and, as they both hungrily attacked their picnic, he pointed out various landmarks. Kate sat listening, relishing every sun-filled moment and the wonderful closeness that seemed to exist between them.

'Do you want the last few bits of crisps?'

'No, you can have them.'

'Let's share.' Kate tipped the last broken remnants into her hand. They both dipped their fingers into the sharp, salty shards to lick off the crumbs. She blushed. It seemed so erotic somehow.

They finished off with the fruit. The pears were sweet and ripe, and the juice dripped down their fingers. Kate made embarrassingly loud sucking sounds as she tried to stop the sweet stickiness from dribbling down her chin. Laughing at her efforts, he gently leant over and wiped her mouth with a crumpled paper serviette. She held her breath, not daring to look at him. Flustered by the intimacy of this gesture, she turned away.

Although all her senses were on high alert just at his very presence, she still felt remarkably relaxed in his company. It could well be that Rob wasn't interested in her, other than as a companion on a sunny day when everyone else was unavailable. But so far she was enjoying herself and he seemed to be as well.

So she just continued sitting soporifically soaking up the sun, full of butties and crisps and gazing dreamily at the cloud patterns slowly unfolding above them. And secretly tingling with desire for the lithe figure lying sprawled beside her.

Chapter Three

Rob sat up and she could feel him watching her.

'So, Miss Kate Caswell, tell me all about yourself.'

She groaned. 'Do I have to?'

OK, she could throw up her usual smokescreen and hide all the upsetting stuff, but she was feeling relaxed and didn't want to make the effort. Although she never actually lied about her background, she didn't want the bother of parrying probing questions.

He looked a bit mystified at her response. 'Well, not if you don't want to, but why not?'

'It's just that I'm dead boring…and no, I'm not being mock modest, I really am.'

He lifted on his elbows and looked at her keenly, 'Why on earth do you think that?'

'Compared to my super sophisticated flatmates, I'm just a naïve peasant.'

'Nowt wrong with that, lass,' he teased in a warm northern accent.

She laughed and thumped him.

'Seriously, why do you think you are boring?'

The last thing Kate wanted was for the conversation to get serious. She had to keep it trivial.

'Oh, it's just everything. Right, for starters all my flatmates are doing interesting double-barrelled posh subjects. Super, slinky Selina is doing French *and* Italian, brainy Dee is 'reading' Philosophy *and* Maths, and even lovely Megan is doing Sociology *and* Anthropology. And I bet you are doing more than one 'ology.'

He laughed, but didn't deny it.

'And I'm just doing English…just English. The stuff

everyone here in England speaks all the time, reads all the time and everyone knows all about without actually having to go to Uni to study it. How boring can you get?'

Rob looked outraged. 'That's just not true. I'll take you to task on the English thing in a minute, but the last thing you are is boring. I've been wanting to get to know you for a while but what with exams and everything…' he tailed off.

'Me? Wanting to get to know *me?'* She gazed at him in astonishment.

'Yes, you. Megan says you're one of the nicest people she's ever met. In fact…' he paused, 'according to her, you're too bloody nice.'

She laughed, 'Yup. She's said it to me often enough… usually when she's cross.'

'Well, you do drive her potty you know. I probably shouldn't say this, but she gets really exasperated by the way you are always trying to stop the squabbles between the other two.'

'I know. They do row a lot, but they can't help it. Dee is overly precise and Selina can be just too dramatic for words. So they are bound to clash. But they have been very kind to me.'

'See. Megan's right. She says you always see the good in people. By the way, she doesn't think they are nice to you at all. She thinks they are interfering busybodies always telling you what to wear and how to flirt and criticising your friends as too loud and boisterous. And they seem to dislike the fact that you are popular because you are so funny and witty.'

She blushed. In fact they *were* always saying she was far too open and too noisy and laughed too much and they hinted that both she and her friends were a bit too 'common'. According to them, she ought to be more alluring and sophisticated and mix more with the right crowd.

'Sorry.' He ran his hand through his already wind-rumpled hair. 'This is very rude of me, repeating what Megan says. But knowing her, she will have said it to your face.'

Kate nodded.

'In fact,' he continued, 'she feels awful and she's not

saying anything anymore because she feels she's interfering as well.'

'Yes. She *has* said all that to me…and she's right. Oh, not about me being too nice, that sounds too wet. But I do hate arguments, especially over silly little things so I do try to calm things down, make them laugh if I can.'

He nodded. 'Yes. I've seen you around the campus and you are always the centre of attention, making people laugh. And Megan says you are full of fun. That's why I offered you a lift. I thought it would be nice to actually get to know you.'

Astounded, Kate just stared at him. Is this how she appeared? Surely not.

Pleased and confused by this image, and not knowing quite how to react, she took refuge in a country bumpkin accent.

'Well, that's very gallant of you to say so, kind sir. But I knows my place, I does.' And she touched an imaginary forelock.

'Woah, we need to do something about your self-image, my girl.'

'Oh no, you don't. You leave my self-image alone. I've had it up to here with people trying to sort me out one way and another. It's true, Selina and Dee have been trying to un-bumpkin me for a year now. Today is my day off from any sort of improvement. I'm going to rebel all day and just be pure, unreconstructed me. Like it or lump it.' And boy did she mean it. But perhaps not the 'pure' bit.

He grinned. 'Oh, I definitely like it.'

'Good.' She flopped down next to him and continued her perusal of the fluffy clouds in the brilliant azure sky, while mulling over what Rob had said. Megan's views didn't surprise her and she had to admit it was true about Selina and Dee.

As a child, she had endured Pa's many angry outbursts and fulminations about the world so she knew she hated confrontation and tried to deflect it whenever she could. But Selina and Dee seemed to actively enjoy quarrelling, both vying for the last word. In vain, she tried to ignore them but always found herself wading in to pacify the disputes. It got very wearing and she could quite understand Megan's irritation with the pair of them.

When she first arrived at Uni, she had loved having her flatmates around her. As an only child from a small isolated village she had always longed for a gang of girlfriends to go around with. She had lapped up the worldly advice from sophisticated Selina and straight-talking Dee on what to wear and how to wear it, what to say and how to say it.

But it had got a little tiresome. OK, maybe her accent was a little strong and, according to them, maybe she was hopelessly quaint and old fashioned in her dress sense and outlook and expressions…but what the hell.

They were horrified by her open friendliness, especially with boys. In order to entice a man, you had to retain an air of mystery, they said. But so far Rob seemed to like her company. She hadn't played any of the flirting games beloved of Selina, or used any of the teasing tactics Dee had tried to teach her. She had just been herself. And she was going to continue like that.

Sod it, he was here now, and so was she.

Suddenly a loud baa-ing close by startled her upright.

'Bloody sheep,' swore Rob, shooing one away. 'Only good with mint sauce.'

Kate couldn't help it and found herself reciting:

'The mountain sheep are sweeter,
But the valley sheep are fatter;
So we therefore deemed it meeter
To carry off the latter.

'Sorry, just made me think of my favourite sheep poem. Don't you just love the pun on *meeter* and *meater*?'

He shook his head in amused bewilderment. 'You really must meet my mum. And my sister,' he added as an afterthought.

'Why? What does your mum do?'

'That's where I take you to task on the studying English bit. My mum's an English teacher and my oldest sister, Fiona, has followed in her footsteps.' He gave her a hard stare. 'And I can assure you they are anything but boring. As you can imagine, I've been surrounded by literary discussions for most of my life. You should hear them as they exchange views on books and poems and plays, in fact anything cultural.'

Kate sighed. How wonderful to have someone knowledgeable to share her passion for literature with. Of course she and Ma had chatted endlessly about books and stuff, but Ma was self-taught so they had to discover things for themselves and neither had the confidence that they really knew what they were talking about. They had both reacted instinctively to the power of the written word and bonded over this shared passion. It had served as a shield from reality and the nasty tittle tattle of the village gossips.

'OK, I admit English isn't boring, not to me at least. But you're a scientist, aren't you? Where did that come from?'

'Hmmn, good question. Possibly from my dad's side. He's a G.P. and my other sister, Rosie, has just finished her medical training. So you can imagine the conversations over meals, if it wasn't books, it was bodies.'

He laughed. 'As the youngest, and the only boy, I suppose I was expected to follow one or the other, which is why, of course, I haven't. Quite fascinated by the workings of the human body but can't be doing with blood and guts and things. So I knew I definitely didn't want to be a doctor. Not of medicine anyway.'

'But I heard somewhere that you were hoping to continue on with your studies and do some research for a Ph. D?' Kate blurted out. 'If you get that, it will make you a Doctor, won't it? Not of medicine, of course, but…' Oh dear, had she just revealed that she had investigated him?

But he was too deep in thought and didn't seem to notice the implication of what she had said.

'Yes,' he said thoughtfully, 'maybe I will.'

Then, shaking his head, he said. 'I daren't think about that just yet. All my plans rest on getting a really good degree.'

'When will you know?'

'I've got a couple of days.' An anxious frown furrowed

across his forehead.

Talking about his exam results had obviously unsettled him. He leapt to his feet and started collecting all the packing from their picnic into the carrier bag.

'Come on, Keswick Kate. Let's go.'

He reached out his hand to haul her to her feet.

'No more idling about. Onward and upward we go. The top's just over that ridge.'

Happily placing her hand in his, Kate was on her feet in a second, ready and willing to follow him to…well, anywhere.

Chapter Four

Aided by Rob's firm grip, the last part of the ascent didn't take long. As they crested the top, Kate suddenly dropped his hand and, to his surprise, outstretched her arms. As usual she began her favourite twirling and singing scene from a S*ound of Music*. Her rendition was loud and heartfelt…only faltering when she saw the look of utter amazement on his face.

'Sorry, I'm afraid it's compulsory whenever you reach the top of a hill. Ma and me always do it.'

'Even when there're all these people around?' he asked, indicating several groups of amused spectators.

'Oh crikes. Where did they all come from?' Crimson with embarrassment, she rushed down a little track and hid in a small clump of trees.

A laughing Rob ran after her.

'What was all that spinning and singing stuff about then?'

'So sorry. Didn't realise there would be people up here. There's never anyone around on top of our local hills. But then, as it is usually raining, it isn't surprising. Pa used to drag us up the hills all the time, saying it would do us good. No matter what the weather. So Ma and me used to do an outrageously dramatic singing and twirling bit when we got to the top as a little blast of triumph. He hated it but it was our small rebellion, I suppose. So I still do it…it's sort of become an ingrained tradition.'

She put her head in her hands. 'I'm so sorry, Rob. I didn't mean to embarrass you like that…or me either. I'm going to need considerably more composure recovery time, I'm afraid.'

A deep chortle convinced her to look up into a pair of

laughing brown eyes. ‘Oh no, you don’t. Out you come. They have all gone now and I want to show you the views. But no more twirling, if you don’t mind.’ He wagged an amused finger at her before seizing her hand again and pulling her back up the hill. At the top, he paused, head to one side as he waited for another spinning outburst. Chastened, Kate just stood sulking, head bowed in mock submission.

Grinning, he said, ‘All right, all right, I give in. You can do a mini-twirl, but no arms and…no singing.’

Kate pouted and did a disconsolate single turn, flopping her arms by her side in a sort of waddling penguin motion.

Laughing, he hugged her, pinioning her flappy arms to her side. ‘I think the full Julie Andrew’s bit was better. In spite of the fact I’ve never seen anyone who looks less like her and… um…less likely to pass as a nun.’

The hug took her completely by surprise. She had a sensation of strong arms, taut chest, a subtle scent of musk and masculinity and felt a flash of desire blaze through her limbs.

Just as swiftly he released her and she went all hot, noticing his frank approval of her curvy form and her dishevelled, wind-ruffled hair. By now distinctly weak-kneed, she had to divert his attention from her flushed confusion.

‘OK, Sherpa Tensing,’ she said indicating the view, ‘now you’ve got me up here, tell me all about it.’

A magnificent panorama spread out before them. As the weather was so bright, they could see for miles. And he lost no time in pointing out the local landmarks.

Too disconcerted by that startling hug, she didn’t really listen, just watched his animated face and enthusiastic gestures as he indicated other hill ranges they could see.

‘Look, it’s so clear today those faint outlines on the horizon are the Black Mountains in Wales. Then over there, that long ridge is the Malverns. And to the north, that’s where we’ve come from today, Birmingham.’

He obviously loved being up high and, in his company, so did she.

'Come on. Let's explore. I want to show you some of the smashing walks up here. It's so good to be out of the city, isn't it?'

He set off and, loving his enthusiasm, she followed him happily as they rambled over the extensive hill side. It was a blissful, sunny afternoon full of aimless chatter, and just walking along, hand in hand, at times in companionable silence. At his prompting, Kate indulged him in her wide repertoire of mountain songs, old and new, from nursery rhymes to hillbilly songs, from Cher and John Denver to Dolly Parton and Tina Turner.

He looked at her in laughing amazement, 'I had no idea there were so many.'

'Those are just the tip of the iceberg of the mountain songs I know, although I think that's a bit of a mixed metaphor. And I haven't even started on hill or valley songs yet.'

'Aaagh,' he gargled.

'But I will if you like,' she threatened with a grin. And to her surprise he challenged her to go ahead and even joined in a few.

At one point, breathless with laughter at her animated rendition of *She'll be coming round the mountain when she comes,* he once again enveloped her in a swift hug. 'This is so wonderfully silly. I love it. It's the perfect antidote to all those dreadful weeks of serious swotting. Thank you so much for coming out with me today.'

He released her far too rapidly for her to react. But she was thrown into such confusion she could no longer remember which verse of the song she had reached and had to threaten to start all over again.

All day she had been determined to relax and just enjoy the easy atmosphere between them but it was getting harder to fight the electric frisson she felt every time their hands touched or their laughing eyes met.

The hugs made it impossible.

Was he as affected by these hugs as she was or were they simply an expression of his exuberance and post-exam euphoria? He seemed to be a very physically demonstrative man and he exuded a sort of pent-up energy and vitality. It was exhilarating to be with him. She felt more alive than she could ever remember.

Towards the end of the day as they began descending towards their starting point, he suddenly turned to her.

'Look, I can't bear to go back yet. Can you?'

Kate shook her head. She didn't want to go back...*ever!*

'And all this rambling has given me an appetite. Do you fancy a meal in that pub where we've parked the car?'

'Sounds great. As long as we go halves. After all, you provided the picnic and…'

'We'll argue about that later. Don't forget you're only a poor little fresher, whereas I am an important, worldly third year,' and here he puffed out his chest, 'so you need to do my bidding.'

'Huh,' Kate grunted, pretending to be unimpressed, but secretly longing to be crushed against his toned torso. And definitely yearning to do his bidding.

Grinning, he held her hand as he loped down the path and, after a reassuring walk round his precious car, he led the way into the low-beamed pub.

'No food songs welling up?' he whispered cautiously as they entered the crowded bar.

'Well, there is the obvious glorious food one from *Oliver*. I'll sing it to you later…but only if you are a good boy.'

He grinned. 'All the more reason to be bad then.'

The twinkle in his eyes made her catch her breath. If that wasn't flirting, she'd like to know what was. Unable to respond without giving away just how much she longed for him to be a bad boy, she followed him to the indicated table.

Although the bar was busy, it was still early so the restaurant part was quiet and they got a good table by the window.

She caught his anxious glance over to the corner containing his car as she perused the menu. She was hungry, but he was right, she was a poor little fresher and, until her flatmates reimbursed her for the shopping, she was seriously short of funds. Would it be obvious if she went for all the cheapest options?

As she scrutinised the prices, she was distracted by the overblown menu descriptions.

'Ooh look, Rob,' she whispered, unable to resist lingering suggestively over the salacious overtones, 'everything is "saucily spiced", or "dashingly drizzled". And you must be tempted by this steak dish, so "lip-smackingly moist" and "awash with jus".'

She was wickedly aware of lingering over the word 'moist', and so was Rob. His eyes were alight with fun…and something else she daren't acknowledge. When she noted the ice-cream was 'playfully stabbed with a banana,' he licked his lips very, very slowly.

A hot torrent of desire swept through her body. With a racing heart, she gazed into his teasing, dark eyes. Yes, he was definitely flirting and totally aware of the effect he was having on her.

A brisk, harassed waiter interrupted for their order and the moment was gone.

But there was definitely an undercurrent of sexy banter that hadn't been there before. Somehow all their utterances seemed to be imbued with double entendres, some intended, and some not.

'Do you fancy a full-bodied red?' Rob asked in faux innocence as he perused the wine list.

She giggled. 'I know anything you want to give me, Rob, will be just wonderful.'

His eyes widened.

Oh no, that really was too forward. She blushed to her roots and hid behind the huge menu.

The wine bottle suddenly seemed very phallic and she had to lower her eyes to fiddle with her cutlery as the waiter popped the cork. Rob seemed to follow her thoughts and shifted uncomfortably in his seat as he carefully draped his serviette over his lap.

This was ridiculous. It was all getting too steamy. She had to change the subject so she began to list her repertoire of food songs. Her offer to sing, albeit quietly, the full *Banana*

Boat Song was hurriedly declined, and swiftly followed by a laughing plea for no songs at all. Nothing daunted, she embarked on Shakespearian lines about 'food of love', quotations and any others she could think of that celebrated eating and drinking and being merry.

And she was, very merry. Some of it was the wine going straight to her head and some of it was the presence of the nicest, funniest, most fanciable man she had ever met.

Suddenly, as they were waiting for their main course, Rob leant forward and grabbed her hand, 'Thank you.'

'What for?'

'For this wonderful day. I can't believe how much I've enjoyed it. Thank goodness I spotted you this morning.'

'It was lucky for me as well. Those bags were bloomin heavy.'

'If I hadn't have met you, I don't know what I would have done today.' His tense energy was back and he let go of her hand. She thought he was going to get up and begin pacing up and down, but instead he passed a worried hand through his hair. 'I've been at such a loose end since my exams finished. The contrast between all those months…well, years really, of intense hard work, then, suddenly, nothing to do, but wait and see how I've done. I haven't been able to settle to anything. I've been down to my parents' but just got on everyone's nerves mooching around worrying. In the end my dad said I could borrow his precious car for a few days and told me to go off and do something. I was just on my way back from home this morning when I spotted you.'

He looked a little shame faced. 'I felt so flash stopping and offering you a lift in my snazzy car, and then, for a minute there, I thought you were going to say no. Were you?'

'Um, yes. I felt so fed up and hot and bedraggled and grumpy, I really couldn't be bothered with anyone.' Dare she confess the other reason? 'And…I assumed you were only befriending me so you could meet Selina, and I was a bit cross about that as well.'

He looked stunned. 'Why would I want to meet such a snooty, self-obsessed person like her?'

Now it was her turn to be stunned. ‘Well, she is gorgeous.’
‘And doesn’t she know it. And you actually thought I was using you for that?’
‘Yup. It’s happened before.’
‘Huh. Well they were idiots if they would rather be with her than you.’
Kate could hardly believe her ears and stuttered her thanks.
‘And you’re an idiot as well,’ he continued, smiling, ‘for not realising just how gorgeous you are too.’
His frank admiration was wonderful…and totally embarrassing. ‘Don’t give me that flannel. You are obviously drunk or…’
‘No, definitely not drunk, I’m driving remember. You really do have a problem with receiving compliments, don’t you? So listen to me, my tantalising Twirly Girl,’ he once again seized her hand and looked directly at her, ‘you have the most amazing green eyes and lovely, shiny reddy-brown hair…is that called chestnut or something? And what a smile. Give me someone as much fun as you any day rather than a vapid, stick-insect bimbo like Selina.’
She was lost for words.
‘And of course, you have the most endearing tendency to blush whenever anyone is nice to you. But it’s true. You are brilliant company. Look at today. You have made me laugh… you have even made me sing…’
‘But not twirl.’
‘No, not twirl. A man must retain some gravitas.’ Suddenly serious again, he swirled his wine thoughtfully round his glass and sighed. ‘It has been so great being outdoors and looking at all that green expanse of countryside. I’ve stored it all up, especially knowing I could be cooped up for the next few years.’
The tense frown had reappeared and his hands clenched round his glass. He took a long drink.
What? Kate jolted alert. Cooped up? Was he going to prison? What was going on?

Chapter Five

'Cooped up?'

'Or not. It all depends on my final exams results. My whole future hangs in the balance.' Rob laughed. 'Oh, don't look so aghast. Sorry, I didn't mean to sound so dramatic. But that's why I have enjoyed today so much. It has stopped me fretting about what's going to happen next.'

'And?'

Just then, their steaks arrived and Rob seemed to lose the thread of what he was about to say.

Kate gave him a couple of minutes as he tucked hungrily into his meal. She couldn't touch hers until she found out what he meant. Today had been too good to be true. Was this where it crumbled?

'Come on, Rob. You can't do that to a girl.' She put her knife and fork down decisively.

He paused with a forkful of chips, 'What?'

'You can't say my whole life hangs in the balance and all that stuff and not explain further. And all that about being cooped up.'

'Oh right, I'm sorry, I was just so hungry but I suppose it was a bit…um...'

'Enigmatic? Doom laden?'

'Oh no, in fact being cooped up is a good thing. I suppose I don't like talking about it in case I jinx it, but it's not fair to half-tell a story, is it?'

'No.'

'OK. If, and only if, my exam results are brilliant,' he paused as if not daring to articulate it, 'I have been accepted on a team that's going to the Antarctic.'

His face as he said it conveyed a huge mixture of hope, excitement, tension and anxiety.

'Wow. You mean like the proper Antarctic? The South Pole and snow and ice and penguins and stuff?'

'Yup. The whole caboodle.' He glanced at her shyly but she could see his amber-flecked eyes shining with suppressed excitement. 'I've been holding my breath, not allowing myself to believe it will really happen as I know how lucky I've been to be accepted. Lots of people applied but we've had to do fitness tests and all sorts to see if we are physically and psychologically suited to living in such isolation in polar conditions.'

'How amazing.' Her meal forgotten, Kate couldn't keep the wonder out of her voice. 'What exactly will you be doing there?'

'Right, it's a bit complicated but I'm going to study... well...the ice. We will drill down through the ice core, take lots of samples and analyse them. From them we can tell all sorts of things that have happened over the past hundreds of years. Put simply, my results will go towards studying the effects of pollution on climate change. As you know there's a big debate going on at the moment about it. The more information we get, the more we can add to the debate.'

Kate's brain was whirring, but before she could ask any more he continued, 'It's not just me of course. The team are a wonderful mix of environmental scientists, meteorologists, geologists, climatologists, penguin-ologists...well...an awful lot of ologists,' he finished quickly as if not wanting to bore her.

'Sounds amazing.'

'Hope so.'

Having broached the subject, it seemed as if he couldn't stem his enthusiasm for the project. As they ate their meals, Rob told her more and more about the expedition's aims and purposes. How they would live in a self-contained pod-like encampment making forays out on to the ice. Eagerly he explained the various aspects of what they were trying to discover and how it would mean living for two years on the polar icecap studying basically ice and the weather.

'Two years?' She tried to keep the dismay from her voice.

'Yes, and maybe more depending on what results we get. I may write up my findings in the field or come back here. I don't know.'

'When do you go?' asked Kate with a sinking feeling.

'If all goes well,' he crossed his fingers, 'I have to go next week for some training, preparation and meet the rest of the team. Then we have about a month to get everything organised before we sail down south on our expeditionary vessel to coincide with the Antarctic spring and set up camp and everything.'

Next week, Kate thought with a thud. So little time. But so little time for what? What could she possibly hope for? They may have only just met but already the depth of her feelings for him were beyond anything she had ever experienced before.

A wave of desolation swept over her. Lowering her head so he couldn't see the tears that were prickling her eyes, she busied herself with cutting up her steak into tiny portions. Not that she wanted to eat anymore.

Rob continued to talk animatedly about the impending preparations, seemingly oblivious to the shock his news had inflicted on her. Which is how it should be, she thought. How selfish of me to spoil his excitement with how all this affects me.

This was so unfair. But, then again, so predictable. *Of course* he was leaving to go and have adventures in the big, wide world. That's what people she cared about always did.

At least forewarned was fore-armed. *And I'm good at waiting for people to come back. I'll just have to bottle up my feelings. Put on a brave face and enjoy the moment.* Looking into his bright, eager face, she thought, to hell with it. I'm here now and I fancy him. If anything, the revelation that their time together was going to be limited made her feel more reckless and heightened her suppressed desire.

She downed her glass of wine and tuned in to Rob's further conjectures.

'Of course, none of this may happen. I'm convinced I made a mess of one of the exams. But, hey, if so I will stick around here and probably join Josh. He's also sweating on getting a good degree but he wants to stay here while Megan finishes her course. So the fall-back plan is doing our research together at this Uni. Which will be fine. It means I will be able to get to know some folk better, and you never know, I might even learn to twirl.'

His eyes met hers as he said it and Kate selfishly crossed surreptitious fingers under the table hoping that he would stay. She could definitely teach him to twirl.

'Anyway, come on, eat up your steak. And finish off the wine. I'm driving remember, so no more for me. I'm really looking forward to my pud. For some inexplicable reason I'm fancying that playfully stabbed banana.'

How could she resist those teasing brown eyes?

The banana splits with their accompanying two provocatively placed balls of ice-cream provoked much glee. Any innuendo was superfluous.

And there was a ray of hope he might not go. Feeling incredibly guilty, she clung to this idea for the rest of the meal.

As Rob went to call for the bill, Kate said, 'It's no good. I'm going to have to go to the loo. But don't you dare pay it all while I'm gone.'

Feeling a littlc tipsy, once there, she surveyed her flushed image in the mirror. 'Oh, what a mess.' She dragged her fingers through her windblown hair in a vain attempt to smooth down the curls. Then ran her wrists under the cold tap before carefully dabbing her forehead and rosy cheeks.

All the time her thoughts were whirling round her head. She fancied him so much but awareness of his imminent departure lurked below her fevered longings. How stupid to fall for a guy who was going.

She sighed. Processing all the day's events was proving too much for her befuddled brain. Suddenly she remembered to check her cash so she could go halves on the bill. Delving into the small cross-body bag she had been wearing all day, she fumbled for her purse. Something silver lurking there caught her eye.

Her condom. The one Megan had given her, and her other flatmates, on their first day at Uni. During this initial getting-to-know each other session, Megan had revealed she had just got back from a gap year in Botswana. She had become gravely messianic about using condoms.

'After what I have seen of Aids in Botswana...and don't attempt to tell me this is England and it won't happen here,' she had said in her lilting Welsh accent whilst eyeing Selina who had tried to interrupt her...'I want you all to solemnly promise you will always, *but always*, get the bloke to use one of these. Let's face it, if you know him well enough for sex, you know him well enough to insist he doesn't go in without an overcoat.'

She had stared emphatically at them all and made them all individually promise.

'Right. And just to show how serious I am, fetch your purses and put one of these in now.'

Cowed by her insistence, they had all dutifully trotted off, fetched their purses and carefully stowed the proffered silver packages away.

'Now, I've got loads because I'm a bit of a boring evangelist on this one, so I'm going to put a few in a drawer in the kitchen for everyone to use when they need them…I know, here under the cutlery tray so you can always discreetly go for a spoon and sneak one into your hand, if you're a bit shy,' here she had pointedly looked at Kate, 'and right now we will make a rule that if you use any, you replace them at the earliest opportunity. OK?'

Kate remembered blushing, suspecting Megan had guessed, correctly, that she had never bought, let alone used, a condom in her life. So she realised it was for her benefit that Megan went on to explain.

'You don't have to get them from shops and chemists. They are free from student services and, if that's still too embarrassing, most student loos should have a dispenser in them.'

'And late-night garages sell them too, you know. They have dispensers in the ladies,' Selina blurted out, then looked embarrassed at possessing this knowledge. 'At least that's what I've heard,' she finished lamely.

Wow, I've never seen them in any Keswick loos, Kate had thought. Do they cater more for sex in the south?

Still the little silver-foiled packet in her purse had made her feel very sophisticated. She was a bit worried about what people would think if she was run over by a bus and they found it there. But it also felt rather naughty and grown-up and full of possibilities. So she had kept it.

Was tonight the night when it would get used at last?

She looked at her excited reflection in the mirror and throwing caution to the winds, she fervently hoped so.

Chapter Six

She emerged to find Rob had paid and would brook no argument, insisting she would ruin his macho credentials if she even so much as took her purse out in his presence.

Stumbling laughing from the pub, they found a soft twilight had descended over the warm June evening. The eggshell-blue sky was shot through with striations of burning reds and glowing yellows from the setting sun. Over the darkening outline of the hills, a majestic golden moon was just sailing into view. Kate gasped at the magnificent beauty of it. That really was the most romantic moon she had ever seen.

She couldn't bear for this perfect day to end. Deep down, she feared that Rob's flirting was leading nowhere. Was this amazing encounter going to end in disappointment? She determined she wasn't going to lose this golden opportunity.

Tonight had to be the night.

She had enjoyed teenage fumbles with her friend Harry on the nearby farm, but was very careful not to cause any tittle-tattle in the village. And, although she had loved the sexy snogs with Simon, her sixth form boyfriend, ever mindful of what had happened to her mum, she had always curbed her longings.

Somehow tonight felt different. Certainly her feelings for Rob were more intense than she had ever experienced before. An unaccustomed spirit of recklessness seemed to have possessed her. Perhaps the wine had helped lower her usual uptight inhibitions.

Impulsively, she said, 'Let's not go back to that stinky city just yet. It's a wonderful evening. Just look at that amazing June moon.'

Giggling, she repeated the phrase, elongating the vowels, for the sheer pleasing sound of it.

'A Juuune moooon. We can't waste it. Come on. Let's just climb up the hill to look at the view one more time. Don't you think it will be incredible, all silvery and shadowy and glowing and mysterious?'

'Kate, Kate what are we to do with you?' He pulled her tight into one of his fierce hugs. Then held her there pressed against him before very slowly releasing her. 'All right, as long as you promise no moon poems. Come on, give us your hand. You'll have to be careful with your footing in the dark.'

It was true. It was a bit hazardous in spite of the bright moonlight and Kate was a bit tipsy. But they weren't the only reasons why she leant on him more than she had done all day. That hug had set her heart racing. His strong arms about her had awakened longings deep in her body that yearned to be fulfilled. Her breath kept catching in her throat as she gripped his strong firm hand.

Half-way up, at the same place as before, he halted.

'From your somewhat heavy breathing I surmise you are either in the throes of uncontrollable passion, or we need to stop and admire the view again while you regain your composure.'

Oh, if only he knew it really is pure passion, or rather impure passion, she thought, ducking her head so he wouldn't see the expression on her face.

'OK, Keswick Kate, let's find "our" spot.'

They had reached the enclosed, gentle, grassy bank which looked even more inviting than it had during their picnic in the afternoon.

Still finding it hard to breathe, she flopped down and stared at the dramatic vista before them. The moonlight was illuminating all the undulations which gave an eerie radiance to every feature. Pockets and spatters of yellow houselights glowed between the dark, uninhabited patches as far as the eye could see.

'Look, Rob. The street lamps on the main roads are like a daisy chain of lights. It's so magical, isn't it?'

He nodded, seemingly as transfixed as she was.

All noise seemed miles away and, save for a warm breeze rustling amongst the leaves, they were cocooned in their own little world.

She settled back on the grass and stared at the star-speckled sky. So romantic, she thought. *If only…*

Rob lay close to her. ‘Yes, you were right. It was worth the climb. It really is magical.’

‘I can’t believe it, a scientist with a soul?’

‘You cheeky thing. I’ll have you know, deep down, I have a very poetic soul.’

‘Prove it. Recite a poem about the moon.’

‘I warned you, no poems about the moon.’

‘You must know the Walter de la Mare one. The one that goes—’

‘I can see there’s only one way to stop you…’ He leant over and his lips closed over hers.

It was a very tender, loving kiss. Tentative at first, and then it deepened and became more passionate and intense. As Kate wound her arms around his neck to pull him closer, she curved her body towards his. She had never been kissed like this before. Ever. All her senses quivered with anticipation as if she had been waiting all day for this. Perhaps she had been waiting all her life.

It felt right. A dam of pent-up desire burst as, melting in the passion of his embrace, her body clamoured for closer contact. She yearned for more.

‘Wow,’ she sighed as they came up for air.

‘And how,’ he murmured, and kissed her again, more hungrily, more urgently.

The atmosphere was suddenly electric. He held her against him in an ardent embrace. And, as their bodies pressed into each other, she felt increasingly light-headed. Entwining her arms around him, she felt the long, lean length of him against her eager body. On fire with her need for him, her kisses were as demanding as his.

Suddenly he pulled away with a groan, ‘Oh, Kate. I think it’s time we went back down, don’t you?’

‘What? Why?’

‘Because I’m only human and the combination of you and the moon…’ He put his head back and gave a long wolf howl.

Grinning, she reached up and insistently pulled him towards her again. Pressing her open lips to his, in a voice she barely recognised as her own, she whispered, ‘It’s nothing to do with the moon, Rob. It’s you I want. I’ve been longing for this all day.’

His eyes widened.

‘Are you sure?’

‘Oh yes, yes, yes, but…oh crikes. How does one do this? Look, could you just pass me my handbag?’

‘Your handbag?’ She could hear the surprise in his voice.

‘Please. I need my purse.’

Mystified, he dragged her bag towards her. She couldn’t bring herself to explain, to spoil the romanticism of the moment, but a promise was a promise, so she just silently opened her purse and the condom shone silver in the moonlight.

He laughed. ‘You old romantic you. Give it here.’

Chapter Seven

Rob lay back, looking dazed as he stared into the star-studded sky. Then drawing her close against his naked chest, he gently kissed the top of her hair. Softly he stroked away the tears that were once again springing from her eyes.

'Oh, Kate, that was…so wonderful. Was it…?' He searched her face.

'Wonderful for me too? Oh yes.'

Had he guessed it was her first time? Driven by pure instinct and need, everything seemed so natural. The build-up of desire had overtaken her and the wild release had been so powerful, it had left her gasping and sobbing with pure pleasure.

And here she was crying again.

He cradled her in his arms while she wept again from sheer emotion.

There were no words so they lay there entwined for a long time. Rob seemed as stunned as she was by the tumultuous sensations unleashed by the intensity of their lovemaking.

Nestling skin to skin, her head fitted perfectly into the hollow of his shoulder. With his arms wrapped warmly round her, she was amazingly aware of the musky scent of his skin, the muscular contours of his bare chest and the strong rhythmic thump of his heart beating against her breasts. A heaviness had descended on all her limbs in the wake of the exhilarating release of such pent-up emotions. Gradually her pulse ceased its frantic beating, leaving a strange euphoria.

Slowly she emerged and became aware of her surroundings. A slight breeze was wafting gently against her bare back and the benign moon seemed to be smiling down on them. Then a fleeting cloud obscured its face and in the sudden chilly darkness, she shivered.

It sort of broke the spell. Rob reached out and draped his discarded T-shirt over her bare shoulders.

Pulling her even tighter into his warm chest, he muttered gruffly, 'I want you to know just how special that was. It was so amazing, so…'

'Romantic?' she offered, snuggling deeper into his embracing arms.

She felt him grin. 'Yes, you're right. That's it, so romantic.'

'For me too. It was the most romantic thing that has ever happened to me in my whole life.'

She reached up for a kiss.

Perhaps one day she would tell him he was her first…but not now. Remembering he was going soon, a huge hand suddenly squeezed her heart. She really mustn't get too involved.

Too late. It had all been so perfect, she had no regrets.

If he is leaving, then I must make hay while the sun shines…or make love while the moon beams in this case.

There and then she resolved to just enjoy Rob's company while she could. With a contented, fulfilled sigh she lifted her head for another kiss. And for whatever might follow.

Chapter Eight

Much later, a blissfully happy Kate giggled back down the hill to the car, leaning on an equally happy Rob to steady her.

As he opened the car door for her, he drew her into him and kissed her tenderly.

'That was truly amazing.'

'Yes, well met by moonlight, proud Roberto.'

'A quote by any chance?'

'Well, a misquote, but I'm too happy to think of anything else.'

'Good. I am indeed proud to have rendered you lost for quotes.' And with a smile he roared the car's engine into life.

There was a deep intimate silence all the way back to the city with her hand resting warmly on his thigh. Every now and then they grinned at each other.

For once she didn't need words, or poems or songs. Everything was perfect. Sighing with complete contentment, she felt utterly fulfilled. As she snuggled down, feeling the car's vibrations purr through her newly awakened body, she couldn't stop smiling.

Neither could he. Until, just before they reached the campus, he slowed down. 'Sorry to spoil the idyll, but I'm going to have to pull in here for some petrol. She's a lovely car, but very thirsty.'

'That's OK. I suppose I ought to pop into the ladies for a quick tidy up.'

He nodded and grinned as he pulled a few strands of straw from her T-shirt.

Slipping into the loos, Kate gazed at her blushing, delighted face and her tousled grass-filled hair. What had just happened there? It wasn't like her at all to be so reckless.

What had possessed her? And she had felt possessed. Taken over by an overwhelming instinctive desire to be in his arms, skin to skin, body to body, making gloriously passionate love. The moonlight had rendered the whole experience surreal and deeply powerful. Gone was the boring, biddable Kate to be replaced by a silver siren who knew what she wanted…and had got it.

She could still feel his lips covering her naked body in kisses, his hands caressing her tingling skin. Her first time. She sighed. She wanted more.

Then her eyes alighted on the condom machine. So Selina was right.

Dare she risk there being none back at the flat or should she buy some more? He just might want to come up to her room. She certainly hoped so. Was she tempting fate by being prepared? But it would be worse if he did want to and she hadn't got any.

With great trepidation she approached the machine and read the operating instructions, dreading anyone coming in and catching her. Fumbling in her purse, she managed to find the right change. But the metal drawer on the machine was so stiff she had to jerk it really hard to open it. The screeching noise it made seemed to reverberate embarrassingly around the tiled walls. Hastily stuffing the contents into her bag, she made her escape through the crowded shop. But as she scurried through, she was uncomfortably aware of some comments and laughter. With horror she thought they must have heard her using the machine, so with flaming cheeks she rushed past Rob paying at till.

When he joined her at the car his shoulders were shaking with laughter. Kate's heart sank. So he heard her using the machine as well. This was so excruciatingly mortifying.

'Look,' he said, reining in a chuckle, 'I don't quite know how to tell you this but... well, you have the most almighty grass stains all up the back of your T-shirt.'

She blushed bright crimson as they drove off into the warm night, laughing.

But thank God. At least he didn't hear the bloody machine.

When he stopped outside her block of flats, Kate steeled herself to sound nonchalant.

'I don't suppose you would like to come in for, um…a cup of coffee?'

'Well, no, not really.'

Her heart plummeted. Of course. She should have known. She was a one-night stand. Well, not even a night, just a hill top tup.

'Coffee tends to keep me awake,' he continued, 'but then again, if you think there might be something worth staying awake for…'

He was teasing. Thank goodness.

He pointed to where the pack of condoms was protruding from her open bag. 'And besides, it would be a shame to waste those.'

Trying to muffle their laughter, they crept into the flat. But just as she opened her bedroom door, a loud cough sounded from the kitchen. On turning round she saw the three faces of her flatmates staring at her, two in astonishment and Megan with a delighted smile.

'Oh, hiyah.'

She wasn't quite sure of the etiquette of the situation. Should she introduce Rob or what? Her speculations on the social niceties got no further. Rob took control and tumbled her into her room…and into bed.

The narrow Uni bed wasn't as romantic as the moonlit hillside, but their activities more than made up for the prosaic surroundings. Kate had lost all inhibitions and giggled with delighted anticipation as they divested each other of their clothes. She couldn't believe how much fun it was as she ran her hands over his taut, toned body and he explored her soft curves.

She was so glad she had bought all those extra supplies at the garage.

As the bright morning light shone through her thin bedroom curtains, she awoke to see Rob lying next to her. Although uncomfortably crunched up against the wall, he was smiling at her.

'Morning, Gorgeous.'

She grinned sleepily. What a great way to start the day.

He kissed her before making a move to clamber over her.

'Sorry, I've got to love and leave you. I must go and see if my results have come through.'

'Oh yes, of course. Oh crikey, Rob. Best of luck although I'm sure you won't need it.' She crossed her fingers, trying not to think disloyal thoughts about a result that would keep him at home.

He cupped her face for another kiss. 'Well certainly, last night took my mind off worrying about them. Can't think why.' He leant over her again and she felt his long, lean torso press into her naked body.

With a groan, he levered himself upright.

'As much as I would love to stay and further sample your delectable delights, my darling, I really must away. See you later for celebrations or commiserations. Should I pick you up at lunchtime? I should know by then. I'm hoping it's just a formality but you never know.' He grimaced, creasing his forehead into a worried frown.

Peering over the edge of her bright red duvet cover, she watched him get dressed, feasting her eyes on his firm, lithe body. Feeling her scrutiny, he looked up and with a lascivious grin he pulled his jeans over the bulge in his shorts. For a moment she wondered if he was going to come back to bed, but with a laugh he shrugged on his T-shirt. Quickly he pulled on his shoes and with a swift kiss and a caress, he was off.

'Here we go. Wish me luck. See you later. OK?'

Oh yes, very much OK.

With a contented sigh Kate snuggled back down into the rumpled bed, hugging herself in delight as she relived the events of the previous day…and night.

How amazing. Twenty-four hours ago she had been hot,

disgruntled and grumpy…now she was alight with excitement and sexual desire from head to toe.

Dying for a pee and a cuppa, in that order, she ended up in the kitchen, to find her three flatmates, faces alive with curiosity, staring at her.

‘So you really enjoyed yourself last night?’

A sleepy, sated Kate was only vaguely aware of the sarcastic note in Dee’s voice.

‘Ooooh yes, and how.’

‘We know. We saw the grass stains on your back,’ Selina snorted while buttering her toast. ‘And are you aware how thin these walls are?’

‘Yes. I bet they heard you in Harborne,’ continued Dee irritably.

‘Hereford more like,’ sniggered Selina, crunching her crusts and eating marmalade from a spoon.

Kate blushed.

But in fact, considering how often embarrassment at her friends’ activities had forced her to turn up the music in her room, the words ‘pot and kettle’ sprang to her mind.

‘Rob’s a great bloke. Ignore them. They’re only jealous,’ Megan observed, pushing back her chair to wash her coffee cup.

‘No, we’re not,’ Selina countered, angry as the barb clearly hit its mark. ‘We’re worried about her. After all he’s a third-year student and bound to be off soon. I just hope she doesn’t get too smitten.’

‘What if she does?’ Megan challenged.

‘Well, it could all end in tears,’ Dee said, loyally supporting Selina’s concern.

‘For God’s sake, she’s a big girl now. Stop interfering. Let her sort it out for herself.’ Seeing the unwelcome reception her words received, Megan turned to Kate with a warm smile. ‘Are you seeing him again?’

‘Yes, he’s just gone back to get his results and change, then we are going out again. He’s got a fantastic little sports car and yesterday he took me up the Clents.’ She giggled at the memory.

'Is that a double entendre?' said Dee suspiciously.

'Well, actually I was going for the triple.' With that Kate swept out to have a long luxurious shower full of heartfelt warbling about love, the moon and June.

Chapter Nine

A quick toot of a car horn alerted her to the presence of Rob's familiar red car, waiting for her outside the flat.

Even though it was another scorching day, Kate took the precaution of taking a cardigan. Just in case she needed to cover grass stains.

Trotting out expectantly, she was aglow with excitement and sexual anticipation. Grinning widely, she clambered into his lovely old-fashioned sports car and leant over to plant a huge kiss on his smiling lips.

'Well. Am I talking to a future doctor of an 'Ology?'

'Still don't know for sure. The official results haven't been posted but apparently my Prof gave Josh a wink and a thumbs up yesterday for both of us. So…'

'So shall we assume a fantastic result and celebrate?'

He groaned. 'I daren't. Not yet. So do you think you can distract me again today?'

'Oh, I'm sure I can manage to think of something.'

Their eyes met and they both burst out laughing.

'OK. What about the Lickeys?' He gave a sly sideways look and grinned salaciously.

'Lickeys?'

'They're another set of local, rather bosomy, hills.'

'Are they suitable for a girl to twirl on?'

'Oh, and a lot more besides. You see I must take you up the Lickeys via Lickey End.'

'You've made that up.'

'Nope, I assure you. There really is a Lickey End.'

Kate gurgled. Pinkly.

And it certainly lived up to its name.

Later, after a wonderful day full of sun and wandering the hills and some very al fresco love-making in a secluded spot, Rob beamed, 'So, fair maiden...'

She snorted. Maiden she most definitely was not.

'...fancy a curry?'

'Love one.'

'I know a very nice Balti house near the Uni.'

Seated in a corner of a very lively restaurant, waiting for their curry, Rob continued the game they had played on and off all day. Picking up a spoon he demanded, 'Spoon poem!'

'Easy. Owl and the Pussycat.

They dined on mince, and slices of quince

Which they ate with a runcible spoon.'

'OK. OK…Um…Knife.'

'Um...*Is this a dagger I see before me*? Lady Macbeth.'

'Uuum. Dagger?'

'Well, it is a knife.'

'OK. I'll let you have that one.' He grinned. 'But I haven't given up yet.' And his eyes searched the restaurant for even more outlandish subjects to test her on.

As their meal arrived, he thought of something. Eventually after much pondering Kate had to admit reluctantly, 'All right. All right. I think you may have beaten me this time. Just for the moment I can't think of a single quote about curry.'

'Yes! Yes, Yes,' he whooped, delightedly banging the table, to the amusement of their fellow diners.

'I thought it was the girl's job to fake the orgasm in the restaurant,' she whispered.

He choked.

Although it was a warm evening, Kate returned wearing the cardigan and this time Rob went into the loos at the garage.

That night in her room she put on some beautiful, romantic music. Very loudly.

Next morning Kate was startled awake, as were the flatmates, by a loud primeval cry.
'AAAAaahahaaAAAAAAYYYYYYYY.'
Astonished, she opened her eyes wide as the dim light filtered through her thin curtains to see a naked man looming over her.
'AAAAAAAAYyyyyyahaahhhhhhhhhhaa,' Rob yodelled again, beating his broad bare chest with his fists.
'Me Tarzan,' he growled.
He glanced down proudly at his manhood and Kate could see something magnificent looming up in the gloom.
'Now can Kate show her Tarzan what to do with a pre-brecky erecky???'
She was able to offer several very acceptable serving suggestions.

Later, a decidedly grumpy Dee surprised Kate in the kitchen making a post-coital pot of tea.
'What on earth was that?' she snapped.
'Er…'
'Yes,' mumbled Selina emerging grumpily from her room. 'I've never heard anything like it. What was he yowling about? Have you no consideration. There're people trying to sleep, you know.'
Thinking of all the many times through the year they had kept her awake with their bedroom antics, Kate smiled sweetly and deftly manoeuvred two mugs of tea and a tray of toast into her darkened room.
'Frankly, my dears, I don't give a hoot.'
She heard Megan chortle. 'About bloody time.'

She snuggled back into bed.
'Mmmn, gorgeous,' he murmured.
'Me or the tea?'
He laughed. 'You of course. Gorgeous…but a bit of a dimwit.'
She hit him.
'Careful, this bed is too small for fisticuffs. It's only just

big enough for very circumspect bonking. I'll swear that the university makes them this narrow to dampen all but the keenest ardour.

'Talking of which, I can feel an ardour coming on...'

Later, crunching their cold toast, Kate became aware of an unfamiliar sound.

'Oh blast. It's raining. I can hear it pelting against the window. It sounds like a right Lake District lash down.'

Rob nuzzled into her breasts. 'Mmmn, I don't care. We can stay here today.'

'I knew it. You've run out of suggestively named local attractions. Admit it.'

'Not at all. I could always show you the Long Mynd.' He glanced down seductively.

She giggled. 'I'm sure you make them up.'

How could she feel so relaxed with Rob? Even though her hair was a tousled mess and she wore no make-up, it didn't seem to matter to him.

Thin university curtains closed against the grey skies, they nestled together.

'I'm going to have to get up soon and go and see about my bloomin result. It's definitely out today, but the notice said they won't be posted till ten o'clock. So I'm not going any earlier to pace up and down. I know, recite me some of your poems.'

'Really?'

'Yes, I love the way you enter into them with your whole spirit. And I'm so impressed you can remember so many off by heart. Yesterday, for example up the Lickeys, you knew the whole of *The Lady of Shallot*. That's amazing.'

'It's one of Ma's favourites. We used to play a game and challenge each other to think of one for everything we did.'

'She sounds amazing.'

'She is,' Kate agreed. But her brain was whirring. How stupid of her to get onto this subject. Rob was bound to ask more about her family now and the last thing she wanted to do was spoil the atmosphere by dredging up her family's past.

'A fresh start,' Ma had insisted. 'Leave all the tittle-tattle behind.' And so far she had successfully deflected any intrusive questions.

Yet here she was lulled by the intimacy between them, bringing up the subject of her Ma and leaving herself open to enquiries. Quickly, she side-tracked to more discussion about poetry.

'I'll tell you the one poem that doesn't fit at the moment, should I?'

'Um, let me see. I really don't know many, especially about lying naked in bed with a gorgeous green-eyed girl with glowing chestnut curls.'

For a moment she was lost for words. What a beautiful description. But obviously he was flattering her. She thumped him.

'What a smooth talker you are, Rob Frazier.'

'No, I'm not. I keep telling you, my lovely Twirly Girl, you *are* gorgeous.'

She rewarded him with a long, loving, toast-crumbed kiss.

'Hmmn, second-hand jam.' He licked his lips. 'Delicious. So what unsuitable poem were you thinking about then?'

She gurgled, '*To My Coy Mistress*.'

'True. Sitting starkers eating toast in bed, cannot in any way be classed as coy. But, oh temptress mine, if you have noticed the bright light through these curtains, methinks the weather has cheered up. So I'm going to go and get my blasted results then, come what may, do you fancy another trip out or should we just laze away here?'

'But if we stayed here, what on earth would we do all day?' she asked in wide-eyed innocence.

'Hmmn, I can't imagine.' But from the gleam in his eyes he was obviously thinking the same as her. 'But tempt me not. If, just if, I'm going to see nothing but white polar ice-scapes for a couple of years, I fancy filling my memory with some rolling green vistas and the sound of you puffing up the hills.'

'I do not puff up the hills.'

‘You do. I can’t believe that someone who lives amongst the mighty Lakeland peaks is so bad at actually climbing them.’

‘I’m bloomin not. It’s just you are half-man half-mountain-goat and you leap up them at a phenomenal pace.’

‘Half goat eh?’ He turned, eyes gleaming.

Chapter Ten

Kate just couldn't settle. She had tidied her room, ironed a couple of tops and was now giving the kitchen a thorough clean. Rob seemed to be gone a long time. Was that good or bad?

She peered out of the kitchen window once again, watching for Rob's familiar loping figure rushing back to give her the news. It wasn't only his future that depended on his results. So did hers. Was she destined to wait for him for two years? Because wait she would, for however long it took. She knew that for certain.

Whoever would have thought a few days ago, I would be standing here looking out for my lover to return? My lover. Oh crikes, my *lover*. The word sent shivers down her spine. Was he her lover? Or just a boyfriend? Somehow 'boyfriend' seemed too prosaic for what she thought they had between them. What they did together seemed more than sex; it seemed like making love. She knew that's how she felt about it. But did it seem like that to him?

If, as predicted, he had got a first in his degree he would return full of plans and excitement about his future. Only days left before he was off to Antarctica to live amongst all those frozen wastes. And it was a waste…of a fantastic man.

Indignantly she wondered why some people felt the need to travel, to explore. Her mum was one such…and look where that got her?

Angrily she tried to push those thoughts aside and continued with her vigil at the window. She'd had a lot of experience in compartmentalising her life. Bad things were put in a box and the lid was closed. Firmly.

But it didn't stop the yearning. The best thing that had

ever, *ever* happened to her and it would only last a bare week.

Hmmn, perhaps the word 'bare' was a touch Freudian, she thought. Anyway there's nothing I can do to stop him going so I've just got to enjoy it to the full for now. In fact, *Gather ye rosebuds while ye may.*

Then there he was. Running towards the flat, waving at her in the window, grinning with arms outstretched in triumph. She thumbs-upped then turned to hide her crushing anguish and just had time to prepare her congratulatory face before he came crashing through the opened door and hugged her so tightly, she could scarcely breathe.

'I take it one has obtained a one,' she murmured, loving the taught strength of him pressed against her body.

Then she felt an almighty shudder pass through him as all the pent-up tension of these last months seemed to drain out of him. He couldn't speak but just sat down on a chair with a thump.

Although her heart was heavy, how could she be so churlish as to spoil his moment of joy?

She bent to kiss him. 'I'm so happy for you. So pleased your dreams can come true. You deserve it…every bit of it.'

'Phew. Thanks. I'm still in a bit of a daze. Everyone has been so nice. Oh, and Josh got his first as well. Thank goodness. You can imagine there was a lot of unseemly whooping from both of us. Even some man-hugging as well. He was off to tell Megan as I left. I phoned my expedition leader and told him the good news. So that's all confirmed and sorted.'

He paused a moment to shake his head in wonderment before continuing, 'Then I phoned my mum and dad. They are so delighted but not surprised. They never doubted it apparently and Dad says I can have his car for another couple of days. I can take it back when I take the final bits of my stuff home.'

He suddenly sprang up. 'Anyway, I've got an idea of how to celebrate. Do you fancy going further afield and staying somewhere overnight?'

'Um…'

‘Right. Pack your bag for a dirty weekend…although I’m hoping it won’t be a *weak end.*’ He grinned as she groaned at the pun.

‘Come on, Gorgeous, stir yourself. Time for some real hills, mountains in fact. What about a trip to Wales?’

‘Wales?’

‘Yes, why not? It’s not far. Don’t worry, I’ll help you up the hills. And given the combination of Wales and mountains you might meet other singers up there. Although I’m not sure if they will be twirling.’

As much as she liked the idea, Kate worried about the state of her finances if they were going to stay somewhere. As if sensing her doubts, he seized her in his arms and looked at her sternly.

‘We are not going to have the ‘going Dutch’ argument again, are we? Look, I know I have the most humongous student debt. But my Antarctic salary will pay it off pretty quickly because my keep is paid for and I can’t exactly pop to any shops to squander it on…well…anything, can I?’

‘But…’

‘No buts.’ Suddenly serious, he looked into her eyes. ‘I had no idea when I stopped to pick you up that it would turn out like this. But I can’t tell you how much I have loved getting to know you. These last few days have been so much fun. And we’ve only got two more. Please, please let me treat you…and me, to just one night in a proper double bed.’

Laughing, she had to give in. And cherished in her heart his words, ‘loved getting to know you.’

As she nestled down into his beloved sports car with an overnight bag duly packed, she patted the dashboard affectionately.

‘I really, really love your little red car.’

‘So glad it meets with your ladyship’s approval.’

‘No, I really do’, she continued. ‘I know lots of people have posher, newer cars…’ He looked at her quizzically.

‘…but I love the old-fashionedness of this one. Not surprising really. The girls are always teasing me about how old-fashioned I am when I say things like *All my eye and Betty Martin*. And when I call the salt and pepper, the cruet set.' She stopped herself abruptly before she said any more. Mustn't give the game away.

But then she suddenly sat bolt upright.

'Of course! That's it!' she exclaimed. 'I know what your car reminds me of. I've been trying to think of it all week. It's really been bugging me. Every time we come back to it I think, where have I seen something like it before?'

'Well?'

'Little Noddy's car,' she said triumphantly. 'I know his car was yellow but it had lovely red bumpers, just like yours.'

He looked aghast. Then started laughing uproariously.

'You don't mind, do you?' she asked anxiously because she knew that men could be sensitive about their cars.

Recovering his composure, he said, 'Do you know what sort of car it is?'

'Well, I've seen the M on the front,' she hazarded, 'so is it a, um…a Morris?'

He groaned. 'Nearly. It's a Morgan.'

He looked as if he expected this to register with her in some way. Nope, no awe at all.

'Well, it's very nice,' she said stoutly.

He just kept driving, his shoulders shaking with laughter.

It was a wonderful feeling motoring along, the sun in her face and the wind ruffling her hair. Deliberately Kate concentrated all her attention on enjoying the present. The here and now with this amazing man was all that mattered. She mustn't spoil his celebration with selfish pre-occupations about his imminent departure. How lucky she had been to have these fun-filled days and these few precious nights with him. A spirit of gratitude swept over her.

The roaring of the car made conversation difficult so she regaled him with relatively tuneful renditions of some of her favourite songs. Especially those from her beloved old movies and musicals. She ranged from Astaire to Judy Garland, tapped her feet on the car floor to *Top Hat and Tails* and crooned one of her all-time favourites from *Casablanca*.

'I suppose I shouldn't be surprised you know all the words to these. Your friends are right. You are such an old-fashioned little thing you know,' he said fondly.

Feeling rather foolish, Kate fell silent for a while. Would this lead into probing questions about why she knew so many old songs?

Perhaps seeing her worried face, he quickly begged, 'No, go on. I love it.'

'Are you sure?'

'Yes. More. More,' he shouted and thumped the steering wheel.

'OK. Give me a subject and I'll give you a song.'

'Oh no, not again. You are incorrigible.'

'Yup. Sure am.'

'OK. You asked for it...Curry!'

Bugger. Not again.

She was still racking her brains as they bowled over the border.

Chapter Eleven

Magically the sun continued to shine as they drove around. Her sexual awakening imbued all the undulating valleys and projecting promontories with sensuous significance.

Once again they picked up a garage picnic and, finding a suitable car park, they set off up a sun-drenched hill. Crackling with energy, as usual, Rob bounded up the hills, dragging her puffing and panting behind him. But she was allowed a full twirl when they got to the top of what she called a mountain and he called a big hill.

They found a suitably isolated spot for their picnic and what Rob suggestively called their 'afters'.

Driving on, it was late afternoon when they found a perfect little pub with rooms. With sweaty glee they tumbled into the bliss of a double bed for the first time. What luxury. Crisp linen sheets and a shower big enough for both of them.

Later they ate at a small intimate table in the corner of a cosy dining room. As Rob wouldn't be driving after the meal, Kate encouraged him to drink more of the wine than her. Sitting there watching his brown eyes glow with enthusiasm, she heard more about his forthcoming expedition and his hopes as to what it might lead to in his career.

Although she listened avidly, something in her face made him stop.

'Don't look so worried.'

Faced with his excitement how could she reveal the absolute devastation she was feeling? She concealed it with her very real concerns about his safety.

'But won't it be a bit dangerous out there? Yes, I know polar bears are at the North Pole, but it must be a bit perilous.'

'No, you're right there are no polar bears but some of those penguins can be pretty fierce.'

She thumped him.

'OK, silly answer I know.' He looked serious for a while. 'No, it's not that perilous but I'm expecting it to be challenging. In fact I hope it is. You never know what you are made of till you've tested yourself a bit. You don't know what's out there till you look and you don't know what you can do until you've tried. You should know this. You're the girl who sings about climbing, till you find your dream.' He grinned at her but his eyes had a faraway look, as if he could already see the glistening ice fields opening up before him.

'Yes,' said Kate sadly, because she knew that climbing mountains with him would be her dream.

'So, Keswick Kate, what is your dream? Come on. You never talk about yourself, yet you sit here and listen to me blethering on.'

'I've told you…'

'Oh don't give me that "old boring me" routine. I've never met anyone less boring than you.'

'No, really. My background is just not that interesting.'

'Try me. I know you come from a small village in the Lake District that no one's ever heard of. You're an only child, you know lots of poems and songs courtesy of your Ma…and that's about it.'

'Well, that is about it.'

'Stop prevaricating. You have never even told me the name of your village or what your parents do, for example.'

Here goes, she thought, deliberately looking down at her meal to avoid looking into his eyes. She had thrown up a smoke screen before and she could do it again. 'Right. My village is called Lower Langbeck. It has a pub, a chapel, a village shop-cum-post office and a small primary school where all the local farm kids go. And not much else. Pa was a Methodist preacher and was the sub-postmaster. Ma used to help him and run the local shop.'

'Used to.'

'Yes, he died eight years ago.'

‘Oh, I’m sorry. Is that why you don’t like talking about your past.’

‘Yes. It was a shock and it sort of changed everything really.’

There was a silence. She thought about explaining more but felt it safer not to.

After a while, Rob asked ‘So did you go to the village primary school?’

‘Yes, and then after that I went on to secondary school in Keswick.’

‘How far away was that?’

‘About ten miles.’

‘So how did you get there?’

‘Well, we all walked to the end of the village road and there was a bus every morning and evening that dropped us off.’

‘That must have been a bit…’

Rob was clearly struggling to find safe questions in the face of her minimal answers.

Feeling sorry for him she offered, ‘A bit isolating? Inconvenient? Bloody awful? Yes it was. School was great. I loved it. Loved all my friends and all the fun. But I only saw them during the school day and never at weekends. I could never join any clubs or go to friends’ houses because I had to catch the bloody bus back. Some friends’ parents were nice and did offer to drive me back, but it’s a fair old trek and I always felt guilty. Sometimes my friend Harry from the farm would stay late for judo and his mum would fetch us both back. So then I could pop into Keswick library or stay for choir. But mainly it was too much hassle, so…sorry, I’m making it sound more miserable than it was. Pa could be very grumpy and storm around the house raging at things which was a bit frightening when I was young. But, as I grew older, I learnt his anger was never directed at me. He had a lot of what you might call moral rectitude and felt he should set a good example to folks in everything he did. And he expected the same of me at all times. And the village gossips would always tell on me if I fell short in any way. It made me a very obedient, goody-two-shoes, I suppose.'

She grimaced knowing it had left her with a life-long worry about what people might say.

'As I got older, me and Ma began to gang up on Pa a bit, and he calmed down a lot. I don't think he realised till then just how…fearsome he sounded when he put his declamatory pulpit voice on round the house. Especially to me as a young child. I think he had too much energy for a small village, which is why he used to drag us up mountains in all weathers. Eventually we put our foot down and he went on his own.'

She closed her eyes and could see his solitary figure, head bent against the driving rain, plodding up the hill outside their back door, while she and Ma naughtily watched black and white musicals on Sunday afternoon TV.

She could see Rob's concerned face so, trying to inject some humour into the account, she grinned, 'And of course, be still my beating heart, there was always an outing to the Pencil Museum in Keswick to look forward to.'

Her smile faded. 'But in a village, everyone knows you and everything about you. We were in a valley surrounded by huge hills. I looked out on one from my bedroom window which blocked out all the light from midday onwards. It was all so…claustrophobic somehow.'

She reached for her wine, not daring to reveal any more. Their last night together wasn't going to be marred by the full tale of her childhood. She couldn't bear to feel his pity.

Rob blew out his cheeks. 'Aaagh. Now you tell me. Oh no. I didn't realise you hated hills. And here's me been forcing you to…'

'No. Don't feel bad,' she reassured him. 'It's a sort of love/hate relationship. Hills in the sun, and with you, are fine. But coming home on the school bus on a dark Friday night in winter, knowing you were stuck there with nothing to do all weekend…' She shivered, remembering the gloom that used to descend upon her.

'Didn't you have any friends in the village?'

'Yes and no. There weren't many of us of the same age.

There was Harry on the farm and his mum would sometimes drive us in to the pictures on a Saturday night. That was OK, as long as we saw the films Harry wanted to see. And, as you can imagine, a fan of musicals he was not.'

'So was he your boyfriend?'

'Um…he was a bit. But he didn't stay on to sixth form and began working on the farm, so we lost touch. So life was… well, let's put it this way you can see why I couldn't wait to get away and start…living.'

He nodded.

She shrugged. 'So that's me really. Nothing much to tell.'

Had she done enough to convince him that there was nothing more to her life than that? She could see Rob was dying to know more but, seeing her downcast face, he obviously didn't want to ask anything that might upset her. She had successfully shut down further lines of enquiry.

But it had cast a sombre shadow over the evening. She had to liven things up again.

'I still haven't found a poem for curry.'

He laughed. But her tale had definitely cooled the atmosphere.

If just the brief outline of her life had depressed the mood, just think what the truth would have done?

Chapter Twelve

Later, in the dark, luxuriating in the big double bed, she lay cocooned in his strong embrace. All her senses were alive, filled with him, feeling his taut skin next to hers, hearing the steady thud of his heart, and scenting his now familiar musky, masculine smell. Through the open attic window they could see the stars flickering in the clear summer night.

'As a boy, I always wanted to be out having adventures,' he confided holding her close. 'I used to sit on the top of my climbing frame and watch the sky and clouds wondering where they came from and went. My mum used to pack me sandwiches and sometimes, in the summer holidays, I would spend all day in my tent in our garden with compasses and maps. And my Action Men of course.'

He grinned fondly and impulsively kissed the top of her head.

'That's why I think I like picnics so much. And I used to love sleeping out at night, just in a sleeping bag, watching the stars. Did you know the stars are different in the Southern Hemisphere, which is part of the reason I want to go.'

He looked a little bashful. 'I hate to confess this, but still stuck on my bedroom ceiling at home are stars and planets, you know, the ones that glow after you switch off the light. My granddad was a navigator in a Lancaster in the Second World War and he had to plot his way by looking at the stars. So he put up all the stars accurately in their constellations. My sisters are older than I am, so he did their room first. They have got the Northern Hemisphere with the pole star and Orion and the outlines of the Milky Way.

'But in my room, I've got the stars of the Southern Hemisphere with the Southern Cross. My grandfather used these as he trained in South Africa all those years ago. Would you believe I can still trace their outline if I close my eyes before going to sleep?'

He did close his eyes and smiled as they obviously appeared before him.

'They're part of my childhood and I can't really believe that at last I'm going to see them for real. Can you imagine seeing the stars from the Antarctic? With no light pollution, they must be so clear and bright. I bet you feel you can reach out and touch them.'

Kate could feel the yearning in his voice.

'Sorry, I'm probably rabbiting on too much, but I've never talked about this to anyone else.'

And she knew he hadn't. In the intimate darkness she had never felt as close to anyone physically or spiritually in her whole life.

And it was their last night together.

Lulled by the wine, and the long, loving sex, Rob eventually drifted off into sated sleep. But she couldn't. As she lay looking at him in the light of the misty moon, he looked so young. She could see the boy dreaming of adventure and felt so privileged to hear his inner thoughts and longings.

But her feelings were in turmoil. At some point she must come to terms with their imminent separation. Looking at his slumbering presence by her side, she knew this was an opportunity, perhaps her last, to gaze and gaze at him for as long as she wanted.

She drank in his brown lashes fringing his closed lids, his rumpled dark hair outlined against the white linen pillow. His face in repose was different somehow, still strong jawed and rugged but without the animation which gave him such vitality during the day. Under her outstretched palm, his chest rose and fell rhythmically. What a contrast this still, peaceful figure was to the daytime Rob with his boundless energy, striding everywhere with those long, muscular legs.

He keeps looking round not realising I struggle to keep up. But I love the way he reaches out to me to help me with those wonderful strong capable hands.

She contemplated them lying relaxed on the covering sheet.

I love those hands. And those lovely broad shoulders that make me feel so protected when he hugs me. I love his dark shock of hair and his laughing brown eyes. I love the way he teases me. And doesn't mind the poems and singing. In fact he eggs me on. And his laugh. Oh, and I love his wicked grin when he is...

With a shock she stopped and held her breath as she suddenly realised. *I love him.*

'I love him.' She said the words out loud slowly as if they were a magic spell you had to say out loud to believe.

'Everything about him I love.'

The thought terrified her.

Is it better to have loved and lost, than never to have loved at all?

The answer was a resounding, yes. Even though he was going, she knew she wouldn't have missed the last few days for the world.

He's going. He likes me a lot, I know he does. But I'm not sure he actually loves me. It's impossible that he could, in this short time. And I know I shouldn't love him. It's too soon...and already too late.

When she woke up in the morning after a heart-searching night, he was curled naked against her back in their usual spoons position. One hand was cradling her breast. As usual. She smiled. Although they had a huge bed, they still cuddled together taking up minimum room. This was the last time though.

This awareness hung heavily over both of them, so, even though they laughed and joked as usual as they clambered up and around the surrounding mountains, it had a sadness about it all. Their drive back was uncharacteristically subdued. For once, they didn't really talk in the car. Apart from the fact that it was always so noisy, the things they wanted to say to each other they didn't want to shout. And Kate didn't feel like singing. She could only think of sad songs.

She appreciated that he obviously thought a lot of her. She knew that seizing this last day together would mean he would be cutting it fine for packing up. He would have to go early that evening and spend most of the night sorting his stuff from Uni. Then he had to drive to his parents' in Worcester to drop off his dad's car, collect the rest of his accumulated expeditionary equipment before travelling down to London to join the rest of the team the following day.

She promised herself, and him, she wouldn't cry or cling. She had known from the beginning he would go and would not come back to England for at least two years, if not longer. She had always known it was a fun relationship. The fact that it had been quite clear it wasn't serious was probably why she was able to be so very relaxed about it from the beginning. It was a wonderful flirtatious fling, full of laughter and fun. Nothing more.

How could she be so foolish as to think she loved him? She must bury that notion.

But Rob obviously noticed her silence as they prepared to say their goodbyes, cuddled together for the last time on the little narrow bed.

'Look, I've talked a lot about me and I've gathered that you don't want to talk about your past, but what about the future. Come on, Kate. What are *your* dreams? What do you want to do? I mean really deep down you must have hopes.'

'Oh, I don't know.'

'Come on. I'll be hurt if you can't tell me. After all I've told you my deepest, darkest secrets,' he teased.

How she longed to reveal that her main hopes for the future centred on him. If he would only return. If they could get back together and recapture what they had now. But how could she say that?

'Go on,' he urged.

There was another secret longing, but to reveal it would mean exposing part of her past. A part she was under strict instructions from Ma not to reveal. She couldn't bear to be pitied. Never again.

'Well, I think I ought to experience a bit more of life. I know I have led a pretty sheltered existence so far. The girls are always pointing this out to me and I suppose they're right. I'm embarrassed by how naive and gullible I am sometimes.'

'No, you are not. You are open and trusting, which are not the same things at all. They are fantastic qualities which is why people like you.'

'You may be slightly biased there, you know.'

'You bet I am. But I'm also right.'

She gave a faint laugh. 'Look, I know myself. I don't want an awfully big adventure like yours. I'm not brave enough for that. But I think I need more experience of people and what makes them tick. I don't really know how I'm going to get it though,' she tailed off lamely. Perhaps her plans needed more formulating.

'Don't worry about it. I'm sure you'll think of something. If I asked you now you could give me ten songs or poems about life so you shouldn't have any problems with thinking of something exciting to do when the time comes.'

Kate hoped he was right, and was grateful for his confidence.

He gave her a big hug and a long lingering kiss.

'Look, really must go.' He hesitated. 'Um…lots can happen in a couple of years. As you know I'm planning to stay on longer if I like it and perhaps visit places down there. You know I want to explore and have…adventures.' He smiled as if knowing she would understand such an old-fashioned word.

'So can I be serious for a moment?' He paused as if not too sure how to continue. 'Look, the last thing I want to do is mislead you or give you false impressions or anything. I know I ought to say I will write, but I'd hate to promise and then gradually we both have full lives and it becomes a chore and sort of tails off. It would spoil what we've had. I would much rather we both remember these few days as very, very special. You do know, don't you, just how magical that first night was for me?'

'And me,' she whispered, trying to suppress a sob. He very gently cupped her face.

'I can't tell you how much fun these last few days have been.' He paused. 'I don't quite know how to say this…and you probably wouldn't anyway, but I don't want you to…sort of wait for me, or anything. I think we are too young really to make any promises…'

Kate was silent.

'Is that OK? Do you agree?'

'Yes, of course. You are right. It's been the most amazing fun. But we need to get on and just keep this week as a wonderful memory.' With a great effort, she managed to keep her voice steady.

He nodded, almost with relief before kissing her tenderly. Then levered himself off the bed.

'Look, Gorgeous, it's no good I've got to go.'

She said bravely, 'I know.

'Parting is such sweet sorrow

We could say goodbye till it be morrow.'

'Shakespeare?' he guessed.

'Yup, *Romeo and Juliet.'*

'Well fret not, I have no intention of ending up like them. This is just the start of our lives and we're going to enjoy it. This has been so special, so much fun. All thanks to you. Bye, love.'

One last lingering kiss, and he was gone.

She waited till she heard his steps leave the flat before she started sobbing.

She knew her friends could probably hear her through the walls but knew there was nothing they could say or do.

It was over.

She had been abandoned…again.

All she could hope for was that, unlike her mum, he would one day return to her.

PART TWO

Chapter Thirteen

June 2000

Bloody rain!

Bloody June!

Bloody Brum!

Kate looked at the summer downpour through her windscreen. Black clouds darkened the evening sky and sheets of rain scudded across the car park. Looking up at her flat she could see flickering lights flashing intermittently through the lounge window. She sighed. That would mean Chris was either watching a macho film or playing one of his shoot-em-up computer games.

Her shoulders slumped. How much longer should she wait for the storm to pass over? She would get absolutely soaked if she made a dash for it now, but if she delayed much longer, Chris would want to know why she was late.

If only his sodding car wasn't parked in my allotted space, I'd only be yards away from the entrance, she thought mutinously. *And then all my presents wouldn't get drenched.*

A wave of anti-climax swept over her. She should be elated that the summer holidays were about to start. The end of another College year. She had just taught her last English Language evening class and they had been so lovely to her. The back seat of her car was full of flowers. She knew Val had been behind the collection for the wonderful bouquet, but Leo had shyly given her a little book of Shakespeare's sonnets and there were so many lovely cards with heartfelt messages of appreciation and thanks.

She had cried, which had embarrassed everyone a bit. Not a little tear but huge gulping sobs. Where had they come from? But the fact that her mascara had run made it easier to refuse the invitations to join them for an end-of-year party in the pub. Chris, of course, had explicitly warned her against going.

Bloody Chris.

She sighed again. June shouldn't be this wet. As she peered disconsolately at the rain, unbidden came memories of that hot June five years ago. She had been feeling fed up then, and lo and behold, along came Rob and the most blissful week of her life. But he had buggered off to bloody penguin land and never come back again.

Of course, at the end of his two years' research, she had hoped and hoped and hoped. But to no avail. Rob was now living happily in Australia with his girlfriend, according to Josh who kept in intermittent touch with him, mainly to talk about science stuff.

She shook herself. Why on earth did she keep the tiny embers of expectation alive? Surely experience had told her that once people go off to have adventures, they never come back. Why should they? Clearly life in the far flung reaches of the world has far more appeal than Birmingham or Lower Langbeck.

She looked in the mirror to check she had wiped away her mascara tears. It would never do for Chris to see she had been crying. He was always mocking her for being too emotional, too romantic about things. So there was no more poetry, no more songs. They had died along with her Rob dreams.

With a huge sigh, she gathered her flowers and presents together and prepared for her dash to the entrance of the flats. She really must make a run for it, in spite of the rain. Chris would be waiting.

He was. He looked up and paused his DVD movie as she came in, clearly noting she was all rain-sodden and laden with flowers and bags of presents.

'Huh. At last. I was beginning to wonder where you were.'

'In case you haven't noticed, it's lashing down with rain. I was waiting for it to stop a bit before I made a run from the car.'

'Humph. I thought you might have gone out with your students but I'm pleased to see you had more sense.'

Not this argument again.

'I don't see why you are so against it. They are all mature students so old enough to drink and they have been a terrific class so why shouldn't I go? They really wanted me to, you know.'

'Don't you think it's a bit sad to go out fraternising? You are a lecturer and have to keep your distance. They would lose all respect for you, especially if you got drunk in front of them…like you usually do.'

'What! I have never been drunk in front of students.'

'Oh, no,' he jeered. 'What about that time after last year's party when you fell over in front of them all.'

'I have told you a hundred times, I tripped.'

'Yea, right.'

'Oh, for goodness sake.' Blazing with suppressed fury she knew better than to engage with him over this old story again.

Flinging her flowers down on the table, she marched into the kitchen to find a vase. She saw his small smile of triumph, as he turned back to the DVD movie he was watching.

Typically, he had made no mention of her flowers and all her presents. In fact she was glad. She didn't want his sneers spoiling them.

'Fetch me a beer, will you? A cold one from the fridge.'

'Get it yourself you shiftless, idle, good-for-nothing parasite,' she muttered under her breath and carried on arranging her flowers.

But she knew it was only a matter of time before she obeyed. The row if she didn't, wasn't worth it. Indeed, the angry gleam in his eyes when she eventually placed it in front of him told her she had pushed it to the limits.

She ostentatiously positioned her bouquet in the middle of the dining table. They really were a gorgeous display. Chris looked at them briefly, then patted the seat next to him.

But no. She wasn't going to join him half-way through a guns and explosions film she had no desire to watch.

'I'm soaked through so I'm going to have a hot bath and bed,' she said, and scooping up her bag of presents she stalked off into the bedroom.

Sod him. Flopping down onto the bed, she began reading her cards again and nearly cried once more.

That Shakespeare sonnet book from lovely, gangly Leo was really sweet. She knew he had a bit of a crush on her and had heard whispered teasing from other class members which made him blush.

Her mature evening classes were her favourite classes. As much as she loved her young students, most of them were straight from school so still treated her like a teacher. Some seemed uncomfortable in calling her by her first name, Kate, and would often revert to 'Miss'.

But the evening students came hot-foot and eager straight from work and were highly motivated. They were there because they needed an English qualification to advance themselves or because they wanted to catch up after a bad school experience or sometimes just to prove something to themselves. Because she believed they could do it, most of them could and did. Her exam results were always proof that her faith in them was justified.

Throughout the year she carefully kept her manner friendly but professional, but after the last class she enjoyed joining them for a farewell drink and to wish them good luck in the impending exam.

Last year, as usual, her class had all insisted on buying her a drink. She had refused most of them but maybe she was just a little tiddly as she left. What a pity that Chris was drinking in the same pub that night and had seen her trip and sprain her ankle as she left. Even more pity that he had rushed to help her and insisted on driving her home.

She knew who he was, having met him briefly in the staff room as he introduced himself as the new head of the College computer system. Once back home, in spite of her insistence she was OK, he had escorted her limping upstairs to her front door. Somehow he had invited himself in for a coffee. Later, she realised, he had cleverly sussed it all out. Then, clearly liking the look of the flat and its location, when her flatmate Zoë moved out, he had wangled his way in, first as a lodger, then eventually weaselled his way into her bedroom as well.

But he had never let her forget her fall that night. In his words, he had come to her rescue when, obviously the worse for drink, she had sprawled across the pavement and clearly needed looking after. Somehow he had wheedled his way into 'looking after her' ever since.

Sitting on her bed reading her cards, she could hear the noise from his film was reaching a final crescendo. So she carefully stowed away her cards and presents in the bottom of her wardrobe, knowing full well he would rifle through them at some point.

Stretching, she grabbed her bathrobe, intending to lock herself away in the bathroom. A long soaking bath beckoned, after which she hoped he might be asleep when she emerged.

She was just padding across the hall when she heard the phone ring. To her surprise, Chris didn't mute the TV and rush to answer it. He always tried to get there first and, to her annoyance, insisted on asking who was calling if it was for her.

'Phone, Chris,' she shouted above the racket from the TV.

Clearly irritated, he shrugged and carried on watching.

So, slightly intrigued, she went to answer it herself.

It was Megan.

'Hiyah. What? Hang on. Chris, I can't hear myself speak with all that noise from the film. Turn it down.'

With a scowl he paused it but his finger was hovering over the button impatient to start again.

'That's better. Oh, hi Megan. How lovely to hear from you. Are you OK?'

'He hasn't told you then,' Megan said flatly.

'Told me what?'

'That I had phoned earlier. I'd forgotten it was your evening class night. I asked him to tell you to phone me back when you got in.'

'No, he didn't mention it.'

Chris just shrugged. He knew exactly what was being said.

'I assume he's there?'

'Yes.'

'Can he hear what I'm saying?'

From the alert way he was sitting, Kate assumed he was trying to decipher what the conversation was about.

'I'm not sure.'

'OK.' She heard Megan sigh. Although her friend had never uttered a word against Chris, Kate knew all too well what she thought of him.

'Right, I'm phoning to say, get your glad rags on, I'm taking you out tomorrow night.'

'Oh thanks, Megan, that sounds great…but tomorrow…'

'I know. I know. It's Chris' night out at the pub with his mates and you go along to drive him home. But just for once he can get a taxi because, my lovely, you *are* coming out with me.' Megan's lilting Welsh voice was insistent.

There was a slight pause. They both knew Chris would object to this arrangement.

'Come on, Kate. It's important. It's a bit of a celebration so get dressed up a bit.'

She took a deep breath and looked across at a scowling Chris. He understood enough to know he wasn't going to like whatever was being discussed. But Megan was her oldest friend.

'OK. That will be great. What are we celebrating?'

'I'll tell you tomorrow. It will be a surprise and probably a late night. You can come back to mine after and we can have a good old chinwag. We haven't caught up with each other in ages, have we?'

'No, you're right.' Kate felt so guilty.

Chris made his dislike of Megan very obvious. But she had remained loyal in the face of all his snide remarks and obstructive behaviour.

Somehow Chris had come between her and all her friends. He began by turning up uninvited to girly nights out and insisting on driving her home early 'before you get too tiddly and embarrass yourself', he said.

He intercepted invitations and 'forgot' to tell her about them till it was too late to go. He arranged 'date nights' to coincide with friends' parties and in the end it wasn't worth the hassle and arguments whenever she wanted to meet up with anyone.

Even inside College, he knew her timetable and would hover around at break times and commandeer her attention in lots of little ways. Her friends had made it clear to him how unwelcome he was when he persisted in joining them all for coffee. But then they began to discover that anyone who crossed him suffered inexplicable problems with their computers and network communications. And it took ages to get them fixed.

But Megan had persevered, just turning up at College and saying, 'Let's go'. So they had escaped for lunches or gone out for pub grub straight after work.

However, recently Megan's job as a social worker had expanded and she was finding the work-load increasingly challenging. As a consequence, she was always pushed for time and Kate realised they hadn't been out together in ages.

Megan's voice was insistent. 'Right. So you will come out tomorrow night, won't you? Just you.'

'Yes, I will.'

'Promise?'

'Promise.'

Chris swivelled round to give her a hard stare.

Megan lowered her voice. 'Right. Be at the top of the steps in Brindley Place tomorrow at eight…and keep your eyes peeled.'

'OK. I'll be there.'

There was a pause as if Megan longed to say more, but decided against it.

'OK, Kate, see you tomorrow.'

'You will. Looking forward to it…and thank you for calling.'

'Pleasure. Bye.'

Chapter Fourteen

'So what was that all about?' Chris stood up and stretched. His grey eyes were hard.

'I'm meeting Megan tomorrow night.'

'But you know that's my night out.'

'Yes, but it's only me that's been invited. So you can still have your night with your mates.'

'But you always drive us home.'

'I know, but you'll just have to get a taxi.'

'How bloody selfish. All the times I drive you into work and you can't even drive me once a week from the pub.'

'I've told you, I'm quite happy to drive myself into work, especially on the days I don't have an early morning lecture...'

'And where would you park then? It would cost you a fortune. Using my designated space saves you money and coming with me saves you petrol.'

She sighed. It was yet another old argument. He was doing her a favour by driving her in. Even though it meant she was often in too early for her lectures or hanging about after work for him to take her home. And, of course, he argued that footing the bill for the petrol meant he didn't have to contribute much to the food bill, which somehow covered all his beer as well.

She could see that Chris wasn't going to let it go.

'Why can't you just meet her for half an hour then come on to us at the pub later?'

'Because she wants to have a good chat and we are going out to celebrate something.'

'What?'

'I don't know. She didn't say. It's a surprise.'

'It'll just be to say her and Josh are getting married. Or she's pregnant.'

'Yes, it might be.'

'Well, why couldn't she tell you on the phone? And where are you going?'

'I don't know, Chris. I just know…' she paused. She saw he would try to spoil it somehow so the less he knew the better. There was no way she would tell him where and when she was meeting Megan.

'Look, Chris, just for once I'm going out with *my* friend. I promised, so I am.'

Before he could say any more, she marched into the bathroom, locked the door and started running a long hot bath.

As she lay there soaking, she began wondering what Megan was celebrating and where were they going? What should she wear? What was it about Megan's voice that sent an unaccustomed thrill of excitement through her?

She was awoken next morning by an almighty crash coming from the lounge.

A sudden dread seized her. Leaping out of bed she raced into the lounge to find her fears confirmed.

Chris was standing by the table and her beautiful bouquet had toppled sideways spilling water and flowers everywhere.

'What's happened?' she exploded.

'It was a silly place to put such a big bunch of flowers.' He shrugged, a mean look on his face. 'It was obviously top heavy and bound to fall over.'

She knew it was a punishment for daring to go and meet Megan.

'It was fine last night,' she snapped. 'You must have done something to make it fall over.'

Rushing forwards, she tried to stop the water dripping on to the carpet.

'Oh no.' Lifting the vase upright, she saw a long crack down the side emanating from a large chip in the rim.

'Look, look what you've done.' She was furious. 'You've

broken Ma's vase.'

'No I haven't. It was an accident. Stop making such a fuss. It was bound to happen putting it there.'

She saw red. 'You know how special this vase was. It was Ma's favourite. How could you, Chris? How could you?' She turned on him and he quailed a bit in the face of her outrage.

'Don't work yourself up like that. You're getting over-emotional again. I told you I was sorry.'

'No, you didn't,' she roared.

'What?'

'You said it was an "accident".' Her voice showed her disbelief. 'But you haven't said you are sorry.'

'Well, I didn't do it on purpose if that's what you mean.'

'Really? Really, Chris?'

'Look, I just brushed past it.'

She stood with her hands on her hips, glaring at him. 'I'm waiting.'

'What for?'

'For you to say you are sorry.'

'Oh, don't be so silly. You are making a fuss again. Is it the time of the month?'

Anger made her voice go cold.

'So if you can't say you are sorry, you obviously aren't. Are you?'

Chris shifted uncomfortably. She had never flared up like this before. But then, she had never felt so angry. Ma's vase had touched an unexpected nerve.

'Come on, Kate. We haven't got time for this.' He edged towards the bedroom door. 'Hurry up and get ready or we'll be late for College.'

'No.'

'What?'

'No, I'm not getting ready. I've got all this mess to deal with first.' She indicated the strewn flowers, the dripping water and the broken vase.

'Well, I'm not waiting for you.'

'Fine. I'll drive myself in.' She shrugged turning her back on him and began to pick up the scattered blooms.

He scowled. 'You'll be late and you won't find a parking space.'

She shrugged again and went to fetch a cloth from the kitchen.

He followed her.

'It's not a good idea for a part-timer like you to be late… especially this end of the term. The head of department is bound to notice and it will jeopardise your chances of getting a job next year.'

His grey eyes gleamed. She knew he would make damn sure the head would notice. Her impeccable record of punctuality would count for nothing once Chris' weasel words insinuated themselves into her head's ear. But she didn't care. Still saying nothing, she pushed past him and went to wipe up the mess on the floor and table.

For a moment he looked nonplussed. Then stomped out to the bedroom to find his jacket. 'I'm going in precisely ten minutes so you'd better get your skates on.'

She kept her back to him and continued mopping up the water. The sight of Ma's broken vase threatened to reduce her to tears, but her overwhelming anger kept them at bay.

Hearing Chris go into the bathroom she rapidly unhooked her car keys from their place by the door and slipped them into her pyjama pocket. She didn't put it past him to take them with him, leaving her stranded. Then slowly and deliberately she found another vase and began reassembling her flowers.

For the next ten minutes, Chris humphed and paced about the flat muttering at her about the dire consequences of being late.

'I think you are being really childish. You will never get dressed and to work on time now. You know what the traffic's like on a Friday morning. Don't blame me if your class complains about you.'

She smiled to herself. He might know her timetable but he didn't realise that this particular exam class finished last week, so there would be no one there. She rather hoped he would make a fool of himself by dragging the head of department down to non-existent complaining students.

Jangling his car keys, Chris stood there as if still waiting for her to capitulate. Finally, he turned to go. She watched through the mirror as his hand surreptitiously reached out to grab her car keys from the hook. An angry flush suffused his face when he saw they weren't there. For a minute she thought he was going to come back and confront her.

Tensing, she turned to face him, instinctively balling her fists ready to defend herself. She had often felt physically intimidated by the way he deliberately invaded her space, but this time she felt defiant. No way was he going to threaten her.

He glared at her, then turned on his heels and slammed the door behind him.

Chapter Fifteen

As she had promised, Kate was standing at the top of the steps in Brindley Place enjoying the buzz in this vibrant new area of Birmingham. It was a lovely soft evening. The water from the nearby fountains was cascading down the slope and the Italianate buildings round the square glowed golden in the evening sun.

I could almost be abroad.

She was really looking forward to seeing Megan, especially as she wanted to recount her day's rebellion to her.

After Chris had left that morning, Kate realised she only had one class that day. It suddenly hit her that her friend, Zoë, owed her many, many favours so if she could cover that class, there was no need to go in to College at all. The mature students were researching stuff in the library and only required the minimum of supervision.

The prospect of a day in her own flat doing just what she wanted, seemed so tempting, she immediately phoned Zoë and begged a favour.

'No, that's fine, Kate. I don't mind at all. In fact happy to pay you back for all the times you've done it for me. But…is everything all right?'

'Yes fine. Just got lots to do today here at home.'

'OK,' but Zoë sounded worried. Rather hesitantly she continued. 'It's just that Chris was in a foul temper this morning and was ranting on about you being childish or something. Are you sure you are OK?'

Horrified, Kate realised Zoë wanted to know if Chris had harmed her in some way and that's why she wasn't coming in.

She knew Zoë hated Chris, making no secret of the fact

that she thought he was a 'devious, manipulative bastard'. She had been Kate's flatmate but when she had moved out to be with Travis, Kate needed someone to help pay the bills. Chris had heard about it on the College grapevine and had been so helpful and obliging it had been difficult to refuse his application. He seemed to fit the bill of being the perfect lodger.

He was far from that now but he was not physically abusive and a shocked Kate hastened to reassure Zoë that Chris hadn't harmed her.

'Don't worry, Zoë, I'm fine. Honest. In fact I'm going to have a lovely girly day all on my own. Lots of primping and unguents galore. Then I'm going shopping this afternoon. I haven't bought myself anything new in ages and I'm meeting Megan this evening for a meal. Just the two of us.' The bit about meeting Megan should reassure Zoë…and it did.

'That sounds great.'

'Yes, really looking forward to it. And thanks for covering that class for me.'

'It's a pleasure. I owe you loads.'

Perturbed by Zoë's suspicions, Kate put the phone down. Without Chris' hovering presence, she had time to think. Gradually her rage at him was replaced with a strong determination to stand up to him more. She had done it this morning and, although he clearly didn't like it, she had won. Now she must do it again.

When he first moved in, he had been so attentive and helpful. He had helped her redecorate the flat and had re-jigged the kitchen so it would accommodate a dishwasher which he had expertly plumbed in. She had been grateful for all he had done and felt looked after.

But thinking back, just when had care shifted to control?

Perhaps it started when, because he always gave her a lift to and from College and even to her evening classes, he began urging her to give up her car as an unnecessary expense. He was very persuasive and nagged away at her but she was fond of her little car and was reluctant to give up the independence it gave her. Eventually she dug her heels in and said no. Once she refused outright, he stopped taking her to her evening classes, but still held on to the flat's designated parking space, leaving her to hunt for somewhere on the nearby street. At first he would have a cuppa waiting but now he barely roused himself from the settee, *her settee*, and only paused the computer game if she was late and he wanted to know why.

She remembered arguing with him over other incidents but gradually he wore her resistance down so now she rarely bothered. But, glancing at the broken vase by the sink, she decided perhaps it was time she began reasserting herself.

Should she start by reclaiming her car parking space?

Pausing in front of the mirror, she took a deep breath and said out loud, 'It's my flat, my rules. If you don't like it, Chris, then you are free to leave.'

Would she dare say it? In her current mood, yes, she would.

Feeling empowered, she actually found herself singing, something she hadn't done for a long time. This liberated mood continued as she set off for an afternoon wandering round the shops. She had carefully propped up a note against her newly arranged flowers telling Chris she wouldn't be home for tea and, as she would probably be going back to Megan's for a chat late into the evening, he mustn't bother waiting up for her. He wouldn't be pleased, but she found she didn't really care.

So, standing there waiting for Megan, she felt good. She had fitted in a trip to the hairdresser and she was wearing a new sea-green top that matched her eyes, an impulse-buy from that afternoon.

She knew it was highly unlikely that Megan would make it on time. The nature of her job meant there was always something cropping up. Kate's admiration for her friend knew no bounds and how she coped with the stress and work-load of being a social worker, she didn't know. Luckily Josh was a perfect partner. His university lecturing post meant he did most of the shopping, housework and cooking. Being totally unmaterialistic, they still lived in their crummy student flat in a rundown area of town. In theory they were saving up for a deposit on a house which is why they liked the cheap rent.

Thinking of Josh's amiable nature brought unexpectedly to mind his ex-flatmate, Rob. These two had kept in touch over the years through their shared scientific enthusiasms and Josh passed on the odd snippet about him. It was with great effort that she kept her questions about Rob as nonchalant as possible.

For two years she had held her breath waiting and hoping. But then there was that heart-stopping moment when she heard the news that he wasn't returning to England. He was going to live in Australia with his girlfriend, Leanne, a fellow scientist he had met during his stay on the icecap.

This news came just as she was already dealing with the death of Ma. A huge black hole had opened at her feet and for months she had been in despair. It was only with the practical and emotional support of Josh and Megan that she had eventually emerged out the other side.

Now, three years later, older, wiser and sadder, she berated herself for the stupidity of all her secret dreams. How foolish to dare to hope that one day he would come back. She, of all people, ought to have known better.

But she had survived. Some days were better than others but she had a job and although Chris' over-protectiveness was a pain, at least she had someone around. OK, life wasn't perfect, but then, whose life was?

Angrily she caught herself in an involuntary sigh. She mustn't do this. Thinking about Rob always brought on a despondent mood and this wouldn't do. She was wearing a new top and it was going to be a fun night out with her friend who had something exciting to celebrate.

Remembering Megan's stipulation about keeping her eyes peeled, she looked around curiously.

In the distance a tall figure striding purposefully into the square caught her eye. There was something about those long legs and the loping walk that looked familiar. The set of his shoulders seemed oddly recognisable.

As she peered at the approaching figure, she felt her pulse began to quicken.

Surely not. How often in the past had she thought she had glimpsed him in a crowd? A turn of the head, a particular physique had often sent her heart racing before realising an instant later it hadn't been him.

But this time… Could it be?

Gasping for breath, she felt dizzy with hope. Surely not… and yet. As he drew nearer, it surely was him.

Although not quite. The figure in her memory did not exactly match up with this tall, dark-haired man with the laughing brown eyes. But then, in a moment, Rob's younger self merged…and morphed…and blended…and there he was…a slightly older, fuller version of his former self. More solid somehow. The manly version of the boy.

But it was, most definitely, Rob.

Chapter Sixteen

As he approached the steps, Rob paused as if he too was trying to match up his memory of her as a young girl with this woman standing stupefied before him. But then, with a grin, he bounded up to her.

His arms opened and before she knew it, she was being hugged against that broad chest she knew so well. Feeling dazed with overwhelming emotion, instinctively she clung to him, all her dormant passion bursting into life. Yes, this was where she felt at home, where she belonged, where she had yearned to be for so many years.

She wanted to weep, to rant, to laugh but all she could do was gasp in stunned wonderment. They stayed entwined for a long time, holding each other close. Her eyes closed, she rested her head on his chest and inhaled his oh-so-familiar scent, revelling in his strong embrace once again.

Eventually Rob gently broke free and held her at arm's length, eyeing her appreciatively.

'Hello, Gorgeous. You look great…but then, you always did.' His warm husky voice vibrated with emotion.

'Rob? What on earth...'

'Woah. Lost for words. That must be a first, Katy girl. From the look on your face I take it Megan didn't tell you I was in the UK.'

'No.'

'Ah. So she also didn't tell you I was coming tonight?'

'No.'

'Hmmn. Well, as you can see, I'm back.'

Grinning broadly, he flung out his arms in dramatic fashion.

But Kate still didn't trust her senses and stood dumbstruck

in disbelief.

'Wow. You really are gob-smacked, aren't you? Unless you recover your powers of speech fairly soon, this is going to be a bit of a one-sided conversation.'

But the shock was still too great. Was this a dream? She daren't, just daren't articulate her feelings. She daren't get her hopes up.

'Right. Still no words from my Twirly Girl.' Rob was clearly a little nonplussed by her silence. 'I suppose I could hum a little bit. There are too many people around for me to actually sing, although I seem to remember it didn't stop you.' He grinned.

And it was that teasing grin that did it. As if a switch had suddenly activated in her brain, Kate jerked alive.

'Rob Frazier. What on earth are you doing here? I thought you were in Australia. I'm going to kill Megan. Why didn't she warn me? And where is she? And how long have you been in England? And…'

'Woah. That's more like it. Now we can start. Hallo, Kate. So good to see you again. I've been looking forward to this all day.'

'And I would have, if I'd known.' But it suddenly clicked precisely why Megan hadn't told her. Her excitement at the prospect of meeting Rob would have been all too obvious. Chris would immediately have suspected something and there was no way he would let her have come to meet an old boyfriend. It also explained why she was told to dress up a bit and keep her eyes peeled.

'So where's Megan hiding? She can come out now. I've forgiven her.'

'Oh, she's not coming.'

'What?'

'No. She thought we'd have so much to catch up on, she's sort of left us to it. But she's expecting us both back at her place later this evening.'

'Oh, right.'

'Sorry, you still look a bit shell-shocked. I've booked us into that restaurant over there so, while you recover a bit, should we meander over and have a drink? I'm dying to have a proper catch-up and find out what you've been up to. Josh is hopeless at passing on personal stuff and Megan hasn't told me much. She says it's better if we get it all from the horse's mouth…as it were.'

He held out his hand, as he always had. As she reached out and grasped it, the sensation was so familiar, so right, so reminiscent of all those times five years ago, she had to stop herself from flinging herself into his arms and never letting go. Still weak-kneed and reeling, she allowed him to guide her to the restaurant overlooking the square.

So many questions raced through her mind. Was he back for good? What had happened to the girlfriend in Australia? In spite of her best intentions, hope blazed through her body.

As they entered the noisy Friday-crowded restaurant, Rob asked, 'What do you fancy to drink? The usual?'

'You remember my usual?'

'Yes, Twirly Girl, I remember everything about you. Except…' he paused, '…I don't remember you being quite so quiet.'

'I'm not quiet, you idiot. I'm still gobsmacked,' she blazed. 'And I maintain the right to be gobsmacked until I choose to unleash the torrents of questions your unexpected presence demands. So you've got a choice, a lady-like stab at polite small talk until we sit down or an inundation of questions while this poor waiter stands waiting for our drinks order.'

'That's more like it. Although I'm totally intrigued by the prospect of lady-like conversation, I'll definitely order the drinks as you suggest.'

While they waited at the bar, Kate pointedly small-talked politely.

'So how are you keeping, Mr Frazier…or should that be Doctor Frazier by now?'

'Oh, just Doc will do amongst friends. And I'm keeping very well, Miss Caswell. Thank you for asking.'

'And I was about to enquire whether you came here often, but I know the bleedin answer to that, don't I?'

Rob choked on his drink. ‘Knew you couldn’t keep up the lady-like for long.’

A petite waitress appeared by his side. ‘Your table’s ready for you, sir. If you’d like to follow me.’

Kate was pleased to see that he had obviously booked a table by the window. They had a great view of the square and while they waited for their menus, Rob made conversation on all the changes he had seen in the city in the past six years.

‘Yes,’ Kate inclined her head graciously, ‘I think you will find, Doctor Flipping Frazier, that crummy old Brum is quite an upmarket cosmopolitan city now.’

Worried her nerves would cause her to burble, she was quite glad of the polite pretence. The old Kate would have launched straight in, but she wanted to keep her guard up. Besides she needed to feel more at ease with this familiar stranger across the table.

‘I see they do a very nice Sole Meunière,’ she commented, perusing the menu, whilst sneaking surreptitious glances at him. She felt he was doing the same.

Seeing his strong capable hands clutching the menu, she remembered the first time she had noticed them on the wheel of his car.

‘Do you still drive the Morgan?’ she blurted out.

‘No. Never felt the same about it after someone called it a Noddy Car,’ he said mournfully.

‘Oh no. Oh sorry. Look, I didn’t realise it was a special car. I’ve found out since I should have been impressed. I really liked it. You shouldn’t have got rid of it just because…’ But then she saw the glint in his eyes and could see he was teasing her.

He grinned. ‘No, seriously. It was a great fun car and yes, I suppose, to the untrained eye it did bear a certain resemblance to a certain yellow toy car but, if you remember, it wasn’t my car at all. It was on loan from my dad.’

He shook his head. ‘I can’t believe you ever thought it was mine. Think about it, Kate. As an impoverished student how could I possibly afford one of those? I was so tickled when Dad said I could borrow it. There I was, driving along feeling really flash and you were decidedly unimpressed and grumpy and, for a moment, I thought I was going to get the ultimate humiliation of you turning me down.'

She blushed, remembering how ungraciously she had accepted the lift and just unceremoniously dumped her shopping in the back of his special car without once giving it a second look.

He grinned at her embarrassment. 'Anyway, I drive a much more sedate car now. I'm all grown-up, I suppose.'

'Me too,' she sighed.

'Awful isn't it?'

'There's this poem about wearing purple and being rebellious before you get too old...' she began, then faltered as a smile lit up his face.

'I wondered how long it would be before you mentioned poetry.'

She coloured. She hadn't quoted anything for years. How amazing that the poetry-loving person she used to be had re-surfaced instantly on meeting Rob again.

'And have you thought of a poem about curry in the last five years?'

She felt her face glow with pleasure. He seemed to remember everything they had talked about during their passion-filled week together. And yes, of course, she now had a poem about curry. But she wasn't prepared to divulge it, yet. She still needed time to adjust to the surreal situation that it was Rob, her Rob, sitting across the table from her. He seemed to assume they could drop straight back into the old teasing banter of that heady week so long ago.

He grinned, 'So no curry poem then?'

'Later. Later.'

She glanced at those warm brown eyes, that familiar curving smile and felt herself melt all over again. Just like before, she felt the flickers of desire smoulder deep in her body.

But what was he doing here in Birmingham? Had he left Australia? His girl-friend? Dare she hope he had come back…for her? And yet, and yet. Was his initial hug and general demeanour more friendly than romantic? She really must keep her guard up till she knew more.

Her mind in overdrive, she looked at the menu without really concentrating on what she was reading. Her stomach was in too much turmoil for food.

'What a crap menu,' he announced. 'None of these food descriptions leave any opportunities for your customary double entendres.'

She glanced again at the classy black menu. 'I agree and I'm so disappointed by the sad demise of gravy.'

'Gravy?'

'I love old fashioned gravy. None of this 'jus' stuff. And I love custard. You see I'm a big fan of *moist* food.' She lingered just a little over the word 'moist' as she had all those years ago and was pleased to see a naughty, responsive twinkle in Rob's eyes.

No. this wouldn't do. She must not be tempted to flirt with him till she knew the lay of the land. It had taken her years to recover from her broken heart last time and she had no intention of going through all that pain and longing ever again.

A waiter hovered meaningfully.

'Oh crikes, I don't know what I fancy.' Kate looked in panic at the huge array of carefully described dishes.

'I know what I want,' Rob said, decisively folding the menu. 'A good old-fashioned plate of fish and chips … with mushy peas.'

'Wow, that does sound good.' For a moment she thought of Chris. He always ordered the biggest steak on the menu and insisted it was well done. If he didn't like the way it was cooked, he sent it back. There had been many mortifying scenes. She suddenly scanned the square. What if he caught her here, dining with a man? Thank goodness she didn't tell him where she was meeting Megan. Thank goodness it was his night out with the 'boys', although he would be furious that she wasn't there to ferry him home.

Rob caught her glance out of the window.

'Everything OK?'

‘Oh yes, of course. Fish and chips it is for me too.’

‘Starters?’ the waiter suggested.

Kate had a quick peek at the long list of suggestions. ‘Um…I’ll go really old- school. I fancy a prawn cocktail.’

Rob‘s eyebrows went up as if waiting for a double entendre but Kate shook her head aware of the listening waiter.

‘No, a step too fishy for me. I’ll have the duck pate, please.’

‘Of course, sir. And wine?’

Rob perused the proffered wine list.

‘Anything you fancy?’

‘I’ll leave it to you. I’m happy with red or white.’

‘OK. A bottle of anything not Australian. Number fourteen, please.’

‘Yes sir.’ And off he went.

‘Why not an Australian wine?’ She tried to keep her tone bland, despite a flicker of hope. Didn’t he like Australia?

‘Just want a change. You really do have a wide variety from all round the world to choose from here.’

‘Don’t you in Oz?’

‘Not so much. Adelaide tends to be a bit insular in many ways and most of the wines are local.’

‘So tell me about Adelaide then?’ How could she find out what she wanted to know without asking him outright?

‘Oh, it’s fine. What’s amazed me is how much Brum had changed over the past five years…in fact everyone has.’ He looked at her as if wanting to hear all her news. But Kate wasn’t going down that path. She already knew how dull her life was. The last thing she wanted from him was confirmation of this fact.

They were distracted by the waiter bringing the wine and the inevitable procedure of the tasting before he poured them a glass each.

Seizing her glass with relief, she took a swift drink hoping it would help ease the tension of suppressed emotion rippling along her shoulders.

A surprised Rob lifted his glass in a toast, ‘Here’s to…’

She waited. Was he going to say 'Us'? or 'Old friends?'. She desperately needed a clue as to what they were.

'…here's to a lovely evening,' he finished.

They clinked glasses.

There was an uncomfortable silence for a moment.

With a sigh, Kate looked at Rob just as he looked at her. There was a flicker of awareness between them. Could they ever go back to how it was?

Chapter Seventeen

Rob settled back with his wine glass clearly ready for a chat.

'So, Megan says you work at a College. How did that happen?'

'Oh, it's a long story. I'd rather hear your news first.'

'No, really. I'm curious. I've heard bits and pieces from Josh over the years but, he's not very good at passing on the personal stuff.'

'Tell me about it,' Kate blurted out. In vain she had interrogated Josh over the years knowing he was in touch with Rob. But while Josh could talk for hours on all the scientific stuff he and Rob had discussed over their university grapevine, he was hopeless at anything more than the bare outlines of what people were actually doing with their lives.

'Megan hasn't told me much either. She said to ask you?'

Kate groaned. 'Yup, typical Megan. She's always had a policy of strict non-interference in people's affairs, but it has got much worse since she became a social worker. Trying to get her to give advice is like getting blood from a stone.'

'Do you need her advice?'

'Oh yes. Don't get me wrong. She has been a brilliant friend. I owe her so much but sometimes I wish...'

'What?'

Kate immediately clammed up. No way was she going to open up about her dark times. Rob seemed to want her to be her funny, old self and to recapture the light-hearted spirit of those heady, youthful days. And she wanted it too. How wonderful to be so carefree again.

'Oh, it's not a criticism of Megan at all. She very much believes in grown-ups making their own decisions. Totally the opposite when it comes to protecting kids, of course. But she...'

She stopped again, not wanting to get into a conversation that might lead to Chris. She was pretty certain Megan wouldn't have said anything much about him. Unlike all of her other friends, Megan had never said a word against him, although, she had never said a word *for* him either.

'What?' he leant forward, clearly keen to hear why she needed Megan's advice.

Something snapped inside her. This was stupid. The tension was killing her. She had to know what was going on. Good or bad.

'Oh no, you don't. We are not here to talk about bloomin Megan, as lovely as she is. I'm dying to hear what on earth you are doing here. Just turning up out of the blue, back in Brum…large as life…' *and twice as handsome*, she said to herself.

'OK. OK. I suppose we'll get the serious bit over first.' He ran his fingers through his hair in a gesture so familiar to her, she was transported back to their narrow little bed with sunlight filtering through the thin curtains. But what was so serious?

'Serious? What's happened?'

'It's my mum.'

'Oh no…is she all right?'

'Well, yes and no.' He frowned. 'She's having treatment for breast cancer.'

'That's awful. How is it going? When did this happen?'

'You might well ask. It's been ongoing for a while and I wasn't supposed to know. I can't tell you how guilty I feel.'

'You mean no one told you?'

'Exactly.' He sighed. 'I wouldn't have known any of it if I hadn't phoned my sister, Fiona. I confess I rarely phone my folks because it's always my mum who contacts me and keeps me in touch with all the family news. I came back for my sister's wedding three years ago but that was it, in all these five years. Too wrapped up in my own life I suppose, so I never suspected anything was wrong. But then Mum made sure I wouldn't.'

From the tension in his face, Kate guessed the next bit was going to be tough for him to tell.

'Looking back, I feel so guilty that I wasn't in touch more. Fellas aren't as good at it, are they? But I'm just excusing myself really. I might never have known anything about her cancer if I hadn't phoned my sister about a present for my mum's sixtieth birthday. Fiona was out, so her husband, Andrew, answered. When I asked where Fiona was, he seemed surprised I didn't know she was looking after my mum. It was the way he stopped short after saying that, it alerted me to the fact that he had let slip something he shouldn't. When pressed, he covered up so badly, I knew something was definitely wrong. I phoned my other sister, Rosie, you remember, the doctor, and wanted to know what was going on. She told me she was sworn to secrecy by Mum but, realising the cat was out of the bag, told me Mum had breast cancer.'

He looked grey at the memory.

'I was devastated, not only by the news, but also the fact that Mum didn't want to worry me so had forbidden anyone to tell me. I felt excluded from family life. I was the only one in the family who didn't know, who wasn't helping her, visiting her, being there for her. I felt so isolated and…sort of the baby brother, who hadn't really grown up, off having his adventures while everyone else got on with adult life and worries.'

Automatically Kate reached out a hand to him and he took it. She could feel his shock and pain.

'This was two weeks ago. Obviously I dropped everything and came back to England immediately. Mum is having chemotherapy and looks so weak and frail. I can't tell you what it did to me seeing her like that.'

His voice choked. 'It's taken its toll on Dad too; he has aged so much. It was a real wake-up call for me. My sisters had been holding the fort of course, but I should have been there as well.'

As he paused to gain control of his voice, she felt her eyes prick with tears. It brought back memories of Ma hiding her stroke so it didn't disrupt her final exams. But now was not the time to tell Rob how well she understood his feelings of guilt.

He gave a wry grimace. 'You never think of your parents as getting old, I suppose. They are just always there, sort of permanent fixtures in your life. You take them for granted until something like this comes along and then suddenly… whoosh…the ground is swept away beneath your feet and you are left feeling vulnerable, sort of unprotected.'

The agonised look in his eyes was matched by hers. She recognised only too well, those feelings of insecurity and exposure, as if standing in a house with no roof.

'Dare I ask? How is she now?'

'They say she's over the worst. She had an operation and they seem to have caught it in time. But she hasn't a lot of energy and she's lost a lot of her hair. That was a dreadful shock I can tell you, seeing her, so pale and frail in that hospital bed...'

Gripping his hand in hers, she saw him shake with anguish. They both sat there, eyes locked together in mutual distress, until he could continue.

'As you know, Dad is a doctor and he reassures me she will be fine. It will take time and there will be regular check-ups, but he's optimistic.' There was still worry etched between his eyes. 'It's really shaken me up. Especially as I'm so far away. But Dad has insisted I go back and the family have promised never, ever to keep me in the dark about anything important again.'

The waiter brought their starters. Reluctantly Kate let go of his hand. She hoped her clasp had conveyed her sympathy. But the phrase about 'going back' hit her hard. An inner voice warned her not to raise her hopes.

Slowly Rob gained control of his emotions. 'I wish I could stay longer. Apart from anything else I've enjoyed catching up with my sisters and their families. There are a couple of nephews and a baby niece I've got to know a bit. Up till now I've only known them from photographs and things Mum had told me about them.

‘Sounds soppy I know, but I began to realise how much I’d missed my family. I’ve stayed with both my sisters for a while and I realise how out of touch I am with their lives. And I’ve got to know their husbands better, both great blokes.’

Deep in thought he stared out of the window.

‘As stupid as it sounds, this all seems so much more real than my life down under.’

Both deep in thought, they picked at their food.

‘Don’t you like it in Adelaide, then?’ She prodded listlessly at a prawn.

‘Adelaide is OK. It’s just not the most vibrant city on the planet.’ He looked round at the busy square as Birmingham came to vibrant life on a Friday night.

‘So why Adelaide?’

‘It’s where my girlfriend Leanne comes from. And I was lucky enough to get a lecturing post there at the university after I finished in the Antarctic. Perhaps it’s a bit staid at times but I can get on with my research. I keep in touch with all my scientist friends back here through the internet so I know what’s going on in the mainstream of science.’

Listening to his tone of voice, Kate thought he sounded far from enthusiastic about his life out there. Or was that just wishful thinking?

‘So when do you go back?’

‘Day after tomorrow.’

She ducked her head swiftly in case he saw the devastation in her eyes.

Suddenly her meal turned to chaff in her mouth and she struggled to swallow as hope died. Again.

Chapter Eighteen

While their half-eaten starters were being cleared away, Kate had time to pull herself together. At least now she knew where she stood.

He was going back to his girlfriend in Australia and this was just a quick catch-up between old friends. So no flirting, nothing suggestive, just regular chat, that's all. With a determined shrug of her shoulders, she told herself she could do that. Of course she could. If only the ache in her heart would die down a little. If only she didn't look at his hands lying so close to hers on the table, just asking to be clasped.

She looked up and caught a lingering look from him. Was that a yearning like hers? Was he too remembering their passion-filled time together?

Rob cleared his throat and deliberately looked away. 'Enough about me,' he said gruffly. 'So how did you end up teaching at a College then?'

Kate knew that to deflect unwonted emotion, use humour.

'OK. If you must know, it was because it was on my bus route.'

'What?'

'I know. All the career advice in the world and it all came down to the number four bus route round Brum.'

He laughed and Kate decided to spice up the tale of how she got her job after finishing Uni. Obviously she was going to miss out all the really upsetting bits. Suddenly, she was impelled by a desire to amuse him as she had all those years ago. Try to be the light-hearted girl he remembered.

'Well, it was the September after I finished Uni and I was living with Megan and Josh.'

Rob filled her wine glass. 'I thought Josh said something

about you staying on and doing a teaching certificate?'

She was a bit surprised that Josh had mentioned this. She looked at him keenly trying to decipher what else he knew about that dreadful summer. Did he know how her friends had to come to her rescue by offering her a refuge after Ma died? But surely he would have asked about Ma's death if he had known.

She sipped her wine. 'Yes, I was considering it but, as you know I've always had to count my pennies and I simply couldn't afford another year without earning a living.'

Rushing on to avoid any more questions, she continued, 'Obviously I needed a job to pay my way at Megan's. But what do you do with an English degree? Then I spotted an advert in the paper for a part-time English lecturing job at the local College. Apparently, although you need a teaching qualification to teach in schools, you don't in Further Education. With a degree, you could start straight away. And, as I said, it was on the bus route. So I applied, never really thinking I would get it.'

'Why not?'

'Well, to be honest I wasn't sure I wanted to get it. Have you read *Wilt*?'

'Um…no.'

'It's a book by Tom Sharpe where an English lecturer tries to teach literature to Meat One but all they want to talk about is sex and violence and cars.'

'Meat One?'

'Well, perhaps not Meat One exactly, but according to this book, you have to teach English to classes of eighteen-year-old students doing motor vehicle engineering or hairdressing or butchery, hence Meat One. Apparently anyone doing a practical subject has to do English as well. And, of course, they all hate it. They try to side-track the lecturer into strange subjects just to avoid doing the work. And I knew I didn't know enough about sex and violence and cars.'

'I can vouch for the fact you know nothing about cars… but sex?' Here he raised an eyebrow and grinned.

She felt herself blush to the roots of her hair. A burning

look passed between them and the years melted away.

Vividly remembering all their outdoor encounters, Kate flushed. 'Thanks to your expert tuition, I could perhaps have waxed lyrical about the local topography and even all the local suggestively named hills suitable for all manner of al-fresco activity.'

'But let me guess? Strangely that didn't come up in the interview.'

'I can't think why.'

His mouth curved in that oh-so familiar grin. Once again, there was a highly-charged look between them.

'Do you remember…?' he began.

But whatever naughty reminiscence he was just about to embark upon was interrupted by the young waiter bringing their fish and chips.

Clearly thinking better of his train of thought, Rob surveyed his plate.

'Oh good. Proper fish.'

'Don't you have fish and chips in Oz?'

'Oh yes. Barramundi is the usual one they serve.'

'Barramundi.' Kate relished the sound of this exotic sounding fish.

'It's nice enough but you can't beat a bit of battered cod. Anyway you were saying about your interview.'

'Huh. Call that farce an interview?'

She blew out her cheeks in exasperation recalling the events of that hot September afternoon. Full of trepidation she had turned up at the somewhat dilapidated and extremely dusty building in a rundown part of the city.

'I should have realised what it was going to be like there just from the so-called interview. I remember being all hot and nervous in my smart new interview suit. I had to wait outside the Head of Department's office and there was this other interviewee in jeans and T-shirt pacing up and down the corridor puffing away on a fag. I assumed she was applying for the same job as me but couldn't understand why she was so scruffily dressed. Then it struck me. Of course. Further Education Colleges were notoriously laid-back hot-beds of left-wing extremism. And I'd turned up for a job in a conventional formal suit. It even had a crisp white blouse, you know, the full Marks and Spencer look.'

She grinned, 'I was really panicked. It was too late to scruff down so I really worried about giving a too-formal image. But this girl seemed more nervous than me so I tried to calm her down and started chatting.

'She said her name was Zoë and when I asked her if she was on interview too she said, and I quote, "Sort off. But the whole thing is a fucking farce." I must have looked a bit shocked because she said, "Well, it *is* a fucking farce. At least for me. Eight fucking years I've been here. Still on a temporary contract so every year they make me come in for a so-called interview to see if they are going to appoint me again for another year.

"I know…and they know…they've got no one else for the job. No one else mad enough to take it on. But every fucking summer I get the letter saying if I want employment for the coming academic year, I should present myself for interview at such and such a time. Each year I say I'm not going to jump through their fucking hoops anymore and every fucking year I chicken out at the last minute and fucking well turn up. Sorry about the fucking language but I am just so fucking mad at myself for being here. One year…you wait and see… one year, I'll not turn up and see if it makes any fucking difference."'

Rob's eyebrows had gone up. 'Wow. That's one angry woman.'

'Yup. And as you can imagine, knowing all that I nearly gave up thinking she was after the same job as me and after eight years in the place, I didn't stand a chance. I said as much.

'She took one astonished look at me in my white blouse and suit and asked, "You mean you teach Sociology?"

'When I said no, English, she grinned, "Relax, you'll be fine. I know they need someone for that since Gareth went back to Wales."'

Kate smiled and took another gulp of her wine. She was

enjoying reliving the experience for Rob.

'I must have looked relieved because Zoë laughed and said, "You weren't nervous about getting the job, were you? Look, if you are upright with a pulse, they'll take you on here. Ooops, sorry that's not very flattering to you, is it? But seriously, they need *you* more than you need *them*. This near to the start of term they get desperate for a body…*any body*, to stand in front of the class. We always reckon that if they've got a class with no teacher they just nip out and grab someone from the nearest bus stop and haul 'em in."

'As you can imagine my face must have been a picture at all this and she obviously felt a bit guilty. She said, "Sorry. I really am. I shouldn't be disillusioning you like this. You probably have high noble ideals about inspiring the little darlings…doing a Robin Williams in *Dead Poets' Society*."'

'And had you?'

'Of course I had.'

'I knew it. Ever the dreamer, and of course you could outdo him on the poems, couldn't you?'

'Yup.' Course I could. Every time.'

He nodded, a faraway glint in his eyes, before leaning forward eagerly.

'So what happened?'

'Just as we were chatting, the door opened and a cheery little man in a short- sleeved shirt and jeans came out and said, "Oh hello, Zoë. Same again this year?"

'She growled at him, "No. This year I want a permanent contract, you miserly old skinflint."

'Then there was a right old ding-dong between them. He said, "Come on, Zoë, love. You know the College can't afford it. The Government's funding is minimal, as you know, and with student numbers as they are…"

'"Cut the crap, Tony. It's never stopped you getting your pay rises, has it?"

'"Now then, Zoë, Do you want to work next year or not?"

'"Not", said Zoë bluntly. "But I will…until I find something else that'll pay the rent."

'Then she turned on her heels, winked at me and strode off

down the corridor.'

Rob looked impressed, 'Wow. One feisty lady.'

'Yup, you can say that again. But a heart of gold. We became flat mates and she's been a lovely friend ever since.'

'So, I take it you got the job.'

'Yup, although the little man, Tony, was obviously very ruffled that I had witnessed this altercation. But Zoë was right. The interview was perfunctory. The Head of English was disaffected and I started work the following Monday.'

Kate sat back with a grin. Rob had been transfixed by her tale.

'And?'

'I've been there ever since.'

'Still temporary.'

'Oh yes, everything Zoë said was spot on. I turn up at the start of every year and I'm offered a temporary part-time contract, usually teaching all the rotten classes that the Head of English and his cronies don't want to teach.'

'Meat One?'

'To be fair we don't have any butchery apprentices at our College but Mechanics One and Hairdressers One and lots of evening classes.' She shrugged. 'It's not as bad as I feared. I'd read all these books about Colleges where the students were anarchic, the lecturers were priapic and the organisation was chaotic.

'And, yup, that more or less sums up our College.'

She sat back. Then thought a bit more.

'Only not quite. I soon discovered the students are only superficially bolshie. In fact apathy is a bigger problem. The male lecturers *talk* a lot about sex but mainly they are apathetic too and mainly spend their time grumbling about all the bloomin admin we have to do. The management is completely out-of-touch and distant so only vaguely aware of the chaos their edicts cause and half the time they don't follow them up anyway. I've noticed old hands know how to lay low and avoid anything too strenuous.'

'Sounds confusing and not very inspiring.'

'You're right. It was a steep learning curve at first, I can tell you. My Head of English left me in no doubt that he expected me to get on with it on my own. I soon learned he was famous for his FOFO style of teaching.'

'FOFO?'

'Telling his students to Fuck Off and Find Out.'

Rob nearly choked.

'I don't think I would have survived those first few weeks if Zoë hadn't helped me out. Now I'm used to all the crazy things that happen.'

'What crazy things?'

'Oh, too many to mention.'

'Go on tell me.'

As they ate their meal, Kate entertained him with tales of lazy male lecturers peeing in sinks in the ladies loos rather that traipsing to the distant male toilets, redundant aircraft seats from the axed travel and tourism course littering the canteen, learning to cough loudly before entering the stationery cupboard and not being surprised when she was the only lecturer still bothering to teach on a Friday afternoon.

'What a place.'

'Yup. It really is.'

The waiter came to take their empty plates away.

'More wine?'

'Um, I will if you will.'

'Sounds like fun.' Rob caught her eye and winked. Then swiftly looked away as if cross with himself for falling into their old flirtatious routine.

She was pleased that he too was finding the friends only relationship as difficult as her. But he was going away again, so friends is all it was. All it could ever be.

Chapter Nineteen

'Pud?'

'Of course.'

Rob opened the menu. 'Now let me see if there are any playfully stabbed bananas.'

Kate gasped. 'I can't believe you can remember so much from all those years ago?'

'Of course I can. It was an amazing time, wasn't it?' Again that special look before dragging back his gaze to the menu.

'I fancy the sticky toffee. Does it come with custard?' she asked the attentive young waiter.

'No, madam. It's cream or ice-cream.'

She sighed, 'OK. Ice-cream please, but can you make it two dollops. I can't bear running out of moistening material before I've got to the end of the pudding.'

Rob grinned. 'For a moment there I thought you were going to be all sophisticated and have the crème brûlée. So, in the absence of our beloved banana split option, it's two dollop sticky toffee for me as well.'

The waiter smiled, 'Two dollops each it is,' and he whisked away.

Rob settled back and gave her an appraising look. 'So if College is as bad as you say, why do you stay?'

'Good question. The College organisation *is* awful, but the students are great. And I've found, to my surprise, I just love teaching.'

'Really?'

'Really.'

'What do you love about it?'

'Well, it's a real adrenalin rush at the beginning of the year getting to know the students and learning all those names. I try to make it fun at first so they relax and look forward to the classes, that's half the battle. And I confess I hadn't realised what an old ham I am. I've discovered a real theatricality in me. In front of a class, you sort of assume a bigger personality. It's like being on the stage only better because you are making up your own script as you go along. And I love having the constant interaction with the audience.'

She paused. 'I feel alive in the classroom because I have to think on my feet and be able to respond quickly to anything they say. And of course, as you know I'm passionate about my subject and I want them to love it too. Let's face it, I like words and I like people so it's great to be able to put the two together. It gives me a real buzz.'

Rob was regarding her with fascination.

Suddenly feeling a bit foolish she stopped and mumbled, 'Sorry, I got a bit carried away there.'

'Yes, you did. And it was great to see. Your face lit up. I can quite understand why your classes love you.'

'I didn't say they loved me.'

'But they do, don't they?'

She coloured thinking about all the gifts and cards she'd got at the end of term.

Then shifted uncomfortably, remembering what had happened to her beautiful bouquet of flowers.

'Anyway enough about me.'

'No. I want to…'

'No more talk about me, do you hear?' she said firmly and gave him the sort of hard stare she reserved for recalcitrant students.

'Wooah.' He pretended to quail. 'OK. But can I ask just one more question?'

'Hmmn?'

'Are you still on a part-time temporary contract?'

'Yes, of course.'

'Aren't you worried you won't have a job in September?'

She thought for a moment. 'No, not really. My exam results are really good. In fact better than the full-timers. And there are loads of classes they don't want to teach so they palm them off on to me.'

'So they should give you a permanent contract.'

'Yes they should, like they should give one to Zoë and Anne and Patience and Sunita. But they won't.'

'Do they ever give out permanent ones?'

'Oh, yes.' Kate gave a bitter laugh. 'To blokes. Sexism is alive and well and living in Halesborne College. All the managers are men, don't forget. And every single one of the part-timers is a woman. Many of them are mothers so want hours to suit school terms so are just grateful to have a job that fits in. And the rest of us keep turning up in September ready to slot in wherever is wanted like the idiots we are. And they know it.'

'But that's illegal.'

'I know. But if we kick up too much fuss, or go to the union, we just won't have a job at all. Bird in the hand etc.'

Rob was indignant. 'But that's not fair.'

'Tell me about it,' said Kate reaching for her wine.

His hand grabbed hers. 'No, Kate, *I am telling you about it*. It's not fair and how long before you rebel and do something about it?' His eyes darkened and bored into hers.

She shifted uncomfortably. 'I know. I know, but…'

'No buts. You're better than this. You are one of the funniest, brightest people I know. You would be an asset anywhere you choose to go.'

'Thank you.' She glowed at the praise. Then stammered, 'I can't think of anything else to do. I'm a bit pathetic, I suppose.'

Rob's eyes flared with anger. 'No, you're not. Far from it. I remember you as Twirly Girl, full of fun, so witty, always singing, so enthusiastic about life.'

She looked down at their clasped hands on the table, torn between delight at this description and utter misery to think none of it applied any longer. He really must think she was a pitiful loser.

'Are there any other Colleges around you could apply to?' He squeezed her hand, trying to make her look at him.

'I suppose.'

'Or schools?'

She shrugged still unable to meet his eyes. 'I would need my teaching certificate for that.'

'And so why aren't you studying for it?'

'Because I can't take a year out to do it because I need to keep earning.'

'What about your bloke. Megan says it's Chris, isn't it? Would he help support you going for it?'

The hollow laugh froze on her lips and instinctively she glanced out of the window, just to check he wasn't out there spying on her.

Then she just shook her head and left it at that.

As if sensing this was a no-go area, he slowly let go of her hand and he too turned to look out of the window.

The square was filling up with groups of people setting out for a night of fun. A young couple caught her eye as they met up and embraced warmly. She looked away rapidly to meet Rob's gaze, a worried frown between his eyes.

'Kate…?'

She couldn't bear any more interrogation that just highlighted how unfulfilled her life was.

'Don't even think about asking me anything else. I said just one more question and you've had it. My turn now.' She might as well bite the bullet so she launched straight in. 'So tell me about your Leanne.'

He shrugged as if admitting defeat in his attempts to galvanise her life.

'OK. As I told you, I met her during my research in Antarctica. She's a meteorologist, four years older than me and had been there for two years already. She very kindly showed me the ropes in those first few months. Talk about steep learning curves…mine was mountainous. The base is quite a claustrophobic environment and you get to know each other pretty well…for better or for worse.'

Her heart sank. Did he realise he had just echoed the wedding vows? Was this where his relationship was heading? Reaching for her wine, she asked nonchalantly, 'What's she like?'

'Quite serious, I suppose. Very intense about her research and we had long scientific discussions about the fate of the planet and pollution.'

For a moment he looked sombre, and she could see he was really concerned. Although she knew he had always taken his work very seriously, she still wasn't too sure what it was he actually did. She really must ask Josh again. But his explanations were usually so scientific and detailed she had lost the will to live long before he finished.

Rob twirled his wine round his glass absently staring at the red swirls. 'Anyway we sort of got together over shared science and stuff. And when my research finished she decided to give up on the base too.'

'You never thought about coming back to the UK after your Antarctic stint?' she asked, eyes lowered, knowing how she had hoped so fervently at the end of this two year period. She remembered vividly the moment when Josh passed on the news that he wasn't coming back. She had been utterly crushed. It had come amidst the sadness of Ma's death. It had been a tough summer as she grieved, both for her past and for all her dreams for the future. But he wasn't to know that, and she wasn't going to tell him.

He paused. 'I did think about it, but Leanne really wanted me to go to Adelaide where her family live. There was a post going at the University which involved some lecturing but also gave me time to write up my research. Luckily I got it and I've been there ever since.'

'It sounds great.' She tried to inject some enthusiasm into her voice.

Obviously without success.

He grinned. 'Actually it's not bad. It sounds a darned sight better than your place. And Leanne has got a meteorological job at the local TV station. Not up front as a 'weather girl'. She's the one supplying the info behind the scenes.'

He sounded proud of her achievements. 'Oh, and did I tell you that she's very, very fit? Goes out jogging before breakfast and is always working-out at the gym. She loves to go hiking and camping at every available opportunity and she can out-climb me up the mountains. Most importantly, she has never *once* embarrassed me by singing and twirling when she got to the top.'

His lips twitched as his teasing eyes gazed at her.

'Sometimes I wish she would.' For a moment, he looked almost wistful. 'But anyway, her family are great and it's a very outdoors sort of place. We've a good social life. The people over there are really easy going...slightly old-fashioned in a way... It can feel a bit like a backwater at times. But, no, it isn't a bad life at all.'

Was she imagining it? Was he trying to convince himself that his life was good out there?

Of course not. Why on earth would he want to come back to the UK? Life here could in no way compare to the one he described. When would she stop kidding herself and finally admit he was gone...and gone for good?

Chapter Twenty

'Right, your turn again. If we are doing the turn and turnabout question thing, then you have to tell me about your fella, Chris.' Rob leaned forward, scrutinising her face.

Involuntarily, Kate's eyes darted to search the busy square outside.

'Why do you always do that?'

'What?'

'Look out of the window whenever we mention his name. Are you expecting him to turn up any minute?'

'No. No. Friday night is when he goes out to the pub with his mates.'

'OK.'

He paused waiting for her to continue. She searched round for what she could say about Chris, and could think of nothing.

He helped her out.

'Well, how did you meet?'

'He's head of the computer systems at the college…' and she stopped again, stumped for anything more.

'So a pretty useful guy to have around?' Rob persevered.

'Oh, yes he's very good at fixing things. When I first got to know him he found out my washing machine was playing up and he came round to fix it. In fact he fixed lots of little things that were going wrong around the flat.'

'Your flat?'

'Yes. I sort of came into some money…an inheritance, so I bought quite a nice two bedroomed flat in Harborne. I shared it with Zoë, from the College, at first to help with the bills. It was great. We had fantastic nights out. She really knows how to party that one does.'

He nodded, clearly waiting for more.

'Well, she started going out with Travis and wanted to move in with him, but wouldn't leave me in the lurch until I'd found another flatmate. When Chris heard about it on the College grapevine...well…he was kind and helpful and he sort of eventually moved in.'

Even to her ears it sounded lame. But that was it, more or less.

Rob was still searching her face. His frown had deepened.

'Dare I say, it doesn't sound very…well…very romantic?'

She flushed with anger. Who was he to question her on her relationships? She wanted to lash out and say, *Of course it's bloody not. You used up all my romance, all my love, all my longings, all those years ago. No wonder I've got nothing left now. It may not be romantic but at least he's not buggering off to study bloody ice and snow. Of course, I don't love him but that means he can't break my heart. Like you did.*

Instead she said stiffly, 'It's very companionable. We get along OK, in our own way.'

Luckily the puddings arrived before she was tempted to say any more that might reveal just how angry she was at him, at his desertion and the devastation he left behind.

'Sticky Toffee puddings with two dollops for you, madam…and for you, sir.' The waiter said with a broad smile as he placed the desserts before them with a flourish.

They began to eat in silence: the atmosphere strained. Kate was facing the reality that Rob would soon be returning to what was evidently a wonderful life in Adelaide. As all hope seeped out of her, so did her energy and she could barely lift her spoon to eat.

Realising he had said the wrong thing, Rob tried to make amends. 'I'm sorry. I shouldn't have said that about you and Chris.'

'It's OK.'

'I mean Leanne and I are hardly what you would call romantic together any more. Like you, we get along. I suppose that's just the way it is after a while.'

'Uhuh.'

‘He sounds like a good reliable chap. Which is what a person needs around the place.’ Rob was floundering on, digging a deeper hole with his every utterance.

Kate put a halt to it. She just wanted the evening to end. ‘So are you going back to Worcester tonight?’

‘No.’ He looked surprised. ‘Didn’t you know? I’m staying at Megan’s tonight. That’s why she wants you to come back to hers as well. She said it would be nice for us all to be together so we can catch up on each other.’

‘Oh, right.’ Normally she would love a long chat with Megan. But not tonight. Not now she was feeling so despondent about Rob, Chris, and her life in general. Rob clearly thought she was wasting her time with her job and her man. Well, maybe she was. But right now, she didn’t want reminding of it.

Looking worried about her monosyllabic replies, Rob began justifying why he was staying at Megan’s.

‘In fact I haven’t seen Megan at all since I got back. She’s so busy with her job, isn’t she? I met Josh this afternoon at the Uni for a while. In fact I popped in on my old professor and had a good long talk with him. He seemed very interested in my research. There’s a lot of new stuff going on about global warming he wanted to know about. He would love to have more input about it on one of the courses he’s setting up so I promised to send him some stuff from what I do in Oz.’

He ploughed gamely on telling her more about his research while she mechanically ate her dessert.

It was almost a relief when the smiling waiter came up and asked them how they liked their dollops.

Kate couldn’t bear to disappoint him so waxed lyrical about how they had been just what the pud needed for the requisite moistness. He went a bit pink round the ears at one point, so she stopped.

‘Can I get you some coffees?’

‘Um, Kate?’

‘No, I’m not right bothered but if you want one, go ahead.’

‘Thank you, but no, it’s all right. I think we can have one

round at Megan's, don't you?'

She nodded.

'So the bill please, if you don't mind.'

'Of course, sir.'

'By the way we are not going to have the going Dutch argument again, are we.' Rob leant forward smiling. 'It's definitely my treat.'

She hadn't the energy to argue so just said, 'Thank you.'

If only the evening could end there. Then she could go back home. Chris would probably still be out so she could just curl into a ball and have a good cry before he came in, probably too drunk to notice.

The last thing she felt like was a trip down memory lane with the three of them reminiscing about their student days. But she couldn't hurt Megan by bailing out. She would just have to plaster a smile on her face and try to look as if she was enjoying it.

Chapter Twenty-One

The taxi dropped them off outside a rambling and dilapidated Edwardian house which, from the numerous bell pushes outside, had clearly been divided up into flats. From the tatty state of the many window coverings, it was clear that some of the residents were far from house-proud and there was a general air of neglect about the whole building. Josh and Megan lived on the ground floor, so that, in theory, Josh could tend the extensive back garden. But Kate knew from its wildly overgrown state that he favoured a low maintenance approach, ostensibly to encourage wild life and butterflies.

The taxi ride had passed in polite safe conversation about the many changes in Birmingham. All the while Kate was desperately trying to think of a good reason why she might not be able to stay long.

Rob had barely rung the doorbell when the door was flung open by Megan who had a strange frazzled look on her face. Her eyes glared a warning, as did her overloud voice of welcome.

'Oh hi, you two. Oh, Kate, I'm so sorry I couldn't make it. And thank you so much for standing in for me, Rob. Poor Kate, I didn't mean to let you down but I'd had a tough day at work which brought on one of my migraines. *As I was telling Chris*, I felt so ill, Josh didn't like to leave me, but luckily Rob offered to go and tell you for me.'

'Chris?' Kate's heart sank. What was he doing there?

'Yes,' said Megan, emphatically waggling her eyebrows. 'He came round to escort you home.'

And there he was, looming behind her. And from the ugly look on his face he was half-cut and spoiling for a fight.

'Hi, Chris,' Kate said carefully.

'Who's this?' he asked, peering at Rob through aggressive,

narrowed eyes. 'Been out on the pull have you?'

Noticing Rob had balled his hands into fists, she stepped quickly between them.

'Not at all. This is Rob, an old friend of Josh and Megan's.' She daren't say, *and mine*. 'Anyway, what are you doing here?'

'Surprised to see me aren't you?'

'Well, yes. I thought you were going out with your mates.'

'Yes, I should still be there but thanks to you, I had to leave early. I've come to take you home.'

'There was no need for that, Chris. I'm quite capable of getting myself home.'

'No. you're not. Especially from this grotty end of town. It's full of druggies and all sorts out there.'

Megan stiffened, about to say something, then thought better of it and just stayed warily in the background, watching events with a keen eye.

Chris was on a roll now. 'I couldn't believe that note you left me saying you would get a taxi back from here. How many times have I told you that it's definitely not safe to do that at this time of night? It's a good job I'm here to look after you.' He lurched forward and grabbed her arm. 'Come on.'

Rob leapt forward but Megan put a restraining hand on his chest and deliberately stepped forward, blocking his access to Chris.

'Actually, Chris, I was going to ask Kate if she wanted to stay here tonight so we could have a real good chat. My migraine's gone now and it's been ages since we've had a good catch-up. And I still haven't had chance to tell you my news. It would be a shame not to share it, wouldn't it, Josh?'

Josh was taken aback by this question and for a moment it looked as if he was going to query it, but a hard stare from Megan kicked him into gear.

'Oh gosh, yes, Kate. You must stay. It's been so long since we saw you.'

'She's coming home with me,' Chris said grimly, still gripping her arm.

'Well, I rather think that's up to Kate, don't you? I've already made up the bed in the spare room, so it's all ready for her to stay the night if she wants to.' Her lilting Welsh voice was being sweetly reasonable but her eyes were constantly flicking between a belligerent Chris and a clearly angry Rob.

'I've told you, she's coming with me.' Chris glared at Megan, who, far from quailing, stood up straight and looked him coolly in the eye.

'Last time I looked, Kate was a grown-up independent woman, quite capable of making up her own mind. Aren't you, Kate?'

Megan turned and looked meaningfully at her friend.

There was palpable tension in the air. Chris still held her arm in his fierce grip. Rob's taut expression showed he was itching to intervene and he could explode at any moment. Obviously, to keep the peace, Kate knew she should submit to Chris' demands and go with him.

But she also felt this was a make or break moment. Megan and Rob were looking at her anxiously.

'Yes,' said Kate, then more loudly. 'You're right, Megan. Of course I can make up my own mind. And I'd love to stay the night here. Thank you.'

With a warning glance at Rob, Megan swiftly prised Chris' fingers from Kate's arm and began hustling him towards the front door. Rob silently followed her ready to take over if needed.

'Such a pity it's only a single bed so we can't invite you to stay as well, Chris,' she said loudly. 'Josh, can you call him a taxi, please.'

Josh rushed to the hall phone and began dialling. There was an angry face-off between Megan and Chris, who seemed a bit stunned by the whole situation as if he couldn't quite compute Kate's non-compliance with his orders. Turning to face her, he snarled, 'You'll regret this.'

'Will she?' Megan said. 'Will she indeed? In what way will she regret it? Are you threatening my friend in front of all these witnesses?'

The air vibrated with hostility. Rob's aggressive stance showed he was clearly longing for an opportunity to have a go at Chris. Sensing this, once again, Megan deliberately put herself between the two confrontational men.

For a brief moment, Kate wondered if she should intercede. After all she knew from long practice how to mollify Chris when he was in one of his belligerent, half-drunken moods. He was all talk. All it took to calm him down was a little conciliation. You just had to say sorry for whatever it was that had upset him and promise you wouldn't do it again. She was sure she could smooth his ruffled feathers in the taxi ride home.

But she stopped herself. He had totally embarrassed her in front of her friends. In front of Rob who must now know exactly what Chris was like. She was ashamed and angry and determined not to give in.

'The taxi is on its way,' Josh informed the bristling group.

'Oh good,' said Megan briskly. 'You had better go and wait outside, Chris, or it will go sailing past.' And with Rob's help, she bundled a befuddled Chris outside.

He stood uncertainly for a moment outlined in the streetlight. Then turned back fiercely to the door. Perhaps it was the sight of Rob's tall frame filling the doorway, fist clenched and shoulders tensed for action that dissuaded him from returning. A mutinous look crossed his face before he slunk away into the darkness.

Chapter Twenty-Two

Next morning as Kate opened her bleary, tear-swollen eyes, she despondently watched the faint light filter under the curtains to illuminate Megan's small spare bedroom. She could see two walls of shelves over-crowded with books and fat, dusty lever-arch files. Stacked in one corner was a pile of large cardboard boxes filled to overflowing with unwanted items which she knew her friend was always too busy to sort out.

Lying there, curled up in misery under the brightly coloured duvet, she became aware of subdued noises of breakfast being eaten followed, a while later, by a flurry of hushed goodbyes before the front door softly closed. The finality of the sound reverberated round her whole body.

So that was it. Rob had gone.

Josh was driving him to the airport and she would never see him again.

Last night, totally shamed by Chris's behaviour, she hadn't dared look at Rob, knowing she would see a humiliating look of pity in his eyes. Instead she had muttered about a headache and, at a nod from Megan, had scurried into the spare bedroom where she had flung herself sobbing on to the bed.

Through her torrent of tears she had been aware of quiet voices in the lounge, clearly discussing the situation. Discussing her.

It was bad enough knowing that Rob was going back to his super-fit, successful girlfriend in Australia, but that he should have witnessed that mortifying scene with Chris hurt more than she could bear.

It had been an awful night. She wanted to howl out loud but knew that Rob was curled up on Megan's sofa only twenty feet away. So she pressed her hot face into the soft pillow and drenched it in stifled, heartbroken tears.

At some point in the night she had got undressed and, crawling into the rumpled sheets, had fallen into a fitful sleep. Now, as the new day dawned, she was drained of all emotion and really hadn't the energy to cry any more.

There was a soft knock on the bedroom door.

'Do you want a cup of tea?'

'Thanks, Megan. I would love one.'

The door opened and her friend came in bearing two steaming mugs of tea which she placed on the small bedside table. She then turned to open the bedroom curtains a little.

Sitting up in bed, Kate said, 'He's gone, hasn't he?'

With her back still turned, Megan nodded.

Kate felt herself slump and she let out a huge sigh. Suddenly she was engulfed in a huge hug, and to her astonishment Megan began to cry on her shoulder. Kate couldn't believe it. She was horrified. What had brought her lovely, down-to-earth friend to tears?

'Megan, what on carth is the matter?'

'I'm so sorry, Kate, so sorry. This is all my fault. I should never have arranged for you two to go out last night. I thought it would be a great surprise because he so desperately wanted to meet you again. But I should have warned you and…'

'No. No, you shouldn't. I would have been in a tizz all day and Chris would have suspected.'

'But I shouldn't have done it like that.' Megan wailed afresh. 'It was naughty of me to leave you on your own. I half-hoped…I shouldn't say this, but I hoped he would see you…and it would all ignite again.'

'And me too.' Kate couldn't help but sigh.

'You two had something special going on when you first met. I have never seen such chemistry. I really, really hoped…but I should have known better than to interfere.'

A fresh wave of tears threatened to engulf her. This was so un-Megan-like, all Kate could do was hug her even more tightly and try to soothe her.

'It's all right. Of course it wasn't your fault. And you totally did the right thing. We had a…a long chat. It was good to catch up. And you definitely weren't to know that Chris would show up like he did.' She grabbed hold of Megan's trembling shoulders and gave her a gentle shake. 'Don't you dare blame yourself. Don't you dare.'

Hearing a huge unladylike sniff, she passed her friend the box of tissues by the bed.

'Listen, Megan, you did absolutely the right thing. Last night told me definitely, Rob and me…it's just not to be. It showed me I can't kid myself any longer. I've just got to face it, he is *never* coming back.' She sighed. 'There, I've said it out loud. He's clearly happy where he is. He doesn't love me and he's never coming back.' In spite of her resolve, she felt her voice quaver. But it had to be faced.

Megan looked at her with red-rimmed eyes. 'I'm just so sorry, Kate. I really am.'

Despite her misery, Kate couldn't help a little laugh. 'Megan Price, who knew you were such a soppy old romantic at heart. But don't you ever, *ever* blame yourself again. You are the truest friend anyone could ever have.' She gave her a tight hug. 'Come on, you sentimental starry-eyed wishful-thinker, let's drink our tea before it gets stone cold.'

After another huge sniff, Megan blew her nose and picked up her cuppa.

As she sipped her tea, Kate could see from Megan's weary face that she too had had a bad night.

'I heard you moving about last night. You didn't sleep much, did you?'

'I don't think anyone did. Rob was certainly restless and I don't think it was just that uncomfy sofa he was on.'

'Oh don't. I feel so guilty at pinching his bed. It was really disconcerting knowing he was so close...yet so far away. It really made me think about things. You know how much I've dreamed that one day he would come back.'

Megan nodded.

'Well, the dream has come true. He *did* come back. But now he is returning to his perfect life in Australia with his lovely, perfect girlfriend.'

'No girlfriend is perfect, you know.'

'Don't, Megan,' she groaned. 'Please don't do that. No more false hopes. I've got to wake up to the fact that I have lived half my life waiting and waiting for people to come back. First my mum and now Rob...and it's all been a waste. I could have been getting on with things, instead I've just drifted. And Rob has made me see what a mess my life is and how pathetic I am.'

'No, you're not.'

'But I am. I keep going over and over in my mind what he must have thought about that scene last night. He had already sussed out I was going nowhere with my career, then he saw what Chris was like. I was so humiliated. He must think I'm such a total loser.'

'That's the last thing he thinks,' Megan said sharply. 'He genuinely cares for you, you know, and was really upset for you. He really wishes you valued yourself more. But he was sure it was something to do with your childhood so he kept asking me about it. He thinks you're hiding something… something that has eroded your self-confidence. He says you've always been very cagey about it.'

'I know. Can you blame me? You didn't tell him about my mum, did you?'

'No, of course not. That's for you to tell, if and when you want to. But I do think...'

'You think I should have told him, don't you?'

'No. Who am I to give advice?'

'In fact I did wonder about telling him about how bad it was when Ma died. But in the end, even though it's been three years now, it's still a bit raw. I knew I wouldn't have been able to tell him without getting upset, and that would have put a damper on the evening. Besides, talking about her could have led to all sorts of questions. It just didn't fit the mood of the evening. I felt he wanted me to be the old me. He kept egging me on to be funny and a bit silly. That's when I realised I hadn't been the "old me" for ages. So I tried to find the silly, poetry-quoting, fun-loving person he used to know. The girl who used to be me. He calls her Twirly Girl.'

'And?'

'And…it felt good. At times I did actually feel a bit like the old me.'

Megan nodded. 'She's not gone. She's just dormant. You've had a shitty time over the last couple of years. It's knocked your confidence. But...'

'Is this where you tell me to snap out of it?'

Megan laughed. 'Ah, the old British stiff-upper-lip clichés so beloved of the bracing "buck up" brigade. As you know, that's the last thing I would say. No. I wondered if you knew the main thing that's stopping the re-appearance of the old you.'

Kate grimaced. Megan knew the answer as much as she did.

'It's Chris. I've got to kick him out, haven't I?'

Despite her best social work training, Megan gave an emphatic nod of her head.

'Yup.' she agreed. 'You have.'

Chapter Twenty-Three

'Yes, I know. He's definitely got to go.' Kate eased the tension in her shoulders. 'I'd already decided that. Especially after what he did yesterday.'

'Why, what did he do?'

'It sounds a bit silly I know, but he broke Ma's vase. I don't even think he meant to do it. I think he just wanted to knock over a lovely bunch of flowers my class had bought me. And somehow I wasn't surprised. Perhaps I had even unconsciously put them on display as a provocation knowing how much he hates it when my classes are nice to me.'

Megan nodded, listening intently.

'Looking back, I can see it as just one in a long line of spiteful little acts of revenge whenever I cross him. But that vase was so special to me...'

Fighting to keep down her emotion, she said, 'I remember Ma always put it on the kitchen windowsill full of bought flowers in the winter so it cheered the place up. And then in the summer, she always picked flowers from the garden and arranged them to brighten up the empty hearth in the living room. Seeing it smashed really upset me and I yelled at him.'

'How did he take it?'

'I think I was so fierce it really startled him, and he sort of backed down. Then, of course, he started his usual sneery comments about "making a fuss over nothing" and stuff about me being unstable.'

'Unstable? You?'

'Yes, I know. It's just one of his usual digs. If ever I argue back at him, it's "time of the month" or I'm being unreasonable and volatile. Well this time I wasn't going to let him get at me and I refused to go with him to College so he left in a huff. Later when I phoned Zoë to ask her to cover my class, she sounded really worried. I suddenly realised she thought Chris had thumped me and I wasn't coming in because perhaps I had bruises or a black eye or something. That really shocked me. I began to wonder what people were thinking.

'So I spent the rest of the day really mulling everything over. It was so nice to have the flat to myself for a change. And I began to think what it would be like without him, and I really liked the idea.'

Feeling a burning sense of shame, she confessed, 'Up till then, I suppose I thought that, although Chris wasn't ideal, I'd rather have someone, even like him, than have no one at all. Sounds silly doesn't it?'

'No. A lot of people would rather put up with very bad situations rather than be alone.'

'How pathetic am I? I hadn't realised how stupid I was until I saw Rob's face last night when he saw what sort of man Chris was. It could have got really nasty. You were totally awesome in the way you handled the whole thing.'

'I just knew I had to stop Rob from thumping him…that could have got complicated in all sorts of ways.'

'I know. Chris would have charged him with assault and he would have loved being the martyr. Thank goodness you were there. It was fantastic the way you stood up to him and managed the whole thing.'

'Thanks, but don't forget I wasn't on my own. I had two men ready to back me up if he'd had a real go at me. I think he realised he was outnumbered which is why he didn't make more fuss. And, of course, like most bullies, he's a total coward.'

The scorn in Megan's voice brought back memories of the look of contempt on Rob's face as he gazed at Chris. She had a job holding back her tears of humiliation. 'Oh Megan,' she wailed, 'Rob must really despise me for putting up with a man like that.'

Megan's tone was sharp. 'No one despises you, Kate, least of all Rob. It's Chris they despise. Moving in on you with his smooth, scheming charm, just when you were at your most vulnerable. Sweet as pie at the beginning then slowly but surely tightening his stranglehold on you. Pulling you away from all your friends and chipping away at your self-confidence so you would rely on him more and more. It's him I despise, with every fibre of my being.'

Kate had never seen her friend so angry. No more sitting on the fence for her.

'But, Megan, I should have seen what he was doing.'

'Of course you didn't. He deliberately picked you because he could see what a naturally trusting nature you have. Which he then exploited for his own selfish purposes.'

Kate shook her head. 'I keep looking back and I've never quite known how it happened. How he had such a controlling hold on me. It's like he invaded my brain space so that I always worried about what he would think about everything I wanted to do.'

'Oh, he's a cunning operator all right; I've seen his type so many times. Oh, Kate, I've been itching to interfere, but I know you would have defended him. You had to see it for yourself.'

Kate hung her head. 'You're right. Zoë couldn't stand him and kept chipping away at him and I just kept making excuses for him. I know last night was a bit dramatic, but in the end, I'm glad it happened. I was coming to the conclusion that I must break free of him but was really worried how to do it. You know how I hate confrontation.'

Megan nodded. 'And he knew it too, didn't he? He relies on your dislike of arguments to get his own way.'

'Yes, but I noticed yesterday when I was really furious, he backed down. All his snidey comments just rolled off me, and he knew it. It made me see I could stand up to him. I think that's why he came round for me last night. He was worried that you would bolster me up and I would come back more determined. Well, it backfired big time. It just fast-tracked what I was going to do. I just wish,' her voice trembled, 'I just wish Rob hadn't seen it.'

Megan put her arms about her. 'Don't beat yourself up

about it. Rob didn't blame you at all. Don't under-estimate him. He totally understood the situation.'

'Really?'

'When we were talking last night, he was livid the way you had been manipulated. He kept saying 'How dare he exploit her like that.' I didn't have to tell him anything about Chris. He could see for himself what a weasel he was, abusing the fact that you are just too bloomin nice.'

'But he must still think I'm a total wimp to let him walk all over me like that.'

'Stop it, Kate. I won't have you talking like that. Don't you see that by blaming yourself you are reinforcing the self-hatred Chris tried to engender in you? That's what these scheming snakes do. They take advantage of all your lovely qualities of generosity and tolerance and kindness, then they make you think that everything that occurs is your fault.'

Kate slowly nodded.

'It'll take some time for you to realise just how much he has eroded your self-worth and for you to unlearn your apologetic habit, but I hope you do.' She paused and said carefully, 'So have you decided what you are going to do about him?'

For the first time, Kate smiled. 'Oh yes. I know precisely what I'm going to do.'

Chapter Twenty-Four

'I'm going to kick Chris out … today. I'm all steeled up to go and confront him and tell him to bugger off.' Straightening her shoulders, Kate said, 'I know it's going to be unpleasant but I've had a long sleepless night to think it all through. And he's out on his ear as soon as I get round there.'

'Woah. And that's the last thing you are going to do.'

'What? But you agree he should go.'

'Absolutely. Get rid of the swine as fast as you can. But you don't do it by just turning up and having a massive confrontation. Don't forget I have a lot of experience in these matters and the most dangerous time of all in an abusive relationship is when the woman finally decides enough is enough, and stands up to him. Things can get really nasty then. And it's always the women who come off worst.'

Kate was shocked. 'Mine's not an abusive relationship like that.'

She saw Megan's eyebrows go up.

'It's not, Megan. I know he's very controlling but Chris wouldn't hit me.'

Although Megan looked sceptical, she conceded, 'You could be right. But don't forget you are throwing him out from a very comfortable situation. He's in a very nice flat in a good area, in which, I suspect, he lives very cheaply. I assume he doesn't contribute half as much as he should.'

Kate hung her head and nodded. He earned far more than her and, at first, happily paid half of all the bills. But these days she had to nag him incessantly for the money whenever the electricity, gas, or other household bills came in. He always protested that the cost of his petrol ferrying her (and him, of course) to College more than covered his contribution.

'Thought as much. Hate to say it, but probably the flat

could have been one of the reasons he homed in on you. As well as the fact he could preen about capturing the most attractive female in the College.'

'Me?'

'Yes, you. As Rob kept saying last night, you don't realise how gorgeous you are. He saw you standing at the top of those steps in Brindley Place and he couldn't believe how…' She stopped suddenly. 'Sorry. Anyway back to Chris. I think he probably is a coward as well as a bully but believe me he's going to be really angry. I assume you will want him to leave straight away?'

'Absolutely.'

'Very wise. But he may not go easily. So let's play it safe, shall we?'

'OK.'

'Right. We need to do it as soon as possible. I don't like the idea of that man wreaking petty vengeance on your prized possessions.'

Kate blenched at the thought of all the spiteful things Chris could do.

Megan clasped her hands. 'Don't worry. Whatever happens he will be out by tonight.'

'Really?'

'I promise. But it's easier if he's not around. Does he go out anywhere on Saturday?'

'Yes. He goes out this morning to play five-a-side with his mates.'

'OK. So we phone first to check he's not stayed behind. Then we change the locks.'

Kate's eyes widened. 'I hadn't thought of that.'

'It's the most important thing. Now I just happen to know a lovely, big, burly locksmith called Barry. I always ask if he will come to help on these jobs. He changes the locks and then he waits around till the bloke gets back. Usually all he has to do is loom over them in a menacing fashion, but he can be quite handy when the need arises.'

'It won't come to that, will it?'

'No, it shouldn't. But as a lad Barry watched his dad beat

up his mum for years so he has a bit of a short fuse when it comes to women being bullied by men. He will often stay over for a few days after, just to make sure the bloke doesn't try to wheedle his way back.'

'What?'

'Oh yes. Don't fret, he's in a lovely gay relationship, so you have no need to worry about advances. And anyway, you are coming to stay with us for a while.'

'Megan, I couldn't possibly…'

'No ifs or buts.'

'I can't…'

'I said no buts. Can't have you sitting all alone in your flat moping and brooding and weeping. Not when you can do all that here amidst smashing company like Josh and me.'

Kate laughed. 'Friends don't come any better than you, Megan.'

'Go on with you. Anyway, you know how much I hate housework and I'm not bloomin washing these sheets after only one night.'

She stood up decisively. 'Now, should we get up and spruce up? I always feel better after a shower and tooth clean. And wear that great green top you wore yesterday. Let Chris see just what he's losing.'

As determined as she was, nevertheless, it was with a thumping heart that Kate climbed the stairs to her flat. She was so glad Megan was with her.

'I don't know why I'm so nervous. He didn't answer the phone and his car's not there so he should be out.'

'If you want, we can wait for Barry. He shouldn't be long.'

'No. Chris will definitely be at the match. He wouldn't let down his mates. He fancies himself as their star striker.'

However, as she tiptoed into the flat, she listened intently, alert to every slight sound. Quickly she checked all the rooms, before breathing out a huge sigh of relief.

'Definitely not here.'

'Good. Right, let's pack up all his stuff in these black bin bags I've brought.'

'Why black bin bags.'

'Because why should he have any of your suitcases? And I quite like the symbolism of his stuff being equivalent to rubbish.'

Kate grinned and nodded as she led the way to the bedroom to begin on his clothes.

'Of course,' Megan said as she unceremoniously stuffed his best shirts into a bag, 'you will have to be strong when you bump into him at work.'

'Hmmn, that's another thing I've been thinking about. In fact…'

The doorbell suddenly rang making them both jump out of their skins. 'Don't worry. That'll be Barry,' Megan said with a relieved smile.

And it was. A giant of a man wearing a black beanie hat and a very cheerful grin filled the doorway.

'Hallo, Megan, love,' he said in a broad Yorkshire accent, before embracing her in a bear-like hug. 'And you must be Katie.' He held out a huge paw of a hand.

'Hi, Barry. Thank you so much for coming out at such short notice…and on a Saturday morning as well.'

He grinned. 'If Megan calls, I come running. I owe her big time.'

'You and me both.'

They both turned and beamed at an embarrassed Megan.

'Give over, the pair of you. Now come on. We should have a couple of hours but we want to be all finished by the time he gets back, don't we?'

It didn't take as long as they thought to bag up Chris' clothes, computer games and stuff and dump it all in bags in the hallway ready for his return.

In the meantime, Barry changed the door lock, chatting as he worked. His big hands were remarkably deft as he replaced the old mechanism with a shiny new one.

'Much better quality this one, Katie love. No one will force this one, I can tell you. And tomorrow I'll come back and put a spy hole in the door for you. That should sort it.'

In response to a query about his accent he explained that

he originally came from Bradford and had to move down south for various reasons. He didn't specify and she didn't ask. But he was fulsome in his praise for Megan's help in turning his life around.

'Any friend of Megan's is a friend of mine. And I know she thinks the world of you, Katie, lass.'

He clearly thought her name was Katie, and she was fine with that.

They were just enjoying a nice cuppa and a biscuit when she glanced out of the window and froze as she saw Chris' car turn into the flats' private car park.

Her mouth went dry. 'It's him,' she muttered.

'Now don't you worry, Katie lass. I've had bastards like that for breakfast,' said Barry grimly, patting her hand. And she believed him.

Megan gave him a warning look.

'Don't worry, Megan love, I won't start anything. I'll be good. I've learnt my lesson. But I won't take no shit either.'

'Right, Kate,' Megan looked her directly in the eyes. 'I know you hate confrontation, but you can do this. Show him he has no hold over you anymore. I'm going to stay out of the way, but I'm here if you need me. OK?' She gave Kate a hug then sat down again and continued to drink her tea.

Kate gulped, but Megan was right. She had to stand up to him.

Looking out of the window, she saw a furious Chris leap out of his car. At Megan's instigation she had parked her car in the flat's designated space so this time it would be Chris who would have to search around for somewhere to park. Except of course, he didn't. Instead he parked very, very close behind her, just touching her bumper and boxing her in.

She heard him pounding up the stairs and heard his key trying to fit in the lock. The new lock.

At this point Barry flung the door open. And just glared.

Momentarily cowed by this large, unexpected figure at the front door, Chris recoiled. Then his anger took over. 'Who are you and what are you doing in my flat?'

'Your flat?' Barry roared. 'Your flat! No, mate. It's Katie's flat and I'm here to tell you to shove off.'

'What?'

'Here's your stuff.' Barry effortlessly lifted a large bin bag and thrust it quite forcefully into Chris' chest. The shock on his face was almost comical.

'You can't do that.'

'Stop me.' Barry picked up the other bags and none too carefully flung them out of the door. There was the sound of something breaking as one of them crashed to the floor.

'Careful,' yelled Chris as he scrabbled on the floor grabbing a couple of his DVDs that had spilled out.

Barry grinned. 'Ooops.'

Chris turned and for the first time saw Kate standing in the hall coolly watching events. She was feeling remarkably calm and in control. How pathetic he looked. And to think he had dominated her life for the past year. A cold anger seized her. How dare he?

'What's happening, Kate? You can't kick me out. You'll never manage without me.'

'Oh yes, I will. In fact I will be so much better off without you. My vases won't get broken for a start off.'

'Oh, that thing. Is that what all this is about?' He stood up with a swagger as if at last understanding the problem. Giving an ingratiating smile that turned her stomach, he stretched out a placatory hand. 'You always were a sentimental old thing. Look, if it means so much to you, I'll replace it.'

'That would be nice, Chris. I would appreciate it. But what you can't replace is the year of my life you've leeched from me like the parasite you are. But no more. The locks have been changed; there's all your stuff. You don't live here anymore.'

His smile turned to shocked incomprehension.

'You can't do this. Where will I go?'

Kate shrugged. 'Not my problem.'

As the reality began to sink in, his face turned puce and he lunged towards her. 'How dare you. You'll regret this.'

'Oh no, she won't.' Barry's big hands grabbed the front of

Chris' T-shirt, and he lifted him up till their faces were almost touching.

'My mum was married to a slime ball like you, and, once I grew up, I did time for what I did to him. I'd happily do it again to stop bastards like you abusing the good nature of innocent women. So if anything happens to my friend Katie here, to her car, to her flat or anything belonging to her…I know who you are. I know your name, your car number plate and where you work. But you don't know who I am, do you? One word from Katie lass to me and you will wish you'd never been born. I will be keeping my eye out for you and if ever I see you with a nice woman, I will make sure I find out where you live, and she will learn all about you. Understand?'

He released him very slowly. 'And for your information, I'm Katie's new lodger so don't even think of sneaking back.'

Looking distinctly shaky after this tirade, Chris backed away, clutching one of the bags. But from the relative safety of the top of the stairs, he couldn't resist a parting shot. 'You'll never work at the College again.'

'No, you're right,' Kate replied. 'I'd already decided that. I've got much more exciting things to do.'

And moving past the bulk of Barry, she was the one who finally closed the door on Chris. It felt good. As if she was closing the door on a whole unhappy chapter of her life.

Time for something new.

PART THREE

Chapter Twenty-Five

September 2000

The sweltering heat hit her as soon as she left the arrivals lounge at Malaga airport. Surely it shouldn't still be so hot in September? At home in Birmingham it had been still warm but she thought the stifling Spanish summer temperatures would have abated somewhat by now.

She was obviously wrong about that.

Was she wrong about everything else as well?

The advert for an English lecturer capable of teaching exam classes in the Carlton International College on the Costa del Sol had caught her eye just as she was giving up hope of finding anything suitable. She had seized on it gratefully, thankful that she wouldn't be forced back to Halesborne College with her tail between her legs.

The sense of relief bordering on euphoria those first heady days after Chris left had convinced her, if she needed it, of how right she had been to kick him out. It blunted the overwhelming sense of sadness and self-disgust after her encounter with Rob.

It also strengthened her absolute determination to start living her own life now she knew Rob would never return. No more waiting.

After a somewhat hedonistic holiday to Ibiza with her College friends, she had returned tanned, stronger and more assured, and started looking in earnest for jobs. It wasn't as easy as she thought it might be. Every lecturing or teaching job she saw demanded a teaching qualification and, of course, she hadn't got one. Even as she contemplated other careers, in her heart she knew she did still want to teach. Not because she didn't know what else to do, but because she knew she enjoyed it and was good at it.

As September drew nearer, she began to despair. Then she saw the advert for a lecturer to teach in a small College near Marbella on the Costa del Sol. Someone with proven exam competence was required to teach English GCSE and A levels to ex-pat students but it didn't mention needing an actual teaching qualification. On the off-chance, she phoned to enquire if a qualification was essential and was put through to a very brisk, posh-sounding Principal. What started out as a simple query from Kate soon morphed into a searching phone interview from the rather intimidating Cassandra Carlton-Smith who seemed delighted when Kate outlined her experience and results.

It seemed that the advertisement has gone in later than the Principal would have wished and it had garnered very few applications, and those mainly from newly-qualified inexperienced teachers.

When the phone conversation ended, to her surprise, Kate found that, subject to satisfactory references, she had obtained a job teaching English on the Costa del Sol starting in just over a fortnight.

Stunned, she had put down the phone and just sat there, mind whirling. But in the pit of her stomach a bubble of excitement fizzed.

Why not? There was nothing keeping her in Birmingham. It would be a fresh start. New people. What had she got to lose?

But two weeks. Her mind raced. How could she sort everything at such short notice? What should she do with her flat?

Then inspiration struck. She began making lists.

That evening, surrounded by her plans, she phoned Megan.

'Hi, Megan. Are you sitting down?'

An exhausted voice answered. 'Yes. Just got in and Josh has handed me a mug of tea whilst he gets on with the meal.'

'Guess what?'

‘Nope, I can’t.’ The snappiness of the reply left Kate in no doubts that Megan was too drained of energy after a day at work to summon up any level of curiosity.

‘I’ve got a job.’

‘Great.’ The tone was still flat but there was a slight flicker of interest.

‘It’s in Spain.’

‘What?’ Now Megan really was listening.

‘Starting soon. In fact in two weeks’ time.’

‘What?’

‘Would you and Josh like to come and live in my flat and look after it for me while I’m gone?’

‘What?’

‘We could sort out a rent, just to cover the bills and it would be much cheaper than what you are paying at the moment. So it would give you a chance to save up for a house as you have always wanted to. And it would be doing me a favour because I could just put all my stuff in the spare bedroom and kip in there if I wanted to come back for Christmas or something.’

In spite of the stunned silence at the other end, Kate couldn’t stop herself rushing out all her plans in a garbled flood of persuasion.

‘You’ve been saying how much you ought to get out of that grotty area and how much you hate all the grungy people in that house who litter up the hallway and don’t look after their places and how the landlord won’t sort that damp patch on the bathroom wall. Think about it. Living here in my flat would be much safer for your car after it was scratched last week because you wouldn’t have to park on the street anymore and in fact it’s on a bus route so Josh could get to work more easily and…’

‘OK. OK, slow down there, my lovely.’ Her friend’s voice interrupted her mid-torrent. ‘You have really been thinking this through, haven’t you?’

‘Oh, Megan,’ she groaned. ‘My brain has been working on overload since I talked to the Principal this morning and started thinking about what’s got to be sorted before I go.’

‘Right. Let’s just rewind here. First tell me what’s the job, which Principal, where are you going and…well everything.’

So Kate started from the beginning and, as she told her friend, it crystallised in her mind and became a reality. This was it, an exciting opportunity to re-invent herself and her life.

At first Megan was a bit sceptical about such a late advertisement and a telephone interview appointing her to a post in a College in Spain.

‘Is it all a bit dodgy? Is it some run-down establishment that’s going to exploit you?’

‘No, Megan. I know you always worry about the seamy side of things, but it looks good. I’ve checked the place out as much as I can, and it seems legit. I get an initial one-year contract and the money is much better than I was getting at the College and it seems I get all exam classes.’

‘OK. It sounds good but I’ll get Josh to check it out on the University network tomorrow to see if the place is above board.’

‘Thanks for worrying about me, Megan but, although I’m excited, I’ve got my head screwed on. I’ll give it a year and see how it goes. After all, how bad can it be? If it truly is awful, I’ll come back and get something part-time again here. After all, if I’ve got the back bedroom here in the flat, I can come back. That’s why it would be sooo good if I rent out my flat to you, not through an agency where I would be trapped if it doesn’t work out. Please say you will come and live here. You will be doing me such a favour and…’

Megan laughed. ‘I do believe you have mentioned that before. I’ll have to consult with Josh of course. But you don’t fool me, I rather think it’s *you* doing us a bigger favour.’

There was a moment’s silence. Kate could sense her friend thinking this whole thing through.

‘Yes. I accept. I agree it suits us both. It will give me a huge kick up the backside to get things sorted. Looking round, I can’t believe the junk we’ve accumulated that just needs chucking. And you are right, this area *is* grotty. We’ve sort of squatted in this place since we were students and it’s time we started living grown-up lives. I can see all the advantages of your location, and of course the spare bedroom is yours, should you need to escape back here.'

As they talked through the ramifications of her plan, Kate sighed with relief. She put a big tick next to the word 'flat' on her to-do list.

Perhaps this was going to work after all.

Chapter Twenty-Six

'Am I speaking to Miss Kate Caswell?' a cultured male voice enquired.

'Speaking. Who's that?'

'My name is Jeremy Jameson. I'm the Head of Humanities at the Carlton International College.'

Kate held her breath. She had made lots of plans but she hadn't officially been offered the job yet. Perhaps her references weren't good enough. She had phoned her old Department Head to ask him to be a referee and he had assured her it would be glowing one and he would be very sorry to lose her. But she didn't really trust him. Had it said bad things in order to force her to stay?

The thought that it was bad news caused her spirits to plummet and she realised just how much she really wanted the post, yearned for the fresh start.

'Miss Carlton-Smith asked me to phone you,' the quiet voice continued, 'to say all your references are excellent and therefore we would like to officially offer you a post at the College.'

'Wow, thank you so much, Mr Jameson. I'm so pleased. That's smashing news.'

'Oh, call me Jeremy, please.'

She could tell he was smiling at her relief.

'Perhaps we could go into some details about your timetable before you arrive. And please ask me anything you want to know.'

Kate reached for her list.

'Oh thanks. In fact I do have one or two.'

One by one, Jeremy patiently answered all her queries. He sounded a really nice man, slightly posh, a little ponderous perhaps in his explanations but very thoughtful about consulting her wishes regarding her timetable. Already this sounded promising.

She was just asking him about renting a flat on the Costa and the costs involved when there was a commotion of boisterous children all talking at once with a woman's voice louder than them all.

There was a sigh. 'That's my wife Maria and our children just arriving home. It could get a little noisy.'

And as if to confirm this prediction, a woman's voice cried out what sounded like 'Hrreremy.'

'Excuse me a minute,' he said to Kate, then called, 'Maria, I'm on the phone.'

'Ah, who ees it?' a very Spanish accent enquired.

'It's Kate Caswell, the new lecturer I told you about.'

'Aha, bueno.' There was a strange clattering as the receiver was obviously being seized by his wife.

'Hola, Kate, I am Maria, Hrreremy's wife.' Kate suppressed a smile at her pronunciation of her husband's name. It sounded so much more mysterious somehow.

'Hello, Maria. I'm looking forward to meeting you.'

'Si si. Has Hrreremy told you…?' there was a muffled conversation between husband and wife before Maria came back on again.

'He say you have nowhere to live. Is that true?'

'Well, no, not yet but…'

'Hokay. We pick you up from the h'airport and you stay with us till you find somewhere.' The tone brooked no refusal.

'That's very good of you, but…'

'No problemo. My sister Gabriella, she is estate agent. She know many apartments. She soon find you a good one and at good price. Not tourist rates.'

'Well, thank you, Maria. That's very kind of you.'

'Hokay.' And she was gone.

'Um, sorry about that, Kate. It will be a bit crowded and noisy here I warn you, but you are very welcome. As you may be able to tell, my wife is a very forceful character, and

I've found it's just easier to go along with whatever she says.'

'But that's very good of her to offer to put me up. Are you sure you don't mind?'

There was a rueful laugh. 'What makes you think I have any say in the matter?

Just let me know when you are arriving, and, as Maria says, we will be there to meet you.'

That was two weeks ago. So now a slightly perspiring Kate was scanning the sea of noisy, tanned, brightly-dressed people at Malaga airport looking for the famed Maria and her husband, Hrreremy.

Trying to appear composed despite her rapidly beating heart, she faced the hot hubbub of noise, and a waving throng of gesticulating hands as the crowd tried to attract the attention of the arriving passengers.

As she peered at a host of handwritten placards to see if any said her name, she was quickly surrounded by several portly taxi cab drivers all offering her a lift. Shaking her head, she suddenly felt a tug on her arm.

A small dark-haired boy grinned up at her.

'Are you senorita Caswell?'

'Yes, I am.'

'Follow me,' he said and darted off through the clamouring throng.

She plunged after him dragging her bulging suitcase and emerged into the relative calm of the wider concourse.

Standing there was a small, stout, beaming woman surrounded by lots of colourfully dressed, bright-eyed children.

'You are Katie. Si?'

As soon as Kate nodded, she found herself enveloped in a tight embrace.

'So you must be…' she began.

'Maria. Si and thees is Carlos.' She proudly patted the head of the small boy who had led her out of the melee. Then she patted the heads of each of her offspring in turn as she introduced them in her heavily accented English. 'And thees is my Sofia, thees my Elena, thees my Bianca and thees, my baby, Antonio.' She flourished a fond hand in the direction of a brown-limbed toddler fast asleep in his buggy, oblivious to all the surrounding noise. All the children were smiling at her, curiosity alive in their huge dark eyes.

'How lovely to meet you all,' Kate said politely, already unsure she would remember all their names.

'Ah, Hrreremy. He is herre at last. We were late so he dropped us off to meet you while he go to park our car.'

A tall, thin, harassed-looking man in a rumpled, cream linen suit and a very English panama hat rushed forward to join the group.

Smiling, he thrust out a hand and grasped hers warmly, pumping it up and down. 'So pleased to meet you, Kate. You have met my family I take it.'

'Yes. I have had a lovely welcome,' Kate said. And she had.

As they drove from the airport, squashed into Jeremy's battered people-carrier, Kate found it wasn't only the car that was battered, her eardrums were as well. Maria, turning round in the front seat, kept up a constant stream of chat, pointing things out as they sped along and asking Kate a torrent of questions. She seemed to be able to absorb the answers without ever pausing in her own observations.

The children talked excitedly to each other in Spanish until Jeremy quietly pointed out that it was rude to do so in front of Kate so they continued in effortless English. All the conflicting exchanges made it difficult to concentrate on what Maria was saying. And it was hot in the car. Her arm was pressed up against the child seat in which the podgy form of Antonio still slumbered, his head lolling back against the side-rest. Apart from that mild rebuke, Jeremy said nothing and simply drove along seemingly oblivious to the cacophony of conversation in the car.

Out of the window, Kate caught her first glimpses of the Costa del Sol, and it truly was sunny and very evidently a Costa. The road climbed up into rocky scrubland as it divided the landscape in two distinct parts. On one side was a barren mountainside rising steeply and totally unpopulated. On the coastal side, the land fell sharply in small uneven undulations, densely packed with a jumble of white houses of all shapes and sizes which filled every available space between the road and the azure blue, sun-speckled sea.

There was so much to take in but as the road dipped down to the slightly scruffy outskirts of a bustling town, Jeremy said, 'This is Fuengirola, where we live and…'

'Si, we have a house not an apartment,' Maria interrupted proudly. 'Hrreremy, he finds apartments too noisy and he is an Englishman so must have a garden. My sister Gabriella, she find it for us. She find you a perfect apartment, very cheap. Not tourist rates.' This latter phrase was a refrain Kate had heard in every phone conversation she had had with Maria over the past week. Indeed, much of what Maria had said throughout the journey she had already been told on the phone. The car journey had confirmed what she suspected, Maria was a relentless talker.

She had only been able to discuss College affairs with Jeremy when Maria was out. She got the impression he was immensely grateful to her for applying for the job and was bending over backwards to accommodate her wishes. He had let slip that it was his fault the advert had gone in so late. The previous lecturer had left suddenly at the end of the term to go back to the UK to be with her boyfriend and he just hadn't got round to writing the job specification. With engaging honesty, he confessed that admin wasn't his strongest suit. As they chatted, she discovered that he had gone out to Spain to teach philosophy and classics at the College ten years ago after a nasty marriage break-up. Maria was the Principal's secretary and she swiftly took him under her wing. And it seemed, after nine years of marriage and five children, he was still more than happy to be nestled there.

'We're here,' Jeremy murmured as he slowed up outside a low white-washed wall festooned with bright purple bougainvillea. Curiously Kate peered out and could see his house was situated in a long street of similar gleaming white dwellings all with arched gateways topped with terracotta tiles.

Clambering stiffly out of the hot, cramped car, she saw the house was fronted by a small paved yard full of bright pots of red geraniums and surrounded by a hibiscus hedge. A tall flowering poinsettia tree gave some shade to the blue front door.

As Jeremy got her case out of the boot, she stopped to marvel at the resplendent tree. 'I have never seen a poinsettia *tree* before. I thought it only came as a small indoor plant at Christmas.'

'I know,' Jeremy said smiling. 'I was amazed by all the colour when I first came. It almost hurt my eyes.'

'Yes, I know what you mean.' As she felt the heat of the sun through her clothes and squinted at the cobalt blue sky, the purple bougainvillea, the bright red poinsettia and the scarlet geraniums against the bright white of the walls, it was like an assault on all her senses.

Unbidden came the memories of the dull brown and greens of her childhood, the grey drizzly skies, the dreary rain-sodden lowering hills and the perpetual gloom of her little back bedroom. She shivered.

Jeremy seemed to know what she was feeling. 'Yes, I was overwhelmed at first. It's all so vivid, so gaudy…'

'Hrreremy…' came the cry down the hall.

'So noisy,' he grinned, 'but so full of wondrous life.'

Approaching the front door, he bowed courteously and gestured for her to enter.

'Mi casa es su casa', as they say round here. And it's true; my home is your home.'

'Thank you so much.'

'Look, if it all gets too much in here,' he whispered, 'just say you have a headache and need a siesta.' He winked. 'Maria thinks we English are a bit frail and prone to headaches so we need to lie down in quiet rooms. It's the only way I get any work done.'

Maria came and bustled them in. She began a voluble tour of her home. First was Kate's allocated room which was a small extension attached to the side of the house and, from the desk and all the shelves of books, obviously Jeremy's study. They had clearly crammed a single bed up against the wall for her to sleep there.

Kate resolved to find a flat as speedily as she could, for his sake, and hers.

With evident pride, Maria continued the tour. She opened each of the rooms with a flourish and Kate got the distinct impression that the children's rooms had been tided especially for this showing. The girls all shared a room with two in bunk beds and Sofia, the oldest, smugly in a single bed. The two boys shared another set of bunk beds. Kate said all nice things and exclaimed how tidy they all were. From the beams on each of their faces this was evidently the right thing to say. She noted that as soon as they moved to go downstairs all the children dived into their rooms and set about delving under the beds for their hidden toys.

There was one large room downstairs with a small kitchen to one side and a spacious covered patio area leading to a sizable square garden shaded by trees from the prying eyes of the houses opposite. One side of the garden was strewn with well-worn sun-faded toys.

'This ees my English garden with an English looon,' Maria was saying, gesturing with a flourish to the other side of the garden.

Bewildered, Kate looked to see her pointing proudly to a large square of grass.

'Oh, yes…a lawn.'

'Si a loon. It is very good, you think?'

'Yes. Very nice.'

'You can stand on it if you like.'

Realising this was a rare privilege, Kate stepped tentatively forward. The grass was strangely spiky and almost spongy to walk on.

Jeremy grinned from the patio. 'It's not quite like English grass but it is hardy and withstands the temperatures. A big bonus is that it rarely needs cutting.'

'But is not for children,' Maria warned. 'It is for looking.'

She turned her back decisively. 'I get lunch now.'

As she bustled into the house, she gave her husband a quick squeeze round his waist and stretching up, she popped a swift kiss on his lips.

As he walked over to join Kate, he whispered, 'What more could a man ask? I've a lovely family and a lovely lawn.'

Kate laughed. 'Look I'm sorry. I seem to have taken over your study.'

'It's fine. Term hasn't started yet so no marking and stuff to do. As I hope you know, you are welcome to stay as long as you want, but I'm aware my family are a bit… overpowering. I've a feeling you might want to find yourself a place soon. Maria's sister, Gabriella,' here he rolled his eyes to heaven, 'is well and truly on the case, so I suspect it won't take long.'

'Vamos a comer,' Maria called, indicating the food-laden table, and a horde of children descended on to the patio to eat a delicious lunch amidst a chaos of conversation.

As Kate tried to respond and think amongst the bedlam, she knew he was right. As welcome as she felt there, she would start looking for somewhere of her own as soon as she could.

Chapter Twenty-Seven

'No. Gabriella, I know this is cheap but it's not got…'

'But Katie, mi amiga, it is so good for price and it is in the middle of the town so everything is so near.'

Patiently Kate tried again. 'I know, Gabriella, it is very nice, as you say but it hasn't got two bedrooms which I need for when my friends from England come to visit.'

Undeterred, Gabriella pointed at a mattress stored under the sofa. 'Ah, but see, there is a cama…er…bed…here under the sofa so you can pull it out to sleep on. Is stupid to pay for a room you don't use.'

'That may be, Gabriella, but I still want another bedroom. And this apartment does not have a balcony or outdoor space for me to sit which I said was essential.'

Maria joined in, 'But why you want to sit outside? Lots of traffic and smells. This is small and cheap and…'

'Please stop, both of you, and listen to me.' Kate's exasperation at last boiled over. She had been battling against a torrent of talking from both Maria and her sister Gabriella all morning as they had trailed her round apartment after apartment in the middle of Fuengirola. All had been cheap and small with no views in noisy concrete blocks occupied by Spanish families. Each time she had politely reiterated why it didn't meet her requirements but she had always been met by a barrage of reasons why this particular apartment was very good value. Gabriella was insistent that Kate should not be ripped off by paying for tourist things like views and balconies and second bedrooms. All the things Kate wanted.

Hot and tired after traipsing round busy, traffic-choked central Fuengirola, she realised that being polite and unassertive wasn't going to get her anywhere. She feared that eventually the pair would wear her down till she just said yes to something she didn't want. A bit like Chris used to do.

It was that thought that prompted her stand.

'Listen.' She seized the still-talking Gabriella by the shoulders and looked her fiercely in the eye. A surprised Gabriella fell silent. 'I am *not* looking at any more studios, and that's final. I have told you what I want. I *am* a tourist and I want *tourist* things. OK? And I will pay tourist prices if I have to. I *must* have two bedrooms, outdoor space, somewhere not in the town, quiet with a view over somewhere green and nice…and, yes, don't suck your teeth like that, I know it will cost more, but I can afford to pay a bit more. Thank you for going to all this trouble, but there is no point in looking at all these places because I will *not* live here.' Then she remembered what Jeremy had said. 'I am English and I get headaches if there is too much noise so it is important to me that I have somewhere peaceful. Just like Jeremy needs his lawn, I need to see something green.'

Maria nodded as if understanding for the first time. Gabriella gave a huge shrug and a sigh, then rolled her eyes at her sister. But it seemed to work. For one blissful moment neither of them spoke.

Seizing the moment Kate put in her final plea. 'In fact I would love to see the sea…'

At the gasp of horror from Gabriella, she added swiftly, 'Just a glimpse would be nice. If at all possible. And I know it will cost me more money but it would be very special if you could find it.'

The two sisters huddled together, both talking at once as they always did. Not for the first time, Kate wondered how they could talk and listen at the same time. There were no pauses to take in what the other was saying, and yet they obviously did.

'Leave it with me.' Gabriella shrugged with the air of someone who used this phrase despairingly on her English clients all the time. It implied they had asked the impossible and, although she held out little hope, she would do her utmost to fulfil their foolish whims.

Later that afternoon, Maria received a phone call from her sister.

She called to Kate. 'Gabriella she says she has found something for you. It is in Calahonda so it is near the College. You can walk there. It has two bedrooms and is… no, I must not tell you any more; she is coming to take you to show you. It is *very* expensive but she get it more cheaply just for you.'

Jeremy, who had heard all about the morning's expedition, several times, just winked before he offered, 'Should I come with you this time and then I can show you where the College is?'

'That would be great. If you don't mind.'

'No, it's a pleasure.'

Kate knew her occupation of his study had shut down his bolt hole, so wasn't surprised that he wanted to escape from the overcrowded house for a while. And obviously, although he was far too courteous to say anything, it was in his best interest for her to find somewhere to live as quickly as possible.

From the minute she walked into the apartment, she knew it was just right. It was four floors up, which was a bit of a climb and might be why it was still not rented out, according to Gabriella who puffed behind them. But the lounge was spacious and led out through wide patio doors to a large tiled terrace big enough for a pretty table, two chairs and a comfy lounger. And, most wonderful of all, being high up on a small hill, it had the most superb view over the swaying palms and red-tiled rooftops, to the sea.

Gasping with delight, Kate gazed at the vista before her. The sun was just setting over the sea and there was a sparkling path of radiance leading up to its glowing circle of fire. Astonished, she saw how rapidly the sun sank below the horizon. In the space of a few minutes it was gone, leaving the most amazing apricot glow in the pale blue sky, turning the thin skeins of clouds all shades of gold and coral.

Gabriella had been talking all the time but she and Jeremy

stood there transfixed, zoning her out and glorying in the spectacular sight. Catching each other's eye, they just sighed with pleasure.

That sunset sold it.

She followed as Gabriella proudly showed her all its other features. It had the requisite two good bedrooms, an en suite in the main one, and a compact kitchen with everything she needed, including a kettle. With a slight huff of disapproval, Gabriella explained it was owned by an English couple, hence the kettle, the big comfy sofa, the large rugs covering all the cold marble floors and the thick lined curtains as well as the thin white gauzy ones. All of these homely features totally suited Kate, giving the place a cosy feel and helping to deaden the hollow sound she had noticed in many of the other apartments.

According to Gabriella, the English owners lived in it over the summer and rented it out for the rest of the year. She had persuaded them to lower the normally exorbitant monthly rent for a secure nine-month tenancy ending in June. However, Kate must agree to leave for two weeks at Christmas and at Easter so they could come out for their holidays. This suited Kate as she could easily go back at these times to stay with Megan in the UK.

But it was a big commitment, a legally binding agreement. What happened if she didn't like the College? Couldn't get on with the staff or students?

She hadn't even met Cassandra Carlton-Smith yet. Jeremy always said her name with a slight tinge of fear so Kate didn't know quite what to expect. She had grilled him about all aspects of the College and had been surprised by the vagueness of some of his answers. He was clearly an excellent subject teacher but not brilliant at admin or the general running of his department.

Still, he was clearly a courteous and gentle man and if he could teach there, she was damn sure she could. After all, she only had a one-year contract so could always leave at the end of it, if it turned out to be wrong in some way. She had endured far worse in her life. Her gut instinct said go for it.

'Yes, Gabriella. I'll take it.' Then impulsively she turned and gave her a hug. 'Thank you so much for being so patient with me and for finding this lovely place. You are so clever. It's perfect. Far better than I could have hoped for. I absolutely love it.'

Gabriella beamed. She waved her arm at the view. 'You have green. You have sea. You have bedrooms. You have quiet.' She waved at the furnishings. 'You have cosy apartment…little England.'

'Yes, Gabriella. You are right. But this is little England… with sun.'

Chapter Twenty-Eight

Feeling languorous with the warm sun on her back, Kate was reluctant to leave her comfy padded rattan chair and begin her trudge back home. She had thoroughly enjoyed her long Saturday morning's walk along the beach from her flat in Calahonda to this pretty little marina of Cabopino.

Looking up from her small corner table in the busy harbour-side café, she surveyed the pretty white villas as they dropped haphazardly down the hillside to the sea. Above their neat ochre roofs loomed the impressive rocky back drop of the rugged Sierra Blanca, its exposed pale limestone outlined craggily against the cloudless blue sky.

It really was an idyllic spot to stop for a coffee. The small curved quay in front of her was fringed by classy restaurants and a few sleek white motor launches rocked gently at their moorings.

Draining the last of her drink with a sigh of satisfaction, Kate resumed her contemplation of the scene…and her life.

One month into her Spanish trip and things couldn't be better. She was still glowing from her interview with Cassandra Carlton-Smith yesterday where the formidable Principal had expressed her approval of Kate's diligence, her rapport with the students, her subject knowledge and the subtle way she was supporting Jeremy by taking on some of the admin and record keeping.

'I took a chance appointing you over the phone like I did, but I warmed to your enthusiasm and honesty. I'm glad to see my instincts were right. I hope you are as pleased with us as we are with you.'

Kate assured her truthfully that she was loving the teaching, the staff and the students. The small classes and the fact that the school day ended at 2.00 in the afternoon meant she could easily do her marking and preparation at College before going home. She was getting used to eating a late lunch at Spanish time with her colleagues and she had been pleased to help Jeremy with the departmental paperwork, which he loathed. Many of the teachers were Spanish and she was picking up plenty of phrases from them to augment the beginner's course she was studying at home.

It also helped that each Friday evening she was invited to a noisy family meal at Jeremy's where, amidst much laughter, she practised what she had learnt, and picked up many colloquial phrases not covered in any book.

And how lucky to find those friends from flamenco. On a whim she had signed up for a beginners' flamenco class run by the fierce, raven-haired Carmen who shouted at them if they didn't hold themselves proud and erect when they danced. At her first apprehensive session she had bonded with three of the younger members of the class and they had since become firm friends.

Birgita was Swedish and stereotypically tall, blonde and gorgeous and managed the family vegetarian restaurant in Fuengirola. Shy Ingrid was Dutch and worked in a florists' in El Zocco, the exotic pink-domed shopping arcade in Calahonda. Both had impeccable English of course. Her third friend, Jody, was little and dark with a strong no-nonsense Newcastle accent and was a freelance dog groomer for the surprising number of expats who brought their pets with them.

As a fitness fanatic, Birgita lost no time in recruiting Kate into her exercise regime and she would pick Kate up in her car and take her to her gym in Marbella where she was introduced to the tough regime of Nordic cross training. This was followed by a swimming session. This was not the leisurely paddling up and down of her youth in Keswick baths, but a powered scything though the pool, counting each length until she had done at least a mile. At first Kate couldn't manage anything like that, but Birgita showed her how to position her body in the water, develop her breathing technique and gradually she improved.

In just a month, all this training made her feel not only fitter, but more confident in her body. Already she could feel the difference during her flamenco classes and Carmen had nodded with approval at her posture. Somehow, the fierce assertiveness of the dance sank into her bones and added to her general feeling of assurance.

She discovered to her surprise that Jody, the tough-talking Tynesider, had escaped an abusive husband and would now stand no nonsense from men. Eventually Kate had been able to confide in her about how she had been manipulated by Chris. Jody's understanding and forthright opinions had soothed any residual guilt she felt at being so weak and feeble. It helped to get the whole episode into perspective.

Ingrid, her third friend and close neighbour, like Kate, was a relative newcomer to the Costa del Sol and they tended to stick together on their Saturday nights out partying in Marbella.

The 'tough two' as she and Ingrid secretly called Birgita and Jody, were well-known figures on the club scene. Kate enjoyed the dancing and the cautious flirting with some very gorgeous men, none of whom she fancied at all. They were all too urbane and worldly-wise for her taste. Although the flattering attention from these suave, sophisticated men was surprisingly ego-boosting, she wouldn't have felt safe going off with any of them.

She watched in fascination as the tall, striking Birgita and the dark-haired elfin Jodie, negotiated their way around. If they picked up with a bloke, it was always on their terms. It was all part of her learning experience.

But as much as she enjoyed all the socialising, she also liked exploring on her own. The local buses were brilliant for getting everywhere but today she had decided to take a walk Ingrid had recommended, starting from her apartment to the picturesque harbour of Cabopino. And she was glad she had. It had been a perfect morning's expedition, a lovely wave-paddling saunter for about three miles along the beach. Then an explore of the charming little village followed by a coffee in this stylish café overlooking the picturesque marina.

The sun today wasn't quite as fierce at it had been and she was enjoying its warmth on her bare back and arms. If only she could show Rob this new tanned, toned and confident Kate. He still lurked at the back of her mind. She often wondered how much of her decision to take the job in Spain was as much to show him she could do it, as to prove it to herself. Then ruefully she realised what was a piddling year on the Costa del Sol to a man who had travelled to the edge of the world and spent two years in the frozen wastes of Antarctica. Who was she kidding if she thought he would be impressed? And anyway, her long talks with Jody had told her that she should not be seeking the approval or validation of men for her actions. It was enough if she felt good about her life. And she did.

A clattering of crockery made her aware that the tables around her were being set up for lunch. She'd had a peek at the menu and knew the meals were a bit pricey, so with a sigh she gestured to the waiter for the bill.

'Tristram, Tricia, come away from the water's edge right now.' A shrill anxious voice pierced the air. A petite, dark-haired, mahogany-tanned woman was yelling at two young children who were cavorting perilously close to the edge of the quay and pointing excitedly at the large fish swimming lazily in the deep water of the marina.

Kate stared in fascination at the small group, especially at the screeching woman. She knew Ma would have immediately identified the woman as 'mutton dressed up as lamb'. Although no spring chicken, she was wearing a fuchsia-pink crop top, gold high-heeled mules, and a short cowgirl suede skirt with long fringes which dangled down her thin dark-brown legs. She was pushing an expensive silver buggy almost as big as she was in which an overdressed baby slumbered beatifically, her pink frilly dress matching her pink cheeks.

Gesticulating fretfully to a large florid man in an equally florid Hawaiian shirt, the woman shouted in a broad Essex accent, 'Ted, get them two away from the edge. My nerves won't stand much more of them messing about.'

Ted, who was holding on to the lead of a tiny pug dog, lumbered over to the kids, who must have been about three years old. Kate guessed they were probably twins because they were dressed in identical expensive looking outfits, just one was in blue and one was in pink.

'Do as your nana says,' Ted boomed and scooped them away from the edge, one in each large arm. No easy feat while holding the dog's lead. So it wasn't surprising that when the two wriggled furiously, with a grunt, he had to set then down.

The boy ran over to his nana where he grasped a handful of fringes from her skirt and tugged hard.

'Want an ice-cream,' he whined.

The girl immediately followed his example and began tugging at some other fringes, yelling, 'And me. And me want ice-cream.'

'Shush, you will wake up baby Tarantula,' the nana pleaded, looking anxiously at the baby in the buggy.

The twins just increased the volume of their demands. Kate noticed the little pug dog was now cowering behind Ted's tanned, tree-trunk legs.

The frazzled grandparents exchanged despairing glances. Heads were turning in the direction of all the clamour. With a weary shrug, they nodded at each other, clearly wanting to avoid a confrontation with the raucous twins. It was equally clear just how much they hated submitting to their noisy demands.

'OK, but only if you stop all that whining,' their nana snapped, her hand hovering dangerously close to their heads, clearly itching to clout them both. 'Follow Grandpops to the ice-cream place over there.' Wearily she heaved the huge heavy buggy round to follow them up the slight slope to a kiosk on the far side of the small curved harbour.

Like the rest of the restaurant, Kate had been fascinated by the little scene. Did that woman really call the baby, Tarantula? Surely not.

Looking round she could see 'Reservado' signs being put

on to the beautifully laid-out tables. Yes, it had been a pleasant morning, but it was time to go back. Leaving the money on the table, with a smile at the approaching waiter, she began to set off for the long walk back home.

Chapter Twenty-Nine

As Kate walked down the shallow steps of the restaurant, a movement caught the corner of her eye. At the far side of the marina a large, unattended silver buggy with sleeping baby was rolling with increasing speed down the slight slope towards the edge of the quayside clearly going to topple straight into the deep water.

'Watch out,' she yelled as she hurtled towards it.

Almost in slow motion she saw the nana turn and scream as she took in what was happening. Ted dropped the ice-creams he was holding and both toddlers set up simultaneous wails. By now the pushchair was picking up speed and Kate was racing towards it faster than she had ever run in her life. As it teetered towards the edge, she flung herself forward with her arm outstretched. Landing with a painful thud on the hot, gritty concrete, her whole body skidded along as she flung out a desperate hand to seize it. Tilting ominously, it caused the strapped-in baby to lurch forwards in her harness which accelerated the buggy's progress over the lip of the quay.

With a frantic lunge, Kate caught the handle and held on desperately as it threatened to plunge into the deep water below.

For a moment the buggy hung there suspended over the sea. The baby's blue startled eyes opened wide as her loose toys cascaded into the marina.

With strained sinews, Kate hung on desperately as it dragged her slowly towards the edge. Her arm was on fire with the tension of holding the huge weight just inches from the water. Then, just in time, a large panting presence grabbed the handle and hauled the whole thing back up to the safety of the quay.

She looked up into the shocked dark eyes of Ted.

Suddenly a cacophony of noise erupted. The nana's screams pierced the air and Kate's eardrums. It wasn't only her eardrums that were hurting. Her whole right side was stinging from the grazes incurred by being dragged across the gritty ground.

There were ragged cheers from the assembling crowd, frantic barking from the little pug dog and angry wails from the twins, furious at their dropped ice-creams. Amongst the hubbub of noise, the only one not making a sound was the baby, who was smiling sleepily up into the face of her grandpop as he deftly undid the harness and cradled her in his big beefy arms.

Gingerly, Kate tried to get up but the excited babbling crowd towered over her, hemming her in.

A pair of strong tanned arms gently lifted her up into a sitting position and then the person squatted down beside her.

'Are you OK?' She found herself gazing into a pair of concerned hazel eyes and a rather handsome face.

'I think so,' she grimaced through gritted teeth. Her side was on fire. 'Is the baby all right?'

They both glanced to where a pink-faced baby was being embraced tightly in a pair of scrawny brown arms by her sobbing nana.

The dishy bloke grinned. 'Oh yes, Tara's OK. She's the most placid baby in the world. It's a good job really.' He gesticulated towards the wildly weeping nana, the agitated yapping dog, the bawling twins and the booming Ted yelling at them to shut up.

'Do you know them?' she asked.

'Oh yes.' He gave a rueful smile. 'Meet the Taylor family. Once seen, never forgotten. But never mind them. What about you?'

Feeling increasingly overwhelmed by the whole situation and the jabbering crowd she tried to stand up.

'Take it easy,' he said helping her to her feet.

All the adrenalin of the last few minutes seemed suddenly

to have leached out of her legs and she staggered a bit. Concerned, the bloke put his arm around her shoulders to steady her and held her against him as a prop.

Kate hated feeling so feeble, especially in front of such a good-looking fella. 'I'm OK, honestly,' she declared and tried to stand unaided, but her trembling legs wobbled under her.

'Oh no you're not,' he said bluntly. 'You are shaking. Come on, you need a drink. Allow me.'

And he gently lifted her into his arms and strode towards the café she had just left.

Astounded, she could only stare at him as the crowd parted to let them through.

He grinned at her as the waiters made a path for him among the crowded tables.

'Hi, Pablo. The Taylor booking. Where are we seated?' he asked, as if it was the most normal thing in the world to carry a woman into a café.

The head waiter bowed a little.

'Señor Troy, you are over there at your usual table.' He waved towards a long table situated at the front of the restaurant.

Señor Troy threaded his way towards it and then lowered her carefully on to a chair. Still a little stunned, Kate blushed at the sheer drama of being carried in the strong arms of such a devilishly handsome bloke.

She looked up into his tawny eyes and saw a definite twinkle in them.

'Wow,' she gulped. 'That was a bit theatrical, wasn't it? You didn't have to carry me, you know.'

'Yes, it probably was a bit OTT but I've always wanted to sweep a maiden off her feet and carry her to safety. It's a bloke's dream. You didn't mind, did you?'

All she could do was laugh at such a frank admission.

'It was quite nice, actually.'

She gazed appreciatively at his broad, gym-toned torso outlined by his close-fitting crisp white shirt with the cuffs neatly folded back to reveal tanned, muscular arms and a gleaming gold watch. From his designer stubble to his shiny tan leather shoes, she could see here was a man who cared about his appearance.

Just then, with a shriek, they were spotted by the wailing nana as she scurried towards them, still cradling the baby and followed by a noisy retinue of a barking dog, still howling twins and a large grim-faced man pulling a cumbersome bedraggled buggy behind him.

Her rescuer groaned, 'Hold on to your eardrums. This is going to get very, very loud and emotional.'

Pausing only to transfer the baby to her grandpop's embrace, the diminutive woman launched herself at Kate with outstretched arms and mascara tears streaming down her face.

'Dahlin. Oh, how brave of you.' Kate was swept into a fierce, scrawny-armed hug. 'Oh, Babes, you are amazing. We can't thank you enough. If you hadn't saved our baby Tara…' and here she broke down again into shuddering sobs.

The little woman was shaking from head to foot with shock, so Kate stroked her trembling back and mumbled into her bony shoulder, 'It's OK. Really it is. I'm just glad I could help.'

The sobs showed no sign of subsiding until Señor Troy gently prised the squeezing arms away.

'Let her breathe, Ma,' he said softly. 'Blimey, she's just survived all that and she doesn't want to be smothered to death.' He lifted his still trembling mum away from Kate and guided her to a chair where Ted flung his burly free arm round her shoulder. Both were still visibly in a state of shock.

Their son turned to a hovering waiter and said quietly, 'Brandy, a whole bottle, and glasses as quick as you can, please.'

The little pug dog was still barking noisily, clearly distressed for his mistress. And the twins were still making a racket about their dropped ice-creams.

With a sigh, Señor Troy leant down and picked up the dog and put it on his mum's lap. She immediately began cuddling it and it seemed to help calm her down. Then he turned to the squalling twins. He held out his hands and they trustingly put their little hands into his.

'Now then, Tristram, Tricia, I want you to be really grown up. Your poor nana is upset and so is your grandpop and you don't want people to think you are little cry-babies, do you?'

Their big tear-stained eyes looked into his. 'I want to be able to tell your mum and dad when they come how good you were. Now I promise you can have an ice-cream, but I want you to show me just what brave soldiers you are and sit quietly at this table. Can you do that for me?'

'Yes, Uncle Troy,' they chorused, clearly not entirely happy. But they did as they were told and climbed onto the big chairs and started to play sullenly with the cutlery. Uncle Troy quietly removed the knives out of their reach and signalled to the approaching waiter for two ice-creams.

There was still a curious crowd standing in front of the restaurant eyeing the group and talking volubly about what had happened.

Troy stood up and called. 'It's all right, folks. No harm done. Everything's fine. Sorry to disturb your morning.' And he sort of waved his arm and the group edged away and began dispersing.

A large bottle of brandy was placed on the table and Ted seized it and poured his wife a hefty slug. She downed it in one go. He swiftly drank one himself, poured them both another and offered a large glass to Kate.

'Here you are, Babes. It will help with the shock.'

'Thank you.' Kate realised she needed it and took a mouthful. The fiery liquid hit the back of her throat and she coughed a little. She felt Troy's amused eyes on her as she lowered her glass.

'Only drink as much as you want,' he advised. 'You don't have to finish it if you don't want to.' He watched as his parents downed yet another large tot.

'It is in fact helping a bit,' Kate confessed.

And it was clearly reviving his mum and dad. The ice-cream had arrived for the twins who were clattering their way through tall glasses of mixed colours and flavours.

The baby had fallen pinkly asleep again in her grandpop's

arms and the little pug dog turned and settled on his mistress's lap.

For a moment all was peace.

Chapter Thirty

In a hoarse shaky voice, Ted leant forward and took her hand, 'Dahlin girl. Thank you. Thank you so much for saving our little Tara's life. Reen and me can't ever thank you enough…' He broke off to wipe the unashamed tears rolling down his face with the back of his hand.

Embarrassed by the big man's evident emotions, Kate mumbled, 'Honestly, it was just lucky I got there in time. I'm sure everything would have been OK.'

'No, it wouldn't,' Ted said, his gravelly tone giving voice to his worst fears. 'She was strapped in and that water is deep and…'

He couldn't go on and Reen had begun quietly sobbing again.

Troy patted his mum's hand fondly and, in an obvious attempt to distract them both, said, 'Should we find out who it is we have to thank.'

'What?'

'Well, we can't really keep calling her Dahlin all the time…even though she is.'

Blushing under his frank admiring gaze, Kate said. 'I'm Kate, Kate Caswell.'

'Oh, and she has one of them lovely northern accents, hasn't she, Troy?' Reen exclaimed.

'Yes she has. My ma loves northern accents. One of her best friends comes from Accrington.'

'I'm just a bit further north. I'm from near Keswick.'

There was a puzzled frown on Reen's face.

'Sorry, Kate Dahlin, I'm not much good with anything north of Watford Gap.'

'That's OK.' Kate smiled, 'I'm not much good with

anything south of it.'

Troy flashed her a grateful smile. 'It's in the Lake District, Ma.'

'Ooh, that's supposed to be nice, isn't it, Troy?'

'Yes, Ma. It is. Anyway, very pleased to meet you, Kate from Keswick,' he said sincerely. Then, as if on impulse, he took her hand with a flourish, and raised it to his lips. His copper-flecked eyes twinkled and she blushed again. He really did have a roguish way with him. Was he really flirting with her in these strange circumstances?

Releasing her hand, he then made a grand gesture towards his family. 'Right, our turn now. Let me introduce you to the Taylor family from Essex, as you have probably realised from our accents. I'm Troy Taylor and this is my mum, Reen and my dad, Ted.' They both beamed at her.

Troy then gesticulated at the guzzling, ice-creamed smeared pair of toddlers. 'Those two over there are the terrible twins, Tristram and Tricia, and this little sweetie,' he chucked the now gurgling baby under her chin, 'is Tarantella or Tara for short.'

Winking at Kate, he continued, 'You may have noticed a certain theme running through the family names.' He cocked his head to one side and eyed his mother fondly. 'This will become even more obvious when I tell you that my two brothers are called Tarquin and Tyrone and their wives are called Tracey and Tina.'

Kate didn't know what to do. She could feel the laughter burbling up inside her and from the grin spreading across Troy's face, he knew just how she was feeling.

'Yup, that's us, the terrible Taylor tribe.' He blew a kiss to his mum who just smiled weakly at him.

'All these T names were Ma's idea, although I think you have a few regrets now don't you, Ma? The baby, Tarantella…'

Reen shuddered, 'Ooh, I hate that name. When they first told me I thought it was one of them spiders.'

'Tarantula?' Kate asked.

'Yes, but they explained it was a sort of Spanish dance…

but I kept getting it wrong in the beginning and saying the spider one. Tracey got so mad at me, that I'm nervous about saying her name anymore in case the wrong one comes out.'

'That's why we just call her Tara,' Troy said squeezing her hand affectionately.

'Oh no,' suddenly Reen's face drained of colour. 'That reminds me, Tarquin and Tracey will be here any minute.'

'Where are they?' Troy asked.

'They wanted to do some last minute shopping before they fly back tonight. Of course, Tracey has to buy some fancy stuff for all her posh friends back home. I knew the twins would be a nuisance so I offered to look after them and bring them here to meet them all for our last lunch before they go back. Oh, Troy,' she wailed, 'what am I going to tell her? She'll never forgive me. She already thinks I'm useless.'

Her brown sparrow eyes looked pleadingly at her big capable son.

'Right. First, tell me what actually happened. I'd just parked the car and arrived in time to see that spectacular save you made, Kate, but how did it start?'

'It was all my fault,' Reen moaned. 'I got distracted by the twins whining for an ice-cream and we went over there to get one. Well you know, I can't work out all the levers on these big new-fangled pushchairs and I can't have put the brake on properly. And with sorting out the money for the ice-creams, I just didn't notice it rolling away.' She was wringing her little tanned hands and her eyes once again filled with tears.

Ted's arm immediately went round her frail shoulder. 'There, there. Don't upset yourself so much, Princess. I should have noticed. It should have been me pushing that thing. It's too big for you.'

'Oh, Ted. It's not a man's job to push babies around.' Reen was obviously of a generation where there was clear delineation between the roles of men and woman. 'I can't believe I didn't check it. I'll never forgive myself.' Reen covered her face with her hands.

Her overwhelming feelings of guilt tugged at Kate's heartstrings.

‘Please don’t blame yourself, Mrs Taylor. It was clearly an accident. You had a lot on your plate…I saw how the kids...um…were…’ Here she paused knowing she would have to be careful how she described the twins’ spoilt behaviour ‘…asking for an ice-cream and that monster of a buggy looks a nightmare to sort out. I bet you just weren’t strong enough to put the brake on properly.’

‘You are such a Dahlin.’ Reen smiled through her tears. ‘And please call me Reen. No one calls me Mrs Taylor.’

‘I think you are probably right about not being strong enough to sort that brake,’ Ted said, shooting Kate a grateful look. ‘So it’s not your fault after all.’

‘That won’t stop Tracey blaming me. You know how she’s always picking me up on everything I do.’

‘I know…’ Ted said suddenly, ‘…I can say it was my fault. Tracey won’t give me such a hard time.’

Troy gave him a doubtful look but Reen’s face lit up. ‘Oh, Babes. Would you really? Tracey doesn’t think a lot of me at the best of times, but you’re right, she will go much easier on you.’

‘So that’s what we’ll do then. After all, no harm was done in the end. Thanks to this brave little lady here.’ Ted reached out and patted her arm. He looked at her so fondly, it brought tears to Kate’s eyes. ‘We are so grateful,’ his voice broke into a gruff whisper, ‘we can’t ever repay you.’

Embarrassed by all this praise, Kate squirmed in her seat. She reached out to cover his big hand with hers, but gasped as a stab of pain shot up her side.

‘Oh, Dahlin, you are hurt.’ Reen shot out of her chair pitching her little dog unceremoniously on to the floor. She peered at Kate’s torn white T-shirt. ‘Look, you are covered in blood. Quick, Ted, phone for an ambulance.’

‘No. No, please don’t. I’m fine, really I am. I’ve just grazed my side that’s all. It looks worse than it is.’

But Reen was aghast as she carefully lifted Kate’s arm and examined the extent of the damage. ‘And your lovely T-shirt is ripped to pieces. And just look at all the blood on your white crop trousers.’

Kate looked and saw it was true. All the right side of her body was covered in long, bloody scratches. They went all down her inner arm, her side and her leg from where she had skidded along the ground in her final lunge to save the buggy. It was stinging like mad.

'Right that settles it,' Troy said decisively. 'I'm taking you two home. You look all done in, Ma, and this little lady is badly injured and in no fit state to go anywhere.'

Turning to Kate he said gently, 'Come back with us, Kate, and you can clean yourself up and we can call a doctor if you need it.'

'No, honestly, I'm fine…' she began protesting as she tried to get out of her chair.

Troy leapt to his feet and towered over her.

'No you're not and it's the least we can do. Right, Pa you stay here and look after the kids. They won't fit in my car and besides they will need feeding a proper lunch when Tracey and Tarquin arrive.'

Reen's face went pale at the mention of Tracey's name.

'OK, Pa, it's agreed we tell them you didn't put the brake on properly and the buggy rolled towards the edge of the quay but keep what happened a bit vague and low key. After all no harm done in the end. Do you think you can manage that?'

Ted nodded. 'Don't worry, Troy my boy. I know what a drama queen that there Tracey can be and I ain't giving her any ammo. Although it might be a good idea if you was to fish Tara's toys out of the drink before you go and try to get 'em dry before we come back. She'll probably want to cuddle 'em on the flight back home.'

'Good thinking, Pops. Will do. Hang on a minute.' Troy bounded off keeping a wary eye out for his brother and wife. Kate couldn't help noticing how well his jeans fitted and how his broad chest filled out his fitted white shirt. Definitely a bit of a hunk.

Reen saw her eyes following her son and smiled. 'He's a good 'un, my Troy. The only one of my boys still single. Clever an' all, isn't he, Ted?'

Ted chuckled and wagged his finger 'Now Reen…'

Blushing, Kate looked away, but it was nice to know the object of her attention wasn't spoken for.

Troy returned, brushing down the front of his shirt where he had lain flat trying to reach all the toys that had fallen into the water. He was clutching a sodden pink bunny, a multi-coloured stuffed elephant and a bedraggled fluffy white horse. 'These are the only ones still floating. There's some more at the bottom I can see but can't get without some sort of fishing rod or something.'

'I'll ask Pablo if he can get them later,' Ted said. 'We are good customers and I'll slip him a few quid. I'm sure he won't mind.'

'Right, we better get going before they arrive. You two,' Troy gave a hard stare at the twins who were just beginning to venture from their seats to explore under the table. 'You be good for Grandpops. I don't want to hear you've been naughty. OK?'

They looked up at him and, sated with ice-cream they seemed more amenable. Nodding, they chorused, 'Yes, Uncle Troy.' They were clearly used to obeying him.

He grinned at them and ruffled their hair 'Good kids. You OK, Pa?'

Ted nodded and patted Reen's arm. 'You go home, Princess. I'll make sure it's all right here.' He did indeed look in control and gave Tara a little joggle which made her giggle.

Troy beamed at his niece before turning to hoist his little dot of a mother to her feet. 'Come on, Ma, up you come.' She looked up at him, eyes glowing with love and linked her arm through his.

He then offered his other arm to Kate. 'Can you make it over there to my car? It's not far. And, as you see, I didn't have any brandy so I'm safe to drive.'

'He is Katie, Dahlin. He don't drink much at all.'

He hooted, 'I think it's all relative, Ma.'

Kate levered herself out of her seat. Her side throbbed but she wasn't going to show anyone how much it hurt. But Troy caught her wince of pain. ‘Are you sure you’re OK?’ he whispered.

‘Yes. Fine. Look, you don’t have to take me with you. I can catch a bus.’

Reen whirled round in horror.

‘Don’t you even think about it, Dahlin. Troy’s right we need to clean that side up properly and I’ll get Doctor Donaldson to come and have a look at it. He’s a lovely man. Sorted my sciatica a treat he did and he’s happy to come out on a Saturday.’

Troy grunted, ‘He should be. You pay him enough.’

‘That’s true, but he can look you over. Check you haven’t broken a rib or something. Then I can find you a nice new top. I’m sure I’ve got something that will fit you.’

Kate saw Troy’s eyes flicker doubtfully from her perky peaks to his mum’s minuscule mounds, but he said nothing.

‘And if you are OK,’ Reen continued, ‘I’m going to put you in our Jacuzzi. All them bubbles will make you feel so much better.’

‘Ma’s a great believer that bubbles make everything better,’ Troy murmured as they turned to leave the little marina and walk slowly towards a row of parked cars.

Kate was glad of his strong arm to lean on. She was surprised how wobbly she felt. One or two curious eyes followed them, but generally people were far more interested in what they were eating and drinking to pay much attention to the participants in a little drama that was now long gone.

Chapter Thirty-One

Arriving at a row of smart cars, snugly parked along the far wall of the marina, Troy fished in his pocket and brought out a key fob which he pressed.

With a beep, the lights flicked on a sleek, white, open-top sports car.

Even to Kate's un-trained eye it looked a very posh car indeed. Low-slung, with luxurious red leather interior and a wide spoiler on the back, it gleamed expensively in the sunshine.

'Wow,' she gasped. 'Is this yours?'

Troy seemed to be hoping for this reaction as he grinned deprecatingly. 'Oh this old thing. Just something I picked up at the showroom today.'

'Oh, Troy.' His mother thumped him on the arm. 'You are a one.'

'It's very nice,' Kate said, whilst unbidden the thought of another open-topped sports car sprang into her mind. But Troy's was clearly in a different class from Rob's more homely Noddy motor.

'Ooh, it's way more than nice,' he smiled, stroking its shiny paintwork, 'it's a limited edition Porsche Evolution GTS Convertible with…'

'That's enough, Troy,' his ma said, obviously unimpressed by all the technical details that were about to flow about the car's performance. 'We just want to get in and get home before Tarquin and Tracey arrive.'

'Yes, Ma. Right you are,' he conceded cheerfully. 'Now I suggest that as you are so little, would you mind if you and Pugsy scrunched up on the back seat. Then we can let our little injured heroine here regale herself in the front.'

'I'm not a heroine,' Kate protested but got no further as once again she was squeezed into a tight Reen hug.

'Oh yes, you are, Dahlin,' said Reen. Then, obviously emotional, she clambered stiffly into the tiny bucket seat in the back of the car. Pugsy followed her and she clasped him to her thin little body.

With a flourish Troy gestured to the front passenger seat and, somewhat gingerly, Kate climbed in.

'Let me help you with the seat belt,' Troy said as he pulled it out from its fastening and reached across her to snap it into its clip. Kate felt a definite tingle at his close proximity and the subtle citrus tang of his aftershave.

Then reaching into the glove compartment, Troy brought out a large plastic bag into which he placed Tara's sodden toys before transferring them to the boot.

'Let's go quickly,' Reen said anxiously, peering at a line of oncoming cars.

With a nod, Troy got in and swiftly roared off up the hill away from the small harbour complex. It wasn't till they had exited on to the main autostrada that Kate thought to ask where they were going.

'Ma and Pa's place in Marbella,' he said as he deftly wove in and out of the traffic till they were in the fast lane.

'Tedreen Villa,' his mum shouted from the back seat against the roar of the engine. 'It's named after us see…me and my Ted.'

Kate thought she saw a grimace cross Troy's face.

'Yup, Tedreen Villa it is,' he said neutrally.

Feeling the warm wind in her hair and seeing a pair of strong, tanned hands on the wheel of an open-topped sports car inevitably took her back to those heady days with Rob. Memories came flooding back of the last time she heard a car vroom like that, but this car was much sleeker and smoother, and so was the driver.

'It's a very posh car, isn't it?' she patted the leather dashboard. She wasn't going to make the same mistake again and not realise how special the car was. 'Um…so what sort of car is it again?'

'It's a Porsche.'

She nodded. 'Aah.' Even she had heard of them. 'So that is quite posh then.'

'You could say that.' He grinned.

'My Troy's a car salesman,' Reen shouted from the back seat.

'Thanks, Ma. Here was me trying to impress a beautiful lady and let her think how rich I was, as well as good-looking.' He winked and gave a theatrical sigh. 'But now you know. Ma's right, it's not mine. But I do get to drive them round. It's sort of advertising. Folk come up and ask me and I tell them a bit about it and if I think they have the spondoolix, I pass them my card, offer to get them a good price…and Bob's your uncle.'

'He's very good at it,' Reen yelled. 'He's their top salesman.'

Troy just shrugged. 'Normally I'd be working today but as we were going to have a farewell lunch for my beloved brother and family at Cabopino, I thought I'd flash up in my swanky car and impress them all.'

'Oh sorry,' Kate said feeling immediately guilty that he was driving her back when he should have been enjoying the adulation of his brother.

'What!' he laughed. 'What are you sorry for? I arrived just in time to see you hurtle across that quay like an Olympic sprinter, then fling yourself heroically forward in a move that would have impressed any rugby player and hang on for dear life to that monster of a buggy while my dear baby niece just laughed at the adventure of it all. Wouldn't have missed it for the world.'

'You make it sound much more dramatic than it was.'

'No, believe me. I can exaggerate with the best of them, but that really was spectacular.'

His eyes crinkled with warmth as he smiled at her. She found herself blushing again. What was it about this man that caused her to feel so tingly?

They became aware that Reen was quietly sobbing in the back seat.

'Sorry, Ma. Stupid of me to bring it up again. Please don't go upsetting yourself. No harm was done and let's look on the bright side. It means I got to meet this gorgeous little lady here.'

He really was a charmer but that was just too much. She pulled a face.

'That's just a bit too cheesy, you know.'

He nodded. 'Yes, not one of my best lines.'

He glanced in the mirror. 'Come on, Ma, pull yourself together we are nearly there.'

Kate looked to see where they were. It looked to be an urbanisation, a bit like Calahonda, but much more spacious and expensive. Large villas were hidden behind white-washed walls and huge iron gates. The roads were broader and lined with palm trees and just as they were cresting a small hill, Reen announced, 'Here we are.'

Kate's eyes were assailed by the vibrant colours of crimson, purple and orange bougainvillea blossoms covering the high walls surrounding the Villa. The gold embellished gates gleamed brightly in the sun and on either side stood mock Grecian columns topped with what looked like rampant lions. The name *Tedreen Villa* was emblazoned on a prominent sign in ornate ruby red writing.

Kate gasped half in wonder and half in amusement. She was aware that Troy was watching her reaction with keen eyes.

'Here we are indeed,' he said flatly. 'Press the button, Ma.'

Reen scrabbled in her handbag and pressed a key fob and the large gates swung open to allow them to drive in.

A sprawling two-storey building stretched before them. Troy drove under a large shady portico shaped a bit like an ancient Greek temple which overhung an arched antique-looking mahogany front door. It was heavily studded with metal bolts and had huge cast iron hinges and wouldn't have looked out of place on a medieval castle.

Kate's eyes were round with amazement at such an incongruous clash of styles.

Troy leapt out and solicitously helped her and Reen out of

the car. Her side had stiffened up during the journey and moving once again caused flashes of pain which she sought to conceal from them both.

Reen was fumbling with a large set of keys.

'Prepare yourself,' Troy said under his breath as the large door swung open.

If outside was a riotous clash of colour and styles, inside was even more so.

There were marbled columns and life-sized ceramic leopards standing guard on either side of an arched opening to a large bright lounge. Huge colourful paintings dominated the walls. There were the swirling red frocks of flamenco dancers, large trumpeting elephants, parades of pink flamingos and fields of crimson poppies. Kate's eyes popped at the swirly electric blue and lime green suite which was buried deep beneath mounds of shiny, multi-coloured silk cushions all decorated with tassels and twinkling jewels. The marble floor was a minefield of intricately patterned rugs of all shapes and sizes. As they entered, a gold ceiling fan was just stirring into life and wafting the gauze curtains into snowy waves against the wide patio doors.

Blinking, Kate had hardly time to take it all in before Reen began fussing round her.

'Now let me have a good look at your side,' she said gently lifting Kate's arm. 'Oh dear. The scratches are full of grit. I think we should call the doctor.'

'No please don't,' Kate begged. 'I'm sure it's all superficial.'

'May I suggest you have a shower and wash away the surface dirt and blood then we can see how bad it is?' Troy said. 'Then if we are not happy and think it is going to be infected, will you agree to us calling the doctor?'

Kate nodded. Her side was in agony and she could feel the tension of trying not to let it show. She desperately wanted some time to herself to inspect her wounds and gather herself together. It had all been a bit too much and she longed to lose herself under soothing jets of water and perhaps have a little weep to release all the pent-up shock.

'Wait a minute,' Reen said and dived out of a door into what looked like an English cottage kitchen, complete with an Aga.

'Here,' she said, clutching a homely bottle of TCP. 'That should help. It always used to sort my boys, didn't it Troy?'

He unscrewed the cap and took a deep sniff.

'Yes, that's it. The pungent smell of my childhood.'

'You daft lump,' his mother said, thumping him on the arm. He seemed to have the knack of lifting her mood.

'Right, come upstairs with me, Dahlin, and I'll show you where you can shower.'

Reen's heels clip-clopped up the broad marble stairs and she led the way into a room that looked like liquid sunshine. The walls, coverlets, curtains and cushions shone with vibrant yellows, oranges and golds.

Beckoning, Reen went over to the large patio door and led the way onto a wide sunny terrace which wrapped round the whole of the second floor.

'Look, Dahlin. Over there,' she pointed proudly. 'You can see Gibraltar.'

And Kate could. There, in the distance a large lopsided triangle jutted out into the sea. But her eye was also caught by the garden below and the long rectangular swimming pool surrounded by various well-padded pink loungers and chairs and, just below the terrace, there was a swinging garden seat plumped to the gunnels with yet more multi-coloured bejewelled silk cushions. And what were those fluorescent pink items dotted about seemingly at random? Were they flamingos?

Reen was still gazing rapturously at the hazy shape in the distance.

'Whoever would have thought that one day we would live in a place where you could see Gibraltar from your bedroom window?'

Troy loomed in the doorway.

'Ma,' he sighed. 'I know you can't resist showing people Gibraltar, but I rather think Kate just wants to have her shower and…'

Reen jumped guiltily and reluctantly closed the patio door. 'OK. OK. Here's the bathroom, Dahlin, and help yourself to all the lovely smelly stuff you want. Have a bath if you prefer. It's got a jet thing in it you can press if you want bubbles and stuff. And please use as many towels as you need. While you are in there, I'll go and see if I've got anything of mine for you to wear. That top of yours will have to be binned.'

Kate looked at the remnants of her favourite white T-shirt and had to agree.

'Nothing too skimpy or fitted, Ma.' Troy warned hastily. 'I think Kate's…' he stopped, not quite sure how to continue.

'Oh don't be silly, Troy. I'm not daft. I can see Kate's jubblies are younger and perkier than mine. But I think I've got a couple of slouch tops or some sloppy jumpers that might do.'

'Right, Ma, let's leave her in peace.'

'Take as long as you want, Dahlin,' Reen said softly as she closed the bedroom door and left Kate on her blissful own.

Chapter Thirty-Two

All Kate wanted to do was to flop on the invitingly soft yellow bed. But she daren't. She knew if she did, she would just doze in the sunshine and also she had to wash away the streaks of blood before she dare touch anything.

As she stripped off in the bathroom, particles of grit and dirt fell on to the large fluffy mat. Wincing, she peeled off her top and looked in dismay at the deep lacerations on her hips and side. She could see dark purple bruising under all the surface blood. Gritting her teeth, she stepped into the shower to do a preliminary rinse of her body so she could better see the extent of the damage. As she switched on the shower, she gasped to find her body was assailed by fierce jets of water coming at her from all directions. But the pummelling was dislodging the dirt and debris from her cuts so she kept it on full flow for a long time before switching it off and examining her side in the mirror.

To her relief, the cuts were clearer to see and looked clean. The purple bruising was emerging but the damage was definitely not as great as she feared. As she flexed her shoulders, she found the powerful jets seemed to have released some of the tension in her body and she ached less than before. To her surprise she had also lost some of her weariness.

As she glanced in the mirror, she noticed her colour had come back and she looked less shocked. But her hair was a bedraggled mess. She couldn't possibly emerge looking such a fright, especially in front of such a gorgeously groomed bloke like Troy. Delving amongst all the shampoos and shower gels arrayed in neat rows on a shelf near the bath, she sniffed their different fragrances. Selecting something peachy, she stepped into the shower again to wash her hair. This time the jets didn't take her by surprise and she found herself giggling at the unexpected places they reached. Quite titillating really.

After drying herself on the thick soft towels, she dabbed the stinging TCP on her cuts then massaged the undamaged part of her body with a gorgeously rich body lotion. It was a soothing relaxing motion and she noticed how much calmer she felt. As she did so, she couldn't stop thinking about Troy. As well as being definitely dishy, he also seemed very caring and considerate. He was clearly very protective of his mum…and her. Giggling, she remembered the sensation of those strong arms as they lifted her up and effortlessly carried her away from that distressingly noisy crowd.

She had been literally swept off her feet. And she had to admit, she had loved it. He had effortlessly dispersed the onlookers from outside the restaurant and even managed to tame the terrible twins. He clearly had a good sense of humour and, according to Reen, he was single. This man ticked all the boxes.

Woah there, girl. Her common sense suddenly kicked in. Not so fast. No falling headlong again. It didn't work last time. Rob went off to Antarctica without a backward glance, so take your time.

Troy was clearly a charmer but it wasn't wise to fall under his spell until she had found out much more about him. How much of his attraction was prompted because driving along in that open-top car awakened memories of Rob?

Nevertheless, a small bubble of excitement rippled up her body. She hadn't felt like this since…well since Rob. Was this a good sign? Did it mean that at last his hold on her heart was loosening?

Deep in thought, she emerged from the bathroom, swathed in a huge fluffy orange bathrobe, to be greeted by an array of clothes carefully set out on the bed.

All were glittery or pink or strapless and all were things she would never normally even look at. Most were too small. But there was a baggy, coral-pink, sparkly off-the shoulder number which would probably have reached down to Reen's knees, which did actually fit her. It hugged her figure a bit more than she generally would have liked, but it was the only choice. Her torn top had disappeared, her white crop trousers had been sponged a little and dried and Reen's top covered all the small rips down one side.

Surveying herself in the mirror with the soft pink, shoulder-revealing top outlining her curves and her dark glossy hair all fluffed up from the dryer, she looked at an unfamiliar girl…but liked what she saw.

Feeling nervous, Kate emerged from her room and padded downstairs.

Troy was just placing something on the huge glass dining room table but his eyes lit up in appreciation as he saw her.

'I don't like to use the phrase about scrubbed up well but…'

Kate felt herself blush but was immediately seized by Reen.

'How are you, Dahlin? Let me see them cuts,' and she unceremoniously began lifting Kate's top. Troy immediately swung round and disappeared into the kitchen.

Totally oblivious to Kate's embarrassment, Reen inspected her injuries.

'They look nice and clean but I don't smell no TCP.'

'Thanks, Reen, I did use it but then I washed it off.'

'The smell put you off, did it?'

'No, all those jets of water had blasted out all the grit and stuff. I think it looked much worse than it actually was.'

'Hmmn,' Reen said, still lifting up Kate's top and peering closely at her side. 'There's a lot of bruising, but you're right, it does look clean. But that is really going to hurt for days so…'

'Lunch is ready,' Troy called from the kitchen.

Kate hurriedly pulled away from Reen's scrutiny just as Troy appeared bearing two huge pizzas.

'I thought as we'd missed lunch at Cabopino, you might be starting to feel a bit peckish. This is all I could find in the freezer. Sorry, it's not much but Ma's kitchen is a bit of a desert when it comes to fresh food stuff.'

'It's true, Dahlin,' Reen confessed. 'I'm not much of a cook and we can order in anything we want from round here if we aren't eating out. But my Troy is a dab hand in the kitchen, aren't you, Babes.'

'Yes, Ma.' Troy rolled his eyes and whispered to Kate, 'Although anyone who can rustle up anything edible is a Michelin-starred chef in her eyes.'

He brought in three large gold-rimmed plates and set them out before pulling out an ornately decorated gold chair for Kate and gestured for her to sit down.

'And you, Ma. You need to eat something as well,' he said sternly.

'I'm just fetching a little drinkipoos for us all,' his mum replied, staggering in balancing three large wine glasses in one hand and a bottle of wine in the other.

'Not for me, Ma, and I think you ought to eat something before you have any more. You've had two or three brandies already don't forget.'

'Oh, they were medicinal…for the shock you know.'

'They still count.'

'Troy doesn't drink you know,' Reen said, sitting down at last having filled two large glasses with wine and passed one to Kate.

'I do, Ma, but not if I'm driving. I daren't lose my licence with my job and I'm taking Tarquin and his tribe to the airport later on.'

It was obviously an ongoing family dispute, so Kate kept well out of it.

'Here you are,' Troy said serving Kate two large slices of Pizza. 'Get stuck in. You must be starving.'

'Actually I am.' And Kate did as she was bid and got stuck into a satisfyingly cheesy quadrant of spicy pizza.

'Now, Babes,' Reen began, nibbling the pointy end of her slice, 'when can we go shopping?'

'Um…I'm not sure…I mean…' Kate was a bit flummoxed by the question.

'Well I've got to buy you a new top and some new crops

to replace the ones that got ruined.'

'Don't worry about that. It's fine.'

'Oh no, it's not,' said Reen, in a voice that brooked no opposition. 'I'm not having any arguments on the matter. I'm taking you shopping and I am buying you some new clothes. You just have to say when. How about tomorrow?'

'Give the girl a chance, Ma,' Troy laughed. Turning to Kate, he warned semi- seriously, 'You'll have to watch out or she will take you over completely.'

Before Reen could protest, they heard a car door bang.

Reen's eyes widened in horror.

'Oh no. Tracey's back.'

Chapter Thirty-Three

A small tawny blonde burst into the room. Her eyes flashed as she saw Reen.

'So what happened then? Ted won't tell me the full story but I know you was behind it. All Tara's stuff in the drink. You didn't put the brake on, did you?'

Reen quailed faced with the fury in those dark eyes.

'Ted says it was him but I know it wasn't. You've never been able to sort that buggy, have you?' Tracey blazed.

'Now look, Princess, don't you go accusing Ma till you've heard the full story.' A big man lumbered into the room. He looked like a younger version of Ted so Kate assumed it must be Tarquin and the fierce woman was the dreaded Tracey.

Tarquin was followed by Ted carrying Tara and then the twins squealed into the room. Smelling the pizzas, they ran over to the table and grabbed a slice each and then decamped to the sofa to eat them, dislodging cushions as they went.

'I take it you didn't stop for lunch then, Pa?' Troy said mildly.

'No, son. It sort of all kicked off and I…'

'You bet it kicked off,' Tracey yelled. 'I knew I shouldn't have trusted you to look after them. From what I gather my baby girl nearly drowned in her buggy because someone…' here she launched another furious stare at Reen.

'Now calm down, Princess,' her husband said, looking anxiously at his mum who was beginning to weep.

Kate couldn't stand seeing Reen bullied by this fierce woman any more.

'Perhaps I can help shed some light on it,' she said stepping forward.

'Who are you?' Tracey whirled round.

'This is Kate,' Troy said. 'She's the one who saved the buggy.'

'We owe her everything,' said Ted emotionally.

'No really. I'm most embarrassed by all your thanks because after all…, 'here Kate took a deep breath, 'As Troy says, I only saved a buggy from going in the water. It was no big deal really.'

Tracey stared at her, clearly spoiling for a fight.

Unconsciously crossing her fingers behind her back as she had done as a child when she was about to tell a fib, Kate continued, 'I know it is an expensive buggy but I'm really uncomfortable with all the fuss everyone made about it. Anyone would think the baby was in it at the time.'

There was a sharp intake of breath and five pairs of Taylor eyes swivelled towards her.

'But…' Tracey began.

It was a risk but she had to save Reen so Kate continued as confidently as she could. 'I must admit, I thought the baby was in it, which is why I lunged forward at it, but, when I looked, there she was, safe in her Grandpa's arms. Obviously, if she had been in it, then it would have been a serious matter, but she wasn't, so no harm was done. Isn't that right, Ted?'

Troy picked up immediately and said swiftly, 'Oh crikey, Tracey. You didn't think Tara was in it, did you?'

From the look on her face, she clearly did.

Kate held her breath. Would they get away with it? What had Ted said?

Sensing her uncertainty, Kate rapidly continued, 'I'm just sorry I didn't get there in time to stop it before some of her toys fell into the water but at least the *buggy* came to no harm.' She carefully stressed the word 'buggy'.

Tarquin's eyes had narrowed but at a meaningful glance from Troy, he picked up the point and turned to Kate.

'Well thank you, Kate. That thing cost an arm and a leg. But nothing's too good for my little girl. It would have been a real shame if it had got dunked in the sea, wouldn't it, Princess?' He put his arm round his wife's shoulder and gave it a squeeze in a gesture reminiscent of how Ted hugged

Reen.

'I've washed the toys I managed to fish out,' Troy said smoothly, rushing the conversation on, 'and they are out there drying in the sun. They might be ready for the flight back tonight. What do you think, Ma? Should we go and check how they are doing?' He then took her arm and hustled a bewildered Reen out into the garden.

From Tracey's face she still seemed uncertain about what had happened and looked suspiciously at Kate. But for the moment said no more.

Kate sighed with relief. It looked as if they had pulled it off. Ted was beaming at her as he joggled Tara in his arms, who to everyone's surprise suddenly let out a wail.

Tracey ran to her and scooped her up.

'Are you OK, baby girl?'

'I suspect she's hungry, don't you?' said Troy, reappearing into the room. 'In fact I think everyone is a bit overwrought from hunger. Pops, can you put a couple more pizzas in the oven. Tarquin, can you get the twins off Ma's sofa with their sticky hands. If they sit nicely at the table, they can have another slice of these I've already cooked.'

Troy chivvied everyone around which diverted them from discussing the Cabopino incident any more.

Then, as everyone got busy with food, he grabbed Kate by the arm and pulled her behind one of the hall columns.

'Brilliant. Brilliant. You clever, clever girl.' His eyes glowed with gratitude and he embraced her in a huge bear-like hug.

'Do you think we got away with it?' Kate whispered.

'Yes, thanks to you we did. That was inspired. What on earth made you think of it?'

'I don't know. I just couldn't stand to see her bullying your mum like that. Poor Reen was trembling.'

'I know. Thank goodness Tracey hadn't given Pops a chance to explain properly. And they are going tonight so they can't ask the Cabopino folk what happened. You are the most absolute genius I've ever met.'

'Thank you, but…'

'No buts. You are. We owe you even more now.' He hugged her again in a warm comforting embrace which caused her heart to lurch a little.

Before he released her, he whispered, 'Can you just nip into the garden and tell Ma everything is OK. I daren't let her back in yet in case she blurts something out. She's still consumed with guilt and we've got to stop her confessing.'

'Yes, can do.'

As Troy let her go, he plonked a huge kiss on her forehead.

Totally embarrassed, Kate made her way to the garden, swerving past an emotional Ted who threatened to crush her in his beefy embrace.

The warm air hit her as she ventured into the extensive garden. And she couldn't help grinning as she was faced with several fluorescent pink plastic flamingos standing jauntily on one leg surveying everything with a supercilious air. The large square pool reflected the brilliant blue of the sky and looked very inviting but her focus was on a small crumpled figure swaying gently in a matching flamingo pink canopied garden seat.

Reen looked up as she approached and held out her bony brown arms. 'Oh Dahlin…,' before bursting into huge gulping sobs.

Kate sat down and was enveloped in a tight embrace. This vulnerable little woman tugged her heartstrings in an inexplicable way. Physically she was the exact opposite of her own sturdy Ma, as was her dress sense. Her Ma was all sensible, hard wearing browns and greens, not sparkly pinks and oranges and all the colours of the rainbow. But Reen was called Ma. The name itself conjured up her own loving Ma who fought for her and loved her unselfishly despite everything. Was that part of her appeal?

'There, there,' Kate found herself stroking Reen's trembling back. 'It's OK. Tracey believes us. She thinks it was just the pushchair that was in danger. You mustn't let on about Tara whatever you do. OK?'

Reen just sobbed more.

‘Look, Reen,’ Kate urged. ‘You’ve got to pull yourself together. If Tracey sees you are too upset, she might smell a rat. Come on. We need to go back in and look as if everything is OK.’

Looking round she saw Tara’s stuffed toys drying on an ornate patio table in full sun.

‘Are those dry yet?’

Reen looked up and sniffed. ‘No, I don’t think so.’

‘Have you got a tumble dryer?’

‘Yes, although we don’t use it much.’

‘Well, shall we put them in and give them a whirl just to speed up the process. I’m sure Tara will want them on the plane, won’t she?’

Gradually Kate managed to get Reen sitting upright and focusing on something else.

Troy came out and gave her a questioning look.

‘We are just going to put Tara’s toys in the tumble dryer, aren’t we, Reen? Can you show me where it is?’

With an effort, Reen stood up. Her eyes were red-rimmed and her mascara had streaked all over her cheeks.

‘Hang on a minute, Ma,’ Troy said and taking out a large red hankie, he gently wiped her cheeks, fluffed up her hair a little and said, ‘Shoulders back, Ma. Come on. Let’s show ‘em what you’re made of. Remember there’s no harm done and Kate here has put her neck on the line for you. You don’t want to let her down, do you?’

That did the trick. ‘No, of course not.’ Reen straightened up and with a bit of a wobble began walking back into the house.

Chapter Thirty-Four

And they did get away with it.

Tracey may have had her suspicions, but she didn't voice them and there was an unspoken bond between the Taylor men that kept her away from Reen for the rest of the afternoon.

As the atmosphere relaxed, Kate noticed the genial banter between the men and the way they gently teased Reen till she lost her haunted look. Perhaps the amount of wine consumed helped with the convivial atmosphere which eventually even Tracey joined in.

How wonderful to be part of a family like this. They included her and wanted to know all about her and how she had ended up in Spain. The questions weren't too intrusive and everyone seemed satisfied with her brief story of wanting a change from teaching in Birmingham. They all looked a bit impressed with her status of lecturer but also looked relieved when she laughingly debunked any pretensions of high academic standing.

Throughout these exchanges she was aware of Troy's approving eyes upon her and, as she surreptitiously checked her watch, he slipped over to sit by her.

'Do you have to get home?'

'Yes, really, I should. I need to get back.' Her side was really aching by now and she wanted to take some strong painkillers before she got ready for her usual Saturday night out with the girls. 'Look, would you mind calling me a taxi.'

He laughed. 'What, you mean my humble little Porsche isn't good enough for you?'

She grinned, 'It's not bad I suppose, but…'

'No buts about it. I'm driving you home.'

‘Haven’t you got to take Tarquin and family to the airport?’

‘Yes, but not yet. I’ve got time to take you first. And besides do you really think Ma would let you go in a taxi? Now brace yourself, leave-taking could take some time.’

He stood up. ‘Right, Ma. Kate has to get back home so I’m…’

‘Oh, Babes,’ Reen immediately rushed over from where she was chatting to Tarquin. ‘Do you have to go?’

‘Yes, sorry, Reen but…’

‘Oh no, I thought you could stay with us and …’

‘No arguments, Ma. If Kate says she’s gotta go she’s gotta go. She does have a life of her own you know.’

‘Yes, but…’

‘Ma!’ Troy raised a warning eyebrow.

‘OK, Troy. Now, Dahling, what’s your address and phone number? We must go out shopping together and… Oh, I know, come for lunch with us tomorrow at Puerto Banus. Ted can pick you up. Can’t you, Ted?’

‘Now, Ma. Let Kate breathe. She might have other plans.’

‘Have you?’

‘Um, well,’ Kate couldn’t think fast enough and also couldn’t bear to disappoint Reen’s eager little face. ‘No, as it happens.’

‘Right. Ted will pick you up at twelve. You will love it there. It’s really posh.’

Troy’s grimace told otherwise.

‘And you can join us, can’t you, Troy? He lives there near his car showroom, you know.’

‘Yes, Ma, I’ll do my best. Now go and grab a pen and write down Kate’s phone number.’

In a protracted flurry of hugs and thanks and goodbyes and yet more hugs, Kate at last managed to get into Troy’s car and drive off amidst much waving and kiss blowing.

Troy grinned, ‘Phew, we escaped. You can relax now.’

‘Thanks.’ How did he know what she was feeling?

They drove along in silence for a while, weaving through the broad avenues of the urbanisation.

'Thanks for what you did, Kate, I…'

'Please, Troy. I get so totally embarrassed about being thanked.'

'I know you do. So I won't say it again. But just one big final thank you for saving Tara as well as your "just the buggy" story, especially as I know you don't like lying.'

'How do you know?'

'I saw your fingers crossed behind your back.'

She laughed. 'Silly isn't it? The childhood belief that it doesn't count as lying if you cross them. But I'm just so pleased I thought of it. I'm amazed we got away with it, though. I thought Ted might have said something about Tara at Cabopino.'

'Tracey wouldn't have been listening. Once she's got a bee in her bonnet, she's off on a rampage. What's so sad is that she wouldn't have dared have a go like that before. Ma wouldn't have stood for it. But since Ma's come out here, she's lost a lot of her confidence and I think Tracey is making the most of it.'

'Do you know why?'

'I think it's a primeval jealousy thing. Tarquin, like all us boys, has always adored Ma and perhaps Tracey is trying to assert herself as top dog now. She didn't used to be like that. I blame the crowd she's with now…all posh, over-privileged, yummy mummies. I think she's a bit out of her depth with them and constantly trying to keep up with the latest thing. Poor Tarquin is working his socks off just to keep up. She doesn't know it, but he's been sussing out escaping down here to see if he can break her out of the back-biting bitchy gang she's in.'

'What does he do?'

'I suppose you could say he's in property. Started small and borrowed from the parents and bought a couple of houses. He's always been very practical, like Pa, so he did them up with his own bare hands and sold them at a profit. He bought some more and it's gradually got to be quite a big concern. Tracey helped in the beginning. She's got a good eye for décor and makes them look good. The twins came along and she stopped work. Then she wanted to move into a posh area and she's now become the not very nice person you see today.'

'What a shame.'

'It is. Tarquin loves her and tries to give her everything she wants, but I can't help thinking he should stand up to her. But, hey, what do I know about things?' He gave a sad rueful smile before asking, 'So tell me more about this College of yours then.'

So Kate happily filled him in about what she did at College, her flamenco friends and her life in Spain generally.

He was a good listener but wanted to know more about her roots 'up north' as he expressed it, so she told him the bits she wanted him to know.

'The reason I ask is it seems like fate, you coming from up there. Ma has a fondness for northern accents…by the way, they all sound the same to her. She was in Nice last winter and made good friends with a girl from Accrington and I think you remind her a lot of Annie.

'Now you are her shining saviour, so she's going to want to shower you with…well everything. She's a warm generous person and you are going to get the full deluge. So watch out.'

There was intensity about the way he said it, a sort of hidden anxiety.

'Once Tracey has gone, she'll bounce back. And she will be looking for things to do, so she will want to take you over. If you want to back out now, just say so.'

Kate could see he was serious.

Before she could ask any further, they were coming off the autostrada and he was wanting directions to her apartment. With a roar he pulled up outside her block and then to her surprise switched off the engine.

Looking troubled, he gazed out across the gardens to the sea.

'It's no good. I'm going to have to warn you about Ma.'

Chapter Thirty-Five

'Warn me?'

Kate was alarmed. What was wrong with Reen?

'What do you mean?'

'You like her, don't you?' Troy wrinkled his brow.

'Of course, I do. Why do you ask like that?'

'Well, I know she's not everyone's cup of tea. We love her, of course, but…' he was obviously choosing his words carefully, '…some people might think her clothes are a bit too loud, her taste is a bit too flashy. You've seen the house and all those bloomin pink flamingos, haven't you?'

Kate giggled, 'Yes, and I love them.'

'Really?'

'Yes. I think your mum, her house and the flamingos are… well, exuberant and fabulous and fun.'

He was scrutinising her carefully as she said all this and seemed to relax at her answer.

He slowly ran his hand through his dark, short-cropped hair obviously thinking through his next words.

'About tomorrow. I meant it. You don't have to come to Puerto Banus if you don't want to. I'll tell her you'd forgotten that you were going out for lunch with friends. I'm not sure Puerto Banus is your sort of place.'

'But you live there.'

'Yes, it's true. But I have to live where the money is, where the contacts are. It doesn't mean I have to like it.'

'Really?' Kate paused, 'Can I ask why you are so worried about me going? Don't you want me there?'

'Oh crikey no. That's not what I meant. I'd love to see you again…' he looked at her sincerely, '…I really would. But you might not want to see us again so soon. I know Ma can be quite insistent because she is a bit…'

'Lonely?' Kate offered.

'Oh yes. Oh, you understand.' He sighed with relief. 'I might have guessed you would. She can come over so needy and clingy and it's just because she's lonely. I think she's been a bit bored and well…lost. Ever since her and Pa gave up the yard…'

'The yard?'

'Yes. Her and Pa ran a scrap metal yard for most of their lives. You'd never guess it to see her now, but she was as tough as old boots. Her ability to drive a hard bargain was legendary. Everyone used to want to negotiate with Ted because they knew he was softer than she was, but woe betide him if he agreed to a deal without her say so. He ran the yard because he's the practical one, which is why Tracey knew it wasn't him who didn't put the brakes on. Ma's hopeless with any machinery or stuff. But she's the sharp one. She's a whizz with figures so she ran the office and did the accounts. Together they made one helluva team.'

'I can imagine. I love the way your dad is so protective of her.'

'They were childhood sweethearts. Married young…it was a bit quick 'cos Tarquin was on the way.' He grinned. 'Pa went to help his dad in the family scrap business and Ma went to join him. Looking back, I often wonder if they'd have done something else, but it was expected that Pa, as the only son, would join the family firm, and so he did. Ma just supported him and a few years later when his dad died in an accident, they took on the whole thing themselves. They lived and breathed that yard. They had to support the three of us and his mum. As you can imagine, Ma was never a conventional mother. Couldn't abide cooking and cleaning and all that stuff but our grandparents pitched in and looked after us and we always felt loved. It was what we knew and it was fine.'

He shrugged. 'We had good holidays. Often used to come down here, especially when my nana met another bloke and came to Spain to live. They used to close up the yard for a fortnight at Christmas and we'd come down to Marbella to stay with them for the whole holiday. Ma used to curl up on a lounger and sleep like a cat in the sun for the whole time. She loved it here. Mind you we all did. Such a contrast to the drizzly cold back home.'

'Isn't it,' Kate agreed. 'I love all the warmth and colour and brightness.'

He grinned. 'Just like Ma. She used to say, "Let that sun get at my bones and warm 'em up". Back home she always felt the cold.'

'I'm not surprised. There's nothing of her.'

He nodded. 'There used to be more. As you can imagine the yard was grey and grimy and noisy. And it was often cold and wet so she would wrap herself up in layers and layers of warm clothes because she was in and out of the office all the time, yelling instructions and stuff. She's always done it. But four winters ago, she got a cold and couldn't seem to shift it. It got worse but she wouldn't take a day off. So stubborn. Then Pa walked into the office one day and found her collapsed and fighting for breath on the floor. It was pneumonia and it was touch and go whether she survived.'

He went grey at the memory. 'Frightened the life out of us all. Lost all that weight, never totally got it back. And she had to stop smoking...well, I think she's stopped. I'm not too sure she doesn't have the occasional crafty drag but at least she's not a twenty-a-day person anymore.'

'So what happened?'

'Pa had a long talk with the doctors and they advised sun and rest but warned her lungs would never be the same again. Pa didn't think twice about it. He sold up immediately. They'd always liked it round here so came to live in the sun. They made a packet on the yard so they could buy this place and they don't ever need to work again...and I think Ma is bored stiff.'

'Really?'

'Yup. I think she enjoyed setting up the place but that's pretty much done now. Sorry about the name *Tedreen Villa* by the way.'

Kate giggled. ‘I have to say I think it suits the house.’

He groaned. ‘I never know what she’s going to do to it next. Growing up they never had any money and all the years at the yard they have always ploughed everything back into the business, so all this money has gone to her head. If she sees something she likes, she just gets it, whether it matches anything or not. And all those colours everywhere…’ He sighed. ‘She’s just too flamboyant, don’t you think?’

He seemed genuinely anxious for her opinion and somehow a bit sad.

‘Well, I must admit her styles are a bit of a mish-mash, but do you think after all those monochrome years in a grey yard under grey skies her soul has just craved for colours and she’s gone for it?’

His eyes widened. ‘I’d never thought of it like that before. I think you could be right. I’m just so glad you like her.’

Why did it seem to matter to him so much?

‘But I think after all those hard working years, Ma is too young to retire and do nothing. Last winter she replaced all the bathrooms and put in Jacuzzis. She had to go and live in Nice while it was being done because of all the plaster dust, but that’s finished now. Then of course she had my brother Tyrone’s wedding to organise, so that kept her busy. But now there’s nothing.’

Kate sat and pondered. What sort of things did retired expats do down here. ‘Could she take up Spanish classes?’

Troy burst out laughing. ‘Sorry. I suppose you don’t realize how funny that is. Ma has enough trouble with English sometimes. As you know she nearly calls Tarantella, Tarantula, she thinks the Spanish dance with castanets is called *Flamingo* and their cream paint on the walls is *Mongolia*. Once, when Stan at the yard fainted, she rushed out and told everyone to put him in the *missionary position* and wondered why everyone fell about laughing.’

Kate grinned. She could imagine it.

‘Oh there’s many more. She can’t bear it when *people cast nasturtiums* on us.’ He shook his head. ’Anyway let’s just say I don’t see her getting to grips with anything too linguistic.

Luckily everyone round here speaks English so there's no real need to torture herself, and others, with anything else.'

'Hmmn, suppose not. What about golf?'

He groaned. 'They did try it. Pa would be OK at it, but Ma would probably kill someone with her swing. Anyway they went to the local golf club, with Ma wearing her usual skimpy crop top and mini skirt and her best high-heeled mules. She came back fulminating about the snotty cows at the club and they never went there again.'

He sighed, 'I just wish I could think of something for both of them. I worry they are drinking too much. I know Pa drove back from Cabopino today even after he'd had those brandies.' He shook his head, 'Sorry, I shouldn't burden you with all this but you're too good a listener. I feel a bit disloyal but I just wanted to warn you that my Ma will suck you in and take over your life, if you are not careful. Please don't let on I've told you any of this, will you? It's just you seem too nice to say no and you've got your own life to lead.'

He looked genuinely concerned.

'Thanks for the warning.' Kate paused for a while to think, then decided. 'I promise I *will* say no if I don't want to do anything she suggests. I can stand up for myself when I want to, honestly.'

He seemed reassured, 'OK. Just so long as you do. I can't believe I've rabbited on so long. I'd better be getting back to drive the Tarquin tribe to the airport.'

Kate looked at the little car. 'In this?'

'No,' he laughed, shaking his head. 'I shudder at the thought of letting the twins' sticky mitts anywhere near this paintwork. And that blasted monstrosity of a buggy alone would fill it. No. I'll use Pa's Range Rover. It's got the child seats in it and everything. I'll try to suggest Ma stays at home away from Tracey and just hope things have simmered down a bit.'

He leapt out of the car and opened her passenger side with a flourish that made her giggle.

'May I see you to your door?'

'Oh no, that's OK. I'm on the third floor and it's a bit of a climb.'

As she tried to clamber out of the low, tight bucket seat, her side spasmed with pain and she winced.

'Ah, that's obviously still bothering you. Have you got some pain killers you can take?'

'Yes, I'll be all right.'

Helping her out, he held her arms before looking deep into her eyes and saying sternly, 'I want you to take it easy. And remember you don't have to go to Puerto Banus tomorrow if you don't want.'

Why was he so anxious about her going?

'OK, Troy. I'll see how I feel.'

There was an awkward uncertainty about how they should bid each other goodbye, so Kate backed away and gave a little wave as she entered her building. He returned the wave with a grin before he climbed back into the car and set off with a roar back to Marbella.

Chapter Thirty-Six

But of course Kate went.

In spite of the dull ache in her side, she couldn't resist the pleading tone in Reen's voice when she phoned next morning to ask how she was and to invite her, yet again, to join them for lunch in Puerto Banus.

Her curiosity had also been piqued by Troy's evident misgivings. And she definitely wanted to see him again. He was an intriguing mixture of roguish charm and observant consideration for others. And, at times, a strange, almost wistful, sadness seemed to peek through his cavalier nonchalance.

She had regaled Megan in her weekly phone call with all that happened yesterday, down-playing her heroic save of the baby. Megan had been as fascinated with the Taylor family as she was. All those 'T' names definitely made her laugh.

At the club, her flamenco friends had been equally engrossed by the day's events and they had examined her lacerations with a mixture of awe and concern. But she made sure they were hidden from everyone else and, bolstered by painkillers, had danced away all night as usual.

Megan had been particularly interested in her reaction to Troy, discerning with her usual acuity that Kate found him attractive.

'So do you think you are getting over Rob then?'

'I don't know, Megan. I hope so, but…' at the mere mention of his name she experienced a wonderful flashback to a tousled bed-warm Rob awakening her with a kiss. As a familiar stab of yearning seared through her body, she sighed, 'Who knows? It's too soon to say. His mum says he's single but…look, all I know is, he's the first fella since Rob that

I've quite fancied. I'm not saying more than that.'

'OK.' There was a pause at the other end of the line. Was Megan about to say more? But she didn't. And they went on to talk about other things.

Next morning at precisely 12.00, Kate was downstairs awaiting the arrival of Ted and Reen clad in her most colourful clothes, which were positively boring compared with Ted's gaudily flowered shirt and Reen's sparkly silver boob tube, orange, animal-print cropped leggings and gold tasselled mules. Heavy gold bangles clattered on her wrists and long, glittering pink earrings dangled from her stretched lobes.

All gone was the shrivelled weeping Reen of yesterday to be replaced by a vivacious excited bundle of energy who seized Kate in one of her fierce hugs and was clearly delighted she had agreed to come with them. They had arrived in a sleek black Mercedes taxi driven by someone they introduced as Carlos. Reen sat in the back with Kate and a dozing Pugsy on her knee and talked almost non-stop all the way to Puerto Banus. Of course she kept returning to the happenings of the day before and was fulsome in her gratitude until Ted, glancing round at an embarrassed Kate, suggested they should talk about something else.

Kate got a lot of the story of their lives and how they ended up on the Costa which was familiar from what Troy had told her. But it was nevertheless interesting to hear it from Reen's point of view. Reen talked adoringly about all three of her boys but, once again, stressed that Troy was the only one still free.

'He's had quite a few girlfriends as you can imagine. He's such a lovely boy, isn't he?' She looked keenly at Kate, who of course nodded her agreement. 'But none of them have been the one. He's quite serious really and the most sensitive of them all. They were all scrappers at school, Tyrone especially, but Troy had a way of talking his way out of trouble. He's bright an' all. Loved helping me do the accounts at the yard.' She tailed off almost nostalgically, before returning to Troy's girlfriends. 'Of course I never thought any of them were good enough for him. Perhaps that's why he kept the last one quiet. I thought he seemed dead keen and I was looking forward to meeting her at Tyrone's wedding but at the last minute, she didn't come. Next thing we know, they've broken up and he's transferred his job from London to down here. But he seems to be loving it. Fitted right in with the Costa crowd, I can tell you. They love him and he's already one of their top salesmen here. I hope he finds time to meet us for a bit. He usually does.'

And on she chatted about Troy and Port Banos as she called it.

They arrived and Kate was intrigued to see that Puerto Banus was a carefully constructed imitation village of artfully haphazard housing clustered round a marina filled with the biggest yachts she'd ever seen in her life. She just gasped open-mouthed as her eye travelled round such an ostentatious display of wealth. The moored mega-cruisers ascended around the quay in ever bigger and more opulent proportions. Parked in front of them were their equally expensive cars. Even she could recognise the galloping racehorse on the front of a red Ferrari. With Reen eagerly pointing things out, Kate gazed in all the designer shops with eye-wateringly expensive items displayed artistically in the windows. This was luxury on a scale she had never seen before.

Reen looked to be revelling in it but was also scornful of the prices in the shops.

'You're just paying for the label, Dahlin,' she said, dismissively as they both stopped to gawp at a shimmering barely-there dress in a window. 'I'll show you some places in the back streets of Marbella that could do that at half the price.'

'But Reen, would you want something so revealing anyway?' Kate asked.

'Nah, not me. But you, with your lovely young figure, you could get away with it.'

'Me!' Kate gasped. 'I would never wear anything as…as

skimpy and as tight fitting as that.' She blushed at the thought.

'Hmmn,' Reen looked her up and down and said ominously, 'we'll see.'

'Come on, girls,' Ted rumbled from ahead. 'Here we are.'

'Quick, Ted, grab that nice table there,' Reen urged as she trotted to catch up with him.

'Miguel,' Ted called and a tall, handsome waiter flashed them a very white smile and pulled out some well-padded rattan chairs at a corner table.

'Hola, Señor Ted and the beautiful Señora Reen.' He fussed around them, twinkling at Kate, till they were seated and then murmured, 'The usual for you, my friends?'

'Yes please, Miguel. And what would you like, Kate?'

'Um, I'm not sure. A white wine spritzer perhaps, if that's OK.'

Reen looked shocked. 'No, Dahlin. Have a nice glass of champers or a cocktail. They do a fantastic Bacardi Breezer. Or one of my favourite tipples is tequila which you can have in lots of different ways.'

Reen began listing all the cocktails on offer when Ted interrupted, 'If Kate just wants a spritzer, that's OK.' And he nodded to Miguel who whipped off with a suggestive wiggle of his pert little bum.

'Ted,' Reen hissed. 'I want Kate to have the best.'

'And so do I, Princess. But I'm guessing you're not a big drinker, are you, Babes?'

'Not really.' Kate gave Ted a grateful grin. Judging from the way those two knocked back the brandy yesterday and then all the booze that was consumed back at the house, she knew she wasn't in their league and wanted to pace herself.

'Well, Dahlin, as long as you are happy. But don't hold back on anything. This is our treat and anything you want… just say. After yesterday…' Reen began.

Luckily Kate was saved from a further outpouring of gratitude by the arrival of a large, boisterous party of super-tanned people who hailed Reen and Ted with extravagant bonhomie.

The men stood and gave manly hugs and back slaps, the women air-kissed and 'darlinged' each other in shrill, loud voices. Kate had to be introduced to Reg and Des and Margo and Ruby and… She lost track but was quite happy to subside quietly after the initial introductions and just people watch.

And it was fascinating. The women were louder, browner versions of Reen with much more jewellery. Their gnarled fingers were encrusted with rings sporting huge glittering rocks. Could they really be diamonds? The portly men flashed their flamboyant wealth with heavy gold medallions and chunky gold bracelets. Their loud braying voices and broad cockney accents made Kate think of gangland villains she'd seen in films. Then, with a gulp, she realised that this was often called the Costa del Crime where East-End gangsters holed up to spend their ill-gotten gains. But then, she couldn't envisage Ted and Reen consorting with villains and reprimanded herself for an over-active imagination. Settling back, she quietly watched the interactions between them all.

Reen tried to include her but as Kate didn't know any of the people they were gossiping about, she whispered to Reen, 'Don't worry about me. I'm loving just sitting here in the sun and watching all the goings on.'

'Are you sure, Babes?'

'Absolutely. I've never seen so many posh cars and yachts and people in my life before.'

'Oh, Dahlin, that's just how I felt the first time I came here. Proper shocked me, especially the prices of drinks and meals. But then my Ted said we worked hard all our lives and we can afford it now, so let's just enjoy it. So we do, just now and again. But I still won't pay the prices in these shops, no way.'

She was just about to say more about the shocking cost of everything when she looked up and yelped, 'Here's Troy.'

Eagerly Kate turned to see a swaggering figure approaching. It took a few moments before she realised it really was Troy. His stance and walk were noticeably different from the day before. He looked devilishly handsome in his designer thigh-hugging jeans with his broad shoulders accentuated by the snug fit of his smart white shirt. Once again, his carefully rolled back sleeves revealed his strong tanned forearms. But somehow he exuded a different air and she didn't at first know why. Then she noticed he had two heavy gold signet rings on his fingers and a thick gold bracelet hanging from his wrist. And was that a diamond stud sparkling in his ear?

As he entered the crowded bar area, he greeted everyone with a broad smile and clasping handshake and a good deal of banter before turning to join their large group. His face froze a little as he noticed her in the corner and, for a moment, she thought he seemed embarrassed. Then he was glad-handing the men and slapping them on their shoulders in macho camaraderie. There was a lot of coy, flirtatious giggling as he kissed all the women, lingering a little on each cheek. Boy could that man work a room. They clearly all adored him.

With a shock, she realised he was dressing to suit the clients in the bar, his potential Porsche customers.

He didn't approach her and just nodded a hallo across the drink-laden table. But then she thought cynically, he knows I haven't got the spondoolix to afford one of his posh cars.

Nevertheless, it was a shock to see this other Troy. And a huge disappointment. Gone was the caring, protective man she saw yesterday to be replaced by a smooth charmer clearly selling himself in order to sell his product.

This is why he didn't want me to come, she realised.

'What's everyone having?' Troy offered, waving Miguel over. The waiter seemed to know the order from long custom and gave Kate a 'same again' look. She nodded.

She noticed Troy drank only sparkling water. He flirted outrageously with the women and could keep up an impressive level of quips with the men. He was the dashingly handsome life and soul of the party. But after a while he excused himself, saying he needed to get back to work.

‘Got some cars to sell, folks. Don’t forget, ask for me and I’ll get you a good motor and a good price.’ He winked as he got up and stretched his magnificent torso garnering quite a few lustful stares from the women in the bar. Was that on purpose, Kate wondered? She wasn’t sure where salesman Troy ended and real Toy began but noticed that once again he made contact with everyone in the place as he took his protracted leave.

As he walked away, she watched his retreating back. He hadn’t engaged with her once during his time there. In fact he seemed to be studiously avoiding eye contact but, as if he felt her eyes on him now, he suddenly turned round to look back. He gave her a sad little wave before striding off again along the Ferrari strewn quayside.

Chapter Thirty-Seven

Totally discomforted, Kate sat in the raucous bar in the hot autumn sun, watching as the glittering group drank and gossiped.

Troy was right. She shouldn't have come. Reen and Ted were clearly at home with this increasingly rowdy braying throng. And she wasn't.

But she was trapped. She had agreed to go for lunch with them and must stay until they ate which, as another round of drinks appeared, no one showed any signs of doing.

She sighed and found Reen's keen sparrow eyes upon her. Leaning forward, her friend squeezed her hand and said softly, 'Are you OK, Babes?'

'Oh yes, of course.'

'Don't pretend, Dahlin. It's not your scene, is it?'

'Well…'

'Don't worry, we will be going in a minute.'

'Oh no. Don't leave your friends just for me.'

'These are not my friends, Dahlin,' Reen confided with astonishing frankness. 'They are just people we know from way back. One or two are old customers from the yard and some are friends from school. We picked up with them again when we first came out here but they aren't really our sort. But we catch up now and again. We've started coming more regular since Troy came out here. We wanted to support him and help him make contacts. But small doses is all we can take.'

She waved across at Ted who nodded. Then she turned and made a phone sign to Miguel who also nodded.

'Right, we'll start saying our goodbyes before the taxi comes to pick us up.' Reen sprang to her feet. 'Miguel just phoned him. Carlos will be here in a minute.'

As she stood up, she picked up Pugsy and began a round of kissing, hugging goodbyes and Ted followed her example, stopping to give a fistful of money to Miguel on his way out.

As the black Mercedes glided to a halt outside the bar, they gave final waves and hustled away towards it.

It was wonderfully cool inside and with a brief nod, Carlos drove off along the busy quayside weaving patiently between expensively dressed inhabitants strolling to be seen and lumpen ill-clad tourists gawping at everything they surveyed.

Reen patted her hand. 'Sorry if that wasn't your cup of tea, Dahlin. Ted did wonder if it was the right place to take you, but I thought you might like to see it, especially as it's where Troy lives and works.'

'Oh yes, thanks, Reen. It was absolutely fascinating as a place to go but so far out of my money bracket, it was difficult for me to relate to.'

Ted turned round and grinned. 'You're right, Babes. I agree. It's for people with more money than sense. That's why we don't eat there very much. The price of drinks is bad enough but the food is worse. Costs an arm and a leg for fancy twirls and twiddles on the plate around a few bits and pieces of proper food. We've worked too hard for our money to waste it on stuff like that. It's good to meet for a chat now and again but all we ever talk about is the old days because they have got nothing else going on in their lives. But it's good for Troy's business, so we play along, don't we, Reen?'

'Yes, Dahlin. If we can help him establish himself out here, then it's worth it.'

'Troy seemed very different somehow,' Kate ventured.

'Oh, he's a right chameleon that one. Always was a charmer. All the ladies love him and he plays up to them something rotten. Naughty boy.' Reen gave an indulgent chuckle. 'But don't you worry,' she patted Kate's hand meaningfully, 'none of them mean anything to him. He'd much prefer a nice girl like you.'

'Now, Reen,' Ted warned.

'Well, he would, Ted. You know he would. None of his past girlfriends have been the flashy sort. Not that he's had that many,' she added hastily. 'He just seems to go for pretty ones with a really nice nature, like you.'

Ted frowned. 'But maybe Kate already has someone in her life.'

'Well, have you, Babes?'

'Um, no…not really.'

'I knew it. Told you so, Ted. But what do you mean by "not really"?'

Kate gave a guilty start. Of course she hadn't got anyone in her life. What on earth made her say 'not really'? She knew in her heart of hearts she still loved Rob but what was the point in wanting someone who obviously didn't want her? Reen was obviously sussing her out for Troy so why couldn't she open herself up to a new relationship? She had come out to Spain for a fresh start and this was a perfect opportunity to meet someone new. And yes, she did like Troy. Perhaps the version of him she had seen today wasn't quite right, but how much of that was just put on for show?

Reen's sharp eyes were on her. This woman seemed to have an uncanny knack of reading her thoughts. But there was no way Kate was going to tell her anything about her past relationships, especially aware that the driver was listening to all this with some amusement.

'No, I mean no. There's nobody in my life at the moment, Reen.'

Her friend sat back with a satisfied grin on her face.

Then they were drawing up at a modest restaurant right on the beach in the middle of a small clump of waving palms.

'This is our usual place,' Ted said. 'Reen likes it because you can see Gibraltar from here. She's got a bit of a thing about Gibraltar.'

'And because it's a nice place, Ted,' Reen bristled. 'Really nice people and nice food. I hope you are hungry, Babes.'

'Actually, Reen, I'm starving.' And she was.

And it was a nice place. Simple, unpretentious and very tasty food, with Ted showing his full approval of the generous portions. The waiters made a fuss of them and even brought out a small bowl of leftovers for Pugsy.

It was a lovely afternoon. They sat outside in the warm sun and chatted as they ate. By the end of the lunch she had half absorbed lots more info about the Taylor family. But with the sheer deluge of chat and drink, she wasn't sure how much she would be retaining. And somehow she had agreed to go clothes shopping next Saturday with Reen to replace her torn T-shirt and ruined crop trousers.

The more she was with them, the more she liked the diminutive Reen and her large husband. He clearly adored her and wanted to protect her. They were a very tactile family. Ted was forever putting his arms round her shoulders and patting her hands. And Reen was a big hugger and patter too. *Babes* and *Dahlings* liberally sprinkled her speech and were directed amiably at Ted, Kate, Pugsy and the waiters. And these weren't just mindless endearments. Reen really did view everyone through affectionate eyes.

For a moment a wave of sadness engulfed her. Ted was so different from her Pa, whose scowl frightened her and certainly sapped the enjoyment out of her childhood. Pa's first thought was to censure and rarely did anything get his grudging approval. Including her. Although she knew Ma loved her, she rarely showed it. She supposed Pa did too, in his own severe way but she remembered her feeling of guilty relief when he died. Then, and only then, did Ma begin to smile and actually express her love through occasional, and vastly cherished, embraces.

Not for the first time, she wished she could just shrug off the crippling effects of her childhood. Being on her own over the past few weeks, she'd had a lot of time to think. And, at last, she was coming to terms with some of the unresolved events in the past. But it was a long journey and she wasn't there yet.

Seeing other families up close, like Reen's, brought out a strange wistfulness in her. How she longed to belong to a clearly loving family like that.

As they dropped her off in the early evening, she had a final lung-squeezing hug from Reen before she staggered up the stairs to flop drunkenly on her bed and woozily contemplate her eventful weekend and all the new people who were now part of her life. Including the sexy but perplexing figure of Troy.

Chapter Thirty-Eight

'But don't you think it's a bit too…too bright. And I'm not sure I've got anything it will go with.'

Kate looked at her glittering reflection in the dress shop mirror. The silver-embossed emerald-green vest top looked amazing. It fitted perfectly and really showed off her figure. But how could she explain to Reen that it was just not her style. It was far too flashy, too revealing and would match nothing in her wardrobe.

She turned to a beaming Reen and realised that *too bright* and *not matching* were alien concepts to the vibrant figure in front of her clad in her fuchsia boob tube, her patterned jade and magenta culottes and lime green moc-croc mules.

Anyway Reen wasn't listening. She was busy poking around a rack of colourful clothes before swooping in on a turquoise T-shirt with a swirling peacock motif all down the back.

They were in a small boutique down a side street behind the famous orange square in Marbella. From the slightly apprehensive way the assistants greeted Reen, she was obviously a regular customer.

'Look, Reen, all I want is a plain white T-shirt to replace the torn one. That's what we agreed wasn't it?'

'No, Dahlin, with your shiny chestnut hair you can take really strong colours. Why do you want such a plain colour like white when you could have this cherry-red one? Or what about this gorgeous peacock colour? You have such lovely blue-green eyes, this will bring out their colour a treat.'

Reen draped it against her and it was true. Looking again in the mirror Kate could see she did look more vibrant. It did enhance her golden tan and match her eyes.

But after a childhood of being told to always look respectable, the image before her made her feel uncomfortable. She could hear Pa scolding her not to make a spectacle of herself. As if he was ashamed of her. Which of course he was.

Cautiously, she turned to the plain, long sleeved navy top she had picked out for herself, only to have it snatched away by Reen.

'No, you are definitely not having that. You shouldn't be hiding your lovely young skin. Show it off. I know my skin's like leather but after all those years in the yard bundled up to keep warm, I love the feel of the sun on my bones. I know folk criticise what I wear, but I just say, sod em. If they don't like it, they don't have to look. Really, Dahlin, with a figure and face like yours, I can't understand why you go around in such drab wishy-washy clothes. Why haven't you got more confidence in yourself? If I looked like you, I would really be strutting my stuff. Ain't I right, girls,' she said enlisting the help of the hovering assistants.

This had been a long morning. When she'd agreed to go shopping with Reen, Kate hadn't realised what she was letting herself in for.

The Marbella shopping scene was like nothing she had ever experienced before. Every shop Reen visited was filled with rails of clothes adorned with glitter and sparkles, bold flowery prints, embossed patterns, studs and sequins. There wasn't a plain item in sight. The colours were loud and cheerful. The prices were extortionate. They seemed to cater for women with time on their hands and money to burn who wanted to show they could afford the best labels.

But Reen was a canny shopper. She knew where she could get something similar at half the price. Sometimes, to Kate's embarrassment, she would barter this knowledge into getting the item she wanted at a discount.

In some shops, Kate could have sworn the assistants quailed as they saw Reen enter.

In vain Kate searched for something simple, insisting that they were only looking to replace one torn T-shirt. Although

Reen seemed to agree, her hands were behind her back. Kate suspected her fingers were crossed because she was being abstemious with the truth. And so it proved.

In the end, she wore Kate down, and by the time they ended up at Reen's favourite tapas bar for a late lunch, she was the embarrassed owner of that gorgeous emerald-green vest top, as well as the turquoise peacock motif one. There was also a gold sequinned strappy one, a shiny silver bomber jacket and a shimmering pink satin off-the-shoulder evening number that secretly she was dying to wear. And, of course, three pairs of crop jeggings, one in fake animal print, one in a sort of ripped denim effect and one in crimson that weirdly seemed to go with everything.

'Reen, this is too much,' she protested each time. But the answer was always a variation on how much pleasure it gave Reen to treat her.

'I haven't got a daughter, so I've never had the chance to go girly shopping. Tracey's always a bit too snobbish about my shops and Tina, bless her…she's the beauty salon/ hairdresser one…she's got lots of the same stuff as me. Besides she can afford to buy her own so it's no treat.'

'I can afford to buy my own clothes as well.' Kate found her tone was sharper than she intended.

'Didn't mean you couldn't, Dahlin. No offence, but on a teacher's money?'

'Well yes. Not as fancy as these of course but…'

'Precisely my point. Just that boring stuff you usually wear. I owe you so much, Dahlin, so please let me show my gratitude like this.'

This tactic was used every time. Kate always protested and Reen always insisted. So the good natured bickering went on throughout their expedition. But Reen always won.

By late afternoon even Reen was all shopped out. She was laden down with lots of glossy posh carrier bags, even though Kate hadn't seen her try much on. There had been some surreptitious goings on at various tills and she suspected Reen had secretly purchased some of the items Kate had rejected as too expensive or too showy.

‘Let’s wait here for Ted to pick us up, shall we?’ said Reen indicating an open-air café in Marbella’s lovely Orange Square. Leading the way to a small table, she plonked down and gave a groan as she slipped her feet out of her moc–croc mules. ‘Ooh, my dogs are barking, and no mistake. Should we have a little drinky-poos just to celebrate the day?’

‘Oh, Reen. You and your celebrations.’

‘Well it has been a lovely day. I haven’t enjoyed myself as much in a long time.’

‘OK,’ Kate sighed. She knew when she was beaten.

As they sipped their champagne cocktails, Reen looked up at the surrounding orange-festooned trees. ‘You know, Dahlin, the first time I saw these trees, I couldn’t believe it. I wondered what these little orange balls were and when I realised they were your actual oranges growing, I got all goose pimples up my arm. I thought it was so strange and foreign, so erotic.’

‘Um…exotic?’ Kate suggested.

‘Yes, that’s it. I still get a thrill to think little old me is living in a place where oranges grow on trees. And what about you, Dahlin? What was it like where you grew up?’

Kate shivered. The last thing she wanted to think about was her cold, damp childhood surrounded by those looming mist-covered hills.

‘Not like this at all. My Pa would have a fit if he could see me now, especially dressed like this.’ She indicated the silver bomber jacket Reen had cajoled her into wearing.

‘Hmmn. Is he the reason you don’t like bright colours and you keep hiding your light under a bucket?’

Kate suppressed her impulse to correct Reen’s expression. After all, hiding your light under a bucket made a lot more sense than a bushel.

‘I suppose so.’ And under Reen’s gentle probing she found she was revealing more than she intended about Pa’s disapproving influence on her life. She stopped short of the reasons why he was so censorious of her and just kept it to his lay-preacher’s desire for respectability and belief that sin was waiting to leap out at you from every corner.

‘Doesn’t sound much fun,’ was Reen’s verdict, as she finished telling her about her life in the gloomy village and the gossiping nosy tattlers who frequented their little post office, always eager to report on anything untoward.

‘Nope, Reen, you are right there. Fun was the last thing it was.’

‘I’m amazed you’ve come out so normal.’

‘Oh, do you think so?’

‘I mean, it explains why you don’t think you are worth all those lovely clothes and are worried about looking nice. I did wonder why no bloke had snapped up such a lovely creature like you. Unless you had a run in with someone awful who took advantage of your nice nature.’

Kate stared. How did this woman know so much?

It only took a couple more questions before it all came tumbling out about Chris. How he had homed in on her and undermined her and how she had eventually got up the courage to chuck him out and how coming out here was her escape from her old life and her fresh start.

Was it the drink, or was it the sympathy that emanated from Reen’s every pore that prompted her to reveal so much?

But whatever it was, she felt so much better after unburdening herself and being consoled by Reen’s motherly words of wisdom and comfort.

Chapter Thirty-Nine

Waiting in the sunshine on her balcony next morning for the usual taxi to take her to Reen's 'Gibraltar View' restaurant for lunch, Kate smoothed down her new turquoise top. She really did feel good in it. Reen was right. Thanks to her she had begun to rethink her whole image and outlook on life.

Why shouldn't she wear the bold colours she loved? Reen was right, she really must shake off the shackles of her upbringing and value herself more. She had accepted Chris' domination of her behaviour because it echoed Pa's. She could see that now. Gradually she felt she was emerging from the shadows into the bright sunlight, both literally and metaphorically.

Her flamenco friends last night were full of compliments for her new wardrobe. As the evening progressed, so did her confidence. She had flirted a little more and danced a lot more. Although she hadn't fancied any of the blokes who had chatted her up, it was nice to feel so sexy and alive.

She hadn't felt so attractive since…well since Rob really. He had definitely made her feel sexy, but that was all in the past. Her new mantra was 'fresh start' and, by repeating it often enough, she would soon forget him. At least, that was the plan.

Her taxi hooted down below. Grabbing her bag, she raced down the stairs wondering what this encounter with the Taylor family would bring.

It brought a first meeting with Tyrone and Tina. As a young man rose to greet her she knew straight away it was Tyrone. He was a younger version of Ted, same barrel chest and taste in loud flowery shirts. It was interesting. Now she had met all three Taylor boys, she could see that, although in physique they took after their father, there was something about the sharpness in their bright brown eyes that reminded her of Reen. As did Tyrone's effusive hug and broad grin.

Tina, to Kate's amusement, was a younger version of Reen. They even dressed the same. The same glitzy, figure-hugging, skin-revealing tops, the same clippy-cloppy mules and the same chatty warmth.

Kate liked them both immediately. Recently back from their honeymoon in the Seychelles, they were obviously so much in love. There was none of the tension between Tina and Reen that there had been between her and Tracey.

They had obviously heard all about how she had rescued 'the buggy' at Cabopino and there was some good-natured teasing of Reen, who no longer looked as stricken whenever the incident was mentioned.

Settling in the sun with the obligatory round of drinks, Kate felt she had known them for years and soon joined in the easy banter. Even Pugsy had given her a little welcoming bark as she arrived and wagged his stumpy little tail in welcome.

They were just ordering food when Troy's tall figure joined them. The old Troy, no earring or gold bracelet. Just friendly natural Troy. Seemingly very conscious of Reen's keen gaze, he gave Kate a swift hug and a peck on the cheek before he sat down on the other side of the table.

Reen had beamed when she saw that Kate was wearing her previous day's purchases and, to their mutual embarrassment, she lost no time in drawing Troy's attention to how good Kate looked. Then, with a wink, she slid a glossy carrier bag across the floor towards Kate.

'Here you are, Dahlin,' she whispered with a conspiratorial grin, 'Just some little extras I thought you might like.'

Surprised, Kate looked at the bag and all the bright, tissue-wrapped contents. She knew exactly what was in there. All the items she had rejected yesterday.

She carefully lifted the bag and plonked it back under Reen's chair.

'No thank you, Reen.'

'What?'

'I know what's in there. And it's very good of you, but no thanks.'

'But, Dahlin…'

'I know you mean well, Reen. And I know how much we both enjoyed yesterday and how much pleasure it gave you treating me to all those clothes…but that's enough. I'm very grateful for it all, but no more presents, Reen. I mean it.'

Thwarted, Reen turned to Ted to back her up.

'Ted, tell her how much I want her to have these.'

'No, don't bring him into it, Reen. I love shopping with you, but I can't go with you again if all the time I'm worrying that you are watching me and secretly buying stuff for me. I hope you can see that. You have more than repaid any debt you think you owe me for saving "the buggy" and we are now quits. OK?'

Her severe look was met with a defiant expression that showed Reen wasn't going to give in that easily. Kate became aware that the rest of the Taylors were watching the tussle with a keen and amused interest.

'Look, Reen, don't you see that yesterday you gave me something more precious than clothes? You have given me your friendship and you made me see myself from a fresh perspective. You dragged me, kicking and screaming, out of my dull conformity into a wonderful bright new colourful world. Your world. In doing so you have stopped me worrying all the time about what people think of me. And I want you to know how grateful I am for that.'

She patted Reen's little brown hands. 'So I will happily go shopping with you again as long as you promise me, no more secret presents. Promise.'

As Reen's eyes welled up, Ted's arm went round his wife's shoulders.

'I don't think she can promise that, Babes. It's just not in her. But I think she's got the message.' He reached over and put the bag behind his chair.

But he under-estimated his wife. Reen rallied and tried one

more time.

'But, Dahlin,' she wheedled. 'You may as well have these few things I've already got. After all what am I going to do with them?'

Kate laughed. 'Good try, Reen. But from the cowed look on those shop assistants' faces whenever you walked in, if you can't get your money back, nobody can.'

There was a gasp, then Tina led the whole family in a hearty round of applause.

'You've met you match there, Ma,' laughed Tina.

Kate blushed, especially as she caught a gleam of approval in Troy's eyes. Approval, and was there something else?

At the end of a wonderfully high-spirited meal, as everyone gathered under the shady palm trees waiting for their taxis, Troy managed to manoeuvre Kate to one side.

'Good work there with Ma. There's not many can deflect her like that. And is it true what you said about her helping you feel good about yourself?'

'Absolutely. I feel like a butterfly emerging from a dull chrysalis.'

'Oh, Kate, you were never dull,' he said warmly. Then hesitated before he continued, 'I don't suppose you fancy spreading your butterfly wings a bit more. I mean…' he hurried on, '…I know you like exploring around here and I wondered if you have ever been to a place called Ronda?'

'Rhonda? You mean the place in Wales?'

He grinned, 'No, it's a wonderful old town up in the hills about twenty miles from here.' Looking down shyly, he continued, 'I rather fancy seeing it. Everyone says it's got a really dramatic setting over a gorge. I'm free next Saturday and I would love to get away from bloomin Puerto Banus.' Gone was the super smooth Troy. He looked genuinely nervous as he asked, 'I don't suppose you would like to come out for a drive up there with me and we can explore it together?'

'I would love to. That would be great.'

He looked immensely relieved.

'I'll ring you. Oh, and don't tell Ma or you will never hear the end of it.'

With a little grin he walked rapidly away as a slightly squiffy Reen called out that their taxi had arrived.

Chapter Forty

The following Saturday a thoughtful Kate paced up and down her apartment waiting for Troy to pick her up. She had spent all week trying to reconcile the two images of the man. There was the schmoozy Puerto Banus man, self-assured, flirtatious, oozing social confidence and supremely in control of himself and his surroundings. And then there was the diffident, nervous man who had shyly plucked up the courage to ask her out for a drive. Which was the real Troy? And how did she feel about him?

She didn't know the answer to either question but was hoping that today might provide some clues. He had phoned her during the week to arrange the time and told her to wear warm clothes as it could be cool in the mountains.

She had had to disappoint Reen by calling off their Saturday shopping trip and, mindful of Troy's instruction, she had invented a lunch date with her flamenco friends.

Feeling slightly nervous, she trotted down to meet him at the appointed time. Although the weather was sunny it was also a bit blustery so she had stuffed a warm pashmina into her shoulder bag in case it was cool in an open top car.

But it wasn't an open top car. It was an ordinary beige saloon car and standing by it was a strangely familiar figure in a blue jumper and blue cords and trainers. She did a double take. Gone was the designer stubble and the gelled hair. This bloke was clean shaven and wearing a prominent pair of black framed glasses. This Troy looked slightly geeky, more serious and somehow more ordinary. Like Clark Kent, not Superman.

She stopped, stumped until the figure smiled shyly, almost apprehensively and said, 'Yes, it is me. This is the real me.'

She laughed, 'For the moment I didn't recognise you.'

Troy slumped a little. 'I know. It's a bit of a shock isn't it?'

'No, just unexpected.'

Looking down at his feet he said quietly, 'Look, if you don't want to come, especially in this non-swish car with this non-swish bloke, just say so. I will quite understand.'

'Don't be silly. I think I prefer this non-glamorous version to…' She stopped short. She was going to say 'Puerto Banus schmooze man', but thought better of it.

He laughed in relief. 'I could tell you didn't like Puerto Banus me. I don't like him either. That's what made me think that perhaps I dare show you the real boring me.'

'I doubt the real you is boring and I'd be happy to get to know him, if you want me to.'

'Your wish is granted.' He grinned, that lovely, familiar, genuine grin. 'Your carriage awaits, Princess,' and he opened the car door with a flourish.

Good. The real Troy is still charming and has a sense of humour. That'll do me.

Although really intrigued by this new persona, Kate sensed his apprehension in opening up to her. So she waited, taking in the view as they approached the long winding road up into the mountains. Either side, as far as the eye could see, the fields of vines were stripped bare ready for the winter.

Eventually she could contain her curiosity no longer. 'So, Mr Troy Taylor, reveal all. How many versions of you are there?'

He paused before answering as if summoning up courage. 'Just two really. This one and the guy who sells Porsches. This guy is short-sighted and Porsche guy wears contacts. This guy is quite shy, the other one can charm the birds from the trees, wears great clothes and sells himself to people with the money to buy flash cars. This one cringes when he hears the other one. This one hates what he does for a living but accepts he's good at it and he gets a good living from it and so is trapped by his success.'

Kate was stunned into silence by the sadness in his voice.

Eventually she said gently, 'What would this one rather

do?'

'This one has been going to evening classes to train to be…don't laugh…an accountant.'

He gave a sidelong glance as if to gauge her reaction.

Kate could sense this was a big admission on his part so refused to look shocked. 'That sounds fine to me. What's wrong with that?'

There was big sigh.

'OK, I'm going to tell you everything. No one else knows all this and the last thing you must do is tell Ma or Pa. Promise.'

Absolutely mystified, Kate promised.

'I saw the way you stood up to Ma the other day so I know you are no pushover. I'll be honest, I really like you and I like the way you fit into my family. That's really important to me.'

Here he paused and looked over at her, 'I think…well, I get the feeling you like me too. Is that true?'

She nodded. Yes, she knew she did and it was great to know the feeling was mutual.

Troy sighed with relief. 'Good. But I wasn't sure so I thought today I'd better show you the real me.'

'You're right, Troy, I do like you. And don't forget, I have already seen the real you. I see him every time you are with your family. He is sincere and funny and very likeable. And I much prefer him to Mr Schmooze man.'

'What! Oh my God, is that what you call the other me.'

'Sorry, yes.'

'He is a bit of a schmoozer isn't he? But you'll find the real me is Mr Boring.'

'Oh no, he's not. You had me when you lifted me into your arms at Cabopino and carried me off into the sunset. And that was the real you, wasn't it?'

He grinned and blushed. 'Yes, I suppose it was. But dressed in Mr Schmooze's clothes.'

'Maybe, but the real you was there, sorting things out, caring for me and protecting Reen. All the qualities a girl looks for in a bloke.'

To her surprise, his face scrunched with anguish.

'Maybe. But don't you think it's much more complicated than that?'

She could tell she had hit a nerve.

'Perhaps. OK, I'm listening. Tell me about Mr Would-be-Accountant Troy Taylor and why he can't reveal his true self. And yes, I do promise not to tell a soul.'

'Thank you. I knew I could trust you.' His warm smile briefly erased the worry lines from his forehead. Then there was a long pause while he obviously thought about what he was going to say.

'I suppose I ought to start by telling you that I never set out to sell cars. I just helped out doing odd jobs in a showroom as a Saturday job. All we Taylor boys had them. Our parents worked hard and so we automatically did too. Our school was pretty rough but I enjoyed going because I liked learning stuff. Not that I ever told anyone. But when I did surprisingly well at my exams, I really wanted to stay on and do A Levels. But coming from our area, well, it just wasn't done.'

'Didn't you think of telling your parents?'

'Ma always said I was the bright one, but I think that's because I loved helping her with the firm's accounts. I found them easy to understand so never thought you had to be particularly clever to do them. It was obvious to me. Looking back I should have realised that it wasn't to everyone. But to do A level maths I would have had to go to the local sixth form College and only posh kids went there. Huh, and if there was one thing I knew about us Taylors, it was that we definitely weren't posh.'

There was a shocking note of bitterness in his voice. 'My brothers had left school early and got good jobs and were bringing in the money and it seemed as if I was getting above myself if went on to study instead of pulling my weight.

So I sort of slipped into the car showroom job. I watched the good salesmen and could see where the bad ones messed up. I knew I could do it…and I could. I can pick up the technicalities easily, the financial aspects are a doddle and I can sort of read people.'

'Yes, you can,' Kate agreed. 'I've noticed you do it all the time, almost instinctively. And not in a bad way so that you can exploit them. I think it's second nature to you because you care about people. Look at you with your family. You are totally in tune with them, especially with Reen.'

Blushing at her praise, he said, 'But you are too. It's great the way you two get on. It's really perked her up. She was on such a down after all the excitement of Tyrone's wedding.'

'Is that why you came out here? To cheer her up? Reen says you transferred to Spain soon after the wedding.' Kate kept her tone light, because Reen had also mentioned a girlfriend he seemed keen on but didn't invite.

There was a long silence. His hand tightened on the wheel as the miles and miles of vineyards slipped past them. He seemed to be thinking something through.

'I came here because I had to get away from someone,' he said eventually. 'Make a fresh start.'

Kate jumped. That was her mantra.

'Once again, Ma doesn't know this. None of them do. It's all because of a girl. I'm sorry, Kate, I want to be really honest with you. But I'm still in love with her and I'm trying so hard to get over her because I know I can never have her.'

Kate gasped. You too, she thought.

Chapter Forty-One

There was a brief silence while Troy manoeuvred the car round some tricky bends. They had started the winding ascent into the mountains. Rocky outcrops lined the road and, in the distance, Kate could see villages of higgledy-piggledly, white buildings clinging to the steep hillside.

'Would you believe she is called Tamsin so she would have fitted in so well…at least her name would.' He gave a strained laugh.

Kate could see the tension in his jaw line.

'You don't have to tell me if you don't want.'

'To be honest, Kate, I wasn't going to but you are such a sympathetic listener and I've got to tell someone. It's been eating away at me for months now and the tension is becoming too much.' He grimaced, 'But I'm aware that it's not the most tactful thing to talk about on a day out with a girl you really like. Is it?'

She put her hand on his arm. 'Come on, Troy. I like to think we are friends. If it will help, I want to hear what is so obviously bothering you.'

'OK.' He stared straight ahead, his voice gruff with emotion. 'Starting at the beginning, we met when I was setting up a big stand for a Porsche event at a posh hotel in London. I don't usually do the hands-on stuff like that but someone was off ill and I enjoy being practical so I pitched in. There I was in shirt sleeves and my old jeans just wrestling with a big backdrop thing when this girl saw me struggling and came to help. We had a laugh as we tussled with it and eventually got it in place. I fancied her right away. Lovely friendly face and big smiling hazel eyes. She had a posh accent but no airs or graces. She was wearing a plain white blouse and navy skirt and I thought she was part of the event organising team, which she was. We finished the stand together and I invited her to join me for a coffee but she said she had to go and get ready for the evening. And to be honest so did I.

'Next time I saw her she was all dressed up and she blew my breath away. A fantastic silver dress…I can see it now. And I was all tuxed up, the full dinner jacket and bow tie.'

'Ooh, like James Bond.' Kate shivered, imagining the stunning impression he must have made.

'That's funny, that's just what she said. Well to say we hit it off is putting it mildly. I can't remember much else about the evening but we tumbled into a taxi and went back to my place.

'And look, I don't usually do that. Not the first night. But we both couldn't keep our hands off each other and it was… well, magical between us. She stayed most of the next day and we talked and laughed and well…you know.'

'Yes. I know.' Images of a narrow student bed and thin curtains and a gorgeous man flooded through Kate's mind.

For the next half an hour he glowed as he talked about his time with Tamsin, a wonderful time of laughing and talking and sharing the cooking, of cosying up in front of films at home in his flat and living in a bubble of love.

'I had a holiday booked in Majorca. I'd always wanted to learn to scuba dive so had signed up to this training school. I offered to cancel but Tamsin wanted to come too, so I managed to get her a place as well. She offered to share the cost but I'm an old-fashioned fella and wouldn't hear of it.' There was a long pause. 'Anyway we had a wonderful time. The place was far from plush but it was a fun crowd and it was great just to be together all the time.

'It confirmed all my feelings for her so I asked her if she wanted to move in with me when we got back. She seemed delighted. I knew she was the one and I nearly proposed while we were there, but didn't want her to feel I was rushing her. I also wanted to get a nice ring so was waiting for my big quarterly commission to come in.'

His voice had become more strained over the last few minutes.

'I suppose it was going to have to happen sometime. Thank goodness it happened before I proposed. So far we had kept ourselves a bit secret because, on my part, she was so special I didn't want any of my mates to make ribald comments or for her to hear any of the crude banter that I know they are capable of. They all knew I was seeing someone, but not who. Anyway Tamsin popped into the showroom to see me one day after we'd got back from holiday. My mate Colin went over to her as she came in and presumed she wanted to buy a car. He could tell she had the money, just as I would have done in a different context. Anyway when he realised she was with me, his eyes popped. I thought it was because she was so gorgeous. But no. Once she'd gone, he said, "You jammy bugger. Landed on your feet there haven't you?"

'I didn't know what he meant so he proceeded to inform me that my Tamsin Fuller was in fact Tamsin Fuller-White, daughter of the millionaire property tycoon, Edward Fuller-White. She was well and truly loaded. Colin knew because he had sold her dad a Porsche as a surprise birthday present for her thirtieth birthday.'

His face had paled as he was talking and his knuckles shone white on the steering wheel.

'I felt sick.'

'Why was that so awful?' Kate asked.

'That's what she said when I tackled her about it that night. She admitted she had deliberately kept me in the dark when she realised I didn't know who she was and she had carefully kept us away from anywhere where she might be recognised. Hence all the cosy nights in and the down-beat holiday. I thought she worked as an event organiser but she just helps out one of her friends if she needs a hostess at a function. Most of the time she was just bored, which is why she loved being with me and doing, I suppose, "ordinary' stuff".'

His voice was suffused with suppressed emotion.

‘I was banjaxed. I’d been proud of what I’d done with my life. No help. Pulled myself up by my boot straps. Proud I’d got a nice little flat, proud I could afford to take her to places and pay for a holiday for us both. What a shock when I realised she was just slumming it.’

‘No,’ Kate blurted out, ‘she wasn’t.’

‘That’s what she said. She was really emotional and said I was the most real thing in her life. She said she loved me and wanted to be with me. Which of course is exactly what I wanted too, but it had all changed.’

‘Why?’

‘I’ve told you. I’m old fashioned. I want to be the provider.’

‘That is old fashioned. I thought you were more enlightened than that.’

‘So did I…till it came to the crunch. Don’t get me wrong. With a role model like Ma, I’m not against my wife working if she wants to…but I still need to feel I’m the breadwinner.’

‘You surely didn’t break up just because of that.’

‘Yes and no, not really. I still loved her and now I knew she definitely loved me, we talked it through. She kept saying she loved the real me, why couldn’t I love the real her.’

‘She had a point, didn’t she?’

He gave a wry grin. ‘Yes. She’s not daft. She knows how to get round me. But it definitely changed things although I really tried not to let it. She wanted me to meet her family, especially her dad. She said he was really down-to-earth. He’d come up the hard way and knew what it was to work your way up and he wasn’t half as rich as people made out. But I didn’t believe her. She’s been to a posh school, had posh friends. How could I meet her parents? They would have suspected I was a gold digger. And they would have definitely looked upon me as their daughter’s bit of rough. I can’t bear being patronised and I worried my hackles would rise and… Oh dear. I’m coming over all macho, aren’t I?’

She laughed. ‘You are a bit.’

‘I tried not to be. I feel awful. It’s all my fault not hers. She said I’d broken her heart. And I think I did.’

‘So you broke up just because you couldn’t bear to meet her father?’

‘No. I broke up because I couldn’t bear for him to meet Ma.’

‘What!’

‘I know. It was Tyrone’s wedding that did it. Ma loved it and was in her element at the reception doing the birdie dance and all sorts of silly stuff. I suddenly saw her leading the okey cokey across the dance floor, slightly tipsy with purple feathers all skew-whiff in her hair…and I couldn’t bear the thought that Tamsin’s folks would just sneer at her. I had a moment imagining what our wedding would be like… the total clash of cultures. Ma all loud and outgoing, covered in bling and feathers, and Tamsin’s side all uptight and condescending and sniggering at me and my family.’

He couldn’t go on. It was such a vivid picture in his mind. ‘I knew for certain at that moment, I couldn’t marry her.’

‘But her folks might love Reen. Most people do. She is a very loveable person.’

‘Bless you. That’s one of the things I like about you, you are so non-judgemental and so obviously like her. But you have to admit your first impressions of her were…?’

Kate blushed. Yes, she had been a bit taken aback when she first saw Reen and Ted at Cabopino. They were loud and flashy and…

He glanced across at her face. ‘Yup, thought so.’

‘But…’

‘No buts. I knew there couldn’t be a wedding.’

‘Couldn’t you just slip away and tie the knot quietly somewhere?’

He grunted. ‘And tell Ma we’d done it because I was ashamed of her meeting Tamsin’s folks. Really?’

Kate was silent.

‘And especially as Ma loves organising big occasions. I don’t know what she’ll do when she runs out of family weddings and christenings and stuff.’

He had clearly wrestled with this dilemma for a long time and sighed. ‘No. I was torn but I couldn’t see a way out. One day the families would have to meet. I've told you I'm old fashioned. I definitely want to get married, not just live together. And it wasn't fair to string Tamsin along. She had to have a chance to meet someone else. Someone from her own class. So when I got back from the wedding I finished with her, saying it just wouldn't work.'

There was a world of anguish in his voice.

'It was awful. She was devastated. I couldn't really tell her why. She accused me of inverted snobbery. I hated it. Couldn't bear to stay in London so asked for a transfer out here and...well, here I am.'

Chapter Forty-Two

Troy eased the car off a hairpin bend and into a strategically placed viewpoint. Clearly drained of all emotion, he sat gazing unseeingly out of the windscreen. He obviously needed some time to recover from his painful story.

Kate followed his gaze and gasped. Before them perched the ancient town of Ronda spanning a spectacular gorge and set high above the surrounding countryside.

Despite being engrossed in Troy's tale, she had been aware of the impressive scenery unfolding before them as they had wound their way into the rugged mountains. At intervals they had passed several of the famous Pueblos Blancos, whitewashed villages of houses, like cubes of sugar, spilling down the hillside. At one of them, an old castle perched on a bare outcrop of rock above the nestling jumble of houses below. As they drove higher there were numerous mirador viewpoints to look over the dramatic valleys below and in some of them she had spotted rustic wayside stalls selling strings of garlic, bright, fresh-picked oranges and a colourful array of fruit and vegetables.

Arriving at the ancient stone city of Ronda was just as stunning as Kate had hoped it would be. She could see the town was set around a wild, craggy, breath-takingly deep gorge. Spanning it was an old arched bridge uniting the two parts of the town, gleaming pale gold in the bright autumn sunshine.

She couldn't help herself from exclaiming, 'It's amazing.' Then, seeing Troy's still stricken face, she guiltily placed a consoling hand on his arm.

But it seemed to draw him out of his daze and, with a resigned shrug, he began to focus on what was in front of him.

'Wow. That's some view.' He was just as awestruck as she was.

Now tuned into his surroundings, he immediately apologised. 'I'm so sorry, Kate. I really didn't intend to tell you all that about Tamsin and me. I've said it before, I seem to be able to talk to you like no one else.' He gave a rueful grin, 'You really are too good a listener.'

Glancing at her, he grimaced. 'But I promise I won't bend your ear any more. The feelings are nowhere near as raw as they were and I'm becoming reconciled to the whole situation…although I must admit I'm not there yet. But I'm determined to put it behind me and I want us both to enjoy today. It looks a great place. Shall we go?'

'Yes, OK. But look, Troy, if you do want to talk some more…'

'Thanks, but I'd hate to bore you.'

'It's not boring, Troy, and if it's any help,' Kate paused, 'I'm no stranger to lost love…if you really do think you have lost her?'

'Oh yes,' he sighed.

'In that case, join the gang. Mine buggered off to Antarctica and then Australia. You couldn't get much further away if you tried.'

'Was he trying?'

'No, in fairness, I don't think he was. But he didn't love me enough to come back. Just like…well, someone else in my life who buggered off. But you are right. It's too nice a day to wallow in misery. Thanks for bringing me here. It looks like a great place to explore together.'

Troy started the car. 'I agree. I've booked lunch at the Parador which I've heard has the best view of the gorge and it means we can park there as well. Vamos. Si?'

Kate nodded and they set off, both determined to enjoy the day. And, in fact, they did.

There was an amiable companionship between the two of them as they chatted and wandered the labyrinth of narrow streets, visited the Mondragon Palace, played mock bullfights in the old Plaza de Torros and explored the House of the Moorish King with its secret passage down to the ravine. Troy was right; their lunch on the terrace of the Parador commanded the best views over the precipitous gorge. Although the weather up there was cooler, they were seated in a cosy sun trap so relished the food and the warmth. And afterwards, hand in hand, they happily poked around the little shops on the wide main street.

It was late afternoon when they finally got back to the car and began the journey home. Although there was a relaxed atmosphere as they twisted back down through the mountains, Kate could sense that Troy was curious about her previous remarks about her lost love. It hung in the air between them.

'I think you and me have a lot in common,' he began, 'especially when it comes to relationships.'

Clearly he was enticing her to reveal more but Kate paused, not sure where to begin.

Mistaking her hesitancy for reluctance, Troy immediately said, 'You don't have to tell me anything you don't want.'

'No, Troy. You have been totally honest with me and I want to be the same with you. It's only fair. Then we both know where we stand with each other.'

He nodded.

Halting at first, Kate began the story of how she had met Rob that beautiful hot summer which seemed so long ago it almost had a golden sepia haze about it. In recounting that wild week, she saw how young and inexperienced she was when they met. Was the reckless way she fell for him an unconscious rebellion against her upbringing? Right from the start she knew there was no future, but yet she still fell headlong into the most blissful week of her life. And there were no regrets. Looking back, she realised how much she had become the person she had always wanted to be. She had felt alive. She had felt free.

'It was fantastic, undoubtedly the best time of my life. But the trouble is, nothing else has matched up to it since. And I'm cross to think I have wasted all this time just waiting and hoping he would come back.'

'But he hasn't.'

'Oh yes, he did.' She tried to suppress the bitterness in her voice. 'Last summer. And all my stupid, damped-down longing came flooding back. I still felt the same...perhaps even more so because I had been yearning for him for so long. It was as if I had been holding my breath, waiting to live again. But of course, it was all no use. He had a girlfriend...a fit, athletic, successful girlfriend in Australia and I was stuck like a loser in a dead-end job with a rotten controlling boyfriend I hadn't the courage to kick out.'

Troy glanced over at her, 'I hope you don't mind, but Ma has told me about your awful boyfriend.'

'Yes, what a fool I was. But at least meeting Rob and seeing my life through his eyes made me pluck up the gumption to kick Chris out.'

Her voice broke as she recounted the painful events of that evening at Megan's. She was still haunted by that pitying look on Rob's face.

'I will probably never see him again in my life.' She couldn't hide the tremor in her voice.

Troy's glance told her how much he understood her distress. 'Looks like we both want a fresh start, don't we? How about we try to help each other? Do you think it might work?'

'Yes. I think I would like that.'

'But let's take it slowly.'

'I agree. Let's start as friends...'

'As very caring friends...'

'And let's be always honest with each other. If it's not working or...'

'Yes, I agree.'

'Promise?'

'Promise.'

They exchanged shy hopeful smiles. But the intimacy of the moment was broken by a sudden thought from Troy.

'But let's not tell Ma yet. Can you imagine...?'

Laughing, Kate could, so it was agreed.

The sun was just setting as they parked in front of her apartment. Escorting her to her door, Troy very tenderly bent down and kissed her. It was a tentative kiss. A sort of exploring what it felt like kiss. And Kate responded in the same way. It was gentle, almost hesitant. She felt no fireworks, no excitement, and she suspected Troy didn't either. But it was caring. There was almost a sigh of relief as they parted. They had got the first kiss over with and both felt good about it.

'Thank you for a really lovely day.'

'It was a pleasure, Kate. It really was. Thank you for listening and…everything.' He kissed her again more enthusiastically as if full of gratitude.

Chapter Forty-Three

Deep in thought about the happenings of the day, Kate poured herself a glass of crisp white wine and went to watch the sunset from her favourite spot on her terrace. As always, she was mesmerised as the sun, like a gold coin, sank swiftly below the horizon. It took barely five minutes before it disappeared completely, suffusing the clouds with glorious shades of rose gold and turning the pale turquoise sky a dusky pink.

So deep was her contemplation of the scene that the ringing of the phone startled her.

It was Megan. 'Ah, at last. I've been trying to catch you all day. Have you been out shopping again with Reen?'

'No. As it happens, I've just returned from a fantastic day with Troy to a wonderful place in the mountains.'

'Wow, you sound really happy. So Troy, eh? Tell all.'

So Kate did. Not only about what they did but about the deep conversations they had had.

'I promised I wouldn't tell anyone about what he actually said, but, in a nutshell, he's trying to recover from a relationship. In fact, he's honest enough to tell me he still loves her but it will never work out so he's trying desperately to move on. And as you can imagine, I could really empathise with that.'

There was a pause. 'So do you still love Rob?'

Kate was surprised at the bluntness of the question from her normally tactful friend.

'What's the point, Megan? I came out here to start afresh and get on with my life. No more waiting around, hoping for the impossible. And Troy feels the same. He really unburdened himself and I feel very honoured he could tell me things he hasn't told another soul. Not even his mum. I could tell he felt so much better and we really bonded over the same things.'

'So you told him about you and Rob, did you?'

'Yes. He was totally honest with me and so I was with him. In fact we have both promised to be open about everything, about our relationship…'

'Relationship?' Megan said sharply.

'Yes. We are going to go out with each other. Do things together but take things slowly. I really care about him and I know he feels the same about me.'

'You sound as if you are falling for him.'

'Well, it's not the mad heady passion I felt for Rob. He doesn't thrill me in the same way at all. But I was young then and he was my first love. You can't expect to feel the same ever again. This feels more companionable, I suppose. I just know I feel safe and protected when I'm with him. He's so caring. Sometimes he calls me Princess which might sound a bit cheesy, but it doesn't coming from him. I know he would never hurt me, emotionally or physically, which is important after Chris. And I know I couldn't bear to hurt him. So we are going to help each other heal and in time, who knows, we could learn to love each other.'

Another pause. 'As much as Rob?'

'Oh, who knows, Megan?' It really wasn't like her friend to probe in such an intrusive way. 'Look, I'm not sure he is Mr Right but I think he is Mr Nearly Right and I want to get to know him better. He's very intuitive with people and he picks up on moods and intentions really quickly. Although he's not book learned, he's very astute.'

'Do you quote poems at him?'

An almost physical pain sliced through Kate's heart as it brought back vivid memories of laughing with Rob. With an effort she pushed all these pictures back in their compartment and turned the key.

Almost angrily she replied, 'No, I don't quote with *anyone* now. Not even my students. That was the old, stupidly romantic me. I'm much more realistic now.'

There was silence on the end of the phone.

'Oh, Megan, I wish you hadn't reminded me of that. But you know I have had my fingers well and truly burnt by romance. I can't keep returning like a moth to a flame so I've decided to settle for a cosy glow.'

It sounded as if Megan was about to say something then changed her mind.

A bit unnerved, Kate laughed, 'Anyway I don't know why I'm telling you all about him. You'll be able to see for yourself when you come out for your visit next weekend. I'm dying for you to meet him and Reen and all my friends.'

'Oh sorry, Kate, that's what I phoned to tell you. I can't come after all.'

'What? Oh no. I was so looking forward to seeing you again. What's happened?'

'It's bloomin work. There's been some issues on…well, it's confidential, but something really nasty is happening on one of the estates and so we are bringing all the residents together for a big meeting on Saturday.'

'Does it have to be then?'

'Yes. We want to get the respectable working residents to come so we can get them on our side and try to put a stop to it.'

'Do *you* have to go?' Kate was desperately disappointed.

'Honestly yes. I'm a manager now, as you know, so I have to take a leading role. Believe me if I could get out of it, I would.'

'Oh, Megan,' Kate wailed. 'I so wanted to show you my place, the sunset and everything. I wanted you to see how much I've changed. The new me. I feel so different here, more colourful like a flower with my petals unfurling in the sun.'

'Yes, I believe you. I know you have changed. I can hear the confidence in your voice. And I wanted to meet all these people you have told me about. I'm as disappointed as you. I could do with some sun, but it's just not possible.'

Kate sighed.

'I'm so sorry, my lovely, but it's not long till Christmas

and you're back here in Brum. Then we can have a proper catch up on *all* the news.'

Why the stress on *all* the news? What was she holding back on? It was difficult to tell, but she knew her friend well enough to know something was going on. Was Megan pregnant? Is that why she wasn't coming?

Damping down her disappointment they chatted on. Kate wanted to probe further but knew there was no point. Megan would tell her in her own good time. She would just have to wait till they saw each other again at Christmas.

PART FOUR

Chapter Forty-Four

Christmas 2000

Christmas songs blared out over the arrivals gate at Birmingham airport. Kate knew it would be cold but was still shocked by the unexpected chill that greeted her as the main doors opened and she searched for Megan and Josh who were due to meet her.

It was just Megan who was standing there waving and she was so bundled up in a thick coat Kate couldn't tell if her pregnancy suspicions were true or not. Certainly Megan had been cagey about something in all her recent phone calls and she was just hoping it was something good.

Megan was beaming.

'Wow, Kate, my lovely, you look good. Really good. I love that new hairstyle and look at that golden tan. That cherry-red jacket is so right on you. I can't believe how vibrant you look. You even walk more confidently. You certainly brighten up this dull old airport.'

Kate laughed as she hugged her oldest and very best friend. She had deliberately put on her brightest clothes and was fresh from Tina's salon, all groomed up ready for Christmas. But Megan's frank approval was manna to her soul. She had intended to show how much she had changed…and she had done it.

'Thanks, Megan, I do feel good. What about you?'

'What?'

'How are you feeling?'

Megan gave her a strange look. 'Oh you know, the usual. Knackered, stressed and totally disillusioned about how much good I'm actually doing against the rising tide of problems in the world. But apart from that, I'm fine…and all the better for seeing you.'

'Where's Josh?'

'He's in the short term car park ready to drive off if he sees a warden. Come on. Let's get you home and warmed up.'

'How do you know I'm feeling the cold?'

'Apart from the fact you are shivering, you mean?'

'Oh blast. And I deliberately layered up so I wouldn't feel the cold. I'm determined not to moan about how cold, how dark and how grey everywhere is compared with the Costa.'

But it was.

The gaudy Christmas decorations adorning some houses were wonderful oases of colour on the drive back through the dark gloom of a December day in Birmingham.

But the conversation was cheerful enough.

Megan asked all about her College life, her apartment, her flamenco classes, her friends, Reen…but nothing about Troy. Not for the first time Kate got the distinct impression that there was something about Troy that Megan disapproved of. This had irked her for a while and was most unusual. Megan was the most tolerant person she knew, very non-judgemental about most people, always aware of how the past might have shaped bad behaviour. So why did she seem to object to Troy? She was determined to have it out with her when they were on their own.

Looking around her flat, it seemed smaller and darker somehow. Admittedly Megan had filled it full of stuff, box files piled against one wall and some of the furniture from her previous place had found its way from their storage facility into the lounge. She didn't say anything because she was sure that Megan had really tidied up for her visit. And anyway it was good to be back home. But was it home now? Or was Spain?

She just knew that, in spite of Reen's pleading for her to spend Christmas with the Taylor family, she wanted to get back to Brum.

As Megan peeled off her coat, Kate could see no

discernible bump but didn't know at precisely what stage a baby would start showing. But then when Megan opened a bottle of fizz to celebrate Kate's homecoming and downed her glass with gusto, she knew her suppositions couldn't be true. So what was it that was causing both Megan and Josh to be so guarded?

'First thing. Do you mind if I ring Troy to let him know I've arrived safely?'

'Don't you dare ask us about that, Kate? This is your flat remember?'

'Not at the moment, it's not. But let's not argue. You are both still at work so I'm going to muck in and help with Christmas planning and stuff. I've brought some Spanish food with me, and my hand luggage is full of duty-free booze.'

'Goody. When we've finished this,' Megan waved her glass in the air, 'we will start on yours. Off you go though. You know the lead from the phone will stretch into the bedroom so give him a ring…and take as long as you want.'

In fact it was a quick call but lovely to hear his friendly, concerned voice, and he promised to let Reen know she had arrived safely. They both ended by sending love to each other. Although they didn't live together, they spent much of their leisure time in each other's company and it was going to be strange to be apart for the two weeks over Christmas.

Sitting down to one of Josh's substantial lasagnes, Megan turned the conversation to Troy.

'So how are you two getting on then?'

'Really well. As I've told you, he's a lovely man. We've had some amazing trips to some wonderful places. I loved our visit to Seville. The Alhambra in Granada was incredible although blooming cold on the weekend we were there, which was good in a way as it kept the crowds down. But my favourite was Cordoba. It has an amazing Mezquita, a Moorish building with a large courtyard of orange trees in front of it. Inside there is a stunning vista of striped Arabic arches, rows and rows of them. Something about the simplicity of it, made me cry.'

What she didn't say was that it was also the first time they had shared a room and their first lovemaking. Not passionate but gentle and tender with both of them still tentatively exploring the relationship and each other.

As she related the details of the places they had been, Kate was slightly unnerved by the unspoken undercurrents that were greeting her account.

'So are you two an item now?' Megan enquired, almost too nonchalantly.

'Well, yes. We only usually see each other at weekends because we are both working and busy during the week. I still do my flamenco and gym sessions with the girls. I still have my Friday night meal round at Hrreremy's house where I practise my Spanish. So noisy and so much fun. But then I spend the rest of the weekend with the Taylors, either out on an excursion with Troy or out with Reen shopping in Marbella or going to Tina's salon for "a bit of beautification" as Reen calls it. Troy's a great dancer and we go clubbing then come back and stay Saturday night in Reen's "Gibraltar view" room.'

She sighed. 'I can't tell you how wonderful it is to belong to such a loving, if slightly bonkers, family. And Troy is just so caring and considerate...' She broke off from her eulogy because as she was talking, she noticed Josh kept his head down busying himself with his meal. And Megan too didn't seem to want to make eye contact.

Perplexed, Kate nevertheless ploughed on. 'Reen, of course, was over the moon when she twigged we were going out together. Flung herself at us both, hugging and weeping and tried to throw one of her big celebrations till Troy told her that by all means throw a party, but we wouldn't be coming.'

'Do you think you will end up in Spain then?'

'Too early to tell. Besides…' should she tell them about Troy wanting to change his job and come back to the UK to finalise his accountancy qualifications? No. That was private between them. No one else knew about his dreams. He was continuing to work at the showroom until he was ready to break it to his family. He needed time to adjust to giving up the security of his well-paid job for the great unknown of a new career. 'I definitely like living there but not sure about it as a permanent thing. I'm going to see how it feels to be back in Brum and, anyway, I don't have to decide till the summer.'

Josh and Megan exchanged glances. Was that it, Kate wondered? If she was going to stay in Spain, were they looking to buy her flat?

Josh got up to clear the table and fetch one of his legendary bread and butter puddings. It was delicious but the conversation became more and more strained. Megan was definitely drinking more than she used to so Kate knew something was preying on her mind.

Almost at a signal from Megan, Josh excused himself saying he really had to catch up with some work on his laptop and went into the main bedroom closing the door very firmly.

'OK, Megan, what's going on?'

'What do you mean?'

'Don't give me that. I've felt for weeks that there was something you weren't telling me. I thought perhaps you were pregnant.'

'Oh, God no. We haven't saved up enough for our deposit yet…although thanks to you we are getting there.'

'So what is it?'

'You're right. There is something I've been keeping from you for a while. Honestly, I've not known what to do, whether to tell you or not.'

'For God's sake, Megan…'

'OK. Here goes. Rob's back.'

'What?'

'He's back here in the UK, in fact in Brum for good.'

Kate felt all the breath leave her body. In a daze she heard Megan explain.

'For all sorts of reasons, he decided to come back to Brum. While he was here in the summer, he heard that his old Prof was trying to get more funding for a research lectureship. It's in his field of expertise so when he heard a post had been approved, he applied. To cut a long story short, he came back a week ago at the start of the long Oz Christmas break. He's been staying here with us till yesterday then he's gone off to Worcester for Christmas with his family.'

Kate still couldn't speak. She could barely breathe.

Megan carried on in a rush as if a dam had burst.

'I've been agonising over when to tell you. I didn't want to upset your relationship with Troy so thought I'd wait till I saw you.'

'Why has he come back?'

The embers of hope had flared into a flame. Had he, could he have possibly come back to see her? But then she remembered the pathetic creature she had been when she last saw him. The flames were swiftly doused. Why would he come back for someone like that?

'As I say, all sorts of reasons but you must ask him yourself.'

'What? Is he coming here?' Panic swept over her and she collapsed on to the settee.

'Not if you don't want him to. But he would rather like to see you. He's asked all about your life in Spain and I've told him everything about how well you are doing with your job and the flamenco and everything.'

Kate automatically straightened her posture at the mention of flamenco. Could her new, assertive self cope with seeing him again?

'He would love to meet you but only if you want. He knows you are a different person, more confident. I haven't told him anything about Troy. That's up to you.'

Megan looked distraught. 'Oh, Kate, my lovely, I've been so torn as to what to do. You know I don't believe in interfering in people's lives unless they ask me too. It's been churning me up for weeks. Please don't be cross.'

'So that's it. I've known there was something. Is that why you didn't come out for that weekend?'

'No, genuinely there was a crisis here, but afterwards I thought it was just as well. You'd have picked up on something and I would have had to tell you and I knew you were trying to make a go of it with Troy.'

'Is that why you've always sounded a bit disapproving of him.'

'Believe me, I'm not. I suppose I was just testing to see what you really felt about him.'

Kate was still stunned. 'I picked up with Troy as part of my fresh start because I thought Rob was out of my life *forever*. I assumed I would never *ever* see him again in my whole life. And I'd almost come to terms with it and was making a real go of my new life.' Putting her head into her hands, she wailed. 'I can't believe it. I simply can't take in that he's here now.'

'I know.'

'Oh, Megan, I've moved on so much in the last three months. I feel a different person from that pathetic creature in the summer. Half of me thinks I should meet him, if only to show him what a changed person I am. But what happens if I haven't got over him completely? I can't hurt Troy, not as we are just feeling so good together.'

Her thoughts whirled about her head.

'Oh, Megan, what am I going to do?'

'You are going to go to bed now and sleep on it. No big decisions tonight. You will know what's right eventually. I know the new you is strong enough to come up with the right solution. I'm just so relieved to have told you at last.'

Chapter Forty-Five

It was all very well Megan saying sleep on it. How could she? So many conflicting emotions swirled through her head all night.

First, she was angry. How could he wait till now to come back? Just as she had reconciled herself to a new life without him. How dare he swan back and disrupt her settled future. She had made a really successful fresh start and now all her feelings were in turmoil again.

Then doubts assailed her. What made her think he had come back for her? Megan had said there were many reasons for his return. Was she one of them? Of course not. Perhaps he and Leanne had broken up. Or, much more likely, she was going to join him once he was settled. Perhaps he wanted a more promising career. Perhaps he had missed his family or was his mum ill again?

How stupid to think she figured in his decisions at all, especially as the last time he'd seen her she was such a pathetic creature he couldn't possibly want to meet her again. Had he returned because he knew she was safely in Spain so he could make his own fresh start without her bothering him?

And yet, Megan said he wanted to meet her. What was she to think of that? How could she see him knowing it might arouse all her dormant feelings? Or should she go as the new her and show him she didn't need his pity anymore?

Just as she had made up her mind on one course of action, the next minute she totally changed her mind. All night long, the reasons for and against seeing him tumbled through her exhausted brain.

In the end she knew she would have to meet him, otherwise he would be an itch she couldn't scratch. He was best friends with Josh and Megan, just as she was, so they would be bound to meet up sooner or later. This way she could get it over with…and on her terms.

She began psyching herself up for their encounter. If she was prepared, she was sure she could handle it. Although she acknowledged his attraction, there was no way she was going to fall at his feet in a lovelorn mess. He could let her down again. She had made a perfectly good life without him, so she mustn't rely on his impetuous impulses. Although Megan said he was back for good, he seemed to have a wanderlust soul. So what would happen if he upped sticks again back to Australia, or even further afield? How foolish to abandon everything she had achieved over the last few months and tie her future to such a wayward star.

And then there was Troy. The thought of hurting him made her feel ill. She cared for him so deeply. Theirs was a new and fragile relationship but it was built on trust and honesty and a deep consideration for each other. She was not going to jeopardise it now for Rob. Yes, their youthful affair had been fun and passionate and wonderful, but it had also been brief and a long time ago. Perhaps she had invested too much significance into it. Had it assumed a romantic glow that threatened to overshadow the rest of her life and spoil a wonderful *real* relationship with a very decent man?

Eventually she slept and awoke next morning, still troubled, but resolute.

Over breakfast she told Megan of her decision.

'Thank you for telling me about Rob. And I can understand why you were anxious about it. But don't worry, I'm not going to make a fool of myself over him anymore. I have decided to meet him, on my own, if you don't mind. He's a friend after all. It will be good to catch up with his doings and I'll tell him about mine so he can see how much I have moved on.'

Her friend gave her a searching look.

'OK, Megan, I confess I will always have a fondness for him and our week together was special, but I'm not risking what I've got now for anything.' She paused, 'I thought perhaps I'd suggest a meal tonight somewhere in town. I know it's a bit rude the first night here…'

'No, do whatever you want. In fact if you want us to make ourselves scarce and ask him round here…'

'No,' Kate said firmly. 'No. I want to meet somewhere neither of us has been before. Neutral ground. There was that new place opening in the summer round near the canal basin. Is it any good?'

'Oh yes, the French Bistro. We haven't been but we've heard good things. Could be a bit busy on a Saturday night.'

'I'll book an early table. If Rob has got to get back to Worcester, he won't want to be too late. I'll ring him now so we can sort things out.'

Megan nodded, seeming to admire her calm composure.

But in fact Kate had to walk up and down a few times to dispel her nerves before she finally dialled Rob's number.

A Scottish voice answered. His dad?

'Is Rob there? It's Kate.'

'Oh hallo, Kate.' The voice answered as if he knew her. Then shouted above the background sounds of a large family at breakfast.

'Rob. It's Kate for you.'

A rather flustered Rob answered.

'Hi, Kate. I was hoping you would ring. You got in all right from Spain?' He sounded so delighted to hear from her that she found she was all of a tremble.

'Yes, thank you. I arrived last night.'

'You must be feeling the cold.'

'Yes, it is a little chilly,' she agreed, trying to keep her voice steady.

There was a pause, then they both rushed to say something at the same time.

'Sorry, after you,' he protested.

'No, no, you first,' she urged, suddenly unsure of how he would interpret an invitation out to dinner.

He laughed, 'I was just going to say I would love to see you again. When are you free?'

‘Well, Megan and Josh are out tonight,’ she lied, ‘dinner with friends. So I’m free this evening if that’s convenient.’

‘That sounds great. Anywhere you fancy meeting?’

She suggested the new French place by the waterfront.

‘Brilliant. I’ll book it. What time?’

‘Early so you can get back to Worcester.’ She wanted him to have no preconceptions of accompanying her home.

He offered to pick her up but she refused. She wanted to get there before him so she was in command of the place, and herself.

He began to chat asking her about her time in Spain but she cut it short by saying she was off out now with Megan. He seemed a bit bemused by her business-like tone, but the warmth in his voice was beginning to undermine her resolve.

She had just about managed on the phone but would she be able to be quite so cool when she actually met him face to face?

Chapter Forty-Six

Alone in the Bistro's elegant ladies' loos, Kate surveyed herself in the mirror. Apart from slightly flushed cheeks, she looked good. Her light tan seemed to accentuate her green eyes and the bright overhead light brought out the copper tones in her sleekly-cut chestnut hair. Yes, she felt sure Rob would definitely notice a difference in her appearance, especially after the miserable figure she cut last summer.

Turning to the full-length mirror, she inspected her clothes. It had been a difficult choice but, in the end, she had decided to be striking, no more drab colours for her. She was out to wow him. He *had* to see how much she had changed. Her cherry-red jacket had a matador cut which showed off her slim waist and neat hips. All that exercise in Spain had toned her figure, as had the dancing. She unconsciously straightened into her flamenco pose. Yes, that was good. It made her look aloof, composed and confident. If only she could maintain that poise when she actually met him.

She had arrived at the restaurant deliberately early so she would have time to calm herself before she saw him. Her nerves had fluttered all day and it had taken every ounce of concentration to chat normally to Megan while out shopping in a busy Christmas-thronged Birmingham. She was looking for something to take back to Reen and family as the Costa shops, to her surprise, didn't really gear up much for the festive season. It had been a real culture shock coming back. She hadn't realised how relaxed her pace of life had become in such a short space of time.

Megan was delighted about her impending evening with Rob but Kate didn't want to discuss it. Quite frankly she didn't know what to think about his return and how she would feel when she saw him again. The overriding point to meeting him was to wipe out his image of the pitiful wimp she had been in the summer. Her plan was to be friendly, but no more than that.

With a last reassuring look in the mirror, she squared her shoulders and stepped decisively out into the busy restaurant. Her plan was to be seated and calmly perusing the menu when he arrived. But she became aware that her entrance had caused a stir and she noticed several heads turn in what seemed like admiration. Adopting her poised flamenco posture, she gazed coolly around looking for her table.

To her annoyance, Rob was already seated there looking through the menu. There was the familiar rugged face, the smiling mouth, the slightly tousled dark hair. His leanly muscled body exuded energy, just as it always had, as his tanned fingers tapped an unconscious rhythm on the white tablecloth. Instantly her heart flipped as she felt a dizzying current of desire race through her body.

Angered by this intense physical response to him, she waited a few seconds to take a few deep calming breaths before she walked slowly and coolly to the table.

He looked up and she saw his tawny eyes widen in awe-struck wonder. Then such a joyful grin split his face, despite her resolve, she spontaneously smiled back.

Scrambling to his feet, he just gazed at her as if mesmerised.

'Wow, you look stunning.' He gasped, then opened his arms wide to give her a hug.

Suddenly shy, she held back a little, blushing, and they somehow executed a strange sort of mismatched dance as he went in for a kiss and she turned her cheek towards him.

Seemingly unfazed by the awkwardness of the greeting, he gazed at her for a long lingering enthralled moment before pulling out her chair.

'You look amazing. I just love that outfit. It makes you look so striking, so Spanish.'

'Thank you.' Although she had hoped to wow him, this obvious admiration overwhelmed her.

His gaze never left her face, as if he was drinking her in.

Unable to meet his eyes any longer, she looked down and murmured, 'I suppose it's the flamenco.'

He blinked and gave one of those quirky lopsided grins she knew so well, setting her heart hammering once again.

'Ah yes. Megan said you were taking classes. I bet that's fun.'

'Yes, it's great.' For a mad moment she was tempted to lift her arms in a sinuous dance move and click her fingers in the air. But of course not. Twirly girl was no more. Straightening her shoulders helped her find her poise. She could do this. She could be composed and cool.

'Well, whatever it is you are doing, it certainly suits you. You look awesome. Like the old you, only more assured.'

He continued to gaze at her full of wonder and another indefinable emotion that set her heart all a flutter. As pleasurable as it was, his frank approval was really testing her resilience to the limits. She must somehow resist falling for him all over again.

The waiter approached to ask for their drink order.

'Do you fancy an aperitif?'

'Oh yes, please. Can I have a Margarita?'

She needed a drink but noticing Rob's surprise, she realised that her favourite Reen-sharing tipple was perhaps a bit too much for this occasion.

'Or perhaps I'll just have a glass of wine.' She instantly adjusted her order, knowing she would need her wits about her.

'OK. There doesn't seem to be any Spanish wine so how about a nice bottle of French red? Can I have this Merlot, please?'

The waiter nodded and departed.

'Rob, are you sure about a whole bottle? If you are driving…'

'Don't worry. I deliberately came by train so I could enjoy myself. I can't tell you how much I've been looking forward to seeing you again.' His dark eyes shone with pleasure.

It was so difficult to stay cool in the face of his clear

delight in meeting up again. But cool she must be and, as soon as she could, she must tell him about Troy.

Picking up the glossy black menu, Rob suggested, 'Shall we choose our food before we launch into all our news?'

'Good idea.' In fact, she was hungry, having been too on edge to eat much all day.

He grinned, 'Like old times, looking at a menu with you.' With a jolt she knew he was talking of their very first meal together all those years ago. He remembered…as did she.

With a glowing face she pretended to immerse herself in the list of dishes. Keeping cool was proving so much harder than she expected.

Chapter Forty-Seven

Food ordered they sat back. Rob clinked glasses and winked at her.

'Right, you first,' Kate said taking a hefty slug of rich fruity wine. It gave her the courage to launch right in. 'Tell me why you came back.'

'I'd rather hear about your life now.'

'Not a chance,' she said. 'I'm just back from Spain for Christmas. Not back from the other side of the world for…is it for good?'

'Yes, it is.'

'That's pretty radical. In the summer you seemed pretty settled out there.' She tried to keep her voice neutral despite a traitorous flare of hope.

'Yes, I was, but coming back here profoundly unsettled me…in every way.' He leant forward, 'I realised how much I cared about...everyone back here.'

He paused as if he was going to say more but then continued. 'Knowing Mum was going to be OK reassured me, but I didn't want to be so far away from her anymore. What would have happened if I hadn't found out about her cancer or things had gone wrong? It really unnerved me.

'Sounds soppy I know, but I began to realise how much I'd missed my family. I stayed with both my sisters for a while and saw how out of touch I was with their lives. So while I was here, I really got to know their husbands, both great blokes. We went out for long blustery walks in the countryside with the kids and I realised how much I feel at home here. And look,' he waved his hand round the busy restaurant, 'Birmingham is now a vibrant, multi-cultural city. I can tell it's going places. As stupid as it sounds, it all seemed much more real than the life I had been living down under.'

He ran his hands through his hair as if trying to find the words he needed.

'I felt really alive over here. More alert. More in touch with the mainstream of things, with world news and events. Josh had told me all about the research he was doing and I wanted to be part of it. In comparison, my life in Adelaide seemed so insular and disconnected from the real world…a bit on the periphery of things.'

He shook his head. It had clearly been a turning point in his life. She suddenly realised, it was happening again. He was confiding in her. It was like all those years ago when they had talked and revealed their deepest feelings to one another. The companionship, the trust was still there. Whatever else, there was still a strong bond between them.

She nodded as he continued. 'Going back made me really restless all over again. But it was different from when I was younger. Then I was restless to get out there and see the world. And now I was restless because I felt sluggish, as if I'd settled for a backwater instead of staying out there and grasping real life by the throat.

'I did some deep thinking. I felt that with Oz and my time in the Antarctic, I had had my fill of remoteness and great vistas. Because, ironically, each time I was actually living in small claustrophobic communities.

'I suppose what got to me in the end, and it's difficult to admit it, but I think I was suffering from homesickness.' He gave an embarrassed laugh. 'I couldn't believe it. Whoever would have thought that I, of all people, would be feeling that?'

He seemed surprised by the power of these tumultuous emotions.

'I think when it comes down to it it's all about belonging. You have to feel you belong somewhere, don't you?'

He looked at Kate who gave a slow nod of recognition.

That need to belong had struck a chord. She thought about the word *belonging*. Longing to be. Longing to be in a certain place. Longing to be *with* a certain person. Perhaps even longing to *be* a certain person. She who was only just learning to belong in her own skin and shake off the constraining influences of her childhood, knew how powerful longing could be. There was a world of wistfulness in the word that went deep into her soul.

Rob suddenly shrugged. 'So here I am. Done my wandering and adventuring. Still not sure I've done the right thing but I feel like I've come home. I want to get on with real life…put down proper roots.'

Here he gave Kate such an intense look, she was forced to look away. He surely couldn't mean…?

No. She couldn't, wouldn't go there again. She wasn't going to hope for something intangible, impossible, not when she had caring, loyal Troy and his warm loving family waiting for her back in Spain. She couldn't betray his trust, couldn't hurt him. Rob had made no mention of his girlfriend. For all she knew it could be Leanne he wanted to put down roots with. Even now Leanne could be flying out to be with him ready to set up their life together in England.

Their starters arrived and as they tucked in, Rob continued in a lighter frame of mind.

'I was in touch with Josh and he told me about this post in his department coming up at Christmas. It was just too good to be true. He was really keen for me to apply so we could work together.'

Leaning back in his seat, a fleeting look of anguish passed over his face. He took a big gulp of wine. 'The crunch came when I talked it over with Leanne. She just couldn't understand it. There I was, surrounded by beautiful scenery, close by the sea, mountains in the background and yet I felt a yearning to come back to scruffy old Brum. But she knew this was a dream job, a really top-notch post in my field, so we sort of agreed I would apply, and if I got it, I would come back to the UK…and if not… We didn't really say anything, but there was a feeling that if I didn't get it, I would do the sensible thing and settle down out there.

'Deep down, I knew I didn't want to do that. Out there

was *her* life, *her* friends, *her* family. She had never even met mine and didn't show much desire to do so. As you can imagine, I was really keeping my fingers crossed. To my surprise, my old professor remembered me and, I don't quite know how… luck I suppose, I got the job, and here I am.'

How modest of him to think it was down to luck, Kate thought, and remembered that back in the old days, for all his reputed brilliance he had always genuinely discounted the idea that he was especially bright.

Not for the first time, she wished she understood precisely what he did.

'It was a bit fraught between Leanne and me after I got the post. But, in the end, she didn't want to uproot and come over here away from her family and friends. Awful thing to say, but I was really quite relieved. But also quite guilty because she was lovely and we had a nice life but…'

Here he paused as if unable to express his feelings quite as he would have liked.

They finished eating in silence. Much unsaid.

The waiter cleared their plates.

Rob leant back. 'So now I've got to find somewhere to live. I stayed at your place for a while with Megan and Josh. But I really must start looking. After all it's a bit embarrassing for a thirty-year-old man to say he's back at home living with his parents. The university has offered me some graduate accommodation but I said no. I remember those narrow student beds all too well, don't you?'

He shot her a teasing look and to her great annoyance Kate felt her colour instantly rise.

She looked away, bracing herself from falling under his spell again. OK, there was no girlfriend anymore. But he mustn't think he could instantly replace her with a Kate. Would she just be a stop-gap till he found someone else? Like a comfortable old slipper to put on for a while before he ventured into pastures new?

He might be free now, but she was not. Troy didn't light her fire in the way Rob did, but he was a good, honest, dependable man. They had made a pact not to hurt each other and she for one intended to abide by it.

In spite of any of her feelings for Rob, she wouldn't, couldn't let them overwhelm her again. She had been hurt too much in the past by people she loved deserting her. It hadn't just been Rob. She simply daren't venture there again. The old adage better safe than sorry sprang to mind.

Yes, she had to admit there was definitely a frisson of mutual attraction between them, but nothing more. Nothing permanent. In the end Rob was just an old friend and it was good to enjoy each other's company and catch up with each other's lives. But that was all.

Just friends. Just friends. She must fight any other feelings.

Chapter Forty-Eight

Rob was looking at her quizzically.

'Even though you look super sophisticated now, I take it the old Kate is still lurking in there somewhere?'

His eyes glinted with amusement.

'Um, yes,' Kate was puzzled by what had prompted this remark.

'Good. So I will definitely ask for the dessert menu then?'

'Oh yes,' she laughed. 'Still a pudding woman.'

'So pleased to hear it. I still can't get over how amazing you look now. Ah, I suppose that implies you didn't before… no, what I meant to say…'

She blushed, 'You mean from that sad wimp you saw in the summer?'

'No, not at all,' he stammered. Clearly he hadn't meant to conjure up that image. 'I didn't mean that. Although obviously, I'm glad you are no longer in that situation.'

'No. That was a low point in my life and I don't ever intend going back there again,' she said, tight-lipped.

He put his hand over hers. 'I'm so glad you got out of that. It took guts to give up everything and start a new life abroad.'

She trembled at the intimacy of the moment. The familiar feel of his hand on hers awoke a maelstrom of emotions. For a moment they just gazed at each other. She felt the years roll away and they were sitting in that pub on the side of Clent before they climbed up the hill to their amazing tryst in the moonlight. Nothing in her life had been as wonderful since. Rob seemed to be just as transfixed as she was. Was he remembering it too?

'Would you like to see the dessert menu?' came a voice from far away.

Jolted back to the present, Kate hastily removed her hand and nodded as the waiter handed her the extensive list of dishes.

Perusing the options, Rob waggled his eyebrows suggestively. 'No playfully stabbed banana, I note,' he whispered.

So he *had* been thinking about their first meeting too.

'And do you still recite poetry at the drop of a hat?'

'No. Not anymore. It was just a silly fad. I'm all grown up now. All my foolish romantic notions are long gone.'

He looked shocked at the note of bitterness in her voice. 'That's such a shame. I loved all your poems. Whenever I think of you, you are twirling and versifying.' His brown eyes twinkled.

This was getting too dangerous. She really must tell him about Troy as soon as possible.

Picking up the menu, he asked, 'So what do you fancy? Not a boring Crème Brûlée I hope. How's about a sticky toffee pudding?'

'OK, you have talked me into it, although I really am quite full.' She felt the tight waistband of her slim red trousers. 'Sticky toffee is not a pud you meet on many Spanish menus.'

'Megan says you have made some good friends out there?' Rob said.

What a perfect opening to bring in Troy. So, in amongst telling him about Hrreremy's family, and her flamenco friends, she recounted her first meeting with Reen's family and how all their names began with T and how she saved 'the buggy' in Cabopino.

'Reen is a fabulous one-off. She thinks she owes me but in fact I owe her so much more. She has brought me kicking and screaming out of my shell, enticing me into these colourful clothes. She is an amazing mix of toughness and vulnerability, of fun and common sense. And she says the most hilarious things without realising it, such as flamingo instead of flamenco. Talking of which, her garden is full of pink plastic flamingos peering out of bushes and standing guard round the huge Greek columned barbeque.'

Unable to suppress her giggles, she told Rob all about the gaudy riot that was Tedreen Villa.

'It sounds amazing.'

'It's totally flamboyant and outrageous and I love it.'

'It sounds as if you love her.'

'Oh, I do. I think she still can't believe she's somewhere so warm, so bright, so colourful. She is so proud of the fact you can see Gibraltar from the guest room, she always points it out. We tease her about it. But me and Troy do worry about how much she drinks. We wish we could think of something for her to do. She has so much energy and business acumen and no outlet for it.'

'Troy?'

Here it comes. She took a deep breath and tried to appear casual.

'Yes, I told you, Troy is her youngest son. We've been going out for a while now.'

'Oh.' Rob looked stunned. There was a long pause 'So… um, what's he like?'

'He's a good man. Very protective of me and his family. We get on so well together. It's a really honest, caring relationship. Nothing like Chris. Troy actively encouraged me to come home for the holidays. He knows it's important for me to keep in touch with my friends. In Spain they don't make as much fuss about Christmas and he only gets a couple of days off from work.' She laughed. 'Reen desperately wanted me to stay with her but my liver couldn't take the booze.'

Their puds arrived.

'What does he do?' Rob hadn't looked her in the eye once since she mentioned Troy. She was torn between hope that he still carried a torch for her and a stirring of anger that he thought he could waltz back in again after all these years and she would be patiently waiting for him.

'He sells Porsches…the posh cars.'

Rob looked surprised.

'And he's very good at it. Everybody likes him. He's very

charming…but with me he's very real.'

She wasn't going to reveal how much Troy hated his job. That was private between them. She respected the fact that, unlike Rob, Troy hadn't had the advantages of middle-class parents and a university education which gave you so many choices. She suddenly felt very protective of him slogging away at an unloved job till he could save up the money to change his career.

'So you really like him…I mean you…' Rob tailed off not sure of what to say. He still looked stunned.

'Yes, obviously I do. It's still early days. We are taking it slowly but we do spend our weekends together.' She wanted him to know that. 'And of course I love being part of his family. Reen is absolutely delighted.'

What else was there to say? Looking down, she carefully scooped up the last remains of her pud, although it had tasted cloyingly sweet in her mouth.

There was an uncomfortable silence for a while as Rob toyed with his dessert. He seemed totally thrown by her revelation. Then, as if coming to terms with the situation, he grabbed her hand. 'I'm so glad you have found someone who really appreciates you, Kate. You are a special person and deserve the best. He sounds like a good bloke and it seems you have a great life out there.'

'Thank you, Rob. I do enjoy it.'

'So you probably won't be coming back here to live.'

'Who knows? It's only a one-year contract and I still have my flat here. I'm just enjoying life at the moment and seeing what happens.'

Despite the slight frown between his eyes, he nodded.

Suddenly they both shivered in a blast of cold air as a crowd of people entered.

'Great to be back, huh, but bloomin cold,' Rob commented and they spent the rest of the evening in friendly, carefully inconsequential chatter about the contrasting weathers of Spain, Australia and Birmingham.

Leaving the restaurant, Rob called for a taxi for her as he set off to the station.

'It's been great seeing you again, Kate.' He hugged her briefly and kissed her cheek. 'We must catch up again.'

Despite an urge to linger in his embrace, Kate steeled herself to say casually, 'Well, I'm back at Easter so I'll see you then if you like.'

'Yes, that would be great.' He opened the cab door for her.

'See you at Easter,' he called as the taxi drove off.

PART FIVE

Chapter Forty-Nine

Easter 2001

This was stupid. What on earth had impelled her to drive all this way from Birmingham to Lancaster hospital on the vague chance she might be allowed to see him.

She wasn't a member of Rob's family so the nurse rightly refused to give her any more news over the phone other than his condition was stable.

They probably wouldn't tell her any more face to face, but she had to try.

Back home for Easter, from the moment Megan had phoned to tell her of Rob's climbing accident and subsequent coma she knew she had to drive up to be near him. She simply couldn't just sit there in an agony of worry, she had to do something. Anything, no matter how futile.

So she had packed a quick bag, left a note for Megan, got in her car and set off on the long drive up north.

Concentrating on driving gave her something to do. And as she neared the Lake District, she recognised the familiar outlines of the mountains of her youth. So many memories were stirred up. What would Ma think of her impetuosity? As a child she had been schooled in restraint and prudence and careful suppression of rash impulses. So why was she ignoring common sense and dashing up north to see him?

Was it the same raw need she had felt the first time she had met him? She had known then that he was the one. Now the same reckless instincts that had led to her making love to him on that long-ago hillside, had overwhelmed her again. What was it about him that made her so foolhardy? Was it intuition? Instinct? Or something deeper?

As Megan told her about Rob's accident, she knew she

couldn't just wait around for news. She had to *do* something. Even if it was only to drive all the way up to Lancaster and back down again.

What precisely had happened wasn't clear, as Megan had got it all second-hand from Josh. It seemed that Rob had been leading a University climbing party up to the top of Helvellyn, when one of the girls in the party had stumbled. Somehow, in trying to help her, Rob had fallen over a ridge. He had landed with a bone-crushing jolt on a small inaccessible ledge. To everyone's consternation he didn't move. Indeed he had remained unconscious throughout the mountain rescue by helicopter and the flight to the specialist unit in Lancaster hospital. His family had been alerted and they had been keeping a vigil by his bed. But, to their increasing alarm, he still hadn't regained consciousness.

Arriving at the busy hospital, Kate shivered as she got out of the car. The sleety cold rain caused her to hunch down even further into her unsuitably light jacket. All through the long drive she had tried not to think of the worst, but now faced with actually walking into the hospital, her nerve failed her. What right had she to be there? She could only claim to be a close friend. What on earth made her think that the nursing staff would let her in to visit a seriously ill patient? He could even be in the life support unit and there they definitely would not want odd bods littering the place up.

How would she explain just turning up? Could she say she was just fulfilling a promise? After all, their last words at Christmas were that they would see each other again at Easter. So here she was.

But there was a chance, and she just had to grab it. If rejected…well she hadn't thought that through yet.

But it was so cold standing there under the hospital portico that, apprehensively, she went in, her thin emerald green jacket attracting curious glances from the warmly clad locals.

Procrastinating, she warmed up over a steaming cup of coffee in the hospital café giving herself a pep talk in the process. Thus emboldened, she enquired at the main desk about Rob Frazier and, after the receptionist had consulted the computer, she was directed along endless shiny antiseptic corridors. With deepening anxiety, she followed the numerous signs till she arrived at the nurses' station of the Intensive Care Unit.

Once again, taking a deep breath, she enquired about Rob Frazier.

No, she wasn't a member of the family, just a friend. And of course, no, she would not be allowed in to visit him. A frosty nurse told her his family had given strict instructions he wasn't to be bothered by any young women.

Puzzled by this specific instruction and totally deflated, it took her a little while to recover enough to ask how he was. No change she was told. And then the nurse bustled off back through the closed doors to the ward.

Kate just stood there fighting back the tears. This was so stupid. She could have guessed this would happen. Would she ever grow up? No, she had let her silly romantic notions rule her life again. She really was a cock-eyed optimist. Buoyed along by her Florence Nightingale visions of sitting by his bed, mopping his fevered brow until he awoke with a smile to her caring, tear-stained face, she had rushed to this frozen place without anywhere to stay and any thoughts of what she would do if she couldn't see him.

She realised with a jolt, real life wasn't like that.

In *real* life, Rob was probably wired up to so many machines you couldn't get near enough to him to hold his hand.

In *rea*l life he was probably brain damaged so wouldn't recognise her even if she were at his bedside.

In *rea*l life she knew she hated hospitals because of long suppressed memories of that smell, that sense of foreboding.

In *real* life, hospitals are where people died, like Pa, and then, heart-breakingly, Ma, leaving her with no family at all.

In *real* life she should give up dreaming right now and face a future knowing she would never see Rob again. Or her mum.

In *real* life, of course, there were no happy ever afters.

Thoroughly distressed by this cold blast of awareness, she

began to search wildly in her pocket for a tissue to wipe her streaming eyes.

'Excuse me, are you the person who was asking after Rob?'

Kate was blowing her nose so fiercely it took a while for her to understand the question from the tired looking woman who had appeared at her side.

'Are you all right?'

'Um…oh yes…and yes. It was me asking after Rob.'

'I thought so. I'm his mum.'

One look into the warm, hazel eyes of the tall, grey-haired figure in front of her and Kate could see the family resemblance.

'Of course you are,' Kate said simply. She felt she knew her already from all Rob had told her.

His mum's eyes were red-rimmed and she looked so exhausted and anxious, that Kate instinctively reached out and hugged her.

It took the look of amazement on her face for Kate to realise that his mum had no idea who this strange emotional girl was.

'Oh, sorry. I'm Kate…Kate Caswell…'

'Of course you are,' said Rob's mum before Kate could explain any further.

'You know about me?'

'Of course I do. You're the girl who went off to Spain to teach in a College. Have you come all the way from Spain to see him?' His mum looked astonished.

'No, I was back in Brum for Easter…we had arranged to meet up…and I heard about his fall so…well…I drove up here…' Kate suppressed a sob, '…but they won't let me see him.'

'Well, we can soon fix that, but they are giving him a bed bath right now which is why I've been sent out. Should we go and have a cuppa together? You look as if you need one nearly as much as me.'

And she put her arm round Kate to steer her expertly down the labyrinthine corridors to the welcome cup of English tea.

Chapter Fifty

Settled at the yellow Formica table, his mum filled her in. Rob was not at death's door. But he was still unconscious, and the longer it went on, the more worrying it became. His mum, 'call me Hazel', had shooed the rest of the family away to get on with jobs and family life.

'We were all just hanging around upsetting each other and there wasn't a lot anyone could do. In fact there's not a lot I can do either but I want to be here, holding his hand and talking to him. The doctors don't know if it makes any difference but I believe he knows I'm there.'

Kate nodded her head vigorously. 'I'm sure you are right. That's why I had to come. Just to be here if he needs me, although I know I've no right to be here really...after all, well...I don't suppose he would expect me to be here. I'm not that important in his life after all…um… She struggled for words under the curious gaze of his mum. 'It's not as if we are…well…in a relationship or anything. We've only known each other on and off since University,' she rushed on, the words tumbling out, 'and obviously there are a lot more important people in his life than me. But I couldn't just sit around so came up on the off chance I could be of some use.'

Hazel laughed. 'Well you are obviously important enough for him to tell me all about you. And you are just as I imagined you would be. If I'm not mistaken, we share a love of poetry and books, oh…and quoting bits of Shakespeare.'

Kate was pink with pleasure. And disbelief. Fancy him telling his mum about her. She could hardly conceal her delight.

'Oh yes,' she blurted, 'he was always moaning about that.'

Suddenly the tiredness descended again onto Hazel's face.

She looked pale and thin. Kate remembered Rob saying something about her breast cancer and chemo. Was she still having it? She certainly didn't look well at all, but that could be worry about her only son lying there so close and unknowing.

'Sorry,' said Hazel rising stiffly from her chair, 'I really should be getting back. Look, they only allow one person in at a time to sit with him. A few unsuitable people have tried to inveigle their way in to sit by him which we have strictly forbidden. They keep hanging around and I think that nurse thought you were the one who keeps pestering about seeing him. But I'll tell them you are a close member of the family and you have my permission to be there. I admit it has been a bit tiring the last couple of days with me being the only one here. You see, I don't like to leave him alone. Silly I know, after all the nurses keep a round-the-clock watch on him. But I want to be there in case he comes to and doesn't know where he is.'

'I could help if you would let me, but of course quite understand if…'

'Actually that would be great, if you are sure.'

And as they walked back to the ward it was settled that she would take a shift at his bedside, so Hazel could have some much-needed sleep.

Kate was amazed that, although initially surprised, Hazel seemed to accept her right to be there. And trusted her to take a place by her son's bedside. All her doubts about coming had been dispelled by Hazel's awareness of who she was. Rob must have thought something of her to tell his mother so much about her. Despite all her worries, she felt a deep inner glow. Which was immediately dispelled as she entered the hushed room.

As they both stood by his bedside, looking at the long, inert figure with an oxygen mask over his grey face and attached to so many softly bleeping machines, they both uttered a deep sigh.

Perhaps, seeing Kate's anguish, Hazel squeezed her hand.

‘It must be a bit of a shock seeing him like this.’

Trying to suppress her tears, Kate could only nod.

‘You don’t have to stay if you don’t want to.’ Hazel looked concerned. ‘As you probably know, Rob’s father is a doctor, so I’ve been exposed to quite a bit of medical stuff in my life, but I know hospitals aren’t for everyone.’

‘No, no. I’ll be fine. I want to help in any way I can.’

‘OK. But please come and get me if there’s any change. I will only have a short break and then…’

‘No, no. Have as long as you want. You look a…well…little tired.’

‘I think you mean absolutely shattered, don’t you? I must admit I’d be grateful for a bit of shut eye, but didn’t want to leave him on his own. As I said, I’ve been talking to him a lot, and I hope you will as well. You could even recite some of those poems he was always telling me about. Oh yes, and even a bit of quiet singing would be allowed, you know.’

Kate went pink with pleasure. This woman really did know her.

‘But look, Kate, don’t feel you have to stay. You must go back to Spain whenever you want to. I have been warned that this…situation,’ she indicated the prone figure, the tubes, the softly whirring machines, ‘could go on for a long time.’

With a worried look at her son and a final reassuring squeeze of Kate’s hand, Hazel slipped away through the dimly lit ward.

Left alone with him, Kate sat down and reached out to grip that so familiar hand, now limp and unresponsive. She looked at him properly for the first time.

Where was the vitality and energy of the man who had hauled her up hills? Where was the infectious grin and tender ardour? Where was the strength, the warmth, the vigour of this love of her life?

Looking round, she confronted the truth of the mechanised world of modern nursing. There was nothing romantically Florence Nightingale about it at all, with bleeps and lights and in-going and outgoing fluids. But she was most shaken by the figure of Rob himself. Somehow she hadn't expected him to be so pale…and shrunken…and…she fought back the word that kept rearing up unbidden, unwelcome and unsuppressable…lifeless.

She sat there squeezing his limp hand and sobbed.

Chapter Fifty-One

A nurse came in to check on him and frowned a little.

'It's OK, Lovie. But the best thing is to talk to him. He wouldn't want to hear you crying, I'm sure. We never know how much they are aware of, but, after they recover, patients often reveal just how much they have heard. Little fragments and sometimes songs especially from a familiar voice.'

She was kind but also a bit brisk. Obviously a sobbing woman by a seriously ill patient's bedside was a hindrance not a help. And she had a job to do.

A bit chastened, Kate pulled herself together. At first it seemed a bit weird, just talking to his inert figure but gradually alone amongst the blinking lights and soft whirring, she began to pour out her heart to him. At each of their meetings, he always remembered so much about that wonderful week together so she thought she would talk about that and sing all the songs they had shared, and the poems too. And as the late afternoon turned into evening then night, mindful of the need to be cheerful, she decided to run through her repertoire of funny poems, sad poems, true poems. And through love poems she told him all the things she could never say to his face and unburdened her heart.

Unlike the nurses, who, as they went about their duties, tended to scrutinise the machines with their dials and readouts and bleeps, she intently watched Rob's pale, still face and felt for the tremor of returning awareness in his hands. But nothing.

Early next morning, an exhausted Hazel came to relieve her.

'I'm so sorry about not coming sooner. I must have slept right through.'

'You obviously needed it. Don't worry about it.'

'How has he been?'

Kate wanted to say something optimistic, 'I think he likes the poems.'

Hazel smiled, 'Yes, he has always had a soft spot for them. He told me you used to have a poem or song for all occasions.'

'Really.' Once again Kate was amazed at how much Hazel knew about her.

'Oh yes. Do you still do it to your classes?'

'No, not really. I'm trying to grow up a bit.'

'That's a shame.'

There was a loud beep from a machine that made them both jump in alarm but before they could do anything a nurse bustled into the room.

'Nothing to worry about, ladies,' she said. 'We just need to change something over.' She deftly switched one of the empty bags holding liquid to another full one.

They both sighed in relief.

'Off you go now,' Hazel said patting her arm. 'Thanks for relieving me. I needed that sleep.'

'Are you better now?' Kate asked, not sure about how strong Hazel was after her cancer treatment and worried at how drawn she looked.

'Well, I'm getting there but it's slow progress.'

'I can come back tonight if you like.'

'Are you sure?'

'Of course. I'll stay as long as you need me.'

'Well Douglas is coming up as soon as he can. He just has to clear his work diary a bit more. But tonight would be great if you don't mind. I couldn't bear for him to wake up all on his own.' Her voice broke a little.

'I feel the same. I will definitely be back later.'

Before she walked back to her car she enquired from the nurses if there was anywhere nearby to stay and was directed to a small B&B, a 10-minute walk away.

The room was a bit chintzy but it was warm and had a

good en suite shower. She explained to the rather fussy owner that she would be coming and going at irregular hours and explained why.

Although seemingly sympathetic, Mrs Pierce couldn't guarantee quietness if she wanted to sleep during the day which Kate assured her was fine.

First thing was to use the phone to tell Megan what was happening. It was a brief call because as always, her friend was rushing out to a meeting.

Then she phoned Troy. He listened patiently as she explained where she was and why.

'I'm sorry, Troy. I just had to come. He used to mean so much to me I just felt…'

'That's OK, Princess,' he said. 'I totally understand.' And she knew he did.

Then she went out to her car to fetch a packet of her emergency biscuits and crunched mournfully on her bed until, too tired to get undressed, she fell asleep.

Later, after eating a solitary meal in the hospital canteen, Kate went to relieve Hazel again for the night shift. Hazel was clearly exhausting herself by the amount of effort she put into her bedside watch, willing her son back into consciousness, afraid of losing him forever.

They spoke in brief hushed whispers aware of the hovering nurse who strictly enforced the one visitor rule. It would have been nice to get to know Hazel more but they were like ships in the night and his mum was too bone-weary to say much after her day's vigil.

As the night wore on Kate once again poured out all her unspoken love for him and fond memories of their time together. Surely if anything was going to penetrate his subconscious it would be the golden glow that surrounded that precious week.

Towards morning Kate couldn't think of anything new to talk to him about so she just kept softly repeating a familiar poem to him. Her eyes were half closed, lulled by the cadence of the lines, so she wasn't sure if it was tiredness or wishful thinking when she noticed a slight flickering around his eyelids.

Suddenly alert, she looked more intently. There it was again. Just a subtle change of expression. Was it almost a smile? She squeezed his hand and held her breath. But nothing happened. She looked at all the machines. Wouldn't they do something if there were a change?

Still nothing. She stared and stared. Yes? No?

No. She had been imagining it. But what if he had been responding to her voice and when she stopped, he had sunk back again into oblivion?

So she started on the poem again. And yes, that was definitely a smile.

She kept talking and rang the bell for the nurse who came running to the door. Kate held her fingers to her lips and kept reciting, then pointed to Rob's face.

The nurse looked puzzled. She obviously could see no change and so began scrutinising the monitors. All the while, to the nurse's mystification, Kate kept on repeating the poem.

As she finished for the third time, Kate whispered, 'Fetch his mum.'

The nurse looked very dubious and continued checking all the monitors.

'Fetch his mum,' Kate said more urgently, and began reciting again.

Plainly unconvinced, the nurse turned and left. Kate continued with the poem and with growing excitement, she noticed a difference in his breathing and felt a movement in his hand.

When his mum arrived, dishevelled and half-asleep from the nearby visitor's sleeping room, Kate was beaming and sobbing as she struggled to keep reciting in the same even voice.

Hazel also didn't need any machines to tell her that her son had started the slow journey back to her. Weeping, she joined Kate in her strange, laughing-crying rendition of *The Owl and the Pussycat.*

Chapter Fifty-Two

Rob opened his eyes for the first time during his mum's shift, just for a moment and with little comprehension in them.

'But they definitely opened,' Hazel said with wonderment.

And then, unwilling to go back to her digs, Kate took on the afternoon shift and experienced the same fleeting opening and closing of the eyes, although they held no recognition of her smiling down at him. But the hands were gaining strength as they occasionally returned squeezes.

And through it all she kept up a barrage of poems, convinced, against all the scepticism of the doctors, that poetry had brought him back from the brink.

'The Dong
The Dong
The Dong with the luminous nose.'

Kate finished her declamation with a flourish.

The tall, grey-haired man at the door laughed.

'It sounds somewhat scurrilous, young lady,' he said with a deep Scottish accent.

'What? Oh a dong. It isn't what you think…it's a poem. He likes Lear…Edward Lear…you see he started to regain consciousness to Lear's *Owl and the Pussy Cat* so I'm concentrating on…' but something was distracting her from explaining her poetic choice to what she assumed was one of the many doctors who dropped by to examine their patient. The voice sounded strangely familiar and Rob's hand was gripping hers in strengthening spasms.

'I'm not sure if all this poetry is good for a scientist like my son, but, as it seems to have done the trick, I'll forgive you.' And Rob's father grinned a familiar grin. Kate jumped up and, to her surprise, his father swept her up in a sudden warm hug.

'Thank you, Kate. Bless you.'

He let go of her just as suddenly as he had seized her and, clearing his throat, he turned to bend over his son.

Hazel had been watching from the doorway.

'I see introductions are unnecessary,' she beamed. 'It was a wonderful surprise when Douglas walked in. But I told him what was happening and he wanted to see for himself and to check everything was well…um…normal.'

This was the big unvoiced fear. Was there any brain damage? Would the returning Rob be the same as the old Rob?

Kirsty, the 'nice nurse', hovered and coughed discreetly. Kate knew she would get into trouble for allowing three people into Rob's room, so with a small wave she left the emotional parents with their son.

'All the indications are good,' Rob's father reassured Kate and his wife later whilst drinking cups of strong tea in the over-bright canteen. He had given them both a lot of medical information, which he could see she hadn't fully understood. 'Put simply, Rob's brain patterns are normal and his other vital signs are better than expected.' He let out a pent-up sigh of relief before continuing seriously, 'I've interrogated all the specialists, and, "as far as is possible to tell in this early stage", I don't think all that poetry will have caused permanent damage.'

Kate hooted with laughter more loudly than she expected and all eyes turned to them.

'Ooops sorry,' she blushed.

'Carry on. I don't expect they get a lot of that in here.' Clasping her hands in his, Douglas continued, 'Now, Kate, I'm going to be able to stay for the rest of the week and do my share of the shifts, and yes…if pushed, I'll probably be able to dredge up the odd rhyme or two. Not to the same standard as your poetic declamations, but I'll do my best. Anyway, it's time someone thought about you. For a start you need a good uninterrupted night's sleep.'

She went to protest but he held up his hand authoritatively.

'Look, with your help, and of course, *the Dong's,* Rob has definitely turned the corner now.'

Hazel put her hand over Kate's. 'We know you have put your own life on hold. And, as you told me, you will have to be getting back to Spain soon for your job at the College.'

It was true. Kate should really be flying back this weekend. It would be hard to explain to the Principal that she couldn't return because she was with an ill friend…just a friend. And besides, now both his parents were there, she wasn't really needed.

But she desperately wanted to stay; to see Rob recognise her; to see him smile.

Douglas seemed to know what she was thinking. 'Look, he's over the worst now and it could be a long, slow haul from here. We would love you to stay. I don't know how Hazel would have managed without you. Not only taking shifts so she could rest, but she knew Rob was in caring hands when you were with him. She said she could relax in confidence when you were there. That's important you know. As was your simple optimism; your unshakeable belief that he would get better. You were a better companion than I would have been. I know too much and…well, to be honest, I feared the worst.' He shook his head as if to dispel a bad dream.

Kate was embarrassed by his sincerity and tried to interrupt, but he fixed her with a stern look and continued, 'You have been utterly indispensable in keeping up my wife's spirits, her morale and her optimism.' He grinned at Hazel who was sipping a cup of stewed tea. 'Not to mention the intellectual stimulation of trying to think of new poems to recite to him.'

Kate hadn't realised that in her nightly phone calls, Hazel had told him everything. And she could see from whom Rob got his teasing gene.

It was true she wasn't needed any more and it was true she ought to get back to Spain. Reluctantly, she got up to go. Giving her a tearful hug, Hazel was effusive in her thanks and Douglas gave her a gruff peck on her cheek and a heartfelt handshake. Their fond goodbyes and gratitude were so warm, an embarrassed Kate had to hurry away with the excuse of the long drive back to Birmingham.

Feeling strangely deflated, Kate trailed back to the B&B and packed her case. Her head was doing the right thing, even though her heart wasn't in it. Leaving now would mean she could still catch her flight back to Malaga from Birmingham. She phoned Troy and told him what had happened and he sounded relieved when she said she would be back on the next day's flight.

'I've missed you, Babes.' He sounded rather sad. She wondered if he was worried about her time with Rob and all the old feelings it might have re-awakened.

'I've missed you too,' she said. And she had.

But she wasn't sure how she felt about him anymore. She would tell him all, of course. They had always promised to be honest with each other. But first she must think through all her emotions of the last few days. She undoubtedly still loved Rob but what were his feelings for her? He had clearly told his parents about her and he had definitely responded to her voice so perhaps… But, there was always that 'but'. Did she love him more than he loved her? If indeed he did love her at all. Was she just an old close friend he could pick up with whenever he came back to Brum?

And meanwhile in Spain, there was a lovely man who had missed her, who needed her.

On impulse, as she left the B&B, she decided to drive to the hospital just once more to have one last look in at Rob in the vain hope he would open his eyes and actually recognise her.

At the intensive care unit, to her surprise, she was told he wasn't there anymore. He was making such good progress they had just transferred him to a more open ward. They needed his bed for a more urgent case now.

Pleased by this news, Kate went to find him in his new surroundings.

Keeping an eye out for his parents to avoid the

embarrassment of yet another goodbye, she enquired at the nurses' station if it was OK just to nip in and see Rob for the last time. The young nurse looked up from her paperwork in surprise when Kate said his name.

'Oh, he's got someone with him already.'

'What? Who?'

'His fiancée.'

'Who?' Kate blurted out far too loudly.

Annoyed, the nurse repeated, 'His fiancée. Look.'

And as Kate peered up the ward, she saw a beautiful, young, slim girl, with long blonde hair, leaning over Rob holding his hand and stroking his head.

And Rob's eyes were open, looking at her.

Kate was rooted to the spot. She didn't believe it. That should be *her*. Who was this vision of loveliness stealing a moment that she had dreamt of, had worked for, a moment that was hers by right?

Enraged, she turned on the nurse.

'What do mean his fiancée? He hasn't got a fiancée.' Her voice in its anger exaggerated the despised word. 'How do know she's his fiancée?'

'Well,' the girl stammered defensively in the face of Kate's fury, 'she said she was…and she showed me her ring. It was lovely…a diamond…she said like her name, Tiffany…like in the jewellers you know…and…' As the nurse searched desperately for further proof, she remembered something. 'She was the one with him when they brought him in by helicopter. She was on the news. Very upset she was. She was the one he was saving when he fell. I remember her being interviewed on the TV. I remember how I liked her name.' She trailed off seeing the effect her words were having on Kate.

All Kate's anger had gone. She was trying to take in what she heard and unsuccessfully fighting her disbelief.

'She's been here before, trying to see him. But they've only just transferred him to this open ward so she can. She gave me her phone number…' The young nurse continued justifying herself, 'I can't really ask her to swop yet, but if you hang on I'll see if the ward sister will agree to two visitors, after all, he seems so much better…really taking notice…'

But Kate had gone.

Chapter Fifty-Three

Several times during the long drive back down to Birmingham, Kate had to pull into a service station as her eyes were too blurred with tears to see.

At the beginning she just drove. Drove to get away from that image seared onto her mind. That picture of Tiffany by Rob's bed. Young, lithe, blonde, looking so stylish in an expensive caramel coat and thigh length boots. Everything that Kate wasn't.

That picture hurt. It really hurt.

But why was she so surprised that someone as good-looking as Rob had a fiancée like that? It made his accident even more feasible. Of course he would risk his life to save someone he loved.

But why didn't she know about her? Why had no one told her about a fiancée? Especially one called Tiffany. She couldn't believe the pure white hatred she felt for this…this hard jewel of a name, this empty vessel of a name, this meretricious concoction of a name…this…she pulled herself up short.

She knew why she was so angry at such a dazzling name. Because it suited its owner perfectly.

Gradually, as the miles were eaten up, she tried to force herself to review the facts coldly and dispassionately. Why hadn't Megan told her? Well, evidently Megan didn't know either. If her main line of communication was Josh, perhaps he wouldn't think to pass on this bit of romantic information.

But why, oh why, hadn't Hazel told her? Or his father?

Well, they wouldn't, would they? They didn't want to hurt her. Or did they assume she knew already?

Hazel had told her she had shooed everyone away because

they were all upsetting each other. And she remembered the nurses had specific instructions to keep a young woman out, presumably Tiffany because she would be more upset than anyone else. Especially if she felt guilty at causing the accident. That nurse wasn't too happy when Kate had sat sobbing by his bedside, so a weeping fiancée really would have been frowned upon.

Burning with embarrassment, Kate thought of her sudden arrival at the hospital, uninvited, certainly unexpected and, let's face it, probably unwanted. What must Hazel have thought, faced with a wild-haired, sobbing girl wearing her heart on her sleeve asking to see her son? Especially one she thought had come all the way from Spain? Initially it was probably pure pity that drove her to ask for help with the bedside shifts.

Although she clearly knew about their affair from long ago, Hazel must have been in a real dilemma about the presence of a besotted ex-girlfriend at the bedside of her engaged son.

Thinking of it further, Kate's cheeks flushed with a scorching shame. How humiliating. Although they were obviously very grateful for her help, look how quickly his dad had suggested she leave once Rob was on the road to recovery.

It was just too much of a coincidence that Tiffany should arrive just as Kate was leaving. Someone must have informed her it was an appropriate time to come and see him; a tactful moment for his fiancée to come and reclaim him from the stalking woman who had driven up, uninvited, from Birmingham.

The only ones who knew Kate was leaving that day were Rob's parents. Cleverly they were both in the canteen to say goodbye to her so Tiffany could be alone with their son, romantically reunited by his bedside. They couldn't possibly have suspected that Kate would sneak back to the ward for a final farewell.

Although she tried to be fair, she couldn't help but feel deeply betrayed by them. And bitterly hurt. She had really liked them, had trusted them.

So wounded was she, that, in spite of all her promises, she would definitely not contact them on her return. They had insisted she keep in touch but what could she say?

Arriving exhausted back at the flat, both Megan and Josh were out. Suddenly knowing she couldn't bear to talk to them, to tell them about Tiffany and see the pitying look in their eyes, she decided to spend the night in an airport hotel. Quickly packing up her remaining belongings, she left a brief note on the table, saying she was back and taking an earlier flight. She then called a taxi and left.

Alone and awake in an anonymous hotel room, she had plenty of time to think, and she began to take stock of her life.

Her revelation in the hospital about 'real life' stuck with her. She knew she must begin to shed a lifetime of romantic notions. She must stop herself every time she caught herself daydreaming or humming a nonsensically romantic song. From now on she mustn't waste a moment in silly reverie about what might be. *This* was her life. And she must take it by the scruff of the neck and get on with it, realistically.

Now Rob was definitely out of her life, she could close that door forever. No more clinging on to hope, no more fantasising about a happy ever after. That must all stop for good.

But of course that night he invaded her dreams. And the next morning she had to endure that sickening lurch as she remembered that fiancée figure by his bed. Her jaw ached with tension and she felt disorientated by the intensity of her dreams.

But thank goodness today she was flying back to her 'other' family. To Reen and the Taylor clan. How she longed to bury herself in the loyal, understanding arms of the faithful Troy.

Chapter Fifty-Four

But one look at Troy's face as he met her from the plane showed he seemed to be in as much anguish as she was.

He enveloped her in a big bear hug and she snuggled into his neck.

'Are you OK?' he asked, searching her face.

'No, not really. Are you?'

'Nope. I've got things to tell you… but Ma is just arriving so can we talk later?'

'Yes, of course.'

And with one accord they both turned and put on brave faces for the waving Reen as she clip-clopped her excited way towards them.

Somehow they both got through the drink-laced welcome-home meal Reen had ordered in from their usual restaurant.

Clearly picking up on their distressed mood, Reen, for once, didn't linger long over the alcoholic night caps.

'You look exhausted,' she said giving Kate a concerned hug.

'I am a bit.'

'Off you both go then. The Gibraltar room is all ready for you.'

'Actually, Ma, I think we will just wander around outside for a while to stretch our legs,' Troy said with a meaningful glance at Kate.

'Oh, OK. Well, see you in the morning then, my Dahlins.' And with an anxious look Reen hustled a confused Ted upstairs to bed.

Kate automatically put on her jacket to go outside, but of course, this was April in Spain and she quickly shrugged it off. It was warm and still without a breath of wind. Wordlessly, they walked hand in hand round the garden almost as if steadying themselves before they launched into what was troubling them. They then returned to cuddle on the padded swinging garden seat.

Through Reen's open patio door upstairs they could hear her heels clipping around the bedroom and her subdued voice talking to Ted. Then her bedroom light went out.

Looking up at their terrace Kate could see a shape peering over the edge into the garden.

'Is that a…'

'Yes,' said Troy with a weary smile. 'It's another bloody flamingo.'

Despite herself, Kate giggled.

Troy pulled her closer, 'Come on, Babes, tell me all about it. I didn't want to go upstairs in case Ma could hear us talking.'

'She's sussed something's wrong, hasn't she?'

'Yes. Not surprising really. I could tell instantly I saw you at the airport.'

'And what about you?'

'What?'

'I could tell you were putting a brave face on something too.'

'Yes. Ma has been fussing round me but I couldn't tell her. But you go first. Is it awful news about your Rob guy? Has he...?'

'Oh no, he is in fact recovering nicely but, oh Troy…he's engaged…engaged to a gorgeous bimbo called Tiffany.'

There was a sharp intake of breath. 'Engaged?'

'Yes, and no one told me. I've made a complete fool of myself. I've been sitting by his bedside talking to him, singing to him and I'm sure it was me who helped him come round but…'

She broke into sobs and haltingly told him all about her vigil, meeting his parents, and about how Rob had gradually come out of his coma and had finally awoken to his gorgeous, sodding fiancée standing by his side gazing adoringly into his newly opened eyes.

She was perfectly honest with Troy about the re-awakening of her dormant feelings for Rob as he lay helplessly in bed.

'I'm sorry, Troy. I couldn't help it. I'll get over it but they just all came flooding back. I didn't realise how much I still felt for him…I'm so sorry.'

'That's OK, Babes. I totally understand. I really do.' He pulled her into his big consoling arms.

As she snuggled weeping into his comfortable chest, she gradually became aware of his ragged breathing and looked up to see he was crying as well.

'Oh no, Troy. What's happened?'

He gave a grimace, 'Tamsin has found someone too.'

'No…oh no.'

'Oh yes. So you see I do know how you feel. I thought I was over her but…it turns out I'm not.'

'How do you know?'

'Huh, my mate Colin from the London showroom, remember the one who told me all about who she was, just "happened" to phone last week and just "happened" to let slip he'd seen a photo of Tamsin in one of the posh, glossy magazines we have hanging around the show rooms. Ma's got the same one so I looked for it yesterday. And there it was. A picture of them both on the society page. Tamsin Fuller-White standing next to her boyfriend, ex-Etonian city banker, Ralph Hepworth-Smythe.'

'Oh no.'

'He looks like a right snobby tosser…not that I'm biased at all. I suppose what really hurts is how quickly she's got another fella. I somehow thought she might still…' His voice broke and he couldn't continue.

For a long time they just wept in each other's arms.

Eventually, Troy sighed, 'I guess it's just you and me now, Babes.'

'Yes. And do you know what…that's fine by me, Troy.'

'And fine by me too, Babe.'

'It means you can give up that job you hate and you can be

an accountant like you want.'

'Yes, I suppose so. But won't you mind being married to a boring accountant?'

What had he just asked? Kate looked up into his lovable face. As marriage proposals went, it might lack a little romance, but she knew the companionship and trust between them would carry them through whatever life had to offer.

'No…and I can't imagine you ever being boring, Troy.' She laughed, 'And at least this way, Reen can wear as many purple feathers as she likes at our wedding without you worrying about it.'

'True, Babes, and I suppose it will keep her occupied for a bit and stop her buying more bloomin flamingos. It might even stop her drinking. But we can't keep having weddings just to give her something to do.'

'No, I suppose not. But it will be great to be part of your family, Troy.'

'You love Ma, don't you?'

'Yes…I wish…'

'What?'

'I'll tell you sometime. Hey, just a thought, we could always double-barrel our names. That wouldn't be boring.'

He groaned. 'Promise me, Babes, we won't do that.'

'OK, only if you promise me that if we have any kids we can call them any T name you want, except Tiffany.'

They sat huddled together for a while, both thinking things over. Then Troy said, 'Do you mind if we don't tell anyone yet…about us getting married and stuff.'

'That's fine. To be honest, I don't think I could cope with all the jollity and celebrations yet.'

'Me neither.'

'I think Ma should be asleep by now. Should we go up?'

Hand in hand they went up to bed, and slept in each other's comforting arms.

Chapter Fifty-Five

'Do you think she knows?'

'About us getting engaged, you mean? No. She can't do.' Troy wove his way expertly through the Saturday morning traffic.

'So why has Reen summoned us to a shindig this weekend?'

'Search me, Babes. I tried to get out of it and say we just wanted a quiet weekend with just the two of us but she was really insistent. She's invited these two old friends from London to stay and she wants us to meet them. Apparently, she was a bridesmaid at their wedding and they have sort of lost touch over the years but now she's contacted them again and they came a couple of days ago for a big reunion.'

'Is all the family coming?'

'Don't think so. Tina's working and Tyrone wouldn't come to a do without her so it's just us. I think she just wants us to fly the family flag. But we don't have to stay long. I'll say we have to go and meet some friends for lunch if you want.'

'Yes, I'm not sure I'm up to too much jollification yet.'

'How's your week been?'

Kate sighed. 'Not good, but it's doing me good to immerse myself back into work and stuff. It's the exam term so the pressure is on. How about you?'

'Same, I suppose. I've really pushed myself this week and got some good sales. Got to get my girl an engagement ring soon.' He beamed at her.

'Oh, Troy, you don't have to.'

'Oh yes I do,' he said sternly.

'We are still not telling Reen though are we?'

'Nope, definitely not. The decibel count would go through

the roof.'

'But she knows something is up between us. Didn't you notice how subdued she was last Sunday?'

'To be honest, Babes, I wasn't feeling too chipper myself, so no.'

'Hmmn.' Kate had a feeling Reen was up to something, but couldn't think what.

It was an excited sparkly Reen who came to greet them at the front door. She seemed a bit agitated and apprehensive about something as she waved them into the lounge to meet her guests.

'Troy, Kate, I'd like you to meet Dot, my old friend from school and her husband, Eddy.'

A portly man struggled to his feet and after giving Troy a piercing stare, grinned and held out his hand in greeting. His matronly wife came forward with a strange smile and, after a similar appraising look, pulled him to her in a warm embrace.

They both nodded and smiled absently at Kate, both clearly focused on Troy who was doing a double-take at Eddy and seemed a bit puzzled as if trying to place him from somewhere.

Reen looked on and seemed to be waiting expectantly. An anxious Ted was also watching everything keenly from the side-lines.

There was definitely something going on. Kate could feel it in the air.

Looking fixedly across at Troy, Reen said, 'My friend Dotty used to be Dorothy *White* and then she married Fast Eddy, as we used to call him. Fast Eddy *Fuller*.' There was a pause as Reen's friends beamed. Then the penny dropped.

Troy gasped, 'Fuller-White. Tamsin's parents?'

'Yes.'

He looked shaken.

'But…'

He looked even more shaken when a figure walked in from the garden.

Kate saw his astonishment as a petite, honey-blonde girl

advanced tentatively towards him with a look of apprehension and love.

'Tamsin! You. Here? What! What's going on?'

'Oh, Troy. You silly sod,' the girl said, 'I told you I wasn't posh. I told you my parents would like you and you mustn't worry about your background. But you wouldn't believe me, would you? You and your stupid pride.'

Then she flung her arms round his neck and kissed him full on the lips.

A bewildered Troy gathered her in his arms, then returned her kiss as if his life depended on it.

'So you *do* still care about me,' Tamsin said mischievously as she released him.

'Of course I do. But I don't understand. What are you doing here?'

'Let's go out into the garden and talk about it, should we?' Tamsin led a dazed and delighted Troy out into the bright sunshine.

Ted had been hovering behind Kate and she was dimly aware of a reassuring hand being gently placed on her shoulder.

As the embracing couple walked into the garden, Reen turned and rushed over to apologise to a totally stunned Kate.

'Oh, Kate, Dahlin. I'm so sorry. I feel awful about this for you. But please understand, I had to help my boy. I just had to. And I know you care enough about him to want him to be happy, don't you?'

Kate nodded dumbly. It was true. She had seen the look on Troy's face when he saw Tamsin and it told her everything about his feelings.

'But I don't understand. How did you know about her?'

Guiding her to sit on the electric blue sofa, Reen took her hand. 'I could see you were both so heartbroken last week, I had to find out what was going on. So I confess I deliberately eavesdropped from the bedroom terrace. I heard every word.'

Kate was frantically wracking her brain to remember exactly what they had said when Reen continued, 'The name Tamsin Fuller-White struck a chord and Troy said the picture was in one of my posh magazines so I searched until I found her. Then I realised who she was. I remembered you had a little girl called Tammy,' she said turning to the beaming round-faced woman sitting on the opposite sofa.

'We had sort of lost touch, hadn't we?' Dot said in a similar accent to Reen. 'It was my fault. We were struggling to have a baby and you had your three boys so quick and easy. I must admit I was jealous. I feel awful now.'

'No, Dot, Dahlin, it was my fault as well. When Eddy sold his garage for all that money, I didn't want you to think we were getting in touch again because you had got so rich.'

'Oh, Reen, I would never have thought that of you, but I do understand. We did get a lot of people suddenly getting very friendly with us. All the wrong sort. My Eddy can't abide these false folk.'

'And, Dahlin, we thought you'd gone all posh on us with your double-barrelled name and all.'

Dotty blushed, 'Yes, I admit for a while we were a bit up ourselves.' She turned to Kate to explain. 'We were just ordinary people, you know, grafters, like Reen and Ted here, just doing the best we could for ourselves. Still are at heart. But the area around Eddy's garage suddenly started getting all gentrified and we were offered a lot of money for the site. Well, at first Eddy refused because the business had come down the family, father to son, and he didn't want to lose the tradition. But we had such a struggle to have our baby Tammy, we realised she was probably all we were having. Then the developers came back offering us even more money, so we had a rethink and realised we'd be daft to hold out anymore.'

She turned to Reen. 'I admit it went to our heads a bit. When we put our Tammy into an expensive school, we thought we'd better up our game, which is when we put our two names together to sound a bit posh. But we tried to make sure she was always very grounded and…' She glanced out into the garden and gasped. 'Oh Reen, just look at them.'

The two mothers reached out to clutch each other as they saw their beloved offspring, Troy and Tamsin, sobbing in each other's arms.

'I can't believe that your Troy thought he wasn't good enough. Our Tamsin was devastated when they finished but would never tell us who it was and why they broke up. Didn't want us interfering. Then when she got involved with that posh, long streak of nothing…all charming to your face and sneering behind your back…'

'A right tosser he was. A proper chinless wonder,' Eddy growled. 'Disliked him from the minute I set eyes on him. Only after my money. I reckoned he'd soon ditch her when he knew I hadn't got as much as everybody reckons.'

'So when you phoned us out of the blue last Sunday, Reen,' Dot interrupted, keen to get the story out, 'and we chatted and put two and two together, we asked her all about your lad…'

Eddy butted in, 'That's when she told us about him and how upset he got when he knew who she was. How he worried he wasn't good enough for her. How he thought we'd look down on him and his family and how he wasn't having that. Well, from what I heard, he's my sort of bloke, hardworking, proud and wanting to provide for her as best he can.' Surveying his beloved daughter in the arms of Troy, Eddy brought out a big white handkerchief and blew his nose loudly.

Ted came forward and slapped him on the back as they both gruffly cleared their throats.

Kate was completely forgotten as all the attention in the room focused on Troy and Tamsin.

'It looks as if it's all going to be all right, don't you reckon?' Dot whispered, reaching out a hand to Reen.

'Yes, Dot, Dahlin, I think it is.'

The relief all round was palpable as both mothers collapsed into each other's arms in tears of joy.

Kate just stood there alone and watched.

Chapter Fifty-Six

'Oh Kate, Babes, I'm so sorry. I had no idea that Ma was planning all this with Tamsin and her parents and everything.'

'I know, Troy, and it's fine. It really is.'

'But…'

'No. Listen to me. I can clearly see the love between you and Tamsin. It shines out of your eyes. How can I possibly stand in your way? I care too much about you.'

Troy's eyes welled up with gratitude as he gazed into her face. He had raced across the room to her as soon as he had come in from the garden, clearly distraught for her and wanting to explain. But Kate had lost no time in reassuring him that she understood completely.

'You truly are a lovely person, Kate.'

'No I'm not. I like to think you would have let me go in similar circumstances.'

'But…'

'No more buts, Troy. I'm really pleased for you and how it's worked out. Tamsin is a lovely girl. I can see why you love her so much. Your mum knew we weren't right for each other. And she was right. Now off you go and get to know your future in-laws.'

With a push, she shoved the clearly guilt-ridden Troy back towards the Fuller-Whites.

Reen had been listening.

'Troy's right. You really are a lovely person.'

'And you are an interfering old bat, Reen Taylor. Listening in to other people's conversations…' She really did need to stop everyone saying what a lovely person she was.

Although this turn of events had hit her hard, there was no way she was going to show it. Not yet, anyway.

'You're right, Dahlin,' Reen confessed. 'And they say the eavesdroppers never hear any good about themselves. And it's true. What you said about me shook me up a lot. So I've done a lot of hard thinking.'

'Oh, Reen. I can't remember what we said but you know…'

'You said about me drinking too much, about not having enough to do, and only living for weddings and family parties and buying too many flaming flamingos. And you were dead right about it all.'

Kate could see Reen's ready acceptance of these comments and a determined gleam in her eye.

'So guess what, Dahlin? I've not just been busy all week with this get-together, I've been sorting myself out as well. I'm going to set up my own wedding and party planning company.'

'What?'

'Yup. Obviously, it's early days but you were the one who gave me the idea. You are right, I *do* need something to do and I am good at organising stuff. So why not do it as a business? Thanks to Tyrone's wedding, I've got lots of contacts. And the whole family can pitch in. Tina would love to do all the beauty/bride stuff. Tamsin has already done event organising in the UK and is keen to be involved. Ted would be good at sorting all the practical side, like putting up marquees and stuff. And after what you said about Troy wanting to be an accountant…'

Kate gasped. She had forgotten that bit of the conversation.

'…I'm rather hoping he will be our finance manager.' Reen beamed with the perfection of it all. 'You never know we might even get Tarquin and Tracey down here as well, away from that rotten set she's in with at the moment. I'm ready to stand up to her now. It will all be new and exciting but it's what this family needs. Don't you think?'

Her eyes sparkled with the thrill of it all.

'Oh, and Eddy and Dot want to come and live on the Costa as well. Eddy has had some heart problems and wants a simpler life. After coming here, Dot wants to feel the sun on her bones like me. It will be great to have a proper friend down here. We all used to get on so well and getting back in touch has made us all realise how close we are. Dot hasn't got any real friends in London…all too toffy-nosed she says, so we've had some real heart-to-hearts, just like the old days.

And, as you can see, Ted and Eddy get on well too.' She glanced fondly over to where the men were having a good laugh over a beer whilst barbecuing the lunch. Round the pool Dot was sitting with Troy and Tamsin clearly hanging on to every word they were saying.

Turning back to Kate, Reen looked sincerely into her eyes. 'I'm so sorry it hasn't worked out between you and my Troy, Dahlin. I really wanted it to and I think you did too. I could see there was a lot of affection between you but there just wasn't any spark. I knew deep down it wasn't right. Was it?'

Kate nodded. It was true.

'But, Dahlin, we've a lot to thank you for. You've been a proper good luck charm for us all. And I want you to know, you will always be a real member of this family.'

That's when the dam broke.

Kate couldn't stop herself. She flung herself into Reen's arms and sobbed as if her heart would break. Because it was breaking. Those last words of Reen's brought it home to her. What she had really wanted was to be included in the Taylor tribe. The main attraction for marrying Troy was so she would be part of a warm loving family…at last.

It wasn't the loss of Troy that was wrenching her apart, it was the realisation that this would never happen now. Reen would never be her mum. How could she watch Tamsin occupy the place she so wanted…the place of Reen's daughter?

Trying to quell her tears, she leapt up, 'Sorry, Reen, I've got to go.'

'No, Dahlin…'

'Yes, Reen, please let me. I can't stay. Not anymore. Don't let Troy see me. Just call me a taxi.'

'I'll do no such thing.' Reen put her arm round her and

helped her to the front door. 'I'll take you home.'

'No, you mustn't leave all your guests…everyone.' Kate was gulping down her sobs, trying in vain to compose herself.

'They are all happy. You aren't, Dahlin…and it's all my fault.'

'Oh, Reen, please don't feel guilty.'

'Shut up and get in the car.' With one swift action Reen had grabbed the car keys from the side table and zapped the doors to her little car. 'I'm taking you home and you and me are going to have a real heart to heart.'

She waved to Ted and did a driving motion with her hands pointing at Kate. He nodded.

As she hustled Kate to the car she said, 'This isn't just about Troy, is it?'

Kate shook her head.

'Thought not. There's some things you have said to me that I want to get to the bottom of. Time you told me everything, my girl. And I won't take no for an answer.'

Chapter Fifty-Seven

Slumped on her settee, Kate was nursing a strong Reen-made cup of tea. She was feeling utterly bereft. All her dreams of belonging to the lovely Taylor family had gone.

'So what is it, Dahlin?' Reen coaxed, peering anxiously into Kate's tear-swollen eyes. 'I've always known there was a hurt little girl inside you. The way you were worried about being flamboyant when we were shopping. You said you were raised not to make a show or something like that. It seems your dad was very hard on you.'

'Yes, he was. He always wanted me to fade into the background as if he was ashamed of me…because of course he was.'

'What! Ashamed of you, his own daughter?'

'Because I wasn't his daughter,' Kate blurted out, glad to unburden herself of her secret at last. 'He wasn't my dad, he was my *grandpa* and I was his *grand*daughter. His *illegitimate* granddaughter.'

It sounded so bare, so blunt. Her upright preacher grandpa hated the fact that she was living proof of what he saw as his daughter's sin. Just by being, she had brought shame on the family.

Kate was rocking back and forth. 'Don't you see, I was born guilty? At least that's how I always felt. I never knew my dad. And I always lived with my grandma and grandpa. They said to call them Ma and Pa to conceal the disgrace. They were the ones who brought me up from when I was five and my mum left me.'

'Left you?' Already shocked, Reen now looked stricken.

'Oh, I don't think she meant to leave me for ever. But she's never come back. It's part of the pattern of my life.

Everyone I've ever loved has left me.' A raw tide of misery engulfed her.

She was immediately wrapped in Reen's loving arms and heard her murmuring soothing endearments as one would to a child.

Years of bewilderment and loss began to escape her wracked body in long shuddering sobs. Bent double, shaking all over and gasping, Kate tried to breathe, but her sorrow consumed her. A pulsating pain squeezed her heart and threatened to crush her. Although frightened by the intensity of her feelings, Kate had no power to control them, and just moaned and keened with overwhelming grief.

Throughout it all, Reen held her close, rocking her backwards and forwards and letting her give vent to her anguish.

Eventually, exhausted, the trembling began to abate. Kate's limbs felt heavy but the storm left her feeling strangely calm as if all emotion had been wrung out of her.

Reen hadn't tried to stem this flood of suffering but waited, clearly distressed; she seemed to understand that Kate needed to pour out all the hurt before she could begin to heal.

Finally, uncurling from Reen's arms, Kate knew it was time to tell someone all about her childhood. And instinctively she knew Reen was the right someone to tell.

'You need to talk about all this, Dahlin. I think you have kept it bottled up too long. I hope you know you can tell me and I will understand, whatever it is.'

'Yes, I do, Reen. You are right. It's time to face it head on. I can't bury it all forever.'

'So what happened, Dahlin?' Reen asked gently.

'I need to go back to where I came from and explain about Ma and Pa. I may have told you that we lived in a small, rainy village, tucked away up a long valley. Pa and Ma ran the local Post Office and shop and they were married a long time before my mum came along. I think Ma was so delighted at having a child at last that she lavished all her dreams and love on this longed-for daughter. Being an avid reader and an incurable romantic all her life, she gave my mum all her favourite heroine names…Guinevere Eloise Juliette Caswell.'

Shaking her head in amusement, Kate said, 'My mum hated it. Apparently, no one could even spell Guinevere. So as soon as she could, she chose the least awful of her names, Juliette, and soon changed it to Julie.'

She sighed. 'I suppose that's why, when she had me, she chose the plainest name she could think of, no frills, nothing fancy, just Kate.'

Reen patted her hand. 'I like the name Kate.'

'I've got used to it now…but Guinevere would have been nice.'

'Hmmn, it's a lot to live up to.'

'Yes, I suppose so. And, in a way, my mum did. Apparently, she was always a restless soul. Very bright but a bit rebellious. Ma said she was always being summoned up to the school trying to explain why her daughter had done this or that. But they were so proud when she got into University, and absolutely devastated when she didn't go. She met a lad and decided to go off on what we would now call a gap year. It was a hippy trip to India "to find herself". Ma and Pa begged and pleaded. They were so worried, but she went anyway. Travelled for a couple of years out there. They never knew where she was. She sent postcards now and again. Ma kept them in an old shoe box.'

Kate could feel her voice grow tight with emotion remembering these links with a mother who went boldly out into the world and wasn't afraid to follow her dreams.

'I've read all of her postcards, of course. I used to pore over them. They are funny and colourful and exciting. She was so adventurous. Much more daring than I've ever been. But I think I was always a bit frightened, especially after what happened to her.'

'She had a bad experience?'

'Oh no, not then. In fact I think she was very sorry to come back. But she had to. She just turned up one day on the shop doorstep, a bit grubby, in sandals and long hair. With a small baby bump. She was pregnant with me.'

Reen nodded slowly. 'So you think she would have stayed living a hippy life in India if she could.'

'Definitely. She always wanted to stay out there but she had split up with my father and was running out of money. She had just enough to get home. So she came back to have me.

As you can imagine, a single parent, no husband in tow, was a bit of a scandal back then, especially in our old-fashioned village. Pa was absolutely mortified. He had been so proud of his intelligent daughter. And, of course, being a very religious man, he felt it contradicted everything he'd ever preached about. But Ma was just glad to have her back, and a new baby on the way.'

'Can I ask? Do you know who your father is?'

'Yes, a New Zealander called Rick Mackenzie. I've seen pictures of him, of both of them together in India. He's tall, sandy-haired, good looking, nice smile and with green eyes like me. But I've never got in touch. Perhaps one day I will. But I'm not sure if I'm brave enough. What if he doesn't want to know me? I don't think I could face the rejection.'

Her voice dropped to a whisper.

Leaning forward to catch her words, Reen said softly, 'Kate, Dahlin, any parent would be proud of a daughter like you.'

'Thank you for saying that, Reen. Ma was always proud of me, but I don't think she dare show too much affection, not while Pa was alive. She also understood why my mum went. She used to say, "Roots and wings. You try to give your children roots to ground them but also wings to fly if they want to." And my mum just wanted to fly.'

Reen nodded perhaps thinking of her own brood and thankful that they didn't seem to want to fly too far from her, the mother hen.

'But your mum did come back home to have you.'

'Yes, and stayed for a while. I can remember her quite clearly at times. Laughing, singing, twirling me round in the kitchen. I've got images of us at the playground. She was on the next swing to me, going higher and higher, her long dark hair flying loose while Ma pushed me gently back and forth. In my memories, my mum is always moving. We have a blurred film of her holding me in her arms and dancing in our garden.'

Kate had to pause. Although she felt a compelling need to bring her past out into the open, she hadn't realised how achingly raw it would make her feel. These scant hazy pictures were so precious, and so painful.

'So, as you can guess, my mum was still restless. She couldn't settle in the village. I realise why now. Like me, she hated its oppressive atmosphere, its small mindedness and those dark, rainy hills always cutting out the light. I suppose after all the colour and sun of India, she must really have felt it.'

Looking out at her terrace bathed in golden sunshine and the cloudless azure blue sky, Kate sighed, 'I totally understand it now, especially after seeing all the brightness of Spain. But it's taken a long time.

I think she tried to stay for my sake. She had lots of jobs but none of them lasted long. Later, I heard lots of gossip about her, but as Ma said, "It doesn't take much to shock the narrow-minded folk round here. Too much to say and not enough to do."'

Taking a deep breath, Kate launched into the most agonising part of her tale.

'She left when I was five. She stayed for my birthday. Ma took lots of photos of that party, even though she couldn't have known my mum's plans. Perhaps she had some sort of premonition that these would be the last photos she'd ever have of her daughter. Who knows?'

Kate exhaled slowly trying to get inside the mind of her mother.

'I suppose mum knew at five I was going to school so I wouldn't be in the way too much at home. She left for India two days later saying she was going to meet some of her old friends out there for a bit of a reunion. She reckoned on being gone for a few months as she wanted to travel round a bit and see some of the things she'd missed when she was last there. But she *promised* me she would come back. I can remember her walking to the garden gate, big rucksack on her back. I was holding Ma's hand. Mum turned and waved and blew me a kiss…and I never saw her again.'

The images all came flooding vividly back. It was a grey day. Her mum was wearing a long multi-coloured hippy skirt, her rucksack had red flashes down the side which matched a red woolly hat from which wisps of escaping dark hair framed her bright laughing face. She looked so happy.

Chapter Fifty-Eight

Kate stopped and looked out at the green waving palms outlined against the bright blue sun-speckled sea. She could understand why her mum longed to swap the grey, rain-laden sky of her village for the warmth and colour of a foreign land.

But to leave her daughter. That hurt. That was the thing she found hardest to understand.

As a child, the happiness in her mother's face as she waved goodbye haunted her. Why was she so glad to be going? Perhaps she didn't love Kate enough to stay. Was there something wrong with her that her mother was so pleased to leave her? Had she been too naughty? If she promised to be good, would her mother come back? Why was she gone so long?

Looking back, Kate realised these bewildered thoughts informed the girl she became, always trying to please, always waiting, always hoping and always knowing there was a huge gap in her life.

Aware of Reen's hands lovingly clutching hers, Kate continued to confront the painful events of long ago, determined to exorcise all her ghosts.

'At first, we got lots of postcards, saying where she was and what she was doing. Ma would read them to me and show me where Mum was on a big map she had pinned on the wall. She had bought some little round red stickers and she would show me where to put them. But after a while the postcards got fewer and fewer. About one a month then gradually they didn't arrive any more. Pa got grumpier and grumpier. He rushed to get the post each day. I don't know at what point he started panicking but I can vividly remember the day he broke down in tears. That really frightened me. Apparently, we hadn't had a postcard for nearly three months and he had a dreadful feeling something had happened.

'He started making enquiries, writing and phoning everyone he could think of, the Indian embassy, the British embassy in India. But they couldn't really help because he didn't know exactly where she was. He gave them her last known location, but that was from months ago. Somehow, he got hold of the addresses and phone numbers of lots of regional Indian police forces and frantically telephoned and wrote to them with pictures of his daughter. Every day he would write. I can picture him now, hunched over his desk where he used to write his sermons, and every day he seemed to get smaller. He wore himself out contacting anyone he could think of. He did it for over a year.'

Closing her eyes, Kate could see him pacing up and down, up and down in the tiny back sitting room of the shop.

'He was forever asking Ma what else he should do. And I can remember him raging at her. He blamed her with all her romantic notions putting ideas into Mum's head so that she wanted adventures. Giving her those damn silly names. All those poems and fancy books. It was all Ma's fault.

'I suppose she must have been just as worried as he was, but she kept reassuring him all would be well.

'But all this frustration and anger and heart-break…well, it did, in fact, break his heart. Ma found him clutching Mum's last postcard and his chest. She phoned the ambulance and he went into hospital. One of my last memories is visiting him and holding his hand…'

She broke down at the memory of this stern, upright man, who nevertheless loved his daughter so much, her loss broke his heart.

Reen stroked her hand, clearly distressed by the story. 'Oh, Babes. This is so awful. If all this is too upsetting, you can stop whenever you want.'

'Thanks, Reen.' Kate scrabbled for yet another tissue from the box by the sofa. 'But I've kept all this suppressed for so long, it's almost a relief to be talking about it at last.'

'I can understand that. I think you will feel so much better if you stop locking it all away as you have done for years. That can't have been good for you.'

'I suppose I was following Ma's example. She dealt with it all in the only way she knew. Ma always said, "What can't be cured, must be endured." And I suppose she was right because she did endure. After Pa died, she took over the post office and tried to shield me from all the gossip and nasty comments about my lack of father and my flibbertigibbet "no better than she should be" mum. But when things got too bad, I used to slip into a daydream where my mum had married an Indian prince and was wearing lots of jewels in her hair and riding on elephants.'

'So did you find out what happened to your mum?'

'No, never have. As I grew up, I stopped imagining she married an Indian prince but I did still fantasise that one day I'd open the door and there she would be grinning on the doorstep in her red woolly hat. She would fling out her arms and hug me and say how I'd grown and she'd come back because she'd missed me so much and what a fine girl I'd grown into.'

Kate had to stop for a moment to compose herself. Those dreams had lasted for years and still sometimes haunted her sleep.

'I think Ma hoped as well. But it never happened. We just never heard anything ever again. It's over twenty years now, so I don't expect we ever will.'

'That's almost worse than finding out that she…' Reen tailed off, not wanting to put it into words.

'That she's dead. Yes, it is, although I assume she is by now. As much as she wanted to explore, I can't believe that if she were alive, she wouldn't have come back to see Ma or me. I've left my address with a village friend so that if ever she did come back, she would know where to find me. Ma always stressed how much my mum loved me and one day she would come back if she could. And I think it's true. So there can only be one reason why she hasn't.'

'Oh, Dahlin, I don't know what to say…'

'Just don't say "Poor Kate". Please don't say that. I don't want anyone ever to pity me. That's why I never told anyone. Ma warned me not to tell because then I would always be "the poor girl whose mother ran off to India and never came back". And I would never have the chance to be the real me. And I think she was right.'

'Oh, I wasn't going to say that. I'm so sorry about what's happened to you. But I wasn't pitying you, far from it. I was admiring your resilience, your fortitude, your determination to get on with your life despite all you have endured. You're one hell of a girl, Kate Caswell.' And Reen once again took her in her arms for a breath-squeezing hug.

'Am I? Do you think so? I always think I'm too timid, too compliant. I don't like to make waves. Everyone says I'm too nice.'

Releasing her, Reen nodded. 'You are a naturally considerate person, very aware of the feelings of others. But considering what's happened to you…'

Kate suddenly shook herself. 'Look, I don't want to make out I had a traumatic, awful childhood. I didn't. We didn't have much money but Pa's insurance paid off the mortgage so we had a roof over our heads. Ma took over the post office which brought in enough, until her arthritis got too bad, but by then she had her pension. And I got a weekend job in the Pencil Museum in Keswick, so we managed.'

In her mind's eye Kate could see the tiny shop she knew so well. 'Ma was the one who said I must call her Ma so people wouldn't know I was being brought up by my *grandma* because then they would ask why and what about my mum and everything. She was the one who insisted I make a fresh start once I got to secondary school away from my bigoted little village.

'I quickly learnt to deflect any questions about me. It's quite easy really, a quick joke or a bit of clowning about. It became second nature. Obviously the other kids from the village knew but they were my friends and were on my side so, as far as I know, they didn't let on to anyone and I began to be myself. Once I got to University it was even easier and

I just never told anyone…except Megan of course. She winkled it out of me early on. Somehow she was never fooled by the slightly old-fashioned, light-hearted Kate, always stupidly romantic and ready with a funny remark.'

Reen took her hand. 'But deep down, there is a seriously hurting Kate, isn't there?'

Kate gulped, 'I suppose so, even though Ma was wonderful. I actually always told her that Ma was short for *Ma*rvellous. We shared so much and there was so much fun, especially after Pa died. It sounds awful but I think we both felt much more free after he'd gone. It meant we could sing and dance round the kitchen if we felt like it. She knew so many old songs, funny songs, sentimental songs. I learned them all from her. And the poetry. She could recite loads off by heart. She loved all the same books as me. And we would discuss them for hours, especially my school books. I'm sure my essays were much better because of her input.

'And she was so funny. She cracked me up. We'd be watching TV, a film or something, and she would make a wicked observation, then we'd miss the next bit because we were laughing so much. Yes, there was a lot of laughter.'

'She sounds a remarkable woman.'

'Yes, I was so lucky to have her.'

'You're a lot like her, you know.'

'Do you really think so?'

'Yes, I do. Strong, funny, spirited and, like you, she obviously hid anything upsetting behind a cheerful exterior and tried not to burden others with her problems.'

Surprised, Kate had to stop and think for a minute. 'It would be fantastic to think I'm even remotely like her. Thank you for that. If I am, it's because of what I've learnt from her.' She sighed again. 'Oh, Reen, it seems as if all my life I keep trying to be me, but I don't know who me is.'

She suddenly found herself sobbing again. Not the paroxysm of grief that overwhelmed her before but more of a mourning for all her losses.

Reen once again reached out for her and embraced her in her bare brown arms and began rocking her gently back and forth whilst rhythmically stroking her back.

It was like being a child again. A child held in the arms of a loving mother.

Yes, she dimly remembered the feeling. Her mother had rocked her like this. So her mother *had* loved her, but not enough.

Just like Rob, really. He also had loved her, but not enough.

And now she had lost Troy too.

Chapter Fifty-Nine

Eventually, the tightness round her heart began to ease and Kate released herself reluctantly from the comfort of Reen's soothing embrace to reach again for the box of tissues. As she wiped her eyes, she was conscious of the huge wet patch her tears had made on Reen's shoulder and the concern in her eyes.

'I'm so sorry, Reen. I really am. I don't know where that came from.'

'That's all right, Dahlin. It was obviously all pent up inside. You will feel better for the release of all that tension.'

And Reen was right. Although the tears still flowed, Kate realised she was somehow weeping with relief. Relief at unburdening herself after all these years, and to such an understanding listener. It was cathartic and she began to feel purged of her past.

Sitting there quietly with Reen, she slowly came to terms with her life and realised that her torrent of grief was not just for what had gone, she was also mourning her future too.

In her heart of hearts, she had to admit, it wasn't the loss of Troy that had hit her so hard, it was the loss of a mother figure, Reen. She knew, as did Reen, that, deep down, her love for Troy wasn't based on true emotion. He was a sensible choice. He ticked all the boxes for a good partner in life, so it was a level-headed decision.

All her youthful yearnings were for poetry and songs and romance, all of which she lavished on Rob and had fallen impetuously and foolishly in love with him. Perhaps in that way she had followed her mother. It was the sort of wild abandon that made her mother seek adventure.

But when her passion for Rob hadn't been reciprocated,

she had fallen back on her childhood upbringing that prioritised practicality. So her head, not her heart, had advised Troy. Bruised by love, she had chosen affection.

Clear-sighted now, she knew it was better to have no man at all, than the wrong one.

All her life she had craved security. This is why she had allowed Chris into her life, why she thought she needed Troy so much and longed to belong in his family.

But she had lived on her own in Spain. Yes, she had loving friends around her, but essentially, she had stood on her own two feet and survived. In fact more than survived. She had earned respect and affection in her own right. This realisation gave her the strength and the will to plough her own furrow. If a man came along for her to love, fair enough, but she would no longer accept second best for fear of being alone.

Another realisation hit her. Troy would always be a loving, caring, dependable friend. But without him as a future husband, she knew she could not be a legitimate member of the Taylor family. Although she knew Reen would still include her and care for her they could only ever be just close friends, nothing more.

Seeing Tamsin and Reen together would remind her of what she so nearly had – a loving family around her. But as Troy's nearly fiancée, it would be too awkward to remain. Troy would be consumed with guilt every time he saw her. Reluctantly she had to let the Taylor family go.

In that instant she knew she would have to leave the Costa once her year's contract was over. One more dream shattered.

But talking about Ma made her realise she shared her tough resilience. She now accepted her mother was never coming back and it was fine. It was time to shed the past and forge her own path in life. And she could do it.

PART SIX

Chapter Sixty

June 2001

To her surprise, Kate found herself humming as she prepared a spicy paella to surprise Megan and Josh when they got home from work. Did that mean she was happy to be home in her flat in Birmingham in spite of no spacious balcony to sit on, no special Spanish sunset to look forward to?

Perhaps it was that the cooler weather of an English June suited her. During those final few weeks of term on the Costa, the Spanish heat had begun to feel oppressive, something to hide from rather than relish.

As the end of her contract approached, knowing that she had to vacate the apartment before the beginning of June, she had made her plans.

But it had been a bigger wrench then she realised leaving all her Spanish friends, especially Jeremy and Maria. There had even been a heart-felt plea from Cassandra Carlton-Smith and a promise of an increased salary should she decide to renew her contract and come back for the new year. It had been very tempting.

But she knew she had to go. It was time to return home, get a proper career and leave all her foolish dreams behind her.

Reen had been devastated to see her go, but as Kate explained, 'You've got Tamsin now and an exciting new project so your life will be too full for all our old shopping expeditions and pamper sessions.'

And it was true.

The Taylors had thrown themselves enthusiastically into their new wedding/party planning venture and the Fuller-

White's had found a villa close by so the two families had eagerly renewed their old friendship. But Reen still begged Kate to be part of family gatherings and to be part of her life. Although she had desperately pleaded with her not to go back to England, the sympathetic look in her eyes showed she fully understood the real reasons why Kate was leaving.

Troy and Tamsin were so blazingly in love that every time Kate saw them, it reminded her of what she was missing. She sincerely wished them well but she could not take Troy's overwhelming guilt at how things had worked out for him and not for her.

Although they had said a fond goodbye, there was relief on both sides at their parting.

Returning to Birmingham, she had felt a new sense of purpose. Megan and Josh would soon be moving out as they had saved up enough to put a deposit on a neat little house nearby. Boxes of their stuff were piled high prior to their imminent move scheduled for when Josh finished his lecturing commitments next week.

As part of her future plan Kate had decided to apply for a teaching qualification at the University. To fund herself through the course, she could do private exam tuition. Once qualified, she would have more choice about where she could go and could start a proper career.

She had asked Josh to pick up the application forms from the education department at the University. Fully expecting him to forget, she was pleasantly surprised when he arrived home with Megan triumphantly brandishing several pieces of paper, clearly delighted he had remembered.

'That smells good,' he said sniffing the air as he peered into the kitchen.

'It's a huge Spanish paella so I hope you are hungry.'

'When is Josh not absolutely starving? I have never seen a meal that could intimidate him. Have you?' Megan began putting the kettle on for a post-work cuppa. 'This is very good of you especially as you've only just arrived back. You mustn't feel you have to cook for us.'

‘I enjoyed it. I’ve much more energy in this cooler weather.’

‘It looks delicious. Just the sort of thing that would be great for a supper party. I was going to suggest a welcome home do, but of course it’s up to you because it’s your flat.’

‘Nope. Not till you’ve moved out. I’m the lodger till then.’

‘Don’t be daft. But how do you feel about having a little shindig? It could be a combined celebration of you coming home and our new house. What about this Saturday? A paella would be perfect for that.’ Megan glanced nonchalantly over her shoulder. ‘Perhaps we could invite Rob over.’

Kate went cold.

It was bound to happen at some point. Obviously, she would have to meet him again. She had heard from Megan that he came out of hospital a few weeks ago and was recovering well in his new city centre apartment. Throughout all their phone conversations about his progress, Megan tactfully hadn’t mentioned his fiancée, and neither had she.

‘As you probably know, he’s still a bit frail,’ Megan said, looking at Kate closely. ‘That long stay in hospital really knocked the stuffing out of him, but he’s gradually regaining his strength. I rather thought you might want to see him again.’

‘I’m not sure I’m up to it just yet.’

‘Up to what?’

Kate took a deep breath. They had to get this out into the open.

‘Seeing him with his fiancée.’

‘What fiancée?’ Gobsmacked, Megan paused her tea-making.

‘Come on, Megan, you surely knew. He’s engaged. Has been for ages as far as I can gather. Her name is Tiffany. I saw her by his bedside in hospital and the nurse told me she was his fiancée. And she’s young…and blonde…and gorgeous.’

Even though she had tried to control her voice, she knew she wasn’t hiding her anguish as she pictured that bed-side scene again. Megan looked stunned.

‘Josh,’ she called sharply. A surprised head poked round the door. ‘Do you know anything about a fiancée? Rob’s supposed to have a fiancée called Tiffany.’

‘Nope. News to me. He’s certainly never mentioned anything like that.’

‘But is it the sort of thing you two would talk about anyway?’ Kate asked despondently.

‘Well, we do tend only to talk about work so he might not, I suppose,’ he confessed.

Megan rolled her eyes and Josh slunk back into the lounge.

Then he re-emerged a moment later to say, ‘Although the name Tiffany does ring a bell, but I can’t remember why.’ He quailed under the gaze of the two women. ‘Certainly not as a fiancée,’ he stuttered and vanished again.

Megan shook her head, clearly still shocked. ‘A fiancée? I really can’t believe it. He would have said something to me when I popped round when he came home. He asked after you. He *always* asks after you,’ she said significantly. ‘I told him you were fine but obviously didn’t tell him about you and Troy splitting up. That’s your business and you know I don’t interfere.’

She plonked down to drink her tea still shaking her head. ‘I’m sure you are wrong.’

Kate haltingly recounted the incident in the hospital and how his parents has got rid of her so Tiffany could visit him at his bedside. ‘The nurse was convinced that Tiffany was his fiancée because she had been trying to visit him for ages but couldn’t while he was in intensive care.’

‘But *you* were allowed to visit him, weren’t you?’

‘Yes. His mum told them I could.’

‘Why wouldn’t his mum allow his fiancée then?’

‘I don’t know.’ Kate was impatient with this line of questioning. ‘Probably because she would have been too emotional, too involved.’

‘More involved than his parents? There’s something fishy here.’

‘His mum did say they had banned some visitors but…

look Megan, I have gone round and round this in my mind ever since. Every time I think of her, all blonde and angelically bending over him, stroking his forehead and him looking up at her…' She couldn't go on. The image still upset her too much.

Seeing her distress, Megan jumped up and gave her a hug 'Oh, sorry, Kate, my lovely. I didn't mean to upset you, but something's not right. I *know* he cares about you. You'll just have to ring him and see how it goes.'

'Ring him! I can't. What would I say?'

'Look, you are friends and you bloomin-well nursed him out of a coma. Even if he *is* engaged, you have a right to know how he is. Just phone him for a friendly chat.'

'I can't,' Kate protested alarmed at the determination on Megan's face. 'Besides I don't even know where he is.'

'Well I do. I'll tell you this much and no more. He was staying with his parents for quite a while but he's now back in his flat in Brum. Been there for about a couple of weeks. He often phones Josh for a manly science chat, doesn't he?'

'Yes,' said Josh cheerfully remembering something. 'We do talk about something personal now and again. And like Megan says, he *always* asks about you, Kate. I told him you were due back from Spain soon.'

'Right, so phone him just to tell him you're back.'

'Oh, no, Megan, I just won't know what to say.'

'For goodness sake, Kate. Last time you saw him he was virtually at death's door and you can't even phone him now you're back to simply ask him how he is. Words fail me. Bloody hell, woman.'

Kate had never seen her friend so exasperated.

'Go! Go and phone him right now.' Or so dictatorial. 'Go on. Just do it. Now.'

Even Josh seemed surprised at the vehemence in her tone.

With a visible effort, Megan calmed herself down. 'Sorry. Sorry. It's no good. Look, I'm breaking all my principles about interfering and meddling in other people's lives. As a friend of nearly ten years I have deliberately made myself stand on the side-lines and watch, but I can no longer stop myself. This is too important. You have *got* to talk to him.'

Kate still stood there irresolute.

'GET ON THAT FLAMING PHONE!' Megan bellowed.

In the silence that followed, Josh and Kate stood there, stunned.

Clearly annoyed at herself for her loss of control, Megan picked up some serving dishes and went to slam them down on the table.

Josh looked at Megan's retreating back, 'Wow, she doesn't often get that way, but it's best to do as she says. We won't listen or anything…in fact I was just going to put that CD on again. OK?'

'Um…I don't know his number.'

'It's in our red phone book...under "R",' came the sharp response from the kitchen.

There was no escape. Sighing, Kate picked up the phone and began trailing the lead into the bedroom.

Chapter Sixty-One

Kate sat on the bed praying, 'Please don't let it be her that picks up. Please, please don't let it be sodding Tiffany.'

It seemed to ring forever and she was just thinking with relief that no one was in, when a sleepy masculine voice answered.

'Hallo?'

Kate melted at the familiarity of it.

'It's me, Kate.' Her throat constricted, strangulating her words.

'Who?'

'Kate, Kate Caswell,' she said more strongly this time.

'Kate?' He sounded surprised, and, dare she say, delighted. 'Wow. Great to hear from you. Sorry, didn't recognise your voice. I had fallen asleep in the chair and hadn't quite come to yet.'

'Sorry to wake you. But, well, I was just wondering how you were.'

'Oh fine, fine now. Not a hundred per cent as you can tell by the fact I'm fast asleep in front of the telly at this hour of the evening, but definitely feeling much better than I was.'

'Good. You sound fine. And anyway, there's nothing on telly these days is there? It's all so soporific, I'm not surprised you fell asleep. I do it myself all the time.' Kate couldn't believe the banality of her remarks.

'Um yes. I suppose it's earlier over there. Or is it an hour later? It's so wonderful of you to phone when it's so expensive for you.'

Of course, he thinks I'm still in Spain. What the hell do I say?

'Kate? Are you still there?'

'Um…yes, I'm here. In fact very here. I'm back in England now.'

'That's wonderful. When did you get back?'

'Oh, not long.' She didn't want to say. If she said she had just got back, would she sound too eager? And if she said ages ago, would it look as if she didn't care? 'It's good to hear you are feeling better.'

'Oh, I'm great, compared to when you last saw me. Oh, Kate,' his voice seemed to wobble a bit, 'I can't tell you how much it meant that you came to visit me in hospital. I suspect you didn't expect to stay so long. It turned into a bit of a marathon stint, didn't it? Mum was just so grateful for your help. She told me about your shift system and how you stayed at my bedside, singing and talking to me all the time.'

I wonder how much you heard, she thought.

'And I can definitely remember hearing your voice and…' It seemed as if he was going to say more but paused before continuing, 'It was very good of you to use up your Easter holiday like that. I'm just sorry you couldn't stay any longer so I could thank you properly.'

'Yes, I had to go.' She felt breathless as that's exactly what she wanted too. 'In fact, I've got to go now.' She rushed on. 'I just wanted to check up on how you were.' Why was she cutting it short when all she wanted to do was listen to his warm expressive voice?

'No, wait. Can we meet? I owe you a drink at least. Are you over for the summer now?' He sounded so eager to see her; it was going to be hard to refuse.

'Um, yes.'

'Well, I haven't been allowed to start work properly yet. I'm trying to build up my strength by walking as much as I can. Look, I don't suppose I could take you up the Clents again?'

She could hear the laughter in his voice and her heart lurched. Not there. No, not there.

'Like old times?' he said. 'Well, perhaps not exactly like old times, of course,' he added hastily. 'Are you at your flat?'

'Yes.'

‘How about tomorrow then? I could pick you up from your place about ten-thirty? Would that be all right?’

‘Yes. Oh, OK’. She was just berating herself for agreeing to something she definitely didn’t want when she heard the sounds of someone entering his flat.

A female voice in the background called out, ‘It’s me.’

‘Got to go,’ she said hurriedly. ‘Bye.’

She replaced the phone with pounding heart. So obviously Tiffany, perfectly-formed, sweet little sodding Tiffany, was still on the scene. Who else would have a key and be just letting herself in like that?

How could he raise her hopes in that way? Why did he suggest going to such a special rendezvous? This wasn’t fair. With a devoted fiancée waiting in the wings, it certainly wouldn’t be like old bloody times.

Angrily she stormed out of the bedroom to be met by an anxious look from Megan.

‘OK, I did it. I asked how he was. We are meeting up tomorrow. And I heard his flaming fiancée came back to the flat while we were talking.’

‘Oh, no, Kate.’ Megan leapt up but was halted by her friend’s fierce expression.

‘No. Stop it, Megan. Remember I can’t bear people feeling sorry for me. Now at least I know where I stand. And we will meet tomorrow as friends. But that’s it. No more hopes and dreams about him. I can’t keep doing this. I am not getting sucked in again. One last meeting then I move on…forever.’

Chapter Sixty-Two

Kate looked desperately at the clear periwinkle blue sky. If only it would pour with rain, then I could cancel. I could plead unsuitable shoes, or no cagoule, or something. Where's a pathetic fallacy when you need one? The Brontës would have conjured up grey louring clouds, stormy winds and driving rain to match her desolate mood.

But no, it was a soddingly perfect June day. The sort Wordsworth would have loved. Perfect for wandering 'lonely as a chuffing cloud that floats on high o'er vales and hills.' All right, she wouldn't be alone, but she knew she would be feeling very, very lonely.

She must not lower her defences. She must keep him, and her feelings, at arm's length. It had been easier at Christmas when she had a lovely Troy as a back-up. She had felt newly assertive with her flamenco poise and the assurance of being accepted into Reen's close loving family. Now she was, as always, on her own again. But she had mapped out her future without depending on anyone. Not Troy, and certainly not Rob.

Last time she had climbed the Clents with Rob she had been a foolish, young, naïve and very romantic Kate. She had spouted poems and songs and twirled in happy abandon. No more. She was all grown up now and somehow she must project a detached image of a coolly rational Kate. One that didn't need a Rob in her life any more.

Although all her barriers were up, her heart gave a lurch when she saw him opening the car door with a flourish. He looked so thin, a tall, pale shadow of his former robust self. But his brown eyes lit up, as they always did, and a familiar grin spread over his rugged face as he saw her. She had to drop her head to avoid her instinctive urge to smile back.

Approaching him slowly, she was unsure of how to greet him. He had opened his arms wide to hug her, but her recoil was so obvious, he dropped them immediately.

There was a strained pause.

'Great to see you again, Kate. You look…wonderful…' he faltered to a halt, clearly deterred by her chilly demeanour.

'Hi, Rob.'

As she returned the greeting, she could see he was bewildered by her coolness. She shook herself. This wouldn't do. Her pride came to her rescue. He mustn't see how deeply hurt she was. Even if he was engaged, they were still friends. So belatedly she pulled herself together and went to give him a friendly peck on the cheek, which he didn't expect and an awkward clash of heads resulted. She groaned inwardly. This whole day was going to be awful.

They made rather strained conversation as they drove the familiar route. He asked her about Spain and she updated him briefly on her friends and colleagues but didn't want to go into any details about Reen or Troy so it all sounded rather flat.

She asked him about his recovery. He was fine; everything was fine. He just needed to regain his former level of fitness after months of relative inactivity.

It was like polite small talk between acquaintances. And yes, it was awful.

They parked the car in the usual place. It was a lovely clear day and the hills looked fresh and inviting. The birds were twittering their busy, busy summer songs.

Everything is conspiring against me, thought Kate. It would have been perfect were it not for the lead weight in her stomach and the tightness in her chest.

'Shall we go up?' he asked. 'Although I warn you I'm not as fit as I was. You might have to pull *me* up this time.' He held out his hand.

With a great effort of will, Kate turned away as if she hadn't seen the extended hand and walked slowly on ahead. This was not working. The memories were too painful. Why on earth had she agreed to come?

They plodded upward for a long while in silence. Kate couldn't trust herself to speak. Inwardly she was fuming. Did he bring sodding Tiffany out here? Did bloody Tiffs hold his hand up a hill?

'Oh, by the way,' he said, panting a little behind her, 'Mum sends her love. She and Dad were so pleased when I told them I was seeing you today. She still talks about all your help in the hospital. I think she was at the end of her tether with tiredness and she knew instinctively she could trust you to take over from her. Not like some who offered to help,' he added darkly. 'She was right about you, of course. I have complete faith in my mum's instincts.'

He was trudging over to a nearby bench as he said this, 'Sorry, I know I said benches were for oldies but I'm just going to have to have rest for a while, "to recover my composure" I think you used to call it.'

Kate realised that he obviously remembered every detail of what was said that day all those years ago.

As she went to sit next to him, he smiled at her with such warmth and something else, was it longing?

Surely not? How could he want her when he'd got Tiffany? Perhaps he was longing to have her as a friend, but this was proving far more difficult than she expected. He seemed so vulnerable Kate nearly melted then and there. But every survival instinct kicked in. No, she must be strong; she must not let this man hurt her ever again. Her emotional strength had been hard won and this man, of all men, had the power to deal her a deadly blow.

She looked steadfastly ahead at the view.

'So…was it getting quite warm out there when you left?' It seemed as if he was going to ask her something different, but thought better of it. In the car his questions about Spain seemed to be probing for something and he was looking at her keenly as he spoke.

'Yes. Much hotter than I expected for early summer.' She couldn't think of anything else to say. The new Kate didn't burble about things like the old one did. Hence the stilted polite conversation and Rob labouring to find topics to talk about.

'So would you say that your time out there was…um, stimulating? Are you glad you went?' he persevered. He seemed uncertain of how to elicit the information he wanted. 'I mean I know you met all those new people, but did you, I mean are you still friends with Reen…and all her family?'

'Oh yes. Reen is still as fabulous as ever.' She couldn't be bothered telling him about the family's new venture which would inevitably lead to her talking about Troy and Tamsin. She definitely didn't want to reveal she had been left again. Didn't want to see that look of pity again, like last summer.

Rob seemed to be watching her intently, then, after a long searching look, his shoulders drooped and he turned swiftly away.

What the old Kate would have revealed was that, although she found Spain different and stimulating, just like him, she had found that, in the end, she wanted to come home. If she was going to be alone, she wanted to bc somewhere familiar.

There was a silence. A long silence. A silence that in the end even the new Kate had to break.

'How's your work going?'

He shook himself and turned back to her. His face had closed down now and his voice was gruffly flat.

'Oh fine, I'm gradually picking up the pieces.' He began a desultory description of how the University had coped with his prolonged absence and he how he was beginning to conduct the odd tutorial.

Silence again. Rob had obviously given up on the questions about Spain. Either he wasn't interested or he had found out whatever it was he wanted to know.

She forced herself to ask, 'How is your mum?'

'Oh, she's fine. Still fussing over me too much of course. As do my sisters. You probably heard one of them arriving on my doorstep last night with some ironing.'

Kate suddenly felt all giddy.

'That was your sister I heard while we were on the phone,' she gasped.

‘Well yes, of course.’ He looked puzzled. ‘Who did you think it was?’

‘Tiffany.’ There, she had said it.

Chapter Sixty-Three

'Tiffany? Why the hell did you think that?' There was a look of complete amazement on his face.

'Well...I know she is your fiancée and…'

'What?' he exploded. 'What? Are you mad? Engaged to Tiffany? What on earth gave you that idea?'

Kate could hardly breathe, but forced herself to say as calmly as she could, 'The nurse in the hospital told me she was your fiancée. She saw the ring and knew she was the girl you were trying to save when you had your fall. I was coming in to see you for the last time before I left, to see if you perhaps might…well…recognise me but this young blonde girl was holding your hand and stroking your hair and you…you were gazing into her face.' She struggled to keep her tone steady so strongly was that image burned on her brain.

Now it was his turn to gasp for breath.

'What? Never. What?'

He looked stunned. Then, leaping up, he strode off a few paces in extreme agitation. Frowning, he shook his head as if dispelling a bad dream. With a face like thunder, he came back to sit next to her.

'So that's it. Of course, that explains everything. Bloody hell.' He looked over the view for a moment, clearly trying to quell his anger…and failing.

'Look, let's get one thing clear. That scheming bloody witch, Tiffany, never has been…and never will be…my fiancée, or indeed anything remotely connected with me.' He was trying to calm down.

Kate was still holding her breath so couldn't have said anything even if she tried.

‘She’s a sly, silly, silly girl. And yes, I can well believe she would lie to that nurse. She’s rightly named after a jewellery store. She wears loads of rings and would think nothing of moving one to the appropriate finger to deceive someone. But how on earth could you have supposed that someone so young and, and well…so insubstantial, could be my fiancée?’

Because she was as gorgeous as you are. You looked like the perfect couple. But the word ‘insubstantial’ stopped her in her tracks. Dare she hope?

He looked earnestly into Kate’s tight face. ‘Tiffany is, well was, one of my students who really fancied me. It was embarrassing the way she followed me around, mooning after me. I alerted my Prof about her and said I didn’t want her on the climbing trip but there was really nothing we could do to prevent her.’

He ran his hands through his hair in that old familiar gesture.

‘I was right to be concerned. It was bloody Tiffany who caused me to fall on the mountain by playing a silly trick to catch my attention. She pretended to twist her ankle and made a lunge for me to hold her up which caused me to lose my footing. I can assure you,’ he said with some bitterness, ‘Miss Tawdry Tiffany Tantrum is far from my favourite person.’

He was still blazing with anger.

‘Then, of course, she revelled in the spotlight, all the media fuss, when they airlifted me to hospital. Gave a gushing interview for the local news. She kept wanting to see me in hospital but my mum deliberately kept her at bay. Mum had soon sussed her for the spoilt little drama queen that she was and sent her packing. It was only when I’d come round and was out of intensive care that she managed to get in to see me. Apparently, she had told a sob story to one of the nurses who phoned her once I was out of intensive care. I hadn’t realised till now she had passed herself off as my fiancée. The conniving little…’ Words momentarily failed him. He seized Kate’s hands in his and looked deeply into her eyes.

'Believe me, my mum gave her short shrift when she caught her at my bedside. But we had no idea you had seen her there.'

A strange look of relief and realisation dawned on his face.

'It's all beginning to make sense now. Mum and Dad were hoping you would keep in touch with them. You know, they really liked you a lot and thought you liked them.'

Still too stunned to take it all in, all she could do was nod, as he leapt to his feet again. The old energetic Rob was back and he began pacing up and down, clearly sorting things out in his mind.

'Of course, everything is starting to fall into place. They were really puzzled and hurt because they were expecting you to phone them. I think you said you would keep in touch. And I thought you really must care for me to do all that, come all that way.' That look of longing returned. 'Then when I heard no more, I eventually assumed that you had your reasons for not contacting me or them.'

He looked earnestly into her face. 'The only thing I could think of was that you and Troy were together. That you'd decided he was the one for you and you no longer wanted anything to do with…well, anyone back here.'

Kate's head pounded as she sought to make sense of everything he was saying.

His voice increased in intensity. 'When Josh told me you were coming back for good, I hoped there might still be a chance. That's why I wanted to come here. I had to have one more try.'

Seizing her hands again, he implored, 'Put me out of my misery, please, Kate. I have to know. Are you and Troy…are you two together?'

Still unable to speak, so profound were her feelings at all these revelations, she just shook her head.

His shoulders slumped as if all the tension was seeping away from him and he gave a huge choking sigh of relief. Head bowed, he clung on to her hands as if she had just saved him from drowning.

Stupefied, Kate was gradually assimilating all this

information and readjusting, well, everything. It was like awakening to hope.

At last she managed to speak. Still dazed she tried to re-assess what she had seen in the hospital. She had to explain to him what she believed had happened.

'I'm so sorry if I hurt your mum and dad. I must phone them and apologise. Yes, I really like them too but I thought they knew about Tiffany and couldn't tell me. I assumed that they didn't know what to do with me…turning up out of the blue like that. I was mortified to think they were embarrassed by me being there, an ex-girlfriend, uninvited and just sort of hanging around. Feeling sorry for me, I thought that's why they gave me something to do. The more I analysed it afterwards, the more foolish I felt about the whole episode.'

How could she convey to him her sense of anger and betrayal at the scene that had confronted her on the ward on the day of her departure?

'I assumed when *she* arrived just as I was going, they had told her I was leaving so the coast was clear for her to come. I sort of came to the only conclusions I could. It was an awful shock to see her there holding your hand…stroking your hair…'

She stopped, unable to go on, remembering the devastating maelstrom of emotions on that day.

Seeing her distress, he drew her close to him as she whispered, 'I did so want you to regain consciousness properly and recognise *me*. I was so angry that she was the first one you really looked at.'

Holding her tightly against his chest, he said, 'If it's any consolation, I don't remember her being there at all. Mum told me afterwards that Tiffany had been in to see me. I suppose Mum soon put that nurse right that Tiffany wasn't my fiancée and so the nurse daren't tell her about your visit.'

'You mean…that day you looked at her…you really didn't recognise her?'

He kissed the top of her head, 'No honestly. In fact the first thing I really remember vividly was my dad booming out something about a "dong". He said it was something he learned from you.'

She giggled. 'Yes. He took a lot of convincing that it wasn't rude.'

'I can remember some things as I kept swooshing in and out of consciousness. I could hear my mum's voice, mainly telling me family stories, of holidays and Christmas presents…and lots of lovely stuff.' His voice broke a little. Kate knew his mum had opened the emotional floodgates and told him repeatedly how much she loved him, how much they all loved him.

'But, young lady,' he said severely, sounding very much like his father, 'I hold you totally responsible for my surreal dreams. I had Owls and Pussycats dancing in the rain. I had a Jabberwocky, a most fearsome beast with scales like a giant Godzilla, whiffling in the turgy wood, dressed, most inappropriately, in full top hat and tails.'

Kate hooted.

'And as for the Dong…not only had he a luminous nose, but another very sizeable part of his anatomy shone very brightly indeed. I was quite envious.'

A blushing Kate couldn't stop laughing. He had heard much more than she thought.

'It's not funny. You do realise that as I was recovering, I kept singing and chanting in my sleep, quite loudly at times apparently, if not very tunefully. And all the songs segued into each other in a messy musical morass. It got so bad at one time they had to move me into a side ward as none of the other patients could get any rest, and the laughing kept bursting their stitches. The nurses said they had never had a patient quite like me before. My parents were torn between apologising profusely, and killing themselves laughing.'

He was grinning broadly, 'As you can imagine they have teased me unmercifully since then about my post-accident penchant for poetry. And, of course, all those sentimental songs from the musicals. It's doing my credibility as a full-blooded scientific male no good at all.'

They were both laughing now. It was a most wonderful release of months of tension for both of them. Hugging and laughing they clung to each in a blissful bubble of joy and relief.

All Kate's anxieties and fears were expelled in great gales of air from her lungs and she just wanted to twirl…and twirl…and twirl.

Giddy with joy, she whispered this urge to Rob who simply groaned.

'Of course. I should have guessed you'd want to do the full "Julie Andrews" job. Actually I'm so elated, I might just join you. But first, my little songstress…,' he enfolded her tightly in his arms and kissed her long and tenderly.

Kate surrendered blissfully to the intimacy of the moment and moulded her body into his. To be held by him and to return his kisses was more than she could have dreamed of as she set out this morning. A wave of happiness swept through her, causing her to feel weak with wonder. It was a miracle. Was this really happening?

He must have been thinking the same because he suddenly broke away and looked at her intensely.

'Oh, Kate, Oh, my darling Kate, I can't believe this is really happening. I had lost all hope.'

'And me. I nearly didn't come today. I feel almost dizzy with relief.'

He grinned. 'And that's before you start twirling.'

'Yes. But just for once I'm going to forgo the twirling because I need to kiss you again…and again until you yell for me to stop.'

'I will never do that.' And once again he entwined his arms around her as if he could never let her go.

Chapter Sixty-Four

Eventually gasping for breath they disentangled themselves, both laughing at the sheer intensity of their euphoria.

'Have pity on me,' he implored, his eyes dancing with happiness. 'I'm supposed to be still recovering my strength.'

'That's a pity because I had wondered if you might be up to a re-enactment of our first foray up these hills.'

His eyes crinkled. 'Oh, you shameless hussy. Tempt me not. But, first I have to ask you a question.' He suddenly became more serious. 'There is something else I half remember. It's been bugging me at the back of my mind. I'm not sure if it's real or...or wish fulfilment.'

Puzzled by his change in tone, Kate held her breath.

'Wish fulfilment?'

'Yes. I know you recited lots of silly poems while I was unconscious, but I thought you also said…well…it could have been a poem or a moon/June thing, but did you also say stuff about love? In fact a lot about love.'

She jumped, electrified. How much had he heard?

He whispered as if afraid to ask out loud. 'Did I hear it right? Did you say you loved me?'

She gazed at him, all subterfuge gone, and nodded.

'Yes, Rob. I always have.'

His face shone with joy. 'It's true for me too,' he said simply. 'I love you, Kate, with all my heart. Stupidly I didn't realise it, but I think I always have too.'

'Really?' Her heart flipped. Was this truly happening at last?

'Yes really, really. Why do you think I came back from Australia? Seeing you again last summer reawakened all my old feelings from the first time we met. It was so intense I just couldn't stop thinking about you and it showed me how much my relationship with Leanne couldn't live up to what we had. And I didn't want to settle for second best anymore.'

'But I looked awful that summer. I felt awful. I'll never forget the way you looked at me that night with Chris.'

'But that's because I knew how much I cared about you. My feelings were in complete turmoil as I realised how I felt. When I saw you with that creep, I was desperate to seize you in my arms and protect you and love you and never let you go.' The sincerity in his nut-brown eyes transfixed her.

'Oh, Rob, I thought you despised me for being so weak. I hated myself so much and seeing my life through your eyes made me feel even worse.'

'Oh, my love.' He seized her in his arms and his voice choked with emotion. 'How could you ever think I could blame you for being with that manipulative bully? You were still you. The girl I remembered. You just took a wrong path for a while, like I did with Leanne.'

She nodded. 'The good thing was, that dreadful evening spurred me on to do something about it. To be bolder and stronger. Which I think I am now.'

He pondered for a while, 'Yes, the same for me. Going back I knew I had sort of drifted into things. It made me more decisive to go for what I really wanted. I wonder if you have to go wrong in order to know when it's right. And this is so right.'

He kissed her again. 'I was glad to hear you had escaped to Spain and I was desperate to see you again when I came back at Christmas. And there you were, standing there in that restaurant so gorgeous, so dramatic in that red jacket, how I stopped myself from leaping up and…' For a moment he seemed lost for words.

She distinctly remembered the look on his face and how hope had flared in her heart, but then how she shrank back, frightened of being drawn into an abyss of misery and rejection again.

'I desperately wanted to tell you I had come back for you and nearly blurted it out straight away, but then you told me about you and Troy. It totally devastated me. But I blamed myself and thought it served me right for not coming back after Antarctica.' He gave a rueful smile. 'When you talked about Reen and how much you loved the family, that's when I gave up hope. I knew I had lost you because I couldn't see how Troy could fail to love you.'

His despair so closely reflected her own when she learnt about Tiffany, Kate eyes welled up in sympathy.

'Oh, Rob, thank you for that. In fact Troy *did* love me, after a fashion, but his heart had already been lost to someone else. Just like mine had with you.'

Rob kissed her tenderly, then squeezed her to him again. 'Even though I wasn't really with it in hospital, I could hear your voice calling to me. I yearned so much to wake up to be with you, I'm sure that's what brought me out of the coma. But when I emerged, you weren't there. It seemed you had gone back to Troy and severed all contact. I was so confused. One day hopeful and certain I heard you say you loved me, the next, thinking it was all a dream.'

Everything he was saying reflected her own conflicting emotions. At Christmas there were all those signs that he cared. Then at Easter, the fact his parents knew all about her and it was the response to her voice that seemed to bring him back from his coma were all good signs. But she daren't hope.

But now she not only hoped, she *knew*. He loved her. He had said so. She could see it in his eyes and feel it as he hugged her tighter and tighter.

'I thought I'd lost you to some Spanish lothario,' he moaned, half seriously.

'Troy is hardly that. He's an Essex would-be accountant. And I thought I'd lost you to a Tiffany-shaped temptress.'

The kisses became more passionate and she eventually emerged, slightly dishevelled and grinning delightedly.

She got up ready to haul him to his feet, 'Come on, I want to do some serious damage to you in the bushes.'

'Young lady!' he expostulated in mock shock.

'You are up to it, I hope?' she asked salaciously.

‘I can safely say the Dong and I are more than equal to any challenge the fair, if very rude, Maiden sets us,’ he grinned.

‘The usual spot do you?’

‘Oh yes. Oh yes.’

Chapter Sixty-Five

September 2001

They were there again in their favourite spot three months later. It was the obvious place to celebrate the end of a wonderful summer together and the imminent start of a new term for both of them. Kate was excited about beginning her teaching training course and Rob had a permanent contract at the University lecturing and researching a subject he loved.

She was looking forward to Troy's wedding next month. It promised to be a riot of gaudiness and glitter, tans and tequila, feathers and flamingos. Well…just a wonderful riot really. It would be great to see all her friends and the Taylor family again, especially now she could show off her hunky Rob.

The man at her side bounding up the hill was fully recovered and full of his characteristic energy as they returned to the site of their first, romantic tryst all those years ago.

'This time can we have something a bit more sophisticated than a couple of garage sandwiches and a luke-warm bottle of Tizer?' Rob had requested that morning with a grin.

'It wasn't Tizer, it was Coke.'

'Well, I possibly had other things on my mind at the time.' He gave a mock leer and attempted to fondle her bosom as she was making the sandwiches.

'Unhand me, sir, if you know what's good for you…and the picnic.'

He had been in a particularly bouncy mood as he had suggested their day out and seemed as excited as a big kid at the prospect.

‘And please try to save some energy for later,’ she sighed in mock exasperation.

‘Why, oh sweety-pie mine, will I need my energy later?’ he asked all innocence. ‘I can’t think that a simple drive and a picnic will take much out of me. Unless of course, I’m driven wild by someone’s amazing allure.’

‘Oh dear, I can see you really are going to be hand-full today.’

Sitting there munching on their picnic, she kept glancing at her wonderful man lounging on the rug, gazing at the view. He had lost his pale and wan look and had filled out again. She loved his broad chest, his long, lithe legs and his strong capable hands. In his blue open-necked shirt he looked brown, fit and sooo hunky, she was having trouble keeping her hands, and indeed whole body, from seizing him then and there. But she supposed it was only polite to let him finish eating his baguette first.

Being in what Kate called ‘their trysting spot’, brought so many memories flooding back, Kate began reflecting on the hopes and dreams of their younger selves.

‘I suppose we were searching for something, but didn’t know what. Do you remember saying it was all about belonging? Well, I’ve thought a lot about that word. About the longing to be somewhere or with someone.’

As she turned to lie next to him and snuggle into his arms, she could hear the birds and the slight rustle of the wind in the bushes and the steady thud, thud of Rob's heartbeat.

I wonder if anyone else is as happy as I am.

She still couldn’t believe her luck that after all these years and set-backs and partings, such a gorgeous man actually seemed to love her. It was a source of great wonder and slight apprehension. She was still holding back a little from him, just in case these last blissful months were too good to be true. Surely he would tire of her. Surely she couldn’t be part of his dreams and plans. That would be too much to hope for.

So she kept her tone light.

'And you, my singalong scientist. When we first met, not even in your wildest dreams, did you ever imagine you would know all the words to *Oklahoma*? Do you remember telling me about all your hopes and plans?'

'Yes, very clearly although you are right that I never envisaged all the singing and dancing it would involve. Not to mention the twirling. And I never dreamt I would be happy to lie in the sun just outside Brum. I wanted adventure and exploration and to make a name for myself. All typical boys' comic book stuff, I suppose.'

'And you've done it.'

'Um…after a fashion but not half as bigly as I thought I would.'

'Bigly?' Kate queried in school-marmy tones.

'Yup. Bigly.' He beamed, pleased with his verbal invention…and foreseeing it would have many future applications. But later. Now he was trying to remember what his younger self had thought and dreamt.

'Somehow actually *doing* stuff wasn't half as adventurous as dreaming about it. Yes, the Antarctic itself was spectacular and beautiful and hazardous and all those things, but most of the time we were cramped up in a stuffy, smelly…and I do mean smelly…hut getting on each other's nerves. And hunched over computer screens number-crunching our results into statistics. And my research didn't change the world or bring me international fame.'

'But you did become an expert in your field,' countered Kate loyally, 'and gained a lot of recognition from the ologists…um…them what knows about these things,' she finished lamely.

He laughed. They both knew full well she was speaking very much from the standpoint of 'them what *didn't* really know much about these things'. His research was so esoteric that after several attempts, he had given up trying to explain to her exactly what it was. He saved the detailed discussions for his colleagues and of course, Josh. Kate and Megan never ceased to marvel at the incomprehensibility of their intense conversations.

'It's OK. I don't regret all that travelling at all. It's just the whole experience wasn't quite as majestic or as grand or, well, as fulfilling as I dreamed it would be. Of course, I'm pleased I did it but,' he continued, biting into one of Kate's muffins, 'these days my dreams are much more realistic and much more focused.'

'Oh. So what are they?'

'Later. Later, my impatient little muffin-maker.'

Would she ever get used to the variety of nicknames he called her. She fervently hoped not.

'It's your turn now,' Rob urged. 'You never really told me about your dreams, did you? In fact I can't believe how much you hid from me.'

'No, I had to come to terms with things myself back then so didn't tell anyone. Especially as, you know me, they were all impossibly romantic. I seem to remember white horses and black knights loomed large.'

His dark brown eyes fixed her with a stern look. 'OK, failing the appearance of either in this modern day and age, what was your fall-back position…and no smut, if you don't mind.'

Kate could see he wanted her to take this more seriously so said simply, 'Here and now, most of my dreams are coming true. I wanted to gain more confidence in myself. Be more the girl I wanted to be. And I think, mainly due to Spain and Reen and my imperious flamenco posture, that has happened.' She clicked her fingers and raised her arms in a sinuous beckoning gesture that never failed to arouse Rob. Grinning, he pulled her down into a passionate kiss, but then released her and commanded her to continue her musings.

'Impossibly, I suppose, I wanted my mother to return, but I now accept she never will, and that's fine. She had to follow her dream. I understand why she had to escape. And I know I wouldn't be here now, the person I am, without her genes, but also the steady upbringing and love Ma gave me. So I'm grateful to both of them.'

Talking about her childhood to Reen had been cathartic. Since then she had been able to open up to Rob and all her friends and had found an inner peace she had never thought possible before.

She turned to gaze at the view. 'Most of all I wanted a good man to love and good friends to laugh with, and I think I've got that as well. So like you, I'm perfectly happy to be up the Clents again with you.'

As she turned to blow him a light-hearted kiss, she noticed a strange, half-excited, half-apprehensive expression on his face.

To her surprise, suddenly, decisively, he pulled her up into a sitting position and knelt in front of her.

'OK here goes.' He braced his shoulders and gazed intently into her eyes. 'In fact, I too have a romantic dream. It's one I've had for quite some time now. It's the main reason I came back to England, and why I suggested we came here today. This place for me is the most romantic spot in the universe, because it's where I met the love of my life.'

And to her further astonishment he asked seriously, 'Do you think we can keep this romance, this love, between us "till death do us part"?'

She held her breath, not quite certain what he meant, not daring to hope he was saying what she thought he was saying.

'Um, I'm not sure.'

'Oh'. He looked astounded...and bewildered...and very hurt.

'I mean I'm not sure what it is you are saying,' she said hastily.

'Surely, as a diehard romantic, you must realise I love you and I'm asking you to marry me?'

And he brought out a little box from his pocket and flicked it open to reveal a beautiful diamond ring.

Now she really was lost for words. No song, no poem sprang to her rescue. She just sat and stared at him and his beaming excited face and the question in his loving brown eyes.

'Kate, my love, will you take this ring...and me as well?' he asked anxiously, clearly unnerved by her silence.

Jolted out of her momentary stupefaction, Kate sighed, 'Oh yes. Oh yes. Of course I will. It's just such a shock.'

'A shock? What? That I love you and want to spend the rest of my life in your twirly world?'

'Yes…um…no. I just didn't think that dreams could come true like this.'

'It *is* rather romantic, isn't it?' A delighted grin lit up his face. He had clearly planned the whole thing for this special place.

As she reached out to him with joyful tears in her eyes, she agreed. 'Yes. Totally romantic.'

They entwined, both too emotional to say any more.

Later, as Kate emerged from the best kiss of her life, she groaned, 'You do realise, don't you, that, as in all the best romance stories, we are going to have to live happily ever after.'

'Yup.'

'And how do you feel about feathers…purple feathers and lots of pink plastic flamingos because I know who is going to insist on doing our wedding.'

'As long as you are there, it all sounds good to me.'

She giggled. Little did he know what he was letting himself in for. But, as he said, if they were together, they could face anything life threw at them, even a Reen wedding.

THE END

45323675R00216

Printed in Poland
by Amazon Fulfillment
Poland Sp. z o.o., Wrocław